THE GYPSY'S PROMISE OF LOVE . . .

Luis possessed a remarkable physical appeal, but when he stepped back slightly to judge her reaction to his kiss, she thought first of magic rather than of something far more precious and rare. "How do you do that?"

"Do what?"

His smile was so dazzling that several seconds elapsed before Michelle recalled the question she had asked. "Is it merely practice with all the women who admire your talents as a singer and dancer that makes kissing you so pleasant, or is it some Gypsy spell?"

Luis nodded thoughtfully, but then shrugged. "How can I possibly say why you enjoy kissing me? You'll have to answer that question yourself."

Michelle could feel his heart beat steadily beneath her palm while hers was thumping wildly within her chest. That wasn't fair. It had to be magic. It just had to be. "I think it's a spell of some kind," she murmured.

PHOEBE CONN

DESIRE

ZEBRA BOOKS
KENSINGTON PUBLISHING CORP.

ZEBRA BOOKS

are published by

Kensington Publishing Corp.
475 Park Avenue South
New York, NY 10016

First Printing: March, 1993

Printed in the United States of America

One

A fiery-eyed *gitana* stepped out of the doorway of a
small café and brazenly offered to tell Michelle Minoux's fortune. The French beauty pretended not to
hear the garishly attired Gypsy's words, took a firmer
hold on the arm of her maid, and continued on her
way. With the wedding of the Spanish Infanta and His
Royal Highness, the Duke of Montpensier, less than a
week away, Madrid had been flooded with French visitors and Michelle wondered if all of her countrymen
suffered a similar misfortune and were accosted by
Gypsies whenever they left their lodgings. If so, she
hoped they were better able to cope with unwanted attentions of the *gitanos* than she was. Perhaps her fair
coloring made her appear younger than her nineteen
years and the Gypsies mistakenly believed her to be
too gullible to know the difference between truth and
their cunning lies. Perhaps it was merely the exquisite
nature of her stylish apparel that encouraged them to
leap out at her at every turn. Annoyed whatever their
motive, Michelle tugged at the lace mantilla her aunt
had insisted she wear to further shade her deep scowl.

Accompanied by Yvette, Michelle had been out
shopping for souvenirs to take back home to Lyon for
her mother and two younger sisters. Talking excitedly

about her purchases, she had apparently allowed them to stray into a part of town that was totally inappropriate for young ladies. Michelle could see a well-traveled boulevard up ahead and hoped once they had reached it they could find their way back to her aunt's home, or a respectable person to show them the way.

Not easily discouraged, the enterprising Gypsy caught up with the elegantly gowned young Frenchwoman. Noting that she wore several pieces of expensive jewelry but no wedding ring, she called to her in a seductive whisper.

"My name is Aurora and I have the gift of prophecy. Wouldn't you like to know which of your many lovers will become your husband?"

Outraged by that insulting question, Michelle felt a sudden rush of heat as her cheeks filled with a bright blush. She stopped abruptly and spun around to confront the raven-haired *gitana*. "I do not take lovers," she denied emphatically. "Not that it is any concern of yours."

Elated to have captured the young woman's attention, Aurora broke into a wide grin. The initial flash of sparkling white teeth against the sun-darkened bronze of her skin was one of predatory triumph, but she quickly controlled that revealing expression and assumed a merely saucy smile which imparted a flattering softness to her features. The angular planes of her face were too sharp for her to be truly pretty, but like all *gitanas,* her confident manner created an illusion of beauty few noticed was as false as her promises.

She placed her hands on her hips and swayed as though she longed to dance to the haunting strains of the guitar being strummed softly inside the café where she spent her idle hours. She looked very pleased with herself as she again spoke in a deliberately hushed tone. "You are mistaken, mademoiselle. Allow me to read your palm and I can tell you whatever it is you wish to know about the men in your life."

6

"I already know all there is to know," Michelle responded flippantly.

Aurora's smile widened. "No, there is a great deal more that you do not know."

"And you think that *you* do?" Michelle scoffed.

"Your life is drawn on your palm as plainly as the streets of Madrid are drawn on a city map." Aurora gestured toward the tables circling the entrance of the café. "Come, sit down with me and I will reveal all the secrets your future holds. Surely you have a few minutes to spare when a lifetime of happiness is at stake."

Michelle was sorry that she did not have a copy of the map the *gitana* had just mentioned. She had heard Gypsies were adept at languages and was not surprised that this one was addressing her in fluent French, though she was unconvinced that the buxom girl had any talent for seeing the future. Yvette was of a different opinion, however, and reached up to whisper a plea that Michelle consent to having her fortune told.

Yvette was a dear girl, but a very superstitious one. Michelle patted her arm lightly as she glanced back toward the café. There were half a dozen tables outside so at least she would not have to enter what was undoubtedly an unsavory establishment to have her palm read. Still, despite Yvette's continued urging, she doubted the wisdom of consulting a Gypsy for advice.

Needing the few coins it was obvious this reluctant Frenchwoman could afford to pay, Aurora made a bold guess. "Your lover is blond," she said suddenly, certain there would be at least one such man among the mademoiselle's male admirers, of which there were many, she was sure.

Startled by the accuracy of that description, Michelle's long-lashed blue eyes widened before narrowing slightly. "I do not take lovers," she reminded the insistent *gitana*.

"Forgive me," Aurora begged with a great show of

humility which brought forth a jingle reminiscent of sleighbells from the profusion of narrow bracelets adorning her slender arms. "Your suitor then is nearly as fair-haired as you, is he not?"

"She's describing Antoine, mademoiselle," Yvette insisted in an awed whisper.

"Antoine?" Aurora repeated. She then closed her eyes and with another intentionally dramatic gesture raised her fingertips to her temples. She appeared to be concentrating deeply, as though straining to hear the voice of some unseen oracle. "Yes, his name is Antoine. He's causing you a great deal of concern at present, but . . ." She stopped there and opened her eyes. "Come. I must study your palm to be sure of the rest."

Antoine Lareau was indeed causing Michelle such deep concern it bordered on despair, and while she would not have sat down with Aurora for any other reason, she grasped at the slim hope the persistent *gitana* might provide some clue to Antoine's maddening reluctance to declare his love. "I can stay only a few minutes," she cautioned as she moved toward one of the outdoor tables.

Her dark eyes now dancing with mischief, Aurora waited for both Michelle and Yvette to be seated before she took a chair opposite them. She cast an inquisitive glance toward the reticule dangling from Michelle's arm and was promptly rewarded with the coins she had sought. "Give me your right hand," she then instructed.

Michelle gingerly held out her hand. "Surely my palm is no different than anyone else's," she posited.

"You are mistaken, mademoiselle. Each one is unique," Aurora assured her. She stroked the back of Michelle's hand lightly as she studied her palm. "You have lovely hands. They're small and delicate."

"What does that mean?" Michelle asked.

Aurora replied without looking up. "It means that you're a lady with fine lineage."

8

That was certainly true, and growing more interested in the *gitana*'s remarks, Michelle leaned forward slightly. "I know my ancestry quite well. You promised to tell me something that I do *not* know."

"I can see that you're a sensitive woman of many moods," Aurora explained as she continued to study Michelle's upturned hand. Experience had taught her that describing what she saw as though it were fact usually made a believer of even the most skeptical woman. Gypsies had their own way of reading palms, but it involved secrets she never divulged. Instead, she related the more common method of discerning what a person's palm revealed.

She traced the line curving across Michelle's palm nearest the thumb and spoke in a deliberately honeyed tone. "This is your life line. It shows you'll live to an advanced age."

"I will?"

"Oh, yes, most assuredly." Aurora traced the next line. "This is the head line. It completely crosses the palm, meaning that you have a lively imagination and a belief in dreams. This line closest to your fingers is the heart line. The way it curves shows that you value love and prize romance very highly."

Because both of those pronouncements confirmed Michelle's own view of her nature, she grew anxious to hear what else the Gypsy had to say. "And what of Antoine?" she prompted. "What can you tell about him from looking at my palm?"

"Be patient a moment longer, please," Aurora pleaded softly, allowing the dramatic tension of the moment to mount. "This line which runs down the center of your palm from your fingers to your wrist foretells your destiny. Do you see all the little breaks in it?"

"Yes. What do they mean?"

"That you'll have many changes in your life." Aurora captured Michelle's gaze and held it, confident in the knowledge a Frenchwoman visiting Spain would read-

9

ily believe her next comment. "You love travel and you'll see a great deal of the world."

Michelle frowned. The vineyards on Antoine's estate produced some of France's finest wines, and devoted to their production, he seldom traveled far from home. He had come to Spain with her, but more to enhance his image among his customers than for pleasure.

A keen observer, Aurora noted the darkening of Michelle's expression and made the most of it. "Antoine does not like to venture far from home, does he?"

"Not as a general rule, no."

Aurora cupped Michelle's hand. "Do you see this tiny line here near your little finger? This is the marriage line. Yours curves very near your heart line and that means you'll find much happiness in your marriage."

"If we ever do marry," Michelle whispered under her breath.

Aurora caught that remark, and after a moment's hesitation, offered advice of another type. "Antoine is being very foolish to postpone your wedding, but a hesitant suitor can become the most devoted of admirers with the proper inspiration."

Instantly suspicious, Michelle withdrew her hand from Aurora's. "What sort of inspiration?" she asked.

Before the Gypsy could reply, a sudden movement at the entrance of the café caught Michelle's eye. She glanced toward the doorway and found the guitarist had moved his chair out into the open. His head was bowed slightly as he plucked the notes of a difficult passage, but he still appeared to be listening more closely to her conversation with Aurora than to his melody.

Seated, it was difficult to judge, but he looked quite tall. His hair was as thick and black as Aurora's and his skin just as handsome a bronze. He was dressed quite conservatively compared to the other Gypsies Michelle had noticed on her walks through Madrid, in

a simple muslin shirt, black trousers, and highly polished black boots. He also had no manners at all, for
he was clearly eavesdropping on Aurora and her.

Disgusted to be satisfying the curiosity of some
Gypsy musician, Michelle abruptly turned her attention back to Aurora. She had not meant to reveal so
much about herself, and now spoke in a far more
guarded tone. "I suppose for a few more coins you can
suggest a proven way to capture a man's heart?"

Startled by the change in Michelle's tone, Aurora
raised her hands in a placating gesture, again setting
her bracelets into a flurry of musical motion. "Please,
it would be my pleasure to serve you, mademoiselle,
and if you wished to reward me later out of gratitude,
I would appreciate your kindness."

The guitarist strummed the final notes of his tune,
and now making no further effort to appear preoccupied with his instrument, stared at Michelle quite
boldly. She shot him a fiercely disapproving glance
that wavered the instant their gazes met. While she
had always preferred fair-haired men like Antoine,
there was no denying this inquisitive ebony-eyed devil
was handsome, extraordinarily so, in fact. Just the
barest hint of a smile played across his lips, but the
expression was so utterly charming it would have devastated a less sophisticated young woman.

"What do you find so amusing?" Michelle challenged.

The musician accented his reply with a dramatic
flourish on his guitar. "If a woman as beautiful as you
needs advice on romance, then the man in your life
must be a pathetic fool."

Shocked that a complete stranger would make such
a bold reference to her appearance and in the same
breath insult Antoine, Michelle was horribly embarrassed that she had ever consented to speak with the
Gypsies. She rose quickly, gestured for Yvette to come
along, and hurried toward the boulevard where she
hoped to find directions.

11

Incensed to have lost the interest of such an obviously wealthy young woman without extracting far more than the cost of reading a palm, Aurora also leapt to her feet, but rather than again following Michelle, she turned her rage on the opinionated musician. "Look what you've done!" she scolded. "Sergio!" she shouted through the doorway. "Come out here and make Luis pay for what he's done to me."

Sergio, a slender young man in his early thirties, soon appeared. As was the custom of the Gypsies, his colorful garb was as fanciful as Aurora's. He wore the same dark trousers, white shirt, and boots as Luis, but with the addition of a brilliant red sash, a satin vest striped in vivid rainbow hues, and a bright-green velvet cap. A single gold earring completed his attire.

"What horrible thing have you done, Luis?" Sergio asked in a mocking tone.

Aurora gestured wildly as she explained in Romany, the Gypsies' own language. She grabbed Sergio's arm and pointed up the street toward the rapidly departing young women. "I could have sold her a dozen charms or perhaps a love potion. She was eager to believe in my predictions until Luis insulted her."

Sergio merely laughed at Aurora's complaint. "You tell a dozen fortunes a day and sell as many charms. One more or less won't matter."

"You did not see her jewelry!"

Chagrined, Luis rose and handed Sergio his guitar. He then reached into his pocket and extracted several gold coins which he placed in Aurora's hand. "There. That will cover whatever the Frenchwoman might have spent."

Aurora counted the money quickly, and although thrilled by Luis's generosity, she pretended to still be disappointed. "You must follow her," she demanded. "Tell me where she lives so that I can call on her tomorrow and finish telling her fortune."

Dismayed by the request, Luis looked to Sergio, expecting him to say such an effort was unnecessary, but

12

the young man thought it an excellent idea and nodded his head. Despite the disparity in their backgrounds and circumstances, Luis enjoyed the company of the dramatic pair, but he had never realized how much a wealthy customer meant to Aurora. Sincerely regretting now that he had chased the young woman away, he shrugged and started off after her with a long, confident stride that quickly allowed him to close the distance between them.

"Mademoiselle!" he called softly as he drew near.

Michelle sent a hasty glance over her shoulder, shot Luis a darkly menacing stare, and increased her pace to a near run. Not nearly so tall and lithe, Yvette was then forced to trot alongside her mistress to keep up. Hoping to recognize their location when they reached the tree-lined boulevard, Michelle looked first left and then right, but nothing was in the least bit familiar. Annoyed with herself for having lost her way, she grew even more ashamed of having tarried to speak with the Gypsies.

"Are you lost?" Luis inquired politely as he reached Michelle's side.

Michelle ignored him, but Yvette was frightened by that prospect and nodded frantically to encourage Luis's assistance.

Luis winked at the plump maid and then leaned down to whisper in Michelle's ear. "A beautiful woman should not wander the streets of Madrid unescorted. Please tell me your address and I will accompany you there."

Refusing to dignify the arrogant stranger's request with a response, Michelle lifted her chin proudly and remained silent. She was certain no respectable woman allowed a Gypsy to serve as an escort and just wanted him to go away. When he stubbornly refused to absent himself, she was forced to speak to him.

"Must I demand that you leave us alone? Can't you see you're not wanted here?"

Her eyes were as dazzling a blue as the waters of the

13

Caribbean. They were ablaze with a temperamental fire, but Luis could not help but wonder if passion did not lend her a far softer, more sultry gaze. Her features contained a delicate perfection, but her manner conveyed the unmistakable impression of one who expected to have her orders obeyed, and promptly. To encounter such a regally cool blonde with such a hot temper was an unusual happenstance. For reasons Luis made no attempt to analyze, he found her disdain for him wildly amusing and had difficulty not laughing out loud.

"I beg your pardon for being so lacking in manners earlier, mademoiselle," he managed to reply with a straight face. "I would be honored to escort you to your home."

Taken aback by his gentlemanly offer, Michelle still hesitated to accept. Even though Madrid was not her home, she did not want to behave in an unseemly fashion, for she was certain gossip traveled with the same rapidity here as it did in France. The friendly man was not only handsome, but cut an imposing figure with his broad shoulders, narrow hips, and long, muscular legs. Despite his appealing appearance he was still a Gypsy, she reminded herself, and not someone whose acquaintance she could justify cultivating, even when lost in a strange city.

"Thank you, but we can make our own way home," she informed him brusquely.

While Luis sincerely doubted that, he again responded with a slight bow, turned away, and started back toward the café. He did not go far, however, before he retraced his steps and returned to the spot where he and the French belle had spoken. He watched her ask directions from an elderly woman and, amused by her insistence to return home on her own when she was obviously lost, he followed her at a discreet distance. He kept close to the buildings that lined the walk, ready to dart into the shadowed doorways should the intriguing young woman cast a back-

14

ward glance, but she was apparently so confident her rebuff had sent him away that she did not once pause to see if she was being followed.

They soon passed the Puerta del Sol and entered the oldest part of the city, where the cobblestone street was uneven and narrow. Luis remained in the shadows and went unobserved. He was sorry that he had not introduced himself, for it now seemed unlikely that he would ever learn the independent beauty's name. When she finally reached her destination, an agile young man alighted from a carriage waiting in front. While Luis was not close enough to hear his words, it was plain from his exaggerated gestures that he was not pleased to find the young woman had been out walking alone.

Apparently unfazed by his criticism, she turned away and entered her dwelling without waiting for her visitor to complete his animated tirade. Not discouraged by her silence, the fair-haired man pursued her into the impressive-looking home. No longer concerned about being seen, Luis crossed the street. Pretending to be in need of·directions himself, he struck up a conversation with the driver of the carriage.

Surprised to be addressed in flawless French by a Spaniard, the driver responded to Luis's polite inquiry with effusive apologies and then explained his circumstance. "We've come to Madrid for the duke's wedding and I am probably more lost than you are."

Luis was unperturbed by that response and with subtle urging, he coaxed the helpful Frenchman into revealing that he was in the employ of a Monsieur Antoine Lareau, a prosperous wine merchant from Lyon. Devoted to his young master, he extolled Antoine's virtues to such an extent that Luis soon grew bored hearing them.

"And the young woman who lives here?" he interrupted to ask.

"Mademoiselle Minoux. She has been his sweetheart since childhood. They are sometimes mistaken

15

for brother and sister, but I can assure you that is not the case," the driver informed Luis with a sly wink.

Luis turned to look up at the imposing residence Mademoiselle Minoux had entered with such arrogant haste. The three-story structure was as elegant in its simplicity as any lining the narrow street. The wrought-iron balconies beneath the second- and third-floor windows were festooned with pots overflowing with bright-pink and orange geraniums while the first floor was dominated by a magnificent set of oak doors framed by a beautifully proportioned arch. Luis was very impressed.

"This is not her family home then?" he prompted with apparent casual interest.

"No, she is a guest of an elderly aunt, a Señora Magdalena Ortiz y Reyes."

From the immaculate appearance of her house, Luis gathered the impression that the woman must be extremely wealthy. Her high-spirited niece would undoubtedly have come from a similarly stately home and have led the easy life of some rich man's pampered daughter. It was no wonder she displayed such open hostility to strangers. Her entire life she must have been taught to avoid the common people. Fortunately, he was not in the least bit common.

His curiosity piqued, he was delighted when he caught sight of Michelle observing him from a second-story window. He responded with a jaunty salute, but she hurriedly drew the drapes rather than return the friendly wave. Luis chuckled to himself as he bid Antoine's driver farewell and turned away. He would be happy to tell Aurora where the young woman lived, but he thought he might find such knowledge far more valuable than she would.

"Mon Dieu!" Antoine complained. "This house is dark enough without your drawing the drapes. Open them at once, please."

Michelle did as he asked but turned away from the window without again glancing down into the street. She had been mortified to find the handsome Gypsy staring up at her and feared now that he knew where she was staying he would return time and again to annoy her. Whatever would Antoine say if he knew she had spoken with Gypsies? she fretted anxiously.

"What is wrong with you, Michelle?" Antoine inquired as he approached her. "You invited me to dine with you and then did not even do me the courtesy of being home. Do you find Madrid so fascinating a place that you no longer have time for me?"

Before Michelle could reply, Antoine veered away and began to study his reflection in the mirror above the fireplace. He took great pride in his appearance and was pleased that despite the fury of his mood, he did indeed look his best. He was dressed in shades of blue and gray which he felt were especially flattering to a man of his fair coloring. He smiled at the perfection of his image before turning back to face Michelle.

"Well, my dearest, aren't you going to offer any excuse for your rudeness before you beg my forgiveness?"

Upset by her morning's misadventure, Michelle merely stared at her attractive guest. He was six years her senior, but today, as he did so often, he reminded her of a spoiled child. When his mood was lighthearted he was a joy to be with, but she refused to take the blame for causing his current distress.

"I'm only a few minutes late, so you shouldn't carry on so. Why didn't you make your presence known to my aunt? You know she would have entertained you until I arrived."

Antoine sent a soulful glance toward heaven. "Oh, please, Michelle, you know she and I have nothing in common. She is very sweet, a dear woman, but I fear rather stupid."

"Hush! She might hear you!" Michelle scolded.

"She is lucky to hear me when I speak directly to

her. She could not possibly have overheard me just now."

"Whether or not she can hear you, she deserves the same respect you would show any woman her age. Besides, she is not lacking in intelligence. She is merely less sophisticated than we are. That is no excuse not to treat her kindly, however. Can't you try to be more understanding?"

Antoine stepped close and reached for Michelle's hand. He brought it to his lips, and after brushing the back lightly, he kissed her palm with undisguised passion. "I treat all women kindly, my darling. You know that."

The seductive warmth of his hand on hers filled Michelle with a painful wave of desire. When Antoine chose to be attentive, she quickly forgave him all his faults. He escorted her everywhere and kept her heart astir with grandly romantic gestures, but he always stopped short of speaking of love or asking for her hand in marriage. Her friends and family all assumed she would wed Antoine one day. Perhaps he assumed it, too, but it was disheartening to be taken for granted when she longed to be courted ardently instead.

The dull thud of her aunt's cane striking the hardwood floor of the hall signaled the elderly woman's approach, and Michelle stepped back to create a more discreet distance between herself and Antoine so as not to draw further criticism of her behavior. The morning had been wretched enough without that, and she braced herself for what would undoubtedly be a strained meal during which Antoine's conversation would be focused almost exclusively on the wines. He had pronounced her aunt's wine cellar magnificent and she was grateful that he had found at least one thing about the sweet-tempered widow worthy of praise.

* * *

Aurora nodded excitedly as Luis described the location of her errant French customer's residence and provided the necessary details to permit her to recognize it. "It's her aunt's home," he added. "Perhaps you can tell her fortune, too, but from the looks of the place, she has all the luck she needs."

"That's all the more reason for her to seek my advice to ensure that her good fortune continues," Aurora claimed with a jubilant smile. "The more wealth a woman has, the more desperate she is to maintain it, and the more eager she is to believe my predictions. You'll see, I'll make enough off them for us to live like royalty all winter. Now come and dance with me. If Sergio could dance half as well as you, we would be the richest *gitanos* in all of Spain."

Not impressed by the mercenary slant of her boasts, or her invitation, Luis responded with a weary sigh. "Not today. I've already done one favor for you and I'll not grant another."

"A favor!" Aurora contradicted sharply. "You were the one who chased the young woman away, so it was rightly your responsibility to let me know where to find her. Do not speak to me of favors!"

Luis merely laughed rather than argue with the volatile dark-haired woman. Like all *gitanas,* she flirted openly with every man she met. Her dancing was as bold as her speech, the wildness of her spirit barely contained, but, despite her blatantly seductive manner, he had never been tempted to sample more of her charms than she shared when they danced.

"I also paid you what Mademoiselle Minoux would have spent. Have you forgotten that?" Luis reminded her pointedly before turning away. "I'll come back when I can," he called to Sergio, and after retrieving his guitar, he strode from the café without a backward glance.

Aurora rushed to the door and watched until Luis was out of sight. Disappointed that he had dismissed her so abruptly, she sighed unhappily, then tried to make light of her admiration for the tall Spaniard when Sergio appeared at her side. "Luis may dance better than you, but it is only a game to him. He doesn't understand how we live. I will get far more from the Frenchwoman and her aunt than he could ever dream of."

Sergio ran his fingertips across her cheek in a sensuous caress. "What are you plotting, a *Hokkano Baro?*"

"Yes, and why not? It is so easy to trick such women out of their wealth that I would be a fool not to try."

"If the young woman has come to Madrid for the royal wedding, you will not have much time."

"Do you think I'm too stupid to realize that?" Aurora snapped with a haughty toss of her long, straight hair. "Besides, I will need only a few days to separate the young woman and her aunt from their gold."

Aurora enjoyed such frequent success with her schemes that Sergio did not doubt her now. Something else did concern him, though. "There is one other thing," he began cautiously. "Luis may enjoy spending time with us, but just as you said, he is not one of us. You are betrothed to me, Aurora. Don't fool yourself by pretending that you can become Luis's bride. It will never happen."

Shocked by that unnecessary admonition, Aurora shrank away from him. "I have been taught since I was old enough to understand that a *gitana's* most cherished prize is her virtue and that only a *gitano* is worthy of her. Luis is handsome and rich, but he is no fit husband for me," she scoffed loudly. "I have not betrayed you."

Before Sergio could respond with another piece of ridiculous advice, she turned her back on him and, muttering a stream of vile curses in Romany, ran toward the back door of the café. Once outside, she kept right on running until the exertion had sapped her anger. She sat down on a low wall to rest, and unable to bear the constant pain of the impossibility of her love for Luis, she used every ounce of her lively wit to devise a scheme to cheat Mademoiselle Minoux and her aunt out of a great deal of money.

Two

That evening, Antoine escorted Michelle to a lavish party being given by the French ambassador to celebrate the impending royal wedding. As on all similar occasions, his unmistakably possessive attitude discouraged all other men who showed an interest in the lively French beauty, but, as always, he wished her good night with no more than a chaste kiss on the cheek. Continuing to be oblivious to her feelings, he failed to notice that she thanked him through clenched teeth.

Distraught that what should have been a wonderfully romantic evening had progressed predictably and ended in disappointment, Michelle climbed the wide staircase to her bedroom with a leaden step. As she undressed and prepared for bed, she described the evening's festivities to Yvette but her manner lacked any hint of enthusiasm. After bidding her maid good night, she no longer had any reason for pretense and abandoned herself to the sorrow that so often haunted her nights after she and Antoine had parted.

Her first thoughts were of her parents, for she recalled their marriage as having been wonderfully romantic. Her father had been the model of devotion and had showered her mother with attention and affection. He had been the best of fathers, too. The dear man had died suddenly four years ago and her mother missed him so terribly that she had only recently been able to speak his name without bursting into tears. Michelle missed him very much, too. She longed to seek his advice about Antoine. He had died believing she and Antoine would one day marry, but Michelle had grown weary of waiting for the man who had been her constant companion since childhood to offer a formal proposal.

Perhaps at twenty-five Antoine felt too young to take on the responsibilities of a wife and family, but she was *nineteen!* She had close friends who had wed at seventeen and eighteen and now had beautiful children. Antoine had given her an endless round of parties where he proudly introduced her to his friends, but did not do her the honor of making her his wife. Thoroughly disgusted with him, Michelle brushed out her long curls with a savage rhythm.

Her mother had counseled patience and suggested appropriate Bible verses for her to commit to memory, but Michelle could no longer repeat them without giving the lyrical passages the heated cadence of curses. She wanted Antoine's superficial charm to become true devotion, for the playful affection he had always shown to deepen into love. She could not bear the thought of returning home to France without having made plans for a shared future.

It was very late, but Michelle remained seated atop her bed in a dejected pose, too angry to fall asleep, too restless to even try. Several minutes passed before she realized the stillness of the night had been broken by what had to be a passionate Spaniard serenading his lady love. His voice was a sensual baritone and he was accompanying himself on the guitar. Michelle had met several of her aunt's neighbors and she assumed one must have a beautiful daughter who had inspired such a romantic gesture.

23

She had heard Spaniards enjoyed serenading the women they loved and she felt even more discouraged that Antoine would never even think of entertaining her in such a flamboyant fashion, let alone do it, although he had a marvelous singing voice. Fighting back tears, she tried to catch the amorous singer's words, but by the time she had translated one line of Spanish into French, he had sung three more, forcing her to give up the chore as futile.

He had chosen songs with almost painfully sweet melodies and she closed her eyes and pretended that he was singing to her. She almost believed it until he struck up a tune that while being as pretty as his others, sounded somehow familiar. Lured by her efforts to give the song a name, she slid off the high bed and crossed the room to the glass doors which opened out onto a small balcony. She supposed enjoying a musical tribute meant for another might be described as eavesdropping but refused to consider it ill-mannered when the singer could undoubtedly be heard all over the neighborhood.

The moon provided ample light for her to see several of the houses on the opposite side of the street, but she could not locate the source of the music. Believing it must be coming from the house next door, she opened the double glass doors slightly and peered out. Instantly the lengthy serenade came to an end.

"Good evening!" Luis called to her. "I was beginning to think that you did not like music."

"Mon Dieu!" Michelle cried out in horror. "What are you doing here?"

Luis made no attempt to stifle his laughter now. "I'm trying to entertain you, mademoiselle. Most women say that I sing very well."

Michelle felt the very same rush of indignation and shame she had experienced earlier in the day when she had seen him talking with Antoine's driver.

24

She had known in that instant that he was going to cause her trouble, but she had not expected it to begin so soon. Thinking it extremely fortunate that her aunt was nearly deaf and that Yvette had a room in the servants' quarters in the other wing, she nevertheless wanted the talented Gypsy musician gone.

"I am not most women!" she pointed out in a threatening whisper. "Now go away!"

Luis responded by beginning another song.

"Don't you understand me? Be gone!"

Luis shook his head as he continued to play his guitar and sing. He was having far too good a time to leave just yet. Michelle turned away but did not close the glass doors, so he raised his voice slightly as he reached the chorus. She soon came back into view carrying a large vase filled with roses and he thought perhaps she meant to toss him a blossom or two. When instead she sent it crashing down on him, he was only able to dodge out of the way at the very last instant.

The vase shattered at his feet, splashing his boots and trousers with water but doing no damage otherwise. A clever man, he shrank back into the shadows, set his guitar aside, and kept still.

Expecting at the very least a shouted curse or two, Michelle leaned over the wrought-iron railing to gauge the accuracy of her aim. When she didn't see the Gypsy or hear him running away, she was at first puzzled and then alarmed. "What if I've killed him?" she moaned. Terrified that the weight of the vase might have crushed his skull, she dashed from her room, flew down the stairs, and raced across the marble entryway.

When she reached the heavy oak doors, she fumbled with the latch and finally managed to throw one open wide. It took all her courage to hurry outside when she was so fearful of what she might find, but she had taken only two running steps before, to her utter dismay, the handsome Gypsy blocked her way. He was wearing what could only be described as an obnoxiously wicked grin.

"You devil!" she shrieked.

Luis handed her one of the bloodred roses she had just rained down on him. "If my songs don't please you, you should have just said so," he pointed out calmly.

Michelle ignored the proffered rose, spun on her toes, and sped back toward the safety of her aunt's home. The agility that had prevented Luis from being injured by a falling vase again served him well and he followed her inside the house before she could slam the heavy door to shut him out.

"How dare you?" Michelle cried.

"How indeed," Luis teased. "Despite being an ill-tempered shrew, you're quite beautiful and I wanted to serenade you. Had you thanked me politely, I would have left you to dream of me. But now . . ."

Michelle backed away. "If you so much as touch me I'll scream so loud that not only everyone in the house will come running but everyone in the *neighborhood* will also come to my defense!"

Luis raised his hands. "I won't touch you unless you ask me to."

Amazed by that response, Michelle pointed toward the door. "I wouldn't ask you to touch me even if my gown were on fire and I needed help beating out the flames. Now, get out!"

Her silk nightgown was the color of rich cream but so sheer it hid little of her spectacular figure from Luis's view. Stripping her in his mind, he regarded her with a mocking glance which lingered appreciatively at the lush swell of her bosom. Her pale-blond hair hung past her waist in loose curls and he could not help but wonder how a young woman with such an angelic appearance had come to have such a fiery temper.

26

"The next time I come to serenade you—" he began.

"There won't be a next time," Michelle swore dramatically.

Again Luis flashed a cocky grin and he continued as though he had not been interrupted. "The next time you'll be far more cordial. You'll toss me some token, a lace handkerchief or silk scarf, as evidence of your admiration. Otherwise, I won't go away."

Michelle first responded to that boast with a withering glance and then with a promise of her own. "First thing in the morning, I'm going to ask the gardener to bring several dozen bricks up to my room. I'll have him stack them out on the balcony and if I so much as see you walking by in the street, I'll hurl them at you."

Amused by her threat, Luis again offered the rose. "I doubt that you really want to hurt me considering you came outside so quickly to make certain that you hadn't harmed me tonight."

Michelle snatched the flower from his hand and then shook it at him for emphasis. "I did no such thing. I simply did not want my aged aunt to trip over your carcass when she leaves for Mass in the morning."

"I think you're the most beautiful liar I've ever met."

"That's no lie!"

"Oh yes it is."

Before Michelle had the presence of mind to stop him, Luis stepped forward, drew her into his arms, and kissed her with a passion Antoine had never even approached in all the years she had known him. Her arms pinned to her sides she struggled to break free and failed. When she tried to kick him, she succeeded only in bruising her toes against his boots. All the while his lips caressed hers with an

27

insistence that swiftly dissolved her initial frantic need to resist.

Sensing her surrender, Luis drew away slightly, but it was merely a ploy, and when she gasped for breath, he sent his tongue into her open mouth, capturing her very soul with a far more boldly ardent kiss. The bliss of that intimate invasion stirred his blood as violently as hers and might have drowned them both in rapture had he not somehow found the strength to end the passionate exchange as quickly as it had begun.

Luis laughed when Michelle swayed as he released her. Not wanting her to faint in a swoon, he slipped one arm around her waist, slid his fingers through her now-tangled hair, and again pulled her close. He bent his head and kissed her throat so thoroughly he knew a telltale mark would remain on her fair skin for several days. Pleased by that further bit of mischief, he led her to the stairs and placed her hand on the banister. If she truly did feel faint, she would be able to steady herself that way. Then, with no more than a teasing wink, he strode from the house. He picked up his guitar along with another red rose as a souvenir of what had been an even more memorable night than he had anticipated.

When Luis had closed the door on his way out, Michelle collapsed on the bottom step. She tried to comprehend what had just happened, but her usually keen intellect was so dazed by the passionate encounter that she could barely think, let alone reason. Aurora had mentioned something about inspiring devotion in a lover. Had the man who'd serenaded her worked some kind of a Gypsy spell? Her whole body ached with what was surely unfulfilled desire and she knew she dared never spend another minute alone with a handsome *gitano* who could so easily turn revulsion to wanton passion.

She rested her head against one of the ornately

carved posts that supported the banister and tried to summon the energy to return to her room. She was amazed to find the red rose he had given her still remained in her hand. Its vivid color provided the perfect reminder of the darkly handsome man. He had said he would leave her to dream of him.

"*Mon Dieu,*" she sighed softly. "How will I ever dream of anything else?"

Aurora anticipated having to use all her charm to gain a few minutes' time with the young woman she now knew was Mademoiselle Minoux. She was also confident that those few minutes would be all that she would require to convince the Frenchwoman that her expertise in matters of the heart was unexcelled. She went to the rear entrance of the residence Luis had described and smiled sweetly at the young servant girl who answered her knock.

"I have come to see Mademoiselle Minoux," she announced confidently. She removed one of her bracelets and handed it to the girl. "Take her this so that she will know who I am. Tell her Aurora has come to help her with the problem she mentioned yesterday."

Astonished by that request, the maid was sufficiently convinced that the Gypsy had met her employer's niece to carry the message. "Please wait here," she said before closing the door.

"I should have asked to wait in the garden," Aurora muttered in disgust as she began to pace in front of the door. It was undoubtedly too early in the day to pay a formal call, but like all her kind, Aurora cared nothing for the conventions of polite society.

She grew quite bored before the maid returned and did indeed take her into the garden where she had only a brief wait before Michelle appeared.

Each time Michelle had fallen asleep during the

night, she had been awakened by echoes of the amorous Gypsy's mocking laughter. It was now long past the hour she could reasonably remain in bed, so she had been forced to rise rather than appear ill and have to endure the solicitous concern she knew would be undeserved. Equally unable to bear Yvette's cheerful company, she had given her some lingerie to launder and had busied herself shampooing her hair.

When she was handed Aurora's bracelet, she recoiled in dread. Then, far too anxious to discover how she might light the same passionate torch in Antoine that the Gypsy guitarist had created within her, she sent word that she would see the woman. Too distraught to don more suitable attire, she came down to the garden still wearing her silk dressing gown and satin slippers.

Aurora rose to greet Mademoiselle Minoux, but she was shocked by the change in her appearance. Pale-lavender circles marred the delicate skin beneath her eyes, indicating a sleepless night. As she handed Aurora back the bracelet, her hand shook so badly, the delicate silver hoop slipped from her fingers and Aurora had to lunge to catch it before it landed on the gravel path. Most surprising of all was the fact that the young woman who had been so meticulously groomed the previous day would appear with her hair damp and the clear evidence of her lover's possession on her throat.

"You slept poorly . . ." Aurora began as soon as she and Michelle were seated on one of the comfortable wooden benches in the garden.

"How did you know?" Michelle asked fretfully. Then her cheeks began to burn with shame as she realized the Gypsy who had serenaded her might very well have told Aurora exactly what he had done and the wanton way in which she had responded. Appalled by that possibility, Michelle looked away

30

and began to fuss with the ends of the sash that secured her lightweight robe.

Aurora recognized the guilt in Michelle's expression and sought to make the most of it. "I know many things. Antoine has disappointed you again," she announced solemnly.

Surprised by that comment, Michelle looked up. Aurora appeared to be merely concerned about her rather than gloating over the cavalier way the Gypsy musician had treated her. Relieved to think that was because the *gitana* did not know anything about the disgraceful interlude, she relaxed slightly.

"Yes, Antoine disappoints me constantly. He treats me as a sister, when I long to be his wife. That's why I wished to speak with you today."

Trying not to gawk at the sign of her lover's kiss on Michelle's throat, Aurora voiced her natural confusion. "A sister, mademoiselle? I do not understand how you can describe his behavior in innocent terms."

"His estate borders ours," Michelle explained. "I have known him all my life and he treats me as though I were still a pretty child rather than a grown woman."

Astonished by that comment, Aurora began to rummage through the deep pockets of her voluminous skirt, the ruffled tiers of which were sewn from a dozen different red-and-fuchsia prints. Her low-cut blouse was of a shade of pale blue not found among any of the skirt's wildly colorful patterns. A fringed scarf whose subdued hues matched none of her other attire served to tame her thick ebony hair and extended past her shoulder blades like a silken mane.

She carried dozens of objects useful to her trade with her and quickly produced a small mirror which she handed to Michelle. "Forgive me if that is a birthmark on your neck, but if it isn't, it does not look like it was left by a brotherly kiss."

31

While she had been too depressed to even glimpse in a mirror that morning, Michelle knew precisely where to look now. "That bastard," she moaned before shoving the mirror back into Aurora's hands. She hurriedly combed her fingers through her loose curls to pull her hair forward and hide the sign of the Gypsy's farewell, but there was no way to disguise her disgust.

"Again, I beg you to forgive me. I did not realize that you were unaware of that mark or I would never have mentioned it. I did not mean to upset you. Oh, no, I came here in hopes of bringing you and Antoine together as you wish."

Barely able to hear the *gitana*'s words for the blood pounding in her ears, Michelle nevertheless nodded as though she could. She did manage to catch Antoine's name, but a full minute passed before she remembered why she had wanted to speak with Aurora in the first place. "You mentioned ways to inspire devotion. How much does such knowledge cost?"

Aurora shrugged slightly. "I never use my gifts for money, but solely to help people. If you would like to reward me, however, I would be most grateful." She looked down as though discussing money truly embarrassed her.

What Michelle wanted most at the moment was advice on how to cast a curse on a Gypsy, but she knew without asking that Aurora would never provide the necessary information to enable her to harm a fellow *gitano*. "What was the name of the man playing the guitar yesterday?" she asked instead. "He was very good."

This time Aurora was not surprised, for women were drawn to Luis the way seagulls flocked to the sea. "His name is Luis, but I thought it was Antoine you wished to seduce."

"I'm positive I never mentioned seducing anyone,"

32

Michelle complained immediately. "I wish to be Antoine's wife, not his mistress."

"Of course," Aurora hastened to agree. "As any respectable woman would." Grateful to have ended any further interest in Luis, she began to concentrate on making a charm that she insisted would soon wring a proposal from Antoine's lips. "You must select your most beautiful lace handkerchief," she began. "Then use it to wrap something that Antoine gave you."

"He's given me a great many beautiful presents over the years."

"Good," Aurora enthused. "Choose a small one, a bit of jewelry perhaps. Then you must get a lock of his hair."

"I already have one," Michelle revealed.

"Wonderful! That is sometimes the most difficult object to obtain and you have already succeeded in getting it. Tie it together with a lock of your own hair. Use a bit of blue ribbon to ensure his fidelity once you are wed. Next you'll need a rosebud."

Michelle's mouth suddenly felt dry. The roses she had dumped on Luis had come from the garden where they sat and a cursory glance toward the once-fragrant rows of bushes showed few still had blooms. "Red, I suppose?" she barely managed to inquire.

"You're very wise," Aurora said. "Red for passion." She again reached into one of her pockets and this time withdrew a small wooden box intricately inlaid with ivory. She whispered a brief chant in Romany before removing the lid and taking out a tiny gold heart. "Place this in the center of the lace handkerchief. Put the locks of hair over the gift, and then add the rosebud. Again use blue ribbon to tie the handkerchief tightly. The magic is in the heart, you see, so it mustn't be lost."

Aurora placed the delicate token in Michelle's

33

palm. "Prepare everything as soon as you return to your room. Keep the handkerchief with you everywhere you go, and at night, sleep with it under your pillow. Save it for a good-luck charm after you and Antoine are married and it will bring you all the precious babies you want. Sometimes it takes a month or more, but my charm is sure to bring you the man of your dreams," she promised.

As Michelle's fingers closed over the golden heart, she wondered if that was merely an unfortunate choice of words, or if by some horrible misdirected magic she might find Luis enamored of her rather than Antoine. Then she realized that was absurd. She was going to use a gift from Antoine, and a lock of his hair, so if the spell worked at all, which she still rather doubted it would, it would bring her Antoine's love rather than some black-eyed devil who in a single day had managed to show her all she cared to see of hell.

"I'll be back in France in less than a month's time, so I want to pay you now. Will you please excuse me a moment?"

"Of course," Aurora agreed, but rather than sitting patiently, she roamed the garden and peered into the first-floor windows. They were really too high to allow her a good view of the interior, but she was convinced there was a treasure to be had there. When Michelle returned, Aurora was again seated on the bench and smiling innocently as though she had not stirred.

The wily *gitana* could tell from the weight of the small pouch Michelle placed in her hand that the Frenchwoman had been generous. Delighted, she still pretended to be reluctant to accept it. "Surely you have given me too much," she protested dramatically.

Michelle's head had begun to ache and she just wanted Aurora gone. "Not if your charm works

I haven't. Come. I'll show you to the gate."

Before they had reached it, however, Antoine came bounding out of the house. "There you are, *chérie*. Yvette has been looking for you for ten minutes." At first mistaking Aurora for one of the household staff, when Antoine drew near he was shocked to discover that she was actually an unusually attractive *gitana*. Normally he would have teased Michelle unmercifully for consulting a fortune-teller, but he suddenly had a brilliant idea and introduced himself instead.

"I'm Antoine Lareau and I'm hosting a party tomorrow evening. As part of the entertainment I'd considered having dancers, but being a visitor to Madrid I've no idea where to hire them. Do you or your friends dance?"

Dismayed, Michelle gave a small cry of alarm, for she feared if Aurora produced a troupe of dancers, Luis would come along to provide their music. Neither Antoine nor Aurora paid the slightest attention to her, however, and in only a few minutes the enterprising woman had promised to produce the finest *gitano* dancers in all of Spain. Antoine promptly produced a handful of coins which Aurora assured him was more than sufficient to guarantee their appearance. She then memorized the location of the party at the home of Antoine's relatives, and saying she would need time to rehearse, hurried away.

Antoine finally turned his attentions to Michelle. "Perhaps such informal attire is permissible for speaking with a Gypsy, but now that I'm here, you must change into one of your gowns. My favorite perhaps?"

At that moment, Michelle could not recall which of her many lovely gowns he favored, nor did she care. "Please, Antoine, I must beg you to forgive me, but after the wonderful party last night, I was too excited to sleep well. I'm afraid if I don't take a long nap today, I might not be able to attend your party tomorrow night and that would be a great tragedy."

"Yes, it most certainly would," Antoine agreed with undisguised frustration. "I had hoped that we could begin visiting the Prado this afternoon. The collection is so extensive that we'll have to go several times."

"Yes, I know the museum is very fine, but I'll exhaust myself if I go today. I simply can't do it."

Antoine stepped close and wrapped the end of one of her long curls around his fingers. "You don't look well, *chérie*, so I shan't argue. I'll leave you alone to nap, but you must promise me that you'll not entertain any other gentlemen callers."

While fetching the money for Aurora, Michelle had taken a moment to tie a piece of ribbon around her neck. Antoine had mistaken it for a pretty accent rather than the desperately needed camouflage it truly provided. She tucked her chin slightly and looked up at him through the thick fringe of her eyelashes.

"Why, Antoine, you know I see no one but you," she flirted shamelessly.

Amused by that sweetly feminine ploy, Antoine brushed her cheek with a feather-light kiss and then offered his arm to escort her into the house. "Do you think you'll feel up to going out this evening?" he inquired.

The yawn that Michelle had to hurriedly cover was genuine. "I'm sorry, but I really think I should go to bed early tonight."

"After napping all afternoon?" Antoine replied in dismay.

"I do so want to be at my best for your party."

"Well, yes, of course. Tomorrow night is far more important," Antoine admitted reluctantly. "Until tomorrow then."

36

"Au revoir," Michelle bid him sweetly, but the instant he left her aunt's house, she returned to the garden. That late in autumn, there was not a single red rose to be found. There were still white and yellow buds on the gnarled old bushes, but all the red ones were gone. She then sped through the house and, although certainly not dressed to be seen on the street, she peered out the front door hoping that the roses she had tossed from her window were still strewn about on the walk. Unfortunately, the wilted flowers and the remains of the vase had already been swept away.

Perplexed, Michelle dared not inspire curiosity by sending one of the servants out for a red rose. As she climbed the stairs to her room, she convinced herself that using the rose Luis had touched would not diminish the power of the charm Aurora had given her. How could it when she would be using Antoine's gift and lock of hair? Those were personal items which conveyed his essence. A rose was no more than a rose. Surely one would be as effective as another.

"I'm behaving like a ninny," Michelle scolded herself. She had no faith in Gypsy fortune-tellers, none at all. She was far too sensible a young woman to believe in their fanciful predictions. What she was doing was merely an experiment. If it worked, fine. If it didn't, it hadn't cost her all that much.

She wanted to at least give Aurora's suggestions a fair trial though, and thus followed the *gitana's* directions closely. She had so many beautiful lace handkerchiefs that it took her several minutes to decide which one to use. She topped it with the tiny heart and locks of hair, then added some pearl earrings Antoine had given her. They were so similar in design to a pair she had received from her parents that he had never been able to tell the difference between them and surely would not miss them.

Next she removed the rose from atop the dresser where it had lain all night. It had been a bud which had just begun to open when it had been cut, and even after several hours out of water it looked surprisingly fresh. She snipped off the stem with her sewing scissors and placed the red rose atop the earrings. She knotted the required items in the handkerchief and tied it securely with a blue bow, but she was annoyed that she had not been able to find an unsullied rose.

Not really in the mood to nap, she spent most of the day in companionable silence with her aunt, and then just as she had promised Antoine, retired early. She placed the love charm she had made under her pillow, but it failed to ease her apprehensions. What if Luis returned to serenade her? she agonized. Even if he had the sense to stay away from her aunt's house, he would surely be at Antoine's party. What if he created some type of ghastly scene by revealing that they had met previously, no matter how informally?

Those distressing questions kept her awake long into the night. She had made up her mind that she would ignore Luis if he dared return, but when he failed to appear, she did not understand why she felt only disappointment rather than relief. Was it only the lingering effects of whatever magic he had used to cloud her senses and make her desire him?

Fearing she would worry all day about her reaction to Luis at Antoine's party, she swore angrily as she punched her pillow into shape. The first cool rays of dawn filled her room before she was finally able to sleep, and it was again the hot-blooded Luis who appeared in her dreams rather than the warm but aloof Antoine.

Three

For Antoine's party, Michelle chose to wear one of the several new satin gowns she had brought with her from France. The low-cut bodice was the deep red-violet of claret wine while the skirt was fashioned of striped fabric in shades of wine, ecru, and forest green. Her kid slippers exactly matched the red-violet hue of her bodice as did her fan. Forest-green velvet ribbon accented her narrow waist and encircled her neck to suspend a small gold locket. Yvette had caught her curls at her crown to create a glossy cascade adorned with green velvet streamers.

With her fair coloring, the stylish gown was spectacularly beautiful on her, but as Michelle studied her reflection in the standing mirror in her room, she was too preoccupied to notice how stunning she looked. Feeling very foolish, she had slipped the trinket-filled handkerchief into her pocket. An attentive host, Antoine would be busy entertaining his other guests most of the evening, but she hoped that when he brought her home, his kiss might have a new-found warmth.

Her aunt Magdalena rapped lightly at the door and Yvette went to answer it. "You look like a princess!" Magdalena exclaimed. Supported by her cane, she entered the spacious bedroom with tiny, shuffling steps. "You're absolute perfection, my darling. Perfection."

"Merci," Michelle responded shyly. "I hope Antoine agrees."

"Who?" Magdalena asked as she came closer.

"Antoine," Michelle repeated in a slightly louder tone. "And I would like to refer to him as my betrothed rather than my childhood friend."

While now white-haired and frail, Magdalena had been a rare beauty in her day and she nodded sympathetically. "Make him jealous," she suggested. "You need not actually admire another man, merely pretend that you do."

"Isn't that dangerous?"

Magdalena smiled with the sweetness of her memories. "Of course. That is the beauty of it."

Unwilling to resort to such a ruse, Michelle shook her head. "No thank you, Auntie. Antoine complicates my life so completely I don't dare become involved with another man even as a romantic ploy." She gave the dear woman's wrinkled cheek a kiss, thanked Yvette for her assistance, and then went downstairs to await the carriage Antoine had promised to send.

Another man? her conscience whispered. *What about the Gypsy?* "Hush!" Michelle ordered although she was alone in the entryway. She would not allow Luis any place in her life. All day haunting memories of him had entered her thoughts with maddening frequency, but she had stubbornly refused to contemplate him at length. She kept a small leather-bound diary in which she recorded each day's adventures, but it contained no mention of him. She had made a notation of Aurora's visit so that she could recall the date should she wish to later, but she had not even attempted to describe Luis's serenade, or how helpless his kiss had made her feel.

The carriage arrived then and Michelle breathed deeply of the night air before entering it for the brief journey to Antoine's lodgings. Like her, he had also been invited to stay with relatives while in Spain and they lived only a few blocks away. His cousin, Francisco Castillo, and Francisco's wife, Maria Lourdes, were a charming couple, and Michelle was looking forward to seeing them again. She had decided if Luis came to the party, she would again complain of fatigue and go directly upstairs to rest until after he had gone. She hoped snubbing him would not only insult and hurt him, but discourage him, too, from ever bothering her again.

When she arrived at the Castillos' home, Antoine rushed forward to help her from his carriage himself. He gave her hand a fond squeeze before escorting her inside where gracefully curved wrought-iron candelabra filled the rooms with a blaze of light. "Your gown is exquisite," he leaned close to whisper. "It's almost as beautiful as you."

As Michelle murmured a sincere thank-you for his praise, she slipped her hand into her pocket to make certain the beribboned handkerchief was still in place. Antoine often complimented her appearance, but had he sounded a bit more enthusiastic that night, she wondered. It was difficult to judge, but she finally decided that he was merely excited about giving a party rather than having become more deeply enamored of her. She stifled a small sigh of disappointment and reminded herself that Aurora had not promised instant success. Apparently what was called for was more of the patience her mother had advised. It was a terrible shame that she no longer had any.

"Are the Gypsies still coming?" she asked Antoine.

"They're already here," he informed her proudly.

Two dozen guests, perhaps half the number that would eventually arrive, were clustered around them, and Michelle scanned their faces with an anxious glance. "I don't see them," she complained. "Where are they?"

Antoine clearly thought her question daft. "They aren't guests, *chérie*, but performers. They're waiting in the kitchen for the time being."

"When are they going to dance?"

"Not until after supper," Antoine explained. "I'm glad that you're so anxious to see them. That means the others will be equally thrilled."

"Oh, yes, I'm sure that they will," Michelle agreed, although *thrilled* was most certainly not the accurate word to describe her mood. "How many did Aurora bring with her?"

"Four others, another woman and three men."

Positive one of the men would be Luis, Michelle raised her fan to hide the grimace she couldn't suppress. Too distracted to move among those attending the party, she stayed by Antoine's side as he greeted the remainder of his guests. The vast majority were French visitors who had also come to Madrid to celebrate the royal wedding, but a few were Spanish friends of the Castillos Antoine had met and admired.

Michelle sat with him during supper, and so as not to insult him, pushed each course around her plate until it appeared that she had eaten something when she had actually taken only one bite. It was quite late by the time he announced they were to have some entertainment and asked everyone to step back to clear room for the dancers. By then, Michelle truly was so exhausted by dread as to really need the rest she had planned to request. Unfortunately, before she could make her exit, Maria Lourdes came to her side.

"Isn't this going to be wonderful?" she enthused.

"Undoubtedly," Michelle responded, still harboring a slender hope Luis might not be among the *gitanos*.

As soon as an expectant hush fell over the room, Aurora entered. With an insolent strut she circled the floor, shaking a tambourine against her thigh in an insouciant rhythm. After one complete revolution, during which she had locked eyes with every attractive man in the room, she blew out the candles in a standing candelabrum to lower the light to a dimly romantic level.

That night she was dressed in a red satin gown with a ruffled skirt. Although still garish, it was the most attractive garment Michelle had seen her wear. The *gitana's* thick black tresses had been pulled off her face with red ribbons. In addition to her usual assortment of bracelets, she wore earrings from which dangled tiny gold coins.

Sergio, dressed in black and wearing a broad-brimmed Andalusian hat, followed Aurora into the room. He struck an arrogant pose, then began to accent each of his steps by tapping his heels and clapping his hands. Moving in the opposite direction from Aurora, he first traced a wider circle than hers, but swiftly narrowed it until she was forced to move in place with tiny, mincing steps. While their eyes never met, the couple still managed to project the heated passion of lovers.

Michelle was not the only woman present who had to resort to fanning herself to tame her blush. Francisco joined his wife at her side, and other guests closed in around them blocking any hope of making a discreet retreat. She smiled weakly at Francisco and wondered if he would be able to catch her should she faint.

"This type of dance is native to Andalusia," he whispered, "but the *gitanos* perform it with more daring."

"Oh, yes, they most certainly do," Michelle agreed. Her breath then caught in her throat as

43

Luis walked in carrying a stool and his guitar. At least she thought it was Luis. The man was tall and well-built like he was. The problem was, he was also dressed in black, and, like Sergio, wearing a broad-brimmed hat which shaded his face completely. He sat down in the darkest corner of the room and strummed not one of the plaintive melodies he had played for her, but a wildly stirring tune to which Aurora and Sergio kept time with their heels.

The couple continued to stalk each other, but at every turn their motions grew more bold. Hands above their heads, Sergio clapping and Aurora slapping the tambourine, the pair brought their hips together and then spun away, clearly pantomiming the kind of passionate encounter Michelle now knew was possible. Rather than being amused, she was horribly embarrassed, for it seemed the *gitano* couple had no concept of the type of dance that ought to be performed for a mixed gathering.

Michelle searched the crowd for Antoine. She had expected him to stand beside her, but he had been caught in the rush to step out of the Gypsies' way and was confined to the far corner. Clearly delighted with the dancers, he flashed a smile and then turned to speak to a man standing nearby. Appalled that he would consider such a lewd dance appropriate entertainment, Michelle watched neither the guitarist nor the dancers, but instead studied the expressions of those standing closest to her. Clearly, many were enthralled, but she found the same revulsion she felt mirrored in several pairs of eyes, and hoped someone would have the courage to leave so that she could follow.

The first dance came to a dramatic climax with Aurora in Sergio's arms. They were rewarded with polite applause and as they withdrew, another pair of dancers appeared. Again the young man was clad in black and his equally youthful partner was in a vivid blue gown with a ruffled skirt. She held a pair of castanets in each hand, raised her arms above her head, and played them with a steady clatter as she swayed in time to the guitarist's beat. Her partner circled her, approached, and retreated in a ritual seduction as old as time.

. Again Michelle felt as though she were watching something she ought not to be viewing. She tried to look anywhere but at the dancers. Repeatedly her gaze strayed to the musician, who, while merely providing accompaniment, seemed to be moving with an all too sensual grace. His hands caressed the strings with a practiced ease, his fingers long and slim, perfectly formed for his art.

Unconsciously she raised her hand to her throat. The velvet ribbon concealed the mottled evidence of her shame, but she suddenly felt as though everyone in the room knew it was there. How dare the man brand her with a kiss? she cried silently. At that precise instant he looked up at her. He had not scanned the crowd since he entered and sat down, but he knew precisely where she was standing. He broke into a taunting smile meant solely for her before again bowing his head and becoming absorbed in his music.

"Do you know him?" Maria Lourdes asked.

Unable to speak, Michelle shook her head.

"I think you've made a conquest," Francisco added, but when he saw tears welling up in Michelle's eyes, he hurriedly apologized. "I beg you to forgive me. I did not mean to suggest something so improper as a liaison with a *gitano*. They never mix with outsiders anyway, so my comment was not only in poor taste but foolish. I am very sorry."

Michelle reassured him that she had not been of-

45

fended, but when she again glanced over at Antoine, she found him staring at her with an angry frown. She smiled, but it failed to lift his mood. He must have seen the smile Luis had given her, but surely he would have noticed it was a mocking grin rather than a friendly one. "Apparently not," she murmured under her breath.

The second dance drew to the same predictable close as the first and Michelle hoped now that everyone had performed, the *gitanos* would bring their risqué program to an end. Instead, Sergio returned to take the guitar from Luis, who rose and, with Aurora, began another dance. While the other two men had been very good, Michelle saw in an instant that Luis's style was truly extraordinary. He not only moved with the same fluid ease he had displayed on the guitar but each pose he struck held a classical elegance.

Every eye in the room was focused on him rather than Aurora, who tried to make up for what she lacked in grace with bravado. She was using castanets this time, but as she flailed her arms, their frantic clicks lacked any hint of a steady rhythm. She and Sergio had been a far more compatible pair in both height and style, but she smiled seductively as she danced with Luis, her clear preference for him plain in her rapt glance.

Tapping his heels, Luis executed a series of turns, but his eyes never left Michelle. His expression revealed no hint of his thoughts to the others crowding the room, but she understood from that silent salute, he was dancing for her. Another dance from another man might have been a flattering tribute, but Michelle had to fight back the panic that made her want to bolt. It was only the sure knowledge that fleeing suddenly would cause more gossip than if she remained that kept her in place beside the Castillos.

She lifted her chin proudly and did her best to ignore the brazen Gypsy's heated stare.

Rather than dampening Luis's mood, Michelle's open contempt inspired him to take the dance to the limit. With as fiery a finale as any pair of dancers could possibly affect, he knelt on one knee and drew Aurora across his lap. When she went limp against him, he used his hat to shield their faces as he pretended to kiss her. The resulting enthusiasm of the crowd pleased him enormously and after helping Aurora to her feet, he held on to her hand as they took a well-deserved bow.

"I've never seen better," Maria Lourdes confided when the applause died down enough for her to be heard, "but there's something familiar about that man. Could we have met him somewhere, Francisco?"

"A *gitano?*" her husband scoffed. "Of course not, my darling."

Michelle first looked down at her fan, then at the floor, and finally at the beaded tips of Maria Lourdes's slippers until she was confident Luis and his friends had left the room. She struggled to take a deep breath, but before she had fully recovered her composure, Antoine arrived at her side. "Your guests enjoyed the dancers very much," she offered with a hesitant smile.

"Not half as much as the last dancer enjoyed you," he hissed angrily.

Stunned by that rebuke which his cousins and several others standing nearby had undoubtedly overheard, Michelle debated her options. She would have preferred to have smacked him across the face with her fan, but knowing how badly that would embarrass the others present, she chose to take a jesting tone instead. "Surely you're not jealous of a Gypsy," she replied with a musical laugh. "Why,

Antoine Lareau, I am truly surprised at you."

With a well-practiced flip of her wrist, she opened her fan, raised it to cover the lower half of her face, and then batted her eyelashes coyly. To behave like a coquette did not come easily to her, but her mother had trained each of her daughters in the art of flirting should the need for such a transparent but effective ploy ever arise.

Charmed by the delightfully feminine innocence of her response, Antoine's anger dissolved in an embarrassed laugh. "Of course I am jealous," he admitted. "Do you think it pleases me to watch other men eye you that hungrily?"

"Hungrily?" Michelle echoed as though his description were absurd. "I really didn't notice, but if they were so starved it showed in their glance, then I do hope that you provided the *gitanos* with some refreshments before they left."

Amused by her witty repartee, Antoine remained in high spirits as his guests began to depart. Michelle waited until the last so that he could accompany her home. He usually held her hand when they rode in his carriage, but that night he put his arm around her shoulders and gave her frequent affectionate hugs. Uncertain whether the change in him was due to the efficacy of the love charm in her pocket or the jealousy Luis had inspired, Michelle nonetheless enjoyed it.

"Will you be too tired in the morning, or do you think we might plan the visit to the Prado that we postponed?" Antoine asked.

Because she had been sleeping so poorly, Michelle expected that she would be suffering from fatigue, but she did not want to miss any of the sights of Madrid. After all, there would be plenty of time to rest once she returned to Lyon. "I'd like that very

48

much," she told him, and he promised to call for her at eleven.

When they reached her aunt's home, she hoped for more than his usual kiss on the cheek and Antoine did not disappoint her. He kissed her on the lips this time, hesitantly at first but then again with the subtle elegance he displayed in all of his actions. It was a real kiss, and Michelle knew she ought to be ecstatically happy to receive it, but she felt no burst of excitement or even a faint hint of the delirious confusion Luis's kiss had inspired. Perplexed, she sat back and stared at the man she had loved for as long as she could remember.

Thinking he had offended her, Antoine hurriedly apologized, escorted her inside, and then left before he made any more serious blunders where she was concerned. Michelle moved to the window to watch his carriage depart, still amazed by her lackluster reaction to his kiss. She climbed the stairs slowly, hoping against hope that the next time he kissed her she would be thrilled clear to her toes.

"How was the party, mademoiselle?" Yvette greeted her.

"It was marvelous. Just what I've come to expect from Antoine." Michelle allowed the inquisitive maid to help her undress, but as usual said that she preferred to brush out her hair herself and dismissed her. She donned her nightgown and robe, sat down on her bed, and removed the ribbons from her curls.

Startled by a sudden noise from the balcony, she glanced toward the glass doors and listened more attentively. When she heard another slight scraping sound, she suspected a stray cat might have decided to spend the night there. Because it would surely begin to howl the instant she got into bed, she hastened to shoo it away now. She reached the doors in three strides but opened them carefully so that

49

the cat, if there was one, would not bolt inside.

At first glance, the balcony appeared to be unoccupied, but as she started to close the doors, Luis reached out and grasped her wrist to stop her. Michelle would have screamed, but she recognized him and cursed him softly instead. "Let me go!" she demanded hotly. "Wasn't having to look at you earlier tonight punishment enough?"

"Punishment?" Luis repeated skeptically. He led her back into her room and then pulled her around to face him. "Most women think that I dance even better than I sing. Were you the only one there tonight who wasn't impressed?"

"Oh, I was most assuredly impressed," Michelle told him, "but if it's compliments you crave, you'll have to go elsewhere."

"I didn't come here for compliments," Luis admitted in a whisper as tender as a caress.

Michelle regarded his smug smile with a furious frown. "Dare I ask why you have come? How did you get up to my balcony?"

"I'll answer your second question first since it's the easiest. I used a rope. As for why I'm here, you already know that, mademoiselle."

When he bent his head, Michelle knew exactly what was coming, but she stood transfixed, no more able to avoid his kiss than she had been the first time he had plundered her mouth and assaulted her senses. Thinking he could not possibly have the same stunning effect on her twice, she was even more shocked by the wanton abandon of her reaction to him than she had been the first time.

She made no effort to escape him, but instead relaxed, unable to disguise her eagerness for more of the delicious kisses he bestowed with such masterful ease. He released her wrist to encircle her waist and she raised her arms to his shoulders. Her fingertips

50

rested lightly on his black silk shirt and she felt not only the warmth of his well-muscled body but also his impressive strength.

He possessed a remarkable physical appeal, but when he stepped back slightly to judge her reaction to his kiss, she thought first of magic rather than of something far more precious and rare. "How do you do that?" she demanded.

"Do what?"

His smile was so dazzling that several seconds elapsed before Michelle recalled the question she had asked. Without realizing why, she left her palms pressed against his chest. "Is it merely practice with all the women who admire your talents as a singer and dancer that makes kissing you so pleasant, or is it some Gypsy spell?"

"Is kissing me merely pleasant?"

Michelle shook her head. "Answer my question, please."

Luis nodded thoughtfully, but then shrugged. "How can I possibly say why you enjoy kissing me? You'll have to answer that question yourself."

Michelle could feel his heart beating steadily beneath her palm while hers was thumping wildly within her chest. That wasn't fair. It had to be magic. It just had to be. "I think it's a spell of some kind," she murmured.

Amused by that completely erroneous conclusion, Luis kissed her again and again, and again, until he was as unsteady on his feet as she. He eyed the bed with a longing glance, but knew he dared not take things that far tonight. He closed his eyes and continued to savor Michelle's flavorful kiss. She was wearing a matching robe over her nightgown that night, but two layers of silk provided little more of a barrier to his touch than one. He moved his hands up and down her spine and over her ribs before using his thumbs to gently knead the beginning swell of her breasts. This was magic all right, he thought numbly. The very best kind.

Aghast that he would take such a shocking liberty, Michelle shoved him away. She looked around, apparently too dazed to recognize her surroundings immediately. She raised her hand to push her hair out of her eyes, and drew in a deep breath. What had possessed her to speak to him in a civil tone and to kiss him again, rather than scream for help?

"You've no right to be here," she finally managed to announce. "It's got to be far easier to go down a rope than climb up one. Please leave."

"I don't believe that you really want me to go."

"Oh but I do! I'm in love with another man. He's the one who hired you to dance for the party tonight."

"Antoine Lareau?"

"Yes, that's him." Michelle moved to the double doors that were still standing ajar in hopes he would quickly walk through them. "Now you must go. You made Antoine very jealous tonight, and you mustn't come near me ever again."

Luis tilted his head slightly and regarded her with a puzzled glance. "I don't believe that you love him."

"It doesn't matter what you believe. Just go."

"If you two are in love, why haven't you married?"

That was an excruciatingly painful question Michelle had asked herself all too often. "I have no desire to discuss such a personal topic with you."

Luis approached her slowly. "No? Why not when you were willing to share something of yourself just now?"

Once again Michelle combed her fingers through her hair to push a wayward strand out of her eyes. "That was different."

"Why?" Luis inquired as he reached her side.

"You asked for Aurora's advice concerning Antoine. Why not ask for mine?"

Fearing what she might see, Michelle had to force herself to look up at him, but his expression was sympathetic rather than cruel. His eyes were so deep a brown they appeared black and were ringed by a thick fringe of long black lashes any woman would have envied. Not wanting to lose herself in him again, Michelle decided Gypsies were a strange lot she ought to definitely avoid in the future.

"Antoine loves me, he just doesn't realize how much yet. As I said, you made him very jealous tonight. That's a good sign."

Luis nodded. "When will you see him again?"

"Tomorrow morning. We're going to the Prado Museum at eleven."

"Good, I'll go there, too."

Instantly understanding his purpose, Michelle objected strenuously. "I absolutely forbid it. He'll accuse you of following me at the very least. At worst, he'll suspect that I've encouraged you."

Again Luis flashed a triumphant grin. "You have."

"I most certainly have not!"

"Do you frequently entertain gentleman callers in your bedroom at this late hour?"

"You were scarcely invited!"

"But I have been entertained."

Michelle felt an incriminating blush flood her cheeks and suddenly recalled she ought to have complained of what he had done to her. She swept her curls aside and pointed to the telltale mark on her throat. "Did you expect me to thank you for this? What if Antoine had seen it?"

"He didn't?"

"No!"

"Then he is indeed a fool and I shall probably

53

have to follow you all through the Prado tomorrow before he notices me."

Michelle raised her hands in a supplicating gesture. "Please. Stay abed late, practice your guitar, do anything you please, but don't go anywhere near the Prado. Now please go."

Luis shook his head and undid a couple of buttons to loosen the fit of his shirt. He spread the collar to expose his throat more fully and then offered a bargain. "You must leave your mark on me as I did on you and then I'll go."

That was such a bizarre request, Michelle could not believe she had heard him correctly. "But what of all the women who admire you so? Won't they be incensed if you call on them wearing the print of my lips?"

"I certainly hope so," Luis teased. "If jealousy works so well with Antoine, it ought to work with them, too."

"That's despicable, Luis."

"I didn't realize that you knew my name," he replied with a delighted grin. He gave a mock bow. "I'm so pleased to meet you, mademoiselle."

Convinced that he was simply an incorrigible rake, Michelle feared he might linger to tease her all night if she failed to act quickly to send him on his way. "If I do it, will you promise to go?"

"You have my word as a gentleman."

Michelle doubted *gitanos* were ever described as gentlemen but did not want to take the time to argue the point. "You'll have to bend down."

Luis responded by picking her up. "There, go ahead. Do it."

Her feet dangling in midair, Michelle had little choice about obliging him, but the instant her lips touched the seductive warmth of his bare skin she realized her mistake. It was too late to turn back,

54

however, and with her arms looped around his neck she began to caress and ruffle his glossy black hair. His taste, his scent, the blissful heat of his skin all made her long for more. Time had no meaning and she might have clung to him for days had he not broken her hold on him by wrenching her arms free. None too gently, he stood her on her feet.

The look he gave her then was one of such wild desire that Michelle felt his need as deeply as her own. As promised, he took a step toward the doors, but then he turned back. With a low moan he drew her into his arms and, choosing the exact same spot, renewed his mark on her throat before leaving her without a word of apology or farewell.

Completely unable to understand what had just happened, Michelle closed and locked the doors and then leaned back against them while she attempted to catch her breath. She kept telling herself what she had just done with Luis was impossibly foolish, if not wicked, but the smile that refused to leave her face belied those thoughts. Luis made her feel so alive. It was a glorious sensation which even now left her filled with a delicious warmth she hoped might never fade.

She had to force herself to go to the wardrobe and remove the love charm from the pocket of the gown she had worn to the party. She placed it beneath her pillow and as she climbed into bed she reminded herself that she would soon be leaving Madrid. She would marry Antoine and spend the rest of her life in Lyon. It was the life she had always wanted, the one she was convinced she was meant to have.

Luis could never be more than a momentary diversion, and in the future, she dared not allow him to be even that. When Antoine called for her in the morning, she would suggest they go somewhere other than the Prado to prevent Luis from causing any further strife between them. She had been a fool to tell him their plans in the first place, but plans could always be changed and she would see that theirs did.

That problem solved, she again allowed her thoughts to dwell on Luis. He possessed a wildly romantic soul, but she imagined that all Gypsies did. From what Francisco Castillo had told her, Gypsies did not marry outsiders any more than well-bred Frenchwomen did. She sighed softly and raised her hand to caress her throat. If only Antoine could set her blood aflame the way Luis did. Believing there was no point in longing for the impossible, she drifted off to sleep on a pillow dampened by a flood of tears.

Four

Early every morning, Magdalena Ortiz y Reyes attended Mass with the Augustinian nuns at the Convent of the Incarnation. A childhood friend had joined the order and Magdalena had supported the sisters with generous contributions throughout her life. After completing her daily devotions, she returned home, where she looked forward to spending some time with her adorable niece. When a Gypsy accosted her as she left her carriage at her front door, she shrank back and had she still been spry enough to manage it, she would have shaken her cane at the young woman to send her on her way.

Fearing she had frightened the elderly woman, Aurora greeted her with a respectful curtsy. "Forgive me for startling you, señora," she began, "but as I was passing your house I suddenly felt an overwhelming sense of excitement. You are about to become the recipient of an extraordinary piece of good luck and I want you to be prepared for it."

Flustered by the Gypsy's extravagant promise, Magdalena responded hesitantly. "I have been blessed my entire life."

"Oh, you most certainly have!" Aurora agreed enthusiastically. "Your niece, Mademoiselle Minoux, told me so. You must know how greatly she admires you."

"You've met my niece?"

"Yes, I am proud to say that she relies upon my advice in matters of the heart. But you are the one I wish to help today."

57

In addition to her hearing loss, Magdalena's eyesight was also failing. The coins dangling from Aurora's earrings were merely a golden blur and the careless stitches with which her colorful costume was sewn went unnoticed, but despite her inability to distinguish detail clearly, Magdalena felt the wildness of the *gitana*'s manner and doubted that she had ever met Michelle.

"My niece has never mentioned you," she argued.

Aurora drew near, cleverly blocking the widow's access to her front door. "I've told her secrets she would be unlikely to repeat to anyone, but I do know her as well as Antoine Lareau. My name is Aurora. You can ask either of them about me, but I fear that unnecessary waste of time would jeopardize your chances to receive the good luck I've foreseen."

Magdalena was growing tired and shifted her slight weight to ease the burden she had to place on her cane. Impressed by Aurora's use of Antoine's name, she struggled to overcome her suspicions. She knew several women as devout as she who had their fortunes told regularly by Gypsies. Perhaps it was time she had hers told as well, she decided. She invited Aurora into her home, but as soon as they had crossed the threshold, the lively *gitana* raised her fingertips to her temples and began to sway.

"You have a beautiful garden," she described. "That's where the magic will take place. We must talk there." Giving Magdalena no time to argue, she took the elderly woman's arm and guided her toward the rear of the house.

"I do so love my garden," Magdalena admitted rather shyly.

"That's because you feel the magic there, too," Aurora enthused.

"I do?"

"Oh, yes, I'm certain that you must. Others appreciate only the beauty and fragrance of your roses, or enjoy the solitude of a sunlit afternoon. You feel something deeper than peace there, though, don't you?"

Deeper than peace? Magdalena mused silently. A childless widow who still mourned the loving husband she had adored, she often felt closer to his spirit in the garden he had designed than she did in the home they had shared. "Yes," she agreed wistfully. "The hours I spend in my garden are precious to me."

Pleased that Magdalena was proving to be so easy to influence, Aurora's smile took on its predatory gleam. When they entered the well-tended garden, she led the frail widow to the same bench where she and Michelle had sat. She pointed toward the roses with graceful gestures and spoke in a low, seductive tone as she described her prediction in more detail.

"The spell will not work just anywhere," she cautioned. "It must be attempted only in a place where the earth's own magic is strong. Your beautiful garden is just such a wondrous place," she confided.

There were times when Magdalena had to strain to catch Aurora's words, but she was soon following the *gitana*'s conversation with an eagerness that made her weary eyes shine with a girlish delight. Her initial skepticism had vanished completely by the time the Gypsy's comments leapt from the loveliness of the garden to the mystical radiance of the moon and the power contained in a million shimmering stars.

"Only a few *gitanas* still know the ancient spells," Aurora whispered dramatically. "You must never tell anyone that I am adept in capturing the magic

59

of the universe, for surely I would be ripped to pieces by men obsessed with greed. You are a gentle woman whose heart overflows with love. That's why fate has chosen you to receive this good fortune."

Flattered by Aurora's praise of her virtue, Magdalena failed to question her motives. She nodded and repeated each of the *gitana's* directions. "Yes, I have a small wooden chest. After everyone has gone to sleep tonight, I'll fill it with gold coins and jewelry. I'll meet you right here with it at midnight."

"The chest must be only half full for the magic to work, señora," Aurora hastened to remind her. "When we bury it, there must be enough room for your treasure to double in size."

"Yes, I understand," Magdalena agreed, feeling very foolish that she had failed to grasp such an obvious point.

"Remember, you must not tell anyone what we're doing. If the chest is too heavy for you to carry, just meet me here in the garden and I will fetch it from your room. Can you keep this a secret? If not . . ." Aurora gave a pathetic shrug, "the spell will be broken and you'll have only what you buried rather than the newfound riches you deserve."

Magdalena's eyes twinkled as she smiled. "I have secrets I have kept for fifty years. You need not worry that I will fail to keep this one."

"You possess great wisdom. I was sure I could trust you. Now I have another secret for you," Aurora leaned close to reveal. "Michelle and Antoine will soon wed. Thanks to my magic, you will be able to purchase a magnificent gift for them."

"How wonderful!" Magdalena exclaimed.

"Yes, isn't it?" Aurora rose and helped Magdalena to her feet. "Now continue your day as you usually do, and tell no one about our conversation. I will meet you again here at midnight." Delighted with her own cleverness, she gave another respectful curtsy, and then hurried out the back gate before the laughter bubbling up inside her became impossible to contain.

Having slept very little, Michelle had great difficulty dressing with any enthusiasm for the day's outing with Antoine. Too preoccupied to select her garments with care, she succeeded in looking her best primarily due to Yvette's attentive assistance. She had to again resort to wearing a ribbon choker, but being able to hide the evidence of Luis's most recent intrusion on her life did not even begin to ease her nervous tension.

Convinced that avoiding all contact with the handsome Gypsy was the only way to rid herself of his distracting memory, she asked her aunt to suggest places she and Antoine might visit that day. Magdalena was happy to list several possible amusements and when Antoine arrived, Michelle was ready for him.

Delighted that his overly eager good-night kiss had not affected the warmth of Michelle's welcome, Antoine nonetheless took care to brush her cheek with a customary whisper-light touch of his lips. "That you've chosen to wear my favorite gown pleases me immensely," he enthused. "I love showing you off and you're even more lovely than usual when you wear blue."

Uncertain what she had donned, Michelle hurriedly glanced down at her bodice and skirt. The flattering lines of her pale-blue silk gown were trimmed with white satin piping and she was relieved to discover Antoine's favorite among her

61

many dresses was also one of hers. Perhaps now she could recall which one he meant when he referred to "his favorite." Her smile wavered only slightly before she offered a change in plan.

"The day is so bright and clear," she began. "Why don't we spend it touring the city and strolling through Retiro Park rather than studying dusty paintings in the tedious confines of a museum? We've gotten only brief glimpses of the Fountain of Cybele. I want the opportunity to enjoy it more fully."

Antoine slipped his arm around Michelle's slender waist and urged her toward the door. "While it does not compare to Paris in my view, Madrid is a lovely city and I'll be happy to see it with you, but I won't delay our visit to the Prado by another hour much less another day. The Fountain of Cybele is on our way, and while it is indisputably magnificent, it certainly doesn't require more than a few minutes' contemplation to appreciate. As for the park, perhaps you and Yvette might go there some morning. It holds absolutely no interest for me."

"But, Antoine —" Michelle beseeched softly.

"Hush, my darling. I have the whole day planned and there's no time for idle strolls."

Feeling trapped, Michelle slipped on her white lace mantilla before stepping out the door. She pulled the delicate veil forward, and wondered if there was even the slightest chance that Luis might not recognize her. Scarcely demure by nature, she thought she might be able to disguise herself with the flowing mantilla and a well-placed fan but not with Antoine strutting along beside her like a gamecock. Certain Luis would readily recognize him, Michelle's expression filled with frustration.

"Pouting does not become you," Antoine scolded. "Please do try and be pleasant. It will make the day ever so much more enjoyable for the both of us."

Michelle forced herself to smile. "I wasn't pouting," she denied emphatically. "I was merely wondering why my wishes are so consistently ignored."

Believing her complaint absurd, Antoine laughed deeply. He helped her up into his carriage and took his place at her side before pointing out her error. "You must trust me to know what is best, *chérie*. I'm well within my rights to ignore your wishes when they are as frivolous as wanting to spend the day in a park rather than one of the world's most prestigious museums. Surely indulging such a foolish whim would leave us both feeling disappointed when we realized what we had missed for mere sunshine and flowers. Don't we have sunshine enough at home?"

"What if I have no interest in paintings?"

"You should keep such a failing to yourself and strive to be an agreeable companion for me. After all, doesn't every woman find her greatest happiness in pleasing a man?"

"It depends upon the man," Michelle answered all too quickly. Then mortified to think that she had just flippantly insulted the man she hoped to wed, she focused her attention on the passing scene rather than her companion's puzzled frown.

"Would you rather spend the day with someone else?" Antoine asked sharply.

"Don't be silly."

"First I habitually disregard your wishes, and now I'm being silly?"

Michelle knew she was making one stupid mistake after another that day but it wasn't her fault. It was the blasted Gypsy's! "I'm sorry if I offended you, Antoine," she begged contritely. "Please forgive me."

"That scarcely sounded sincere."

"Well, it was!" Half expecting Antoine to order his driver to take her back to her aunt's home, Michelle held her breath, but the opinionated Frenchman did not speak again until they entered the plaza where the Fountain of Cybele stood.

Antoine leaned across her to point toward the impressive stature of Cybele in her chariot at the center of the large fountain. "The lions pulling the chariot are symbols of harmony and elegance. You would do well to cultivate those virtues," he suggested with the bitter sarcasm he frequently turned on others, but seldom on her.

Michelle was positive that if she was lacking in either quality at the moment, it was Luis's fault. Confident in that belief, she strove mightily not to lash out at Antoine when it was the Gypsy who deserved her wrath. She inhaled deeply and fanned the uncomfortable warmth from her cheeks. When she glanced toward Antoine, he was eyeing her with undisguised amusement. He was such a handsome man, and especially so when he smiled, but their trip to Madrid had provided ample opportunity for him to display the proprietary attitude she had always found annoying. It was fast becoming absolutely intolerable. Again, she blamed her ill humor on Luis rather than Antoine.

"I don't recall your ever criticizing me for being lacking in virtue before today," she replied with a knowing smile which readily conveyed her double meaning.

Preferring to flirt rather than fight, Antoine took her hand and brought it to his lips. "I admire your charm far more than your petulant anger."

"Then you would do well to cultivate that mood in me," Michelle advised sweetly.

Amused that she would use his own words to mock him, Antoine forgave her earlier defiance.

"Sight unseen, I'll wager that while the Prado contains portraits of many beautiful women, not a single one compares to you."

Accustomed to his effusive compliments, Michelle was nonetheless flattered. "Thank you, Antoine, but I have no desire to bet against you on any point, and most especially not on that one."

"Somehow I knew that you wouldn't."

Despite the new playfulness in Antoine's mood, Michelle was still apprehensive as they strolled toward the columned entrance of the Prado. A rose-colored palace, the museum had been opened in 1819 to display the royal art collection. They paused to read the plaque identifying the statue of Goya before going inside and Michelle made a silent vow to concentrate all her energies on appreciating the works of art rather than worrying about who else might be visiting the Prado that day. She had always enjoyed touring museum collections, and as she slipped her arm through Antoine's, she grew determined to examine each and every treasure the Prado contained.

Her plan worked quite well for the first few minutes but was instantly forgotten when she caught a glimpse of Luis up ahead. Again dressed entirely in black, he appeared to be studying the work of the German painter and engraver, Albrecht Dürer, but she wondered if a Gypsy knew enough about art to recognize a masterpiece when he saw it. Appearing able to read her thoughts, Luis turned and nodded slightly.

Appalled by that silent show of recognition, Michelle stepped closer to the painting Antoine was admiring and willed the insolent Gypsy away. When she finally dared risk taking another look toward the Dürer display, Luis was gone. It was only a temporary absence she was sure. They would undoubtedly cross paths repeatedly, and anticipating the worst of confrontations, Michelle clung more tightly to Antoine's arm.

Antoine gave Michelle's hand a distracted pat and led her to a portrait of an unidentified man by Dürer. He pointed out the subtle shadings and exquisite brushwork and mistook her noncommittal reply for agreement. "You see, I knew that you would enjoy the Prado far more than the park."

"I enjoy everything we do," Michelle reminded him, but his resulting smile failed to banish her fears. She made no effort to scan the faces of the other visitors until the weight of the Gypsy's gaze became as oppressive as a sodden cloak. She glanced over her shoulder and found him standing less than ten feet away. He winked at her this time, but she responded with a horribly hostile grimace. Convulsed with soundless laughter, he walked into the next room, where he knew she would have to face him again.

A man with an intense love of beauty, Antoine was so absorbed in the delights of the royal collection that he had escorted Michelle through the galleries for more than an hour before he finally noticed a tall, dark-haired man turning the corner just ahead of them. "Wasn't that the Gypsy musician who's so fond of you?"

"Who?" Michelle responded innocently, as though she had no idea to whom he might be referring.

Antoine reminded her of the entertainers at his party the previous evening. "It was only last night, *chérie*. I can't believe that you've forgotten the man so completely."

"Oh, *that* musician," Michelle murmured absently. She swallowed hard, and prayed that now that Antoine had finally noticed Luis, the Gypsy would swiftly depart. She gazed about the room but saw no sign of him. "He was quite tall, wasn't he? I don't see anyone who even resembles him."

"He just stepped into the next room," Antoine informed her. "Come, let's catch up to him."

Michelle hung back. "Why would we want to do that?"

"I'll not have him following you, Michelle," Antoine swore with a disgusted frown.

"How can he possibly be following me if he's ahead of us?"

Antoine opened his mouth to exhort her to take his comment more seriously, and then realized that it had sounded absurd. "Well, he may not be following you in the strictest sense of the word, but loitering here and waiting for you to pass isn't acceptable, either."

Apparently dismayed, Michelle opened her eyes wide as she looked up at her old friend. "How could he have guessed that we'd be here today?"

"He was probably watching your aunt's home, and followed us. Gypsies are extremely clever. Perhaps he follows beautiful women simply to amuse himself, but I'll not allow him to come this near to you ever again."

Michelle made a great show of studying the people who stood nearby. "He's not all that close, Antoine. If that really was him."

"Well, of course it was!"

"You saw him that clearly?"

Antoine took her arm. "Yes, I most certainly did," he insisted, but when they entered the next room, there was no tall, dark-haired man to be seen. There were several well-dressed young couples, not all that different from themselves, two elderly men, and four women with a female guide who were studiously taking notes and speaking in hushed whispers.

"You see?" Michelle teased. "It was merely your imagination."

Dismayed not to have found the man, Antoine shook his head. "No, I saw him," he repeated. "He's here."

Seized with a sudden inspiration, Michelle stepped close. "Would you rather leave than continue our tour? You won't enjoy yourself if you're worried about being followed."

"I am not worried," Antoine scoffed through clenched teeth. A sudden flash of ebony caught his eye and he looked up in time to see a male in dark attire, the Gypsy he believed, walk by the doorway at the end of the room. He took Michelle's hand to pull her along with him. In their haste, their footsteps echoed with a hollow ring across the highly polished marble floor.

"Come on, he's just ahead of us," the Frenchman urged. "We'll find him this time."

That was the very last thing Michelle wished to have happen, but Antoine gripped her fingers so tightly, there was no way that she could hang back. They rushed into the adjacent room, and then hurried on into the next, but Luis, if he had been there, was gone.

Michelle took a deep breath and let it out slowly before encouraging Antoine to look at the brightly painted triptych hanging nearest the door. She did not even care what it was when she pointed it out, but upon closer inspection found Hieronymus Bosch's *The Garden of Earthly Delights* so amazingly complex she was utterly fascinated by it. In the first panel, God was presenting Eve to Adam, but the Dutch artist had chosen to portray the biblical scene against a landscape filled with plants and creatures of the most imaginative sort.

In the center section, crowds of small nudes were

68

engaged in a wide variety of activities both repugnant and captivating. Some were riding animals in a circular procession. Others were bathing in serene pools. Michelle was reminded of nightmares where everything is strange, for nothing in the scene was ordinary. The final panel illustrated Adam and Eve's fall from grace and the earth was now filled with hellish visions. Meticulously painted in shades of vermilion, aqua, and gold it was easily the most bizarre work of art she had ever seen.

Annoyed to have missed the Gypsy, Antoine reluctantly turned his attention to the three Bosch panels. What he saw unnerved him completely and he immediately pulled Michelle away. "That's not anything I want to see," he complained. "Come, let's find the Spanish painters. I've heard that Velázquez's work is especially fine."

While she would have preferred to spend far more time with the Bosch, Michelle knew Antoine's mood was too foul to tolerate a plea for patience. That it was just another example of how he continually put his interests ahead of hers also occurred to her, but that was most definitely not an argument she would use now, either. As they left the room, she glanced back over her shoulder. Luis was now standing beside the fantastic Bosch work and he sent her a jaunty salute.

Completely infuriated with the arrogant Gypsy, Michelle was tempted to put a stop to his ridiculous game of hide-and-seek by pointing him out to Antoine. Unable to predict how Luis would respond, however, she had second thoughts about taking such a risk. Moving with a graceful elegance, she kept pace with Antoine and hoped the Velázquez paintings were indeed so magnificent, he would not care if Luis boldly stood right beside him.

Don Diego Rodriguez de Silva y Velázquez had

been the court painter to Philip IV and his paintings proved to be so exquisitely beautiful that Michelle loved each and every one. She and Antoine stood for a long while in front of *Las Meninas*. It featured not only the petite blond Infanta, Margarita, and her numerous attendants, but Velázquez himself appeared on the left of the painting apparently pausing briefly while he worked on a large canvas. The reflection of the king and queen could be seen in the mirror in the background.

"Simply astonishing," Antoine whispered reverently. "Velázquez took a simple palace scene, made it extraordinarily complex, and rendered it superbly."

Equally awed, Michelle agreed *Las Meninas* was a masterpiece, but their opinions diverged sharply when they began to view El Greco's work. "It has none of the delicacy of Velázquez," Antoine disparaged. "His colors are harsh and his figures appear to have been stretched to their limits as though they were tortured on the rack."

"The colors and proportions are unusual, that's true, but don't you think his work has more passion?" Michelle inquired thoughtfully.

"Passion does not have to be ugly."

Michelle was still in a conciliatory mood. "It's merely a matter of taste," she pointed out. "Obviously the Spanish people consider El Greco a genius or his work wouldn't be so prominently displayed here."

That was an opinion that could not be disputed, but Antoine fell into a resigned silence rather than concede the point. He was then disturbed to find that while he preferred the sentimental tone of Murillo's pastel religious themes, Michelle admired the macabre Goyas. Thoroughly convinced his lovely companion was totally lacking in artistic sensibilities, he turned away suddenly and this time caught Luis off guard.

Luis was perhaps a dozen paces away, leaning against the wall and observing the French couple's debate with sly amusement. When Antoine suddenly noticed him, he nodded politely to acknowledge the Frenchman's presence. After all, he was a Spaniard and had no reason to apologize for spending the day admiring his nation's art treasures.

"Look!" Antoine commanded in a fierce whisper. "The Gypsy is right over there!"

Bracing herself for a horribly embarrassing confrontation, Michelle dropped her fan and hoped the few seconds it took Antoine to retrieve it would provide time enough for her to devise a clever way to avoid it. Once he had slapped the fan into her palm none too graciously, she turned slowly in the direction he had indicated.

Again, Luis was gone.

"Is this some sort of a game, Antoine?"

Following her gaze, Antoine was appalled to again find the handsome Gypsy had vanished. He took a few steps toward the corner where Luis had stood, hesitated a second, and then returned to Michelle's side. "Yes, it most definitely is, but you and I are taking no further part in it. We're leaving."

"Weren't there some Italian painters whose work you wished to see?"

Antoine regarded her with a furious scowl. "Do you honestly believe that I can continue to ignore the fact that a Gypsy is boldly stalking you? Need I remind you that your mother has entrusted your welfare to me? I'll not encourage such an unsuitable admirer by remaining here another instant."

He offered his arm, and Michelle took it willingly. She was grateful the visit to the Prado had not produced the mortifying confrontation she had dreaded, and was relieved to be leaving rather than annoyed their visit had been cut short. By the time they stopped at an exclusive café off the Plaza de la Cibeles for refreshments, she was relaxed enough to be hungry and smiled easily at Antoine while they ate.

Antoine's mood, however, had continued to darken. He organized his thoughts with deliberate care, and as soon as their plates had been cleared away, he began a stern reprimand. "I realize I have no one but myself to blame for hiring Gypsy entertainers in the first place, but I cannot help but feel that there is more to the musician's fascination with you than is readily apparent."

Fearing that he was about to again blame her for Luis's interest, which was undoubtedly the worst sort of mischief on his part, Michelle leaned forward to speak up in her own defense, but Antoine hurriedly continued. "No, don't interrupt me. This is too important a matter to allow it to deteriorate into petty bickering. You are not only a rare beauty, Michelle, but a warm and friendly young woman as well. Perhaps it was no more than the sweetness of your smile which encouraged him, but you should have realized Gypsies aren't respectful and well mannered like we are and acted accordingly."

Michelle was not merely insulted by Antoine's assumption, she was also heavily burdened with guilt. "I did not encourage that man!" she responded with a seething anger she could not control.

Antoine shrugged. "I am not accusing you of doing it intentionally, *chérie,* but obviously it was done."

His reworded account of her relationship with Luis was too close to the truth to be denied and

72

Michelle glanced away rather than continue to meet his perceptive gaze. She did not even consider confessing the truth when it was so damning. No, she would be far too ashamed to admit Luis had visited her room twice when Antoine's reaction would surely be hideous to behold, and quite naturally so. She might never have smiled sweetly at Luis, but she had returned his passionate kisses with an inexcusable ardor that was doubly appalling in the clear light of the charming café.

Michelle was sure the Gypsy had worked a spell on her, some evil, cunning spell she was just too naive to recognize or overcome. She could fight Antoine's suspicions, though, and did. "I don't want to waste my time speculating as to why some Gypsy musician is infatuated with me," she insisted dramatically. "If indeed he is. He must be an extremely shy soul, for he didn't make his presence known to me."

"Are you calling me a liar?" Antoine cried. "Do you honestly believe I would say he was following you if he weren't?"

Michelle reached out to pat his arm with a soothing caress, but Antoine pulled away, so only her fingertips brushed his sleeve. Ignoring how rudely he had just avoided her touch, she opened her fan with a sharp flick of her wrist. "Spain is filled with tall, dark-haired men and I have made no attempt to distinguish one from the next. Perhaps you did see the Gypsy today, but you could just as easily have seen half a dozen other men who resembled him. Even if it *was* the Gypsy, he wasn't forward. He didn't annoy me in any way, but you're behaving as though he crawled along behind me reciting poetry written by lovesick fools."

When stated that way, Antoine had to admit that he did sound more jealous than he cared to admit,

73

and he was furious with Michelle for pointing it out. "Last night's party has left you overtired," he said instead. "I'll take you home now and I suggest that you take another lengthy nap and go to bed early again tonight. I want you to look your best for the wedding and I hope that your mood will have improved greatly, too."

Unwilling to listen when he took such a mocking tone, Michelle strode from the café with a buoyant step. She had never been so glad to see an outing end, but her happiness was short-lived when she thought of the night ahead and what Luis might ask of her this time.

Five

It was not fatigue that kept Michelle confined to her room for the remainder of the day but a palpable anxiety that made being pleasant company for her dear little aunt an intolerable burden. She had dismissed Yvette pleading a desire for privacy, but she could find no solace in the comforts of her beautifully furnished room. The spacious chamber now held taunting memories that refused to fade but instead grew more horribly vivid with each passing hour.

When Luis again climbed a rope to reach her balcony, he found the glass doors unlocked and Michelle waiting for him. "Good evening," he greeted her warmly. "What did you think of the Prado?"

Still dressed in her blue gown, Michelle paced the room. "Surely you did not come here to engage in idle conversation about art," she countered crossly.

Too curious to wait any longer, Luis had come to visit her quite early this evening and after closing the double doors, he took the precaution of drawing the drapes to avoid the neighbors' scrutiny. "I was merely attempting to be polite. If a discussion of art does not interest you, what would?"

Michelle stared at him coldly. "Last night I asked you not to cause trouble. No, let me rephrase that. I begged you to be anywhere but the Prado. Why couldn't you have stayed away?"

Luis's smile filled with a cocky nonchalance. "I

couldn't resist the temptation to make Antoine jealous," he revealed with a sly chuckle. "There was also the opportunity to see you again. Why should I have denied myself that pleasure?"

Pausing momentarily, Michelle clenched her fists at her sides. "You sent Antoine way beyond jealousy. He was infuriated that you'd 'stalk' me, as he described it. As for the pleasure of seeing me, I'm not so vain as to believe such insincere flattery from a brigand."

"I'm no bandit," Luis denied, "although I've been called much worse. I don't think you're really trying to insult me. A woman of your intelligence should be able to call me far more imaginative names."

Michelle shrank back as he took a step toward her. "Stay where you are!" she hissed. "You'll no longer amuse yourself at my expense."

Luis gestured expansively. "I had absolutely no idea that I was the only one being entertained."

After kicking her flounced skirt out the way, Michelle resumed pacing with a restless stride. She also continued to speak her mind. "You are a Gypsy, so it is no wonder that you have the blackest of hearts, but I'll no longer allow you to twist my emotions as brutally as you must wring out your wash. Go away and cease to bother me. I intend to wed Antoine and I'll not abide the interference from you that merely enrages, rather than inspires devotion in the man I love."

Luis had kept a close watch on Antoine as well as Michelle that day. That they were far from the ideal couple was so readily apparent to him that he did not understand how she could have failed to notice such an important fact. "How can you love a man who can't walk past a mirror without stopping to primp? He is constantly stroking his hair, adjusting the fit of his collar, or brushing bits of lint from his sleeves. It's clear that he's too deeply in love

76

with himself to be the husband you deserve."

Michelle was well aware of Antoine's foppish habits but had simply chosen to overlook them. "He's very handsome," she argued. "Why shouldn't he take pride in his appearance? His appearance is greatly admired."

"By whom?" Luis asked incredulously. "I don't know anyone who could possibly admire any individual who was so taken with himself as to neglect the beautiful woman on his arm."

"Well, at least you admire one thing about the man. He's able to escort beautiful women wherever he goes."

"That's easy enough," Luis discounted agreeably. "I do it myself."

Michelle did not rise to that bait but merely kept pacing with a slow, rhythmic stride as though she believed mere physical exertion would eventually result in the composure which eluded her when Luis was near. Lean and muscular, he was standing in a relaxed pose, but she knew how quickly he could move. She would not stand still and meekly wait for another of his disgusting kisses. Her conscience chided her for that lie, but she would admit only to herself that his kisses were sublime.

"Michelle," Luis called with a husky sweetness.

"What?"

"Look at me."

Michelle swallowed hard to force down her fright before glancing toward him. He was smiling at her, and for once his expression held what appeared to be affection rather than a blatantly predatory disdain. In the soft light, his hair glowed with an ebony sheen and his deep brown eyes held an admiring sparkle. It was not only his dark coloring that provided such a sharp contrast to Antoine, though. Luis was an arrogant Gypsy and the man she adored was a refined gentleman. She was ashamed

77

to have wasted even a second of her time comparing the two men.

"Please go," she commanded.

"In a minute," Luis promised. "First I want to know what you thought of Bosch's painting, *The Garden of Earthly Delights.*"

Surprised by what struck her as a completely irrelevant question, Michelle nevertheless answered truthfully. "I thought it was extraordinary in every respect. Monsieur Bosch must be a remarkable man. I'd like to hear him talk about his work."

"So would I," Luis agreed. "Unfortunately, he's been dead for more than three hundred years."

"Oh, I didn't realize."

"How could you? Antoine pulled you away before you'd had more than a passing glance at the card identifying the work. He was embarrassed by it, wasn't he?"

"Embarrassed might not be the right word," Michelle hedged.

"Appalled, aghast, disgusted, revolted?" Luis suggested as alternatives. "Whatever his opinion, it's obvious that your tastes are far more sophisticated than his. I'll bet he didn't care for El Greco or Goya's work, either."

"Well, no, he didn't," Michelle admitted reluctantly. "But that's really not the issue here. I asked you to leave."

"Just when our discussion is becoming interesting?" Luis teased. "Besides, the fact Antoine can't recognize a masterpiece unless the subject isn't in the least bit controversial or offensive is an issue worth debating. The man is totally self-absorbed and rigid in his views. He'd make the worst of husbands for a high-spirited woman. I shouldn't even consider marrying him if I were you."

Michelle's temper flared. "It's lucky for us both that you are not me," she countered.

"That's it!" Luis complimented. "That touch of fire is precisely what makes Antoine such a poor choice for you."

Michelle refused to even consider his assumption. "No, you're wrong. We've known each other our whole lives. We're the perfect couple. Everyone says so."

"Really?" Luis asked with pronounced skepticism. "It doesn't appear that Antoine shares that view."

"But of course he does!"

"He can't, or you'd already be his wife."

"And we've already had this argument. Please go."

Luis's glance turned insolent, but his words were matter-of-fact. "You aren't dressed for the evening. Why aren't you seeing Antoine tonight?"

Amazed he had to ask such an obvious question, Michelle glanced toward the heavens before replying. "He was enraged by your mischief. He had the audacity to accuse me of encouraging you somehow and chose to avoid me for the rest of the day. I hope you're proud of yourself. I came to Madrid with such high hopes and you've dashed them all with your willful disregard for my feelings. My romance is no more than a game to you, but I'll not allow you to make further sport of my life."

Impressed by that impassioned rebuke, Luis drew in a deep breath and exhaled slowly. Both his posture and expression became more relaxed. "Have I really caused trouble between you and Antoine? You're not simply imagining it?"

"Am I merely imagining that I'm alone tonight? Besides, why would I lie about such a thing? What possible point would there be in that? I love Antoine dearly and I hope to marry him soon. That you've caused him to be angry with me was the very last thing I'd ever want." Michelle bit her lower lip in a vain attempt to control the flood of emotion Luis's question had aroused.

Touched by the distress mirrored in her tearful gaze, Luis moved slowly so as not to startle her. "I'll put everything right," he offered. "Do you know where he'll be tonight?"

"You can't possibly expect me to help you make more mischief."

Luis shook his head. "There won't be more trouble, *querida*. Just tell me where I might find Antoine and you have my word that I'll send him back to you a devoted lover."

Michelle licked her lips as she debated whether or not to object violently to Luis's reference to Antoine as her lover. What she wanted from Antoine was a poetic marriage proposal, but she did not want to provide Luis with any excuse to stay and argue the point. There was also the question of whether or not Luis could be trusted to do as he promised. She had absolutely no faith in him in that regard.

Her dilemma was so easy to read in her agonized expression, and Luis did not hesitate to voice it. "Don't be afraid to trust me. I'm a man of my word."

While she sincerely doubted that, Michelle at last realized answering his question might be the only way to inspire him to leave. With that hope, she finally replied. "You must have met his cousin, Francisco Castillo, when you went to his house with Aurora for the party. I believe Francisco is as fond of gambling as Antoine. They'll probably be at Francisco's club tonight. I doubt that they'd admit you, though."

"I know the type of gentlemen's club you mean," Luis assured her. There were several in Madrid and he was confident he would be able to locate the one to which Francisco belonged. "You let me worry about how I'll get inside. It will take only a moment or two to convince Antoine that he is mistaken about us both and that we have absolutely no interest in each other. But before I go, I want you to be certain that's the truth."

"Of course it's the truth," Michelle insisted indignantly. "Or at least it's the truth from my side. I'm in love with Antoine. My future lies at home in France with him, not in Madrid with some, well—"

"Gypsy devil?" Luis supplied the words when she fell silent.

Michelle nodded, but when he reached out to embrace her, she was unable to summon the will to escape his grasp. As before, she knew she ought to fight him, to scream, scratch, and spit, but resistance was impossible when his sly smile was so incredibly appealing. In the next instant his mouth caressed hers and her mind ceased to argue with her heart. His lips were warm, soft, and yet insistent as he kissed her with a tenderness he had not previously shown. Michelle melted against him, and with an insatiable thirst drank in the abundant affection that poured from him in endless waves.

When he broke away, it was only for the few seconds it took to remove the ribbon encircling her throat. She felt the heat of his breath caress her fair skin as he renewed his mark. When he slid his fingers through her hair to force her mouth against his deeply tanned throat she felt his pulse pounding through his jugular vein with a thundering beat that echoed the throbbing of her own heart. Nearly faint from desire, she glimpsed the vivid brand she had left on him as he turned away. He was gone before she could call out to him, but she knew she would not have been able to say goodbye.

Emotionally drained, she reached out for one of the posts at the foot of the bed to steady herself. "It's a Gypsy spell," she murmured absently, but she had again carried the charm Aurora had helped her make with her, and whatever power it contained had yet to make itself known. She closed her eyes and raised her hand to her throat. Perhaps it was only that Luis's magic was far stronger than Aurora's, but Michelle knew she would never forget him.

She remembered the Bosch painting of paradise then, and finally understood why forbidden fruit is always the sweetest.

A few discreet inquiries among his acquaintances soon brought Luis the name of Francisco Castillo's private club. Luis had been a guest there on several occasions and he had no difficulty convincing Ramón Guerrero, a friend who was a member, to accompany him there that night. While not his equal in height, Ramón was a handsome young man with dark-brown hair and lively green eyes. He was well known for his charm, and as he and Luis strode through the club's door, they were given a far more enthusiastic welcome than many of the members received. Clad in elegantly tailored black evening clothes, they responded to admiring glances and friendly greetings with broad smiles and clever replies. It was the eve of the royal wedding, and their spirits were as high as those of all the citizens of Madrid.

After a brief perusal of the gaming rooms, Ramón laid his hand on Luis's sleeve. "I believe Castillo is seated at the far table," he revealed in a hushed whisper. "Why are you so interested in meeting him?"

"I'm not," Luis responded flippantly. "Just come with me and listen. You'll see what I'm after. Just remember to call me Augustín tonight. It's only my family and friends who know me as Luis and I want to keep it that way."

"Whatever you wish," Ramón promised. There were two vacant chairs at Francisco's table and Ramón led Luis over to them.

Antoine loved the game of faro with a passion and was eager to welcome new players, but his smile froze on his lips when he recognized Luis. Appalled to find a Gypsy dressed as a gentleman and staring at him from across the table at one of Madrid's most exclusive clubs, he turned to his cousin expecting him to put an immediate stop to such a disgrace. Equally dismayed, Francisco did no more than stare numbly at Luis.

Surprised to be greeted with shocked looks rather than welcoming smiles, Ramón nonetheless began the introductions. Both he and Luis knew the dealer and the two other men seated to Francisco's right, but not the Frenchman at his left. "Francisco Castillo, this is my guest, Augustín Aragon. He manages his family's shipping line from Barcelona, but like so many others, he is in Madrid for the wedding of La Infanta. We'd both like to meet your guest," he prompted when Francisco failed to respond.

Antoine barely nodded as Francisco spoke his name. Ignoring Ramón, he directed his question to Luis. "I beg your pardon," he began, "but didn't we meet last night at Francisco's home?"

Luis responded with a suitably baffled expression. "You are mistaken. Shall we continue the game?"

The hostile intensity of Antoine's stare did not lessen. "No, there's been no mistake. You played the guitar and danced with a group of Gypsies."

Luis reacted with a boisterous laugh as though what Antoine described were totally absurd, as did the other gentlemen at the table who knew him. He then leaned forward slightly. "Are you saying that you've met a Gypsy who resembles me? If so, then you're fortunate that I'm in such a fine mood tonight, for that's not an insult that I'd tolerate otherwise."

Antoine was not only positive his identification was correct, he was also too proud a man to back

83

down. "I don't suppose you were at the Prado today then, either?" he challenged accusingly.

Luis appeared to be taken aback by that question. "Why, yes, I did visit the Prado today," he admitted. His gaze narrowed sightly as he studied Antoine more closely. After a brief hesitation, he broke into a reckless grin. "I saw you there, too. You were with an exquisitely beautiful young woman dressed in blue. Is she your wife?"

Luis's candor confused Antoine completely. Michelle had repeatedly suggested that he had been mistaken about sighting the Gypsy, and if this Augustín Aragon and the Gypsy were two different men, then he most certainly had been in error. That was such an unusual occurrence that he was completely flustered by it.

"No, she isn't," he finally replied.

"Your fiancée then?" Luis asked.

Antoine shook his head. "She is a childhood friend who wished to attend the royal wedding."

"And nothing more?"

Antoine considered Augustín Aragon's suggestive question an indication of a most unwelcome interest in Michelle and he hurriedly changed the subject. "I apologize if I insulted you in any way, but the Gypsy we saw last night resembled you so closely that you could be brothers."

Luis nodded in a gracious acceptance of Antoine's apology. "I do have three brothers, but they live in California rather than Spain. If there really is a Gypsy who resembles me as closely as you claim, I shall have to search him out as it would be amusing to find someone who looks like me." He glanced toward Francisco then. "Do you share Monsieur Lareau's opinion? Could the Gypsy have been my twin?"

Unlike Antoine, Francisco knew exactly who Augustín Aragon was and he was so intimidated by the powerful man that he could barely think let alone render a coherent opinion. He had to clear his throat noisily before he spoke. "The man in question had your height and build, but he wore an Andalusian hat which shaded his face much of the time," he hastened to explain. "My wife did mention that he resembled someone, however, so apparently she was reminded of you."

"I don't believe I've ever had the pleasure of meeting your wife," Luis pointed out. "Perhaps tomorrow, during the festivities?"

"We'll look for you," Francisco promised.

Ramón was uncertain what had just transpired, but when Luis gave him a nudge under the table he spoke up. "We did not mean to interrupt your game. Why don't you continue, and we'll join in the next round."

Antoine nodded along with the others, but he found it difficult to concentrate on his bets with Augustín Aragon seated opposite him. He glanced at him as often as good manners allowed, constantly comparing him with what he recalled of the Gypsy. Finally he decided that Michelle had been right. There were a great many tall, dark Spaniards, and he had not really gotten a good enough look at the amorous Gypsy to identify him the next day. He felt very foolish then, but Señor Aragon had been so gracious about the misunderstanding that he did not allow it to spoil the evening.

One of the oldest banking games, faro required engraved counters, purchased from the dealer and used to place bets. The club's insignia decorated those in use that night. The same intricate design also appeared on the deck of cards lying faceup in the dealing box.

Luis watched Antoine place his counters on The Layout, a suit of spades enameled on green cloth. If the Frenchman had some sort of system, Luis was unable to discern it. Thinking it probable Antoine used birthdays or some other numbers significant only to himself, he concentrated on placing his own bets. He favored the odd numbers to win himself while his friend, Ramón, was equally fond of the even.

When the players were prepared, the dealer removed the initial pair of cards from the dealing box. He placed the first card, The Soda, about six inches from the box. The next card was The Loser and went right beside the box. The third card, which was now visible at the top of the dealing box was The Winner for that turn. To begin the second turn, the dealer placed the previous winner on the pile begun by The Soda. The following card drawn went on the losing pile and a new winner was revealed in the dealing box. Both groans and appreciative murmurs greeted each card as money could be won by accurately predicting both winning and losing cards.

Faro had always struck Luis as too passive a game to excite much interest, but it was plain from Antoine's whoops and shouts that he found it wildly exhilarating. The first round ended with Luis and Ramón slightly ahead, Francisco and one of the other men gloating over their winnings, and Antoine and the remaining player morosely contemplating their losses.

As the evening progressed, luck passed equally among the men and the winnings paid out by the dealer moved between them with the ebb and flow of the tide. Although wealthy, Luis never carelessly risked more than the average man on a wager, but Antoine continually bet larger sums than he could afford to lose. He won frequently enough to stay even, but not without considerable mental strain, and the anguish showed in his tortured expression each time the dealer turned a card that caused him a loss.

86

With only three cards remaining in the dealing box, the men began to bet on the order with which they would be drawn. Known as Calling the Turn, Luis considered it the highlight of the game. He bet a large sum and then sat back to watch the other men squirm as they debated the wisdom of attempting to recover their losses, or risk losing their winnings by matching his wager.

Luis caught Antoine's eye, and with a taunting glance silently goaded him into betting the last of his money. All six men leaned forward as the dealer revealed the last pair. Luis and Francisco had won and were rewarded with four times their bet by the dealer. Having bet on other combinations, their four companions cursed their bad luck in a mournful chorus.

"I've had enough," Ramón announced as he pushed back his chair. None of the others were inclined to remain, either. After cashing in their counters, they all started toward the door.

"If you should see that Gypsy," Luis called to Antoine, "be sure to give him my name. I would be glad to hire a double so that I didn't have to attend tedious meetings with attorneys and such."

Antoine forced himself to smile, but he made no such promise. The Aragon carriage was the first to be summoned and Antoine shook his head sadly as it rolled away. Disgusted with himself for losing so much money, his expression was sullen as he turned to his cousin. "How stupid of me," he complained. "I didn't even mention the word *wine* to him, and I'll bet I could have sold him a dozen cases."

"You've bet on enough for one evening," Francisco admonished.

Knowing that was certainly true, Antoine fell silent, and as they rode home, he pondered how best to deliver the apology he now knew he owed Michelle.

* * *

Ramón was not so easily fooled as Antoine and Francisco and he was eager to know what game was afoot. When the Aragon carriage reached his door, he refused to get out before hearing the truth. "I know that you play the guitar," he reminded Luis. "I also know that you've befriended a Gypsy or two. Have you actually begun dancing with them, or was that French dandy really mistaken about who he saw perform last night?"

Luis chuckled slyly to himself. "The story's too long to repeat, but I'll admit only that what began as a harmless masquerade has caused Monsieur Lareau's lovely friend more trouble than I'd anticipated. I promised to help her and that's why I had to deny that the Gypsy and I are one and the same. Now I trust you'll be discreet and not repeat that confession to anyone but a priest."

His curiosity merely aroused rather than satisfied, Ramón could not agree. "I want the whole story before you leave Madrid."

Luis leaned forward to unlatch the door and swing it open. "Good night, Ramón. I'll see you tomorrow, but don't pester me for details about my private life. I've already told you too much."

Ramón knew just how futile it was to argue with Luis, but as he entered his home, he vowed to learn just what his friend had been doing even if that meant masquerading as a Gypsy himself.

Like many people of an advanced age, Magdalena required only a few hours' sleep a night, so she had no difficulty remaining awake to meet Aurora. She had located several small wooden chests among her household furnishings and was then forced to choose between them. One was quite old and she feared the sides might crumble and cave in as it was buried and her promised increase in wealth then would be unable to occur. Another of the chests was new and that brought the concern that it might be too solid and secure for the Gypsy's magic to work properly.

Confused, the sweet little woman finally selected a chest that was neither old nor new. It was not the largest available, nor was it the smallest but of a size she could easily carry in her arms. Lined with blue velvet that was only slightly worn, Magdalena was finally satisfied that it was perfect for the task at hand.

Next came the decision of what was to be put into the chest. Her first selections were her most precious treasures. There was a ruby necklace and matching earrings that had belonged to her mother, a gold ring of her late husband's, an exquisite silver rosary, and an ornate gold chalice that had been in her family for generations.

She had bags of gold coins, too, and used them to cushion the jewelry and chalice as she packed the chest. By eleven she was ready. Seated in her favorite chair in the corner of her bedroom, she waited anxiously for midnight to arrive. The minutes passed with an agonizing slowness and she began to fret. What if despite Aurora's praise of her virtue, she wasn't really worthy of such good fortune? Would the precious stones she was about to bury turn to glass? Would the gold and silver turn to brass?

At a few minutes to midnight, Magdalena tried to pick up the chest and discovered now that it contained her treasures, it was much too heavy for her to lift. Something would have to be removed, but what? she worried. The chalice was heavy, so she set that aside with a reverent caress. As she began to rearrange the jewelry and bags of coins, fears of her worthiness for such a miracle returned and she removed the jewelry and rosary rather than risk their diminishing in value.

She had to remove one of the bags of coins as well before she could manage to raise the chest from the bed. It still looked half full to her, though, and not wanting to be late for her meeting with Aurora, she closed the lid, picked up the chest, and, unable to make much use of her cane with her arms full, made her way slowly down the stairs and out to the garden.

Michelle heard each of the clocks in her aunt's home strike the midnight hour. Some had low, mellow tones while others chimed with the beauty of silver bells. She had known when Luis had left that he would not return but she could not stop reviewing their last conversation over and over in her mind. He had promised to put things right with a confidence she was tempted to believe, but what if his words had been no more than an arrogant boast? He was, after all, a Gypsy, and everyone knew they said whatever they wanted the listener to hear.

Disheartened by that possibility, she wondered about the other things Luis had told her. It was true that Antoine was overly fond of his own image, but what handsome man wasn't? She was then embarrassed to recall that while there were two large mirrors in her room, Luis had not shown an interest in either of them. She finally decided that the Gypsy was merely so conceited that he knew how handsome he was without any need to reassure himself by studying his reflection. Surely such arrogance was just as offensive a trait as the one Antoine displayed.

Luis had been correct about Antoine's taste in art, though. He had hurried her away from the Bosch painting, and several others, too, she would have liked to have observed longer. The Gypsy had definitely been right that Antoine often showed little regard for her interests or feelings. But what man did put a woman's needs before his own? Her father had adored her mother, but there had never been any question in her mind as to who came first.

"The Gypsy's no better," Michelle complained. She punched her down pillow and attempted to find a more comfortable pose in which to sleep but she was still too preoccupied to rest. Luis had noted Antoine's faults and she could not deny that the elegant Frenchman certainly had them. But who didn't? She was not without flaws herself and had always believed that loving someone meant forgiving them their faults rather than dwelling on them.

Perhaps jealousy had prompted Luis to be so critical of Antoine, but that was silly when she would soon be gone and they would never see each other again. He would definitely be among the most exciting of her memories of Madrid, but that was all he would ever be: a memory.

Thoroughly convinced of that, Michelle began to think about the royal wedding. She could not help but wish she and Antoine were the ones being married tomorrow rather than a Spanish princess and a French prince. That was a wonderful dream, and with its unlikely beauty filling her thoughts, she was at last able to forget Luis long enough to fall asleep.

Six

Aurora was already in the garden when Magdalena left the house. She rushed toward the frail woman, and with an elaborate show of concern eased the wooden chest from her grasp. "This is much too heavy for you," she admonished gently, but actually she was elated that it weighed so much. "I told you that I would fetch it for you. What if you'd fallen? Not only would you have had to suffer that pain, you would also have failed to meet me and missed out on tonight's magic. That would have been an even worse tragedy."

"I didn't fall," Magdalena argued, for she hated being fussed over as though she were an invalid. Still, she knew she was very lucky to have made her way through the house safely in the dark. Now that she was able to use her cane, she felt far more secure but was much too proud to admit it. "Where are we going to bury the chest?" she asked instead.

"Come, I'll show you," Aurora whispered, and she led her along the gravel path. Their way was lit by the pale moonlight filtered through the leaves of the large oak tree growing in the center of the garden. The Gypsy had to shorten her stride to match Magdalena's, but that was not nearly so difficult as keeping her excitement from appearing too keen.

"Let's stop here," she finally said. "The sundial will provide the perfect marker for your treasure. I've brought a small trowel to dig the hole. It doesn't have to be deep, just large enough to keep the chest from being discovered while the spell is working its magic."

She bent down to place the wooden chest on the ground, removed the trowel from her pocket, and began to dig. An eerie silence filled the garden, and she feared each time the trowel entered the earth, the scrape of the metal blade against the soil was loud enough to wake the whole neighborhood. She hurried, and took courage from the fact that she had worked this same *Hokkano Baro* often enough to know her lively imagination was making more noise than the trowel.

She stopped occasionally to judge the depth she was excavating, and was finally satisfied. "There," she breathed with a grateful sigh, "that's done." Laying the trowel aside, she brushed the dirt from her hands and recited a verse in Romany that would guarantee success for her enterprise. She knew Magdalena would believe her incantation was designed to double the fortune they were burying and did not disabuse her of the idea.

The magic spell now apparently complete, she lowered the chest into the ground, and then carefully covered it with dirt. She scattered the excess soil displaced by the chest under the nearby rosebushes, then stood and gave Magdalena a final warning. "Our part is done," she informed her confidently. "Enjoy your garden as you always have, but don't disturb the chest until I come back and tell you it's time to unearth it. The magic may take only a few days, or several weeks, and it's impossible to say now which it will be."

After replacing the trowel in her pocket, she took Magdalena's elbow to escort her back to the house. "Remember, this is our secret. You mustn't tell anyone what we've done or it will destroy the magic.

The spell is fragile. Even to whisper that it's been performed will doom it to failure. I alone will know when the transformation is complete and I'll meet you at your front door as I did this morning. We can come out here to the garden and recover the chest in the light of day. Won't that be exciting, to see it brimming over with your riches?"

"Oh, yes," Magdalena agreed with a girlish giggle. "It will be wonderful."

"Yes, it certainly will," Aurora enthused. After a final caution not to reveal their secret to anyone, she announced she would leave by the back gate as soon as Magdalena entered the house. When they parted, she actually did go out the gate, but she came right back through it in a matter of seconds and nearly danced as she hurried to the sundial. She hummed softly to herself as she removed the layer of soil atop the chest. Fortunately, the wooden box had no lock and the lid swung up easily as soon as she had brushed the dirt aside.

Aurora had brought not only a trowel with her that night but also a canvas bag she now filled with the coins she and Magdalena had buried. Not wanting to leave the chest empty, she tossed in a couple of scoops of dirt before closing the lid and refilling the hole. She again smoothed out the dirt atop it, and left the yard at a run. It wasn't until she was several blocks away that she could give in to the thrill of her trick and shout for joy, but the weight of the canvas bag convinced her that she had made her own fortune that night.

Knowing Sergio would still be at their favorite café, she went there eager to have him help her count Magdalena's money. Intending to surprise him, she concealed the canvas bag in the folds of her skirt and slipped in the back door. When she found the *gitano* talking with Luis she hung back a moment, but anxious to see the tall Spaniard, she kept

94

the bag of coins hidden as she approached their table.

Sergio knew precisely where Aurora had been and sent her a questioning glance. When she responded with an ecstatic smile he caught her wrist and pulled her close. "Luis has just been telling me how poorly Antoine Lareau did at faro tonight. It doesn't sound as though he will be hosting any more parties before he leaves Madrid."

Luis was so handsomely dressed, Aurora knew he could not have passed himself off as a Gypsy that night. "You played cards with the Frenchman?" she asked with a puzzled frown. "Wasn't he surprised to see a Gypsy owned such a magnificent suit of clothes?"

Luis smiled with the memory of how totally he had confused Antoine. Because the Gypsies did not know who he really was, either, he gave no details. "No, at first he thought that he recognized me, but I convinced him that he was mistaken."

"You have a natural talent for deceit," Sergio praised him easily. "You should have been born a *gitano*."

"No," Luis argued. "I am exactly who I was meant to be." The only problem was that there were times when the heavy load of responsibility he carried became tiresome and he enjoyed escaping into the carefree world of the Gypsies where no important decisions had to be made. He could relax with Sergio, Aurora, and others of their kind in Barcelona, and then return refreshed to his own far more demanding world. Fooling Antoine Lareau had been a harmless bit of fun, but he had no desire to give any further practice to his talents for deception.

He frowned as he recalled Michelle's stubborn insistence that she loved Antoine. He doubted the lovely young woman understood what love was, with the supercilious Frenchman serving as her only

95

guide. Perhaps he had been too harsh with her, but if wedding her childhood sweetheart was such a cherished romantic dream, it was a great pity that Antoine was unworthy of her. Luis was surprised to discover it was quite painful to think of the willful beauty entering into what would surely be a nightmare of a marriage.

Insulted by Luis's preoccupied frown when she craved his attention, Aurora called out to him. "Did Lareau mention Mademoiselle Minoux? I sold her a love charm and I'd like to know if it's working."

"He described her only as a friend, so apparently it isn't."

Sergio pulled Aurora down on his knee. "Aurora's love charms are very effective," he boasted to Luis. "They will turn even the most reluctant suitor into a woman's devoted slave."

Luis was about to reveal that Michelle and Antoine's love affair appeared to be very one-sided, but when he realized he would have to explain how he had arrived at that opinion, he thought better of it. "Save your extravagant promises for the fools who believe in Gypsy spells, Sergio. I prefer to rely on my own charm when it comes to winning a woman's heart."

Well aware of the power of his masculine charm, Aurora tried not to sound as jealous as she felt. "Do you think you could take Mademoiselle Minoux away from Monsieur Lareau?"

Surprised that she would ask such an absurd question, Luis was even more astonished by the reply that came to his lips. "Yes, but since Michelle is relying on one of your love charms to bring her the husband she desires, I'd have to battle your magic as well as Antoine's. I can think of far more enjoyable ways to exhaust myself."

Knowing precisely to what type of exertion Luis was referring, Sergio threw back his head and

laughed, but believing the men were making fun of her, Aurora frowned sullenly. "You'd not defeat my magic," she finally declared petulantly.

It was growing late, and Luis had to cover a wide yawn before rising to his feet. "Let's not argue the point, since I won't put it to the test. I'll stay in Madrid only a day or two after tomorrow's wedding. If I don't see you two again before I leave for home, let me wish you good luck with all your ventures. I'll look for you the next time I'm in Madrid."

Sergio felt Aurora shift her weight, but rather than allow her to leap to her feet, he kept a firm hold on her waist to prevent her from leaving his knee. "We wish you good luck as well," he offered graciously, then waited until Luis had strode from the café without a backward glance before he spoke to his hot-tempered fiancée.

"Now perhaps it will be easier for you to pay attention to me as you should have been doing all along," he scolded. "How much did you take from the widow?"

His taunt about Luis tempted Aurora to wallop him a good one with her bag of coins, but she controlled that reckless impulse and let him feel the weight of it instead. "Here, how much do you think it is? Do you want to guess before we count it?"

Sergio's eyes widened appreciatively, but he knew they dared not open the bag in a public café. He set her on her feet, and rose to his own. "Let's not talk of it here," he cautioned, but he was enormously pleased by the riches they would share. He was also greatly relieved to have told Luis goodbye, and as they stole out the back door he vowed to make Aurora his wife before the handsome Spaniard reentered their lives.

On the morning of October 11, 1846, dawn

97

bathed Madrid in a spectacular light and her citizens were in a jubilant mood as they anticipated the royal wedding. Every theater and square was filled with performers eager to amuse their equally enthusiastic audience. Dancers clothed in the brightly colored costumes associated with each of Spain's fourteen provinces were cheered wildly as they tapped their feet in time to the restless beat of their castanets.

In one square, turbaned Moors reenacted their battle for Granada against descendants of crusaders mounted on horses draped in bright blue. Trumpets accompanied by drummers kept the spirits of both the combatants and the audience at a fever pitch. The spectacle was both wild and wonderful and in many respects a peculiar amusement for a royal wedding, but none present deemed it inappropriate.

In another square, a troupe of Chinese actors entertained. Dressed in silk adorned with silver bells, each of their moves created its own musical accompaniment. Elegant in both gesture and step, the controlled moves of their routine presented a sharp contrast to the aggressive display presented by the scimitar-waving Moors.

Michelle had awakened early, and despite requiring more than two hours to bathe and dress, she was ready when Antoine called for her. Surrounded by reveling Spaniards who clogged every street, their coach moved so slowly they could have arrived at the Church of Atocha much sooner on foot. The journey held such delirious excitement, however, that Michelle did not complain about how long it was taking. She had come to Spain expecting the royal wedding to provide one of the most memorable days of her life, and she eagerly drank in the exotic sights and sounds swirling around them.

Her attention focused on the boisterous antics of the crowd, she smiled frequently at Antoine and was pleased to see that he was also enjoying himself. He was so much more relaxed than he had been when they had parted after their difficult trip to the Prado that she scarcely dared hope his good mood would last out the day. "This was worth the trip," she leaned close to say.

Michelle was wearing a white satin gown shot through with so many gold threads, it constantly sparkled with an iridescent shimmer. Antoine had also worn new clothes that day, and attired in white and dove gray, he thought they made a stunning couple. He had expected her mood to still reflect the previous day's argument, but her smile was so warm and lovely he did not doubt its sincerity.

"I owe you an apology," he began with uncharacteristic candor. "I behaved very badly yesterday and you had every right to be angry with me. It appears that you've already forgiven me for being so jealous that I behaved stupidly, but I still want to tell you how sorry I am to have spoiled the day for us both."

Michelle could not recall the last time she had received such an effusive apology from Antoine, but she was positive it had been a long while ago. She toyed with her gold fan a moment before responding with what was truly in her heart. "I have never loved any man but you, Antoine. I wish that fact gave you more confidence. You've really no reason to be jealous of other men when my devotion to you is so complete."

While he was somewhat surprised by the boldness of Michelle's declaration, Antoine nonetheless recovered quickly. He leaned over to kiss her cheek and then took her hand for the remainder of the trip to the church where both Spanish princes and Infantas were traditionally wed. Also greatly amused by the antics of the colorful crowd filling the streets, he was in high spirits when they finally arrived at their destination.

The church was already so crowded that Michelle feared they might be crushed as they made their way to the seats reserved for French dignitaries. A prosperous merchant rather than a man of royal blood or one holding a position of great importance in the government, Antoine had had the contacts to secure an invitation to the church service and they were finally seated near the center aisle where they would have an excellent view of the ceremony.

Michelle made liberal use of her fan as they waited for the nuptial Mass to begin. When at last it did, she was as dazzled as the others present by the handsomeness of His Highness the Duke of Montpensier. The French prince was dressed in the splendid uniform of a brigadier general, complete with a red sash and a diamond emblem of the Order of the Golden Fleece at his throat. He was accompanied by his brother, who was equally dashing in a similar military uniform.

Michelle was impressed by the regal bearing of the Spanish king. She caught only a brief glimpse of his queen, but thought La Infanta as beautiful as a princess should be. Grateful for the opportunity to attend the royal wedding, she sent Antoine many a delighted smile and hoped that he would not guess how eagerly she was looking forward to their own wedding. The Gypsy love charm was in her pocket, and each time they joined in a prayer, she added one of her own to ensure its magic.

At two o'clock, when the nuptials drew to a close with the benediction, she was sorry to see the extraordinary event come to an end. "It was wonderful!" she whispered to Antoine.

Readily agreeing with her, Antoine raised her hand to his lips. It was not until that instant that he saw Augustín Aragon on the opposite side of the aisle. Already making his way toward the exit, the Spaniard had apparently not noticed them. In a teasing mood, Antoine pointed him out. "Do you recognize the man nearest the pillar?" he asked.

It took Michelle a few seconds to focus her attention on the right location, but then her astonishment showed clearly in her befuddled gaze. To find the Gypsy at a royal wedding would have been shocking enough, but Michelle was flabbergasted by the elegance of his apparel and the easy manner in which he was conversing with those around him. Surely no Gypsy could pass among the Spanish nobility with the nonchalance Luis was displaying. She gasped in spite of her best efforts to retain her composure.

"He does closely resemble the Gypsy musician, doesn't he?" Antoine inquired. "I can assure you that it's a different man altogether, however. His name is Augustín Aragon and his family owns a fleet of ships. Francisco says he's wealthy almost beyond imagining. I played faro with him last night. He's the one who was at the Prado. It's a good thing I didn't manage to confront him there. He would not have known what I was talking about and he most certainly was not 'stalking' you." That Augustín had described Michelle as "exquisitely beautiful" was something he kept to himself.

Antoine had seen Luis only once in a room dimly lit by flickering candles, while Michelle had seen him on several occasions, including the light of day, and she wasn't fooled by the tale he had spun for Antoine. The man named Augustín Aragon did not simply resemble the amorous Gypsy, they were one and the same! She watched him bend down slightly to speak to a much shorter man. When he straightened up, he flashed an all too familiar smile and she could barely contain her rage.

She had called Luis a Gypsy more than once and he had not bothered to correct her, but obviously he wasn't one. Apparently he was a man of such incredible wealth he wrongly believed he could trifle with the lives and emotions of others for sport. How dare he! she seethed. As a respected citizen of Madrid, he could have called on her as a gentleman should, but instead he had chosen a far more flamboyant approach and she had not once doubted he was behaving with a Gypsy's natural reckless disdain for convention.

The gold ribbon that encircled her throat burned with a shame that threatened to choke her and she feared falling into a faint which could not be blamed on the press of the crowd that surrounded them. If Luis was not simply a handsome rake who had taken advantage of her by the use of a Gypsy spell, what excuse did she have for welcoming his affection so eagerly? When none sprang to mind, she grew all the more furious with him. He had simply played a part while she had been sincerely moved and had lacked the strength to send him away.

Surely manipulating a woman's emotions as he had hers was a heinous crime for which he ought to be punished, but she had no interest in revenge. All she wanted was to leave with Antoine and go somewhere Luis or Augustín, or whoever he really was, could never touch her again. She laced her fingers in Antoine's and attempted to project a lightheartness she no longer felt.

"It's only his height, I think. The Gypsy had an insolence about him that man lacks."

"You may be right." Happy to dismiss the matter from his mind, Antoine gave his full attention to protecting Michelle as they inched their way toward the door.

In all her nineteen years, Michelle could not recall anyone else ever telling her a lie. She knew there were people who would stoop to any depths to achieve their own selfish ends, but Luis was the first of that ilk she had ever met. That he had been able to project such a heated passion when surely she had meant less than nothing to him brought an anguish

102

unlike anything she had ever known. She supposed that to him she was nothing more than a pretty tourist he had expected to return to France before she discovered his deception. How he must have laughed at her! she agonized.

The day had lost its splendor, but as she stole a glance at Antoine, he responded with a teasing wink and she knew she could not ask to be excused from the rest of the festivities without inspiring far more curiosity, and perhaps wrath, than she could bear. She would have to pretend that she was enjoying every second or Antoine would question her mood and she dared not reveal how deeply betrayed she felt. *Betrayed* was the perfect word. At that moment she despised Augustín Aragon with a virulent hatred, but she had absolutely no desire to speak the insults he deserved to his face.

It would be enough to send him a letter, she decided. It would be brief but no less deadly in its intent. *I know who you are.* That was all she would have to say. *I know. You despicable bastard, I know.* She held her head high as they made their way to Antoine's carriage. They would return home to change their clothes and then join the throng already making their way down the Alcala Road to the bullring. The prospect of viewing a bullfight had not appealed to her before that very instant, but now the fury of her anger ran so deep it seemed the perfect amusement and she did not keep Antoine waiting more than a few minutes while she changed her gown.

There were twenty thousand spectators crowding the tiers of the bullring and Michelle was grateful Antoine had secured seats for them in the shade. Each time he spoke to her, she thought the blue of his eyes more appealing. She had always regarded his angelic coloring as handsome, but it was especially so that day. The openness to his expression and warmth to his smile assured her that lies never crossed his lips. He was vain, she had never deluded herself in that regard, but he was also honest, which was far more important.

Her attention was diverted from her attractive companion as shouts from the crowd greeted the entrance of the three *picadores* into the ring. Armed with an iron-tipped lance and mounted on old nags both padded and blindfolded, their task was to enrage the bull by gouging him with their weapons. Fearless, the first of the afternoon's bulls burst into the ring. Seven years of age, he was in his prime and his glossy black hide shone with a luster that reflected the pride of the men who had raised him specifically for that fateful day. In a matter of seconds, he had gored one of the hapless old horses, then flipped the second *picador's* mount into the air where his hooves thrashed wildly before he fell back to earth with a resounding thud which crushed his rider.

Michelle was both shocked and sickened by that gruesome introduction to what she had naïely assumed would be an entertaining spectacle, while all around her Spanish citizens applauded the ferocious bull's bravery. Lured away from the fallen horse by a dozen men waving their capes, the massive black beast circled the ring searching for fresh prey. When at last he sighted three men attempting to aid the wounded *picador,* he charged them with his head low, aiming his horns with deadly precision. Only the quick intervention of the third *picador* saved the injured man, but his horse was mortally gored in the process.

With three horses dead and one man gravely injured in the opening minutes of the fight, Michelle feared the ring would soon be awash in blood. She turned to voice her concern, but Antoine was shouting as wildly as the natives of Madrid and she knew he would call her hopelessly silly and refuse her request if she begged to leave. Grateful that this would undoubtedly be the only bullfight she would ever see, she drew in a deep breath and willed herself to remain calm.

She wondered if Luis was among the spectators. Now knowing what a scoundrel the black-eyed devil truly was, she was certain that this was precisely the type of entertainment he enjoyed. He would undoubtedly think the death of three aged horses of little consequence and give no more thought to the welfare of the wounded *picador* than he had lavished on her. She did not bother to search the crowd for him when she could hear him screaming for blood in the hoarse shouts that echoed all around her.

Three *toreros* were on the program: Cuchares, Lucas Blanco, and Salamanchino. They were attired in bright costumes in shades of red, blue, and green. Their short jackets, waistcoats, and breeches had been heavily embroidered with gold. Silk stockings, flat satin slippers, and small black hats completed their outfits. Michelle wondered who had devised such colorful attire for the deadly sport and succeeded in convincing others it suited the bullring when the *toreros's* brilliantly colored clothes seemed so horribly inappropriate to her. They were dressed like clowns or acrobats in her view, not like men whose occupation was ritual murder.

A daring individual, Lucas Blanco was already in the ring even though the first bull was not his to fight. In his mid-twenties, he had more bravado than experience, but managed to distract the bull with skillful use of his cape until the injured *picador* could finally be carried out of the ring. Enraged to have lost one victim of his brutal rampage, the bull now charged Lucas but the wily *torero* jumped into the air, placed one foot between the bull's horns, and leapt clear over his back.

Astonished to see that Lucas had the talent, as

well as the costume of an acrobat, Michelle gasped sharply with the crowd as the bull rushed toward him again. Lucas obscured the beast's vision with his cape and backed toward the edge of the ring, seeking safety behind a protective barrier. The bull was in no mood for such teasing, however, and ripped the cloak from his horns. Lucas would still have made the barrier had he not slipped on a bouquet tossed by an admirer and fallen in the sand.

The deafening noise that had filled the ring was suddenly stilled as the bull lowered his head, and, using all the strength in his mighty shoulders, lifted Lucas up and then tossed him high into the air. Michelle braced herself for a hideous shriek as the *torero* fell to the earth, but he did not utter so much as a low moan. Fearing the brave young man was dead, she did not want to see his lifeless body whipped to and fro by the vicious bull. Before the bull could again attack Lucas, however, the first *picador* reentered the ring on a fresh horse and distracted the bloodthirsty beast.

To the amazement of everyone in the ring, when the bull turned away, Lucas Blancas sprang to his feet and gave a jubilant wave to the crowd. "How can he possibly be alive?" Michelle asked Antoine.

As delighted as Michelle herself, the Frenchman leaned close to explain. "His body must have hit between the bull's horns, so he was merely thrown, not gored. Is this too much for you?"

Michelle nodded numbly. "Yes, it most certainly is."

Antoine caressed her cheek and patted his shoulder. "Then close your eyes and rest. I'm too anxious to see what happens to this bull to leave just yet, but I promise I will take you home early."

Michelle would have been content to do just that, but the arrival of the Queen Mother was announced with a dramatic trumpet fanfare and all activity in the bullring came to a respectful halt. With the bull shunted off to the side, the *toreros, picadores,* and *banderilleros,* who would soon drive their *banderillas,* a streamer-decorated dart, into the bull's withers, formed a proud parade. They marched to the royal box and knelt on one knee. Suitably impressed by their splendor, the Queen Mother accepted their humble tribute and the bullfight began anew.

Bored with being ignored, the bull had turned his attentions to one of the fallen horses, but he was quickly distracted when the *banderilleros* rushed him and began to plant their colorful arrows in his hide. One man was too slow and fled the ring trailing blood from a slashed arm. Certain she was viewing the bloodiest bullfight ever to take place, Michelle grasped Antoine's arm with both hands.

"It's almost over," he promised. "Look, the others are leaving the ring and Cuchares will face the bull alone now."

Armed with a sword hidden in the folds of a *muleta,* a red cloth supported by a short stick, Cuchares first approached the Queen Mother for permission to kill the bull. Once that had been received, he began to stalk the beast with an arrogant step. A seasoned *torero,* he was known for his bravery and daring. When he struck bone in his first attempt to stab the bull and saw his sword go flying away, he fought on with only the *muleta,* gracefully directing the bull's passes with the small red cape until he was finally able to retrieve his sword and strike again. This time his aim was true and he plunged the sword clear to the hilt in the bull's withers.

Unable to comprehend his own death, the bull did not immediately fall, but when he did, the band began to play and the crowd burst into enthusiastic cheers for Cuchares's prowess. Four mules in fancy harness entered the ring and swiftly removed the carcasses of the three dead horses and the bull.

Then, grooms carrying rakes and buckets of sand appeared to repair the surface of the arena.

With no appreciable break in the afternoon's festivities, the second fight began with the entrance of the next bull. Hoping to leave, Michelle turned to Antoine, and was pleased to see an amused smile rather than the harsh expression that accompanied his sarcastic moods.

"Are you ready to leave?" he asked politely.

"Yes, if we may, please. I'd like to go."

As they made their way down the aisle, Michelle focused her attention on the steps and looked neither to the right nor left. Still thinking it likely Luis, or Augustín Aragon, as he was apparently calling himself, would be there, she had no wish to watch him smirk if she succeeded in catching his eye. Perhaps he was very proud of himself for having tricked her so completely, but she would just as soon plunge a wickedly barbed *banderilla* in his hide as forgive him.

Seven

After a brief rest and another change of clothes, Michelle and Antoine spent the evening of the royal couple's wedding day attending parties given by other French visitors to Madrid. At each fete, the attractive pair drew more than their share of attention which thrilled Antoine and barely stirred Michelle's notice. She masked her preoccupation with Luis's treachery with a pleasant smile and forced herself to concentrate on the amusing conversations she and Antoine joined so that she would be able to laugh at the appropriate times.

At every celebration, Michelle was surrounded by happy laughter, but her companions' joyous moods did little to lighten the darkness of her own outlook. She knew a lady displayed the best of manners at all times, but it was a terrible chore when the suffocating sensation of betrayal continued to tighten her throat to the point of tears. She was from a fine family. Her parents had raised her to consider the feelings of others before she spoke or acted in a way that might hurt them, but she was dreadfully inexperienced when it came to affairs of the heart.

That a man who enjoyed what appeared to be considerable respect in Spanish society would masquerade as a Gypsy was such an outrageous act, it was past the realm of belief. No wonder she had been so easily deceived. Any straightforward person who expected honesty in return would also have been misled. How many times had Luis said that he was a man of his word? she asked herself. That was perhaps the most damning lie of all.

Michelle had donned a new gown of pale-blue satin embossed with a lacy filigree design for this last round of parties and Antoine's heart swelled with pride each time he glanced her way. He had had to discourage more than one man's overly attentive manner where she was concerned, but he was inordinately pleased that Michelle had shown nothing more than polite interest in the gentlemen who were so eager to impress her. She was the perfect companion: beautiful without being obsessed with her appearance, bright but content to listen attentively rather than point out the lack of logic in the arguments of others. That she was not enjoying the parties as much as he completely escaped his notice.

When Antoine at last took Michelle home, she relaxed against him as he kissed her, but she was again disappointed by the lack of passion his embrace aroused. She smiled, rather faintly, and after again whispering sweet words of appreciation for the marvelous day, slipped through the door. Yvette had been anxiously awaiting her return and rushed to the bottom of the stairs to meet her.

Exhausted by the weight of pretense, as well as by the strenuous nature of the day, Michelle nevertheless promised to describe every party she and Antoine had attended. "But it will have to be tomorrow," she confided between yawns. "In another few minutes, Antoine would have had to carry me through the door." She swayed on her feet as the plump maid helped to remove her gown, and then she collapsed on the side of her bed.

"It's very late. I want you to go on to your room. You know that I can prepare for bed and brush out my own hair."

110

"But mademoiselle," Yvette complained. "It is not merely my job to assist you. It is my pleasure as well."

"Thank you," Michelle responded, "but please go."

Familiar with Michelle's preference for privacy rather than pampering, Yvette gave a small curtsy and took herself off to bed but she was deeply disappointed to have to wait until morning to hear about the parties she was certain had been among the most exciting ever given.

Michelle rose and began to peel off the first of several layers of petticoats, then hurriedly crossed to the double windows to make certain they were locked. Satisfied that they were, she closed the drapes again and continued removing her lingerie with fingers that shook with both embarrassment and dread. Once she had put on her nightgown, she could not bring herself to climb into bed. Not in that room where every shadow reminded her of a dashing Spaniard who had played her for a fool, she couldn't.

The adjacent guest room was much smaller than the spacious accommodations she had been given, but Michelle was more concerned about not having her sleep interrupted than the suitability of her lodgings. She grabbed her dressing gown, and secure in the knowledge that no Gypsies, or anyone else, would disturb her rest, she went next door to spend what was left of the night.

Luis and Ramón had been separated by the press of the crowd as they entered the Church of Atocha for the wedding but they had met again at Luis's carriage after the ceremony. They rode to the bullring together, and spent the rest of the day in each other's company. Each accused the other of being overly fond of parties, but the truth was that both

111

men enjoyed the day's lavish entertainments just as much as any other citizen of Madrid.

In the evening they went to the Circus Theater for a special program by the National Ballet. The featured dancer was a Frenchwoman, Madame Guy Stephen, who held the audience enthralled with her brilliant interpretations of Spanish dances. Even before she had completed the last of several encores, Ramón had announced that he intended to go backstage to meet her.

While Ramón enthusiastically described Madame Stephen as the epitome of beauty and grace, Luis responded with a distracted nod. When barely out of his teens, he had been infatuated with a dancer who had been so eager to take the Aragon name that she had been the most agreeable of mistresses, but he had not even been tempted to offer marriage as a reward. She had been followed in his affections by an actress, and then by a young woman who had fancied herself a poet. She had read verse after verse of her shockingly ill-conceived rhymes while he lay sprawled across her bed too sated by pleasure to voice the criticism she so richly deserved.

The memory of that silly girl made Luis smile, but in truth, he had known so many beautiful women that he had forgotten the names of most and had no desire to make Madame Stephen's acquaintance that evening. He wished Ramón good luck with his quest to meet the celebrated dancer and left the theater in his carriage. He was nearing home when another destination struck him as far more appealing and he asked to be dropped off at the end of the street where Michelle's aunt lived.

Memories of the impassioned farewell kisses he had exchanged with Michelle Minoux had intruded on his thoughts throughout the day. Each time he had succeeded in forcing the feisty French beauty from his mind, however, she had stubbornly refused to stay away. "How like her!" Luis had laughed to himself, for she had never shown any inclination toward obedience.

She had had no idea who he was, he reminded himself, but he did not think she would have been sufficiently impressed to change her behavior even had she known he was the scion of the Aragon family. He was not simply related to King Ferdinand of Aragon, who with his wife Isabella of Castille, had united Spain. On his mother's side, his heritage included the Bourbon rulers of France. Born in the New World, there were those who dismissed him as a *criollo* rather than a true Spaniard but none who dared repeat such an absurd insult to his face.

Keeping to the shadows as he had on his previous visits, Luis approached Magdalena's home unnoticed. By the time he reached it, he had convinced himself that he could again call on Michelle to inquire how she and Antoine were getting along now that he had convinced the snobbish French dandy that he had only imagined Michelle was being followed by a Gypsy. It was a feeble excuse he knew, but it would provide another opportunity to kiss the lissome beauty and that was too enchanting a prospect to miss.

It wasn't until Luis stood beneath Michelle's balcony that he realized he had failed to bring along a rope to reach it. Her room was dark, however, and after a few minutes' wait, he decided that if she had not returned home by then, she was unlikely to arrive before dawn. Should she appear any sooner, he did not want to risk being seen pacing beneath her balcony like a spurned lover. He turned away and started back up the street, but he had passed only two of the impressive homes on the block before he nearly tripped over a bouquet of roses someone had dropped during the day's festivities.

He plucked it from the cobblestones, and after ascertaining in the dim moonlight that the buds had not been crushed by passing carriage wheels but were still remarkably fresh and fragrant, he carried them back to Magdalena's house. Possessed of a keen eye as well as a muscular arm, he had no difficulty tossing the lost bouquet up to Michelle's balcony. He hoped Michelle or her maid would open the window and discover the flowers before they were hopelessly wilted, and was sorry that he had been unable to hand them to the defiant beauty himself.

He whistled as he again started off toward home. He was going to miss the enormously entertaining Mademoiselle Minoux. He knew that already, but Antoine Lareau was the one she wanted and he would not waste his breath again by pointing out the man's faults when she was blind to them. He hoped that she stayed that way, for if she did, she would make the egotistical Frenchman the perfect wife.

Although she had gone to bed quite late and slept fitfully, Michelle awakened early. She took care to make up the bed she had used so neatly that no trace of her brief presence in it remained in the room. Upon returning to her own, she rumpled the sheets of her usual bed, crushed the pillows together and tossed them about to make it appear that she had spent a restless night. While there was no reason to justify her actions to Yvette, or take such a precaution to fool her, Michelle did not want to arouse the maid's curiosity and risk being pestered by questions which had no credible answers.

She flung back the drapes to let in the clear morning light and the day was such an exceptionally pretty one that she opened the double glass doors, too. Still in her nightgown, she had not intended to step outside until she saw the bright-red roses, their

114

stems tied with white satin streamers that lay softly coiled at her feet. That a bouquet which appeared to have been prepared for the previous day's wedding celebration should have ended up on her balcony startled her for a second. Then she realized only one person could have placed it there.

That Luis had returned and left such a beautiful token unnerved her completely. The man had to know that Antoine would have repeated his story and that she would now know who he really was. Apparently there was simply no end to the man's audacity! He would swagger into her life as Luis the Gypsy, bid her a boldly passionate farewell, and then return to introduce himself as the gentleman he should have been all along.

"Gentleman!" she mouthed deliberately, giving the word the hint of a curse. She did not care how vast Luis's personal fortune was, he was no gentleman. Despite her hearty dislike for the giver, she fondled the roses' velvet-soft petals and could not bring herself to toss the flowers out into the street. They were perfection even if Luis was not, and she felt that she had every right to enjoy them. There was a crystal vase on her dresser, and she removed the previous day's flowers to insert these. When Yvette arrived a few minutes later, Michelle was still admiring the pretty bouquet.

"What lovely roses, mademoiselle," Yvette said. "Did Monsieur Lareau send them this morning?"

"They arrived without a card," Michelle replied truthfully. "But who else could have sent them?"

Yvette's eyes grew wide. "Surely all of his friends know that he regards you as special. The roses could have been sent by no one else."

"I'm sure that you're right," Michelle agreed sweetly. "But I'd rather that you didn't mention them to him on the slight chance that they did come from someone else. I would hate to make Antoine jealous

115

unnecessarily. You understand, don't you?"

"But of course I do," the maid insisted. "If Monsieur Lareau sent the roses, then he will be sure to ask if you liked them. If he did not send them, then he need never know that you've received them."

Michelle rewarded the clever girl with a delighted smile. "Precisely," she agreed. "I believe that Antoine still wishes to leave for home the day after tomorrow. Have my trunks brought upstairs and begin packing the gifts I bought to take home for my family. I'll make certain that he hasn't changed his plans before you begin packing my clothes."

"Oui, mademoiselle, but first, won't you please tell me about last night's parties?"

Grateful for the distraction, Michelle described in lush detail the things she knew would please her maid. She mentioned the elaborate decorations, the beautiful gowns, the handsome men, the sumptuous food, the lilting music. Attending the royal wedding and so many splendid parties had been a thrill, and she practiced now so that she would be able to describe the excitement in an accurate and entertaining fashion when she returned home. That while in Madrid she had also had a scandalous adventure with a rich Spaniard who had hidden his identity with a Gypsy's guile was a secret she would never share with another living soul.

Once she had answered Yvette's last question, Michelle bathed and dressed with a languor that belied the true agitation of her mood. Each time she caught a glimpse of the vase of red roses, she blushed with a deeper shade of shame. Thank God they would soon be leaving for home. With every mile they traveled she would feel more safe and secure.

Hoping to lift her spirits, she selected a gown in a cheerful apricot shade. Rather than slip the love charm Aurora had given her into her pocket, she

116

tossed it into the drawer containing her lingerie. She was finished with Gypsies and their silly spells. Infuriated to have been duped by Luis, she no longer had any faith in Aurora's abilities, either.

A thoughtful look in the mirror revealed the print of Luis's last kiss was still too vivid on her pale skin to be left uncovered. She had a pearl choker she had not worn in several days, and was relieved to find that it hid the spot perfectly. Satisfied with her appearance, she went downstairs to talk with her aunt about the evening's parties, for she knew that while Magdalena was past the age where she had the physical stamina to attend such lively gatherings, she still loved to talk about them.

Magdalena was delighted by her niece's amusing conversation and frequently interrupted to ask questions. "You mentioned that Antoine hired Gypsy dancers the night of his party. Were there any such exotic entertainments last night?"

"No," Michelle responded much too quickly. "While the Gypsies were popular with most of Antoine's guests, apparently his friends' curiosity about them was satisfied and none wished to hire them again. That's just as well. The Gypsies danced with a certain skill, but their manners were crude."

Startled by that opinion, Magdalena leaned forward slightly. "I spoke to a Gypsy woman yesterday, or perhaps it was the day before. You must forgive me, but there are times when I find it impossible to tell one day from the next. No matter, whenever it was, she said that her name was Aurora and that she was a friend of yours and Antoine's."

Michelle shook her head emphatically. "That's exactly what I mean!" she exclaimed. "She told my fortune and arranged for the dancers at Antoine's party. That scarcely makes us friends in my view, but it obviously does in hers. If she should ever come here again, she'll probably be up to some trick. Send her

117

away without speaking to her and then you can't possibly suffer any harm."

"A trick?" Magdalena gasped.

Antoine was announced then, and unmindful of the fears she had just set in motion, Michelle turned her attention from her aunt to him. "We were just talking about last night. I doubt that the guests at the palace had as wonderful a time as we did."

Adept at carrying on inconsequential conversation, Antoine added to Michelle's comments to provide a more detailed account of their day. He spoke slowly, and in what he hoped was a loud enough voice. Magdalena seemed distracted, however, and soon excused herself, leaving him to fear that he had merely confused the elderly woman. After she had left the room, he sat down beside Michelle and breathed an exasperated sigh.

"There, I did my very best and still your aunt would prefer to be elsewhere. I fear that she simply does not like me," he mused with a puzzled frown.

While it was clear the popular young man found that a difficult happenstance to believe, Michelle thought nothing of her aunt's abrupt departure. "We had been talking for some time before you arrived. She probably wished to rest before we eat. You shouldn't look for insults where none exist."

"We'll be gone soon, so whatever she thinks of me, it really doesn't matter."

"I'm sure that she likes you very much, Antoine." Michelle folded her hands in her lap and wondered if he had just recently begun to complain of especially silly things, or if she had simply failed to notice that he had always done so. He looked well rested and handsome that morning, but as usual he was fidgeting with his collar and cuffs and flicking away nonexistent lint. It was amazing that Luis could have noticed so many of Antoine's annoying habits while he followed them through the Prado.

Luis might have no sense of honor, but he definitely had a very keen eye.

This was not the first time of late that Antoine had noted a certain preoccupation on Michelle's part and it was most unflattering. He cleared his throat noisily to gain her attention, but she did not even glance his way. She had always been a most devoted companion and it pained him to think her interest might be slipping away.

"Do you find my company less than entertaining?" he asked accusingly.

"I beg your pardon?"

"You're obviously paying no attention to me. Would you rather that I left? Perhaps you're expecting someone else, another caller?"

The clear blue of Antoine's eyes burned with an uncharacteristic fire and Michelle stared at him for a long moment before replying. The man could be such a jackass at times, and she was tired of coddling him in an attempt to soothe his temperamental moods. Besides, there was no reason for him to be jealous or suspect she might be expecting other callers when he kept everyone else away.

"I came to Madrid with you because I enjoy your company, not to look for someone else," she explained. "Surely you don't believe that my manner is too flirtatious when we're with your friends. Not that it would matter when you make it so obnoxiously plain that I am to be considered your property."

As Antoine's eyes widened in horror, Michelle realized that she had just said far more than good manners allowed. It had been so exhilarating, however, that she continued without drawing a breath. "We have known each other our entire lives, Antoine. If we're to share a future as well as a past, I think we ought to begin planning it now. Forgive me if I sound too forward, but with my father unable to ask the proper questions, you've forced me to speak for myself."

While Antoine was deeply shocked, he could not deny that he did regard Michelle as his future bride and deliberately gave that impression to everyone they met. "Have you grown bored with me?" he asked fretfully.

"Must you be so insufferably dense?" Michelle countered rudely. "I am not bored with *you,* Antoine, only with the life we lead. I want a home and family, but you show me off as though I were your mistress rather than doing me the honor of making me your wife. If you have no intention of ever marrying me, I wish that you would say so now so that I may make other plans before I'm too old to carry them out."

"You're only nineteen!"

Michelle shook her head as though he had just proven that he was hopelessly stupid and looked away. Crushed by this hostile show of indifference from the young woman who had always lit his life with joy, Antoine wondered if perhaps he had been selfish and considered only his own feelings rather than hers as well. Not convinced that he had, he nonetheless moved off the velvet settee and knelt in front of her.

"I had hoped for a more romantic time and place," he began, but when Michelle's frown did not lighten, he knew that was no longer an option. "Obviously I assumed too much," he apologized. "I believed, apparently wrongly, that because we knew each other so well there was no need for haste, that we would marry one day when it appealed to us both."

He paused again, hoping for some small sign from Michelle that she would accept him, but she gave him no such encouragement. He could not recall even one line of all the poetry he had read and blurted out his question in what he feared was dreadfully trite style. "Will you do me the supreme honor of becoming my wife?"

Michelle had waited to hear those words for so long that she was dismayed by how little emotion they created. In many ways, Antoine behaved like a demanding child, but all young men of his class suffered to some extent from that same failing. He was attentive, and he had just proven his love by proposing the first time that she had even hinted he had been remiss in that regard. It had been no mere hint, either, she scolded herself. She had demanded a proposal and she had gotten one. Why didn't she feel elated that, just as she had wished, the next wedding she attended would be her own?

When Michelle finally looked directly at Antoine, she was mortified to find his eyes were filling with tears. It was clear a refusal would devastate him, and she threw her arms around his neck and gave him the most enthusiastic hug she could manage. "Of course I'll marry you," she swore with convincing fervor. "You're the only man I've ever loved."

Antoine had to grab the arm of the settee to keep from being knocked off balance, but he was too thrilled by Michelle's show of warmth to complain. When she released him, he again took his place at her side. "I have a lovely sapphire-and-diamond ring at home. It's an heirloom that I'd like to give you as an engagement ring. Had I known I was going to propose to you here in Madrid, I'd have brought it with me. I hope you won't mind waiting until we get home to receive it."

Michelle had already waited so long to become engaged to Antoine that another few days' wait for a special ring made no difference at all to her. "No, of course not," she assured him. "But I would like to tell my aunt the news rather than mention it in a letter once I return home."

121

Antoine leaned forward to kiss her cheek. "I'll tell my cousins, too. We're dining with them tonight, and we can have a small celebration. It will be only the first of many."

While he might have been goaded into proposing, Antoine appeared to be sincerely thrilled by the prospect of marriage, which made Michelle's strange sense of detachment seem all the more inappropriate. Hoping that she was merely too tired from the previous day's excitement to appreciate her good fortune, she forced herself to stop worrying and keep smiling. When her aunt rejoined them for the noon meal, Michelle attempted to project the proper demure enthusiasm as she reported her engagement.

Magdalena was delighted by Michelle's announcement and also greatly relieved that one of Aurora's predictions had already come true. She had spent the last hour fretting over whether or not she ought to have cooperated with the Gypsy's scheme. Having come to the conclusion that she could not possibly lose money buried in her own yard, her fears had been quieted somewhat, but Michelle's news cheered her even more. She asked to have a special wine served in order to give a proper toast, and by the time the meal was finished, Magdalena and her guests were all more than a little tipsy.

Antoine had confirmed his plans to depart for France in two days' time, but rather than begin packing, Michelle napped the entire afternoon. She awoke refreshed, but the happiness she had always expected to accompany her engagement was still sadly lacking. She felt guilty for having forced Antoine to propose rather than ecstatically happy that he had finally done so. That the life she had longed for was finally within her grasp and yet surprisingly unappealing disturbed her badly and she spent far more than her usual time preparing for the evening.

Having learned of her mistress's betrothal from

the servants who had overheard the luncheon toasts, Yvette wanted to talk about who would design her wedding gown and arrange shopping expeditions for a trousseau, but Michelle brushed aside her comments. "I'll make no plans until my mother has given her consent for the match," she stated firmly.

Yvette was astonished by that remark. "She allows you to travel with Monsieur Lareau, certainly she will permit you to marry him."

"That's not the issue," Michelle scolded. "Call it superstition, or a matter of luck if you will, but I'll not make any wedding plans until my family has been informed that Antoine and I wish to wed. Please don't pester me about it again. Get your own things ready to pack tonight, and tomorrow we'll spend the day packing mine."

Distressed by her mistress's rebuke, Yvette made a decidedly sullen curtsy before leaving her room to go to her own.

With Antoine due to arrive any minute, Michelle smoothed out the folds of her skirt and paused for a final look in the standing mirror. She had chosen to wear a gown she had always regarded as powder blue, but that night it appeared to be pearl gray. Surely it had to be the light in her room, for the gown could not have changed colors, but now that it was too late to select something in a brighter hue, she feared the dress was more suitable for mourning attire than celebrating an engagement.

"Whatever is wrong with me?" she asked herself. Rather than the confident young woman she was accustomed to seeing in the mirror, her reflection revealed her downcast mood all too clearly. What should have been one of the happiest days of her life was being marred by troubling anxieties. That she was having such difficulty coping with them worried her all the more.

She was wearing the pearl choker again, and

flipped open her fan to practice hiding her smile so that she would not appear to be gloating if Maria Lourdes and Francisco were to compliment her on having the good sense to accept Antoine's proposal. She looked properly demure, but she was far closer to tears than laughter. Her visit to Spain had not proven to be the frivolous jaunt she had expected and what she really wanted to do was go home.

"That's all this is," she murmured softly to herself. "I'm just homesick." Thinking Antoine would soon arrive, she went downstairs and found that he had already been shown inside.

"You're wearing blue!" he exclaimed. "If I weren't afraid that you would soon tire of it, I'd insist that you always wear my favorite color."

Relieved that her gown looked blue and pleased him, even if it appeared to be gray to her, Michelle gave his arm an affectionate squeeze as he escorted her through the door. She was certain she would become used to the idea of finally being engaged to Antoine in a day or two. Then surely the unexpected cloud of despair that had dampened her spirits would disappear and she would arrive home filled with the most delicious happiness possible. She held that thought all the way to the Castillos' house, but she did not truly believe it.

Magdalena ate very little in the evenings, and as was her custom, went to her room early, but she was far too restless to prepare for bed. She kept thinking about the magic spell Aurora had attempted and whether or not enough time had elapsed for the promised doubling of the chest's contents to be complete. Aurora had suggested that she use the new wealth to purchase a wedding gift for Michelle and Antoine. How was she to do that if the pair had already left for France before Aurora returned?

Now wishing that she had made a note of the date, Magdalena could not recall how many nights it had been since she and the Gypsy had met at midnight in the garden. Only two nights, she thought, or perhaps three. Was that enough time for the magic to work? Aurora said only she would know, but wasn't that simply because she wished to be on hand to claim a reward when Magdalena unearthed her riches?

Convinced that was the case, Magdalena went downstairs and asked one of the footmen to accompany her out to the garden. He quickly dug up the wooden chest, but when Magdalena opened the lid and found her coins gone, she was far too embarrassed to admit what had happened. She sent the footman away, and, seated alone in the garden, cried for the foolish old woman she had become.

When Michelle and Antoine returned, Yvette again met her mistress at the bottom of the stairs. "Something is dreadfully wrong with your aunt," she informed her. "She refuses to come in from the garden and she's much too frail to stay outside all night."

"Oh, dear," Antoine moaned. "This doesn't sound good. Would you like me to stay?"

"Please!" Michelle called out as she rushed by him. She followed Yvette out to the garden where she found Magdalena staunchly refusing the solicitous attentions of half a dozen servants. She quickly waved them away and sat down on the bench beside her aunt. Antoine was only a few seconds behind her, but he remained at a respectful distance.

After several minutes of sympathetic prompting, Magdalena finally revealed what was troubling her. "I was too impatient, you see, and the spell hadn't had time to work."

While she was absolutely livid, Michelle managed to hold her tongue until her aunt had finished her tale. Then she turned to Antoine. "What do you think really happened?"

The Frenchman shrugged sadly. "There was no magic. The Gypsy, or an accomplice, stole the coins," he stated confidently. "Probably right after they were buried."

Her expression now mirroring disbelief as well as anguish, Magdalena looked first at Antoine and then at Michelle. "You mean Aurora lied to me?"

Michelle knew precisely how betrayed her dear aunt felt. "Yes, she lied in order to gain your trust and trick you out of your money. Do you know how much you put into the chest? Did you count it?"

When she mentioned an amount, Antoine quickly calculated the sum in francs. "That's a thousand francs. Can you afford to lose that much?"

Magdalena shook her head, and Michelle gave her a comforting hug. "You'll not lose a single coin. I'm going to find Aurora and get it all back. Now, come on," she coaxed. "I want you to go upstairs to bed. Antoine and I will take care of everything for you, won't we, Antoine?"

When Michelle glanced toward him, Antoine's chest swelled with pride. He had absolutely no idea how to go about recovering Magdalena's gold, but he could not disappoint his new fiancée by admitting it. "Of course, my beloved," he bragged. "Consider it done."

"Merci," Michelle cooed sweetly as she eased her aunt to her feet. She could hardly wait to find Aurora. She was going to wring the scrawny woman's neck and then go after the arrogant Augustín Aragon, who entertained himself by deceiving others. It was high time the man learned there was a price for that game and he was about to pay it.

Eight

Too furious with Aurora's duplicity to delay the search for her, Michelle rejoined Antoine as soon as she had seen her aunt safely to her room. She took his arm and urged him toward the door. "It's still early enough for us to look for Aurora tonight. Yvette and I met her outside a café while we were shopping. Even in the dark, I think I can still find the place."

Michelle propelled Antoine toward the door in such a determined fashion that he was readily caught up in her quest. As soon as they were seated in his carriage he began to question her. "Was she speaking to all the patrons of the café, or did she single you out?"

Impatient to find the larcenous *gitana*, Michelle hurriedly corrected his misconception. "We were merely walking by, not seated in the café. She offered to tell my fortune and, against my better judgment, I allowed her to read my palm. But as her answers were vague, I soon grew bored with her and Yvette and I came home." She hesitated then, and took care not to make any unintentional reference to Luis.

"She must have followed us, because the very next morning she came to the back gate and again begged to tell my fortune." Too embarrassed to tell Antoine about the love charm Michelle brought him into the story. "That's when you arrived and asked about hiring dancers. You know as much about her as I do after that."

Antoine patted Michelle's hands lightly as he tried to think of something comforting to say, but he was too preoccupied with the possibility of earning a reward from Magdalena to offer abundant sympathy. He had lost far more playing faro than he had had any right to risk and was in such desperate need of funds that even a small reward would be greatly appreciated. Certain that Michelle's father had left her a substantial dowry, he made a mental note to suggest a holiday wedding at the earliest opportunity.

"I wish I had known then that she was not to be trusted," he agonized softly.

That they both should have known better than to trust a Gypsy was too obvious a comment and Michelle kept still. She had given their driver a general description of the area she wished to search, and she peered out the window as they entered the Puerta del Sol. The first street she chose branching off from the wide plaza looked promising, but there were no cafés on its numerous side streets and they had to return to the square and select another. This time the street quickly became so dark and narrow that she knew she had made another mistake.

"Perhaps we should wait until tomorrow," Antoine suggested.

"No. I should have brought paper to make a map."

"It's too dark to draw an accurate one anyway."

"That may be true, but let's look just a little while longer. Please?"

Michelle appeared so genuinely distraught that Antoine readily gave in. "Of course, since it allows us to be together, I'll be happy to look all night. Can you recall the name of the café?"

"No. If it had a sign I didn't see it."

"What a pity." He brushed her lips with a light

kiss, but rather than responding to his romantic gesture with the affection he had expected, Michelle drew away.

"Wait. I see a light up ahead," she said. "Does that look like a café to you?"

Annoyed that she had avoided his attentions, Antoine leaned across her to peer out the window. "Yes, it does. I'll go in alone. A café is no place for a fine lady in broad daylight, let alone the dark of night. Whatever were you doing in this neighborhood in the first place?"

Michelle had been expecting that question and was grateful that this time she could give a truthful reply. "Yvette and I had been going from shop to shop and had inadvertently strayed away from the main boulevard. I want to go inside, too. Surely I'll be safe with you."

"No, *chérie,* you'll wait here in the carriage. I know what Aurora and her friends look like. I'll handle this by myself."

Antoine signaled to his driver, but after the carriage had come to a halt, Michelle took a good look at the café and realized it was the wrong one, since its front door was recessed in a deep arch rather than flush with the building's facade. "No, don't bother getting out. This isn't the place."

"Are you certain?"

"Positive. The door is wrong."

"The door?" Antoine saw nothing distinctive about the door. "Why would you have noticed the door?"

That Luis had been seated in the doorway was not something she wished to reveal. "People were going in and out. I couldn't help but notice and this just isn't the place."

"Well, even if it isn't, someone here might know which café Aurora and her friends frequent." Rather than conduct such an inquiry himself, however, Antoine sent his driver inside to ask for the Gypsies.

129

The man was gone more than five minutes, and returned with the desired information.

"We took a wrong turn," he called to his passengers.

Again Michelle sat forward to have the best view. "If Aurora's there, I want to talk with her, too. I want to ask her how she could brazenly cheat an elderly woman and not die of shame."

"No, I will speak with her," Antoine insisted again, certain that it was imperative for him to assert his authority now rather than to wait until after they were married. "Believe me, if it's possible to recover your aunt's money, I will do it."

Angered by his parental tone, Michelle folded her arms across her bosom. "I don't want to discuss, 'ifs.' We are going to get back every last coin!"

"Of course." Antoine agreed through clenched teeth, but he was not at all pleased that Michelle had suddenly become so demanding. Although his driver now had directions, Antoine was thoroughly lost by the time they stopped at the second café. "Well," he prompted crossly. "Does the door look familiar here?"

Michelle heard the guitar music before she turned to look. This was the café all right, but she felt no surge of elation at their arrival. Instead, she was greeted by a dreadful sense of foreboding. "Yes, this is it. If Aurora isn't here, you had better say that you want to hire dancers again, so she won't be suspicious of your motives and stay away."

"I had already thought a ruse preferable to the truth," Antoine countered snidely. "Really, Michelle, I wish that you'd give me some credit for knowing how to handle this."

"I had no idea you had experience dealing with thieving Gypsies."

Antoine regarded her with a menacing glare, but did not dignify her sarcastic comment with a spoken

130

response. He entered the café and a cursory glance revealed Aurora and her friends were not among the dozen patrons scattered among the tables. Rather than a dashing Gypsy, the lone musician was a heavyset Spaniard who appeared to be lulling himself to sleep with each strum of the strings.

While Antoine had not complimented Michelle on the ploy, an offer of work for the Gypsies did seem like the best way to contact them without arousing their suspicions. He described Aurora and her friends to the barkeep and his supposed purpose for seeking them, but the man just shook his head.

"I know who you mean, sir, but I haven't seen any of them since the day before yesterday," he explained. "They might be here tomorrow, or not for a week. I don't keep track of their comings and goings. You can leave a message here for Aurora if you like, but I can't predict when she'll be here to get it. She's the one who tells the future, not me," he added with a hearty laugh.

Antoine tipped the man, but hesitated to leave. "Perhaps you know of any other cafés where she might dance or tell fortunes?"

"No, I don't want to know too much about her and Sergio. Gypsies have their own ways and it's best not to be too curious about them."

"Sergio?"

"Her fiancé. He plays the guitar."

"Tall man, quite handsome?" Antoine asked.

"No, that's Luis, but he's no Gypsy."

Alarmed by that revelation, Antoine added several more coins to the barkeep's tip. "This Luis, he plays the guitar and dances very well. What makes you think he's not one of the Gypsies?"

Growing bored with their conversation, the barkeep scooped up the money Antoine had offered and slipped it into his pocket. "I know how to tell the difference between Gypsies and my own countrymen," he scoffed. "I would no more confuse them than I would a stallion and a bull."

Antoine ignored the insulting implication that he was incapable of making such a distinction. "Do you know where I might find Luis then? He may know of other dancers available for hire." He saw something akin to fear in the barkeep's eyes then, and when the man insisted he knew even less about Luis than he did about his Gypsy friends, Antoine did not believe him. Disgusted that he was no closer to finding Aurora and winning a much-needed reward, he returned to his carriage in a sullen mood.

He repeated the gist of his conversation with the barkeep to Michelle, then added his unfortunate conclusion. "Aurora is obviously a clever young woman. I doubt that she'll return to this café until she is certain you've left for France and your aunt will have no one to trace her whereabouts. Luis might know something, but I've no idea how to locate him."

Michelle knew that she was treading upon dangerous ground, but she was too angry to be cautious. Now that Antoine knew the name he had used, she no longer had to avoid it. "Do you recall the man you pointed out at the wedding?"

"Augustín Aragon?"

"Yes. Perhaps I was mistaken. His resemblance to Luis might be more than coincidence. If we both thought that we recognized him as one of the men who danced at your party, then it's possible that we were right and he was lying when he denied being there."

Antoine mulled over that possibility for a long moment and came to an unsettling conclusion. "If Luis and Augustín are the same man, then he *was* following you through the Prado, wasn't he?"

"I suppose he could have been, but he could just as easily have been following someone else for all we

132

know. Who can predict what a man who would pose as a Gypsy and then deny it would do? Besides, it's not him we're interested in anyway. It's Aurora. Do you have any idea where Augustín Aragon lives?"

"No, but my cousin must."

"Then let's go back to his house and ask him right now. We haven't a moment to waste, Antoine, not if we want to recover my aunt's money without delaying our trip home."

Antoine was as eager to return to France as Michelle and twice as anxious to confront Augustín Aragon. As a wine merchant, he had frequent dealings with rich men and regarded them as no better than himself simply because their families had amassed wealth. Good manners, culture, refinement—those qualities were what made a gentleman and they transcended wealth. He had met many a rich man who was crude in the extreme. He always sold them expensive but inferior wines and laughed to himself at how easily such obnoxious imbeciles were convinced quality and price were synonymous.

While he could readily justify his behavior as giving arrogant men precisely what they deserved, he was infuriated by how smoothly Augustín had lied to him. The Spaniard had laughed as though mistaking him for a Gypsy was ridiculous, but now, with Michelle's encouragement, Antoine believed his first impression had been the correct one. More importantly, he also knew that Augustín Aragon lied with the same lack of conscience as his Gypsy friends.

"Aragon is apparently as unscrupulous a character as Aurora. We're unlikely to get the truth out of him, either, but at least I will try."

Already convinced Luis was no more trustworthy than a poisonous snake, Michelle suggested the only choice that occurred to her. "I doubt that he would want it known that he amuses himself by masquerading as a Gypsy and performing at parties for pay. Spaniards are far too proud to admit to that sort of thing, aren't they?"

A slow smile played across Antoine's lips. "That is a brilliant idea, *chérie*. If we must, we will shame him into helping us recover your aunt's money."

Pleased that he had finally agreed with her, Michelle snuggled against him. "You are an honest man, Antoine. I've always admired that about you."

While he knew he was not nearly as honest in his business dealings as she assumed, he saw no reason to admit it. *"Merci,"* he whispered softly before bringing their conversation to a close with a lengthy kiss. This time Michelle welcomed his affection and he wondered why he had put off marrying her for so long.

Francisco Castillo had no idea where Augustín Aragon might stay when he visited Madrid, but after repeated urgings from Antoine, he located a friend who did. It was close to midnight when Antoine and Michelle reached the address they had been given, but neither was discouraged by the lateness of the hour. If anything, their desire to avenge the wrong Aurora had done Magdalena had grown more keen.

"I'll not threaten him," Antoine mused aloud. "I'll begin with a gentlemanly plea for his assistance."

"Clearly he is no gentleman," Michelle reminded him.

"True, but I have spoken with him and you haven't. If he fails to respond with the help we require when asked politely, then I'll threaten to make it common knowledge that he associates with Gypsies."

Because she dared not admit that she had already had several heated arguments with Augustín, Michelle nodded as though she agreed with her fiancé, but she doubted a gentlemanly approach would have any value with a man who was clearly a rogue. "I'm going inside with you," she announced firmly instead.

Antoine reached for her hand. "I wouldn't think of leaving you out here in the carriage when Augustín was so taken with you. We'll use that weakness against him now. You needn't speak. Just appear to be as distressed as you truly are over your aunt's misfortune and we may get exactly what we want without having to resort to threats."

That Antoine would coolly order her to manipulate Augustín's emotions as cruelly as Luis had played upon hers both shocked and hurt Michelle. She wanted to accompany him too badly to complain about his reasons for inviting her, however. She squeezed his hand and kept still as he helped her from the carriage. The home where they had been told Augustín Aragon could be found was easily three times the size of her aunt's house, but Michelle refused to let the magnificence of the dwelling intimidate her.

Their knock was answered by a startled servant in his nightshirt, but Antoine and Michelle were such an attractive couple and so beautifully dressed that their request to speak with Don Augustín Aragon was immediately granted. They were shown into a parlor decorated with dark tapestries and though they were not offered refreshments, they were kept waiting only a few minutes.

Michelle's breath caught in her throat as she heard someone approaching the door, and knew it had to be Luis. His stride was long, his footstep sure as he crossed the marble entryway. She despised him, and yet the prospect of seeing him again brought an inexplicable sense of exhilaration. She tried to turn away, to feign interest in the nearest tapestry, but her body refused to give her even a moment to hide before she had to face Luis again.

Told a French couple had come to call, Luis knew they had to be Antoine and Michelle. Amused that the pair would wish to visit him at such a late hour, he nonetheless did his best to make them feel welcome. "I arrived home only a few minutes ago," he began. "Had I known that you wished to see me, I would have arranged to be here much earlier. Would either of you care for some brandy?"

When Michelle reacted with a startled glance, Luis realized his mistake. "Forgive me, Monsieur Lareau, I should have asked to meet your lovely friend first."

As Antoine supplied the introductions, Luis took Michelle's hand and brought it to his lips. He not only kissed it too ardently and held it a moment too long, he winked before releasing his hold on her.

Even knowing to what lengths Luis would go to embarrass her, Michelle was shocked by his lack of discretion. Antoine had seen nothing more than an overly affectionate greeting, and from the way he was smiling, it was plain that he was actually pleased that Augustín still found her appealing. "This is not a social call," she blurted out.

Rather than appear to be surprised by that news, Luis simply inclined his head slightly and nodded to encourage her to state her business. His expression was one of polite interest, but his dark eyes danced with a taunting mischief.

It had been easy for Michelle to hate him when she had not had to suffer the abuse of his mocking stare. Now she could barely recall why they were there. With a great force of will, she turned away, and while she knew Antoine had wanted to be the one to speak, she explained the reason for their call.

"Don't bother to deny that you often pose as a Gypsy named Luis because we know that you do.

136

Your habits, strange as they may be, are your own concern, however. We're looking for Aurora. She cheated my aunt out of a thousand francs and we mean to get it all back tonight. I'm sure that you know where she is."

Apparently unfazed by her accusation, Luis turned away. "I believe that I'll have a brandy. Would either of you care to join me?"

"Señor Aragon!" Antoine called out angrily. "Either you help us recover Magdalena's money or I will see that all of Madrid knows that your morals are no higher than your lying, thieving Gypsy friends."

Luis did not bother to pour any brandy for his guests, but he took a generous portion for himself and drank it in one gulp before he replied. "I am no more responsible for the actions of others than you are, Monsieur Lareau, but I would like to know why you believe Aurora cheated Mademoiselle Minoux's aunt. You must have more information than you've provided thus far."

While Michelle regarded Luis with a murderous stare, Antoine repeated Magdalena's description of how she had been duped. "She was robbed just as surely as she would have been had Aurora taken the money at knife point. I would go straight to the authorities, but we hope to settle this matter quietly before we return to France. However, we can prolong our stay if we must, as well as bring your name into the investigation. It's really up to you."

A considerate host, Luis encouraged his guests to be seated, but neither did. Tired, he rested his arms on the back of a chair. "The Gypsies call what you've described a *Hokkano Baro*, or 'great trick' in their language. There are any number of variations, but the goal is to relieve some trusting person of his valuables. Widows seems to be especially vulnerable to Gypsies' schemes and I'm sorry to learn that your aunt has become one of Aurora's victims."

"We expect you to be a great deal more than sorry, Señor Aragon," Michelle interjected sharply. "We want Aurora to return the money she stole and no later than dawn tomorrow."

"A thousand francs would be a fortune to a Gypsy."

"It is also a fortune to my aunt!"

Luis refused to respond in kind. "I'll see what I can do," he promised calmly.

His reaction struck Michelle as far too controlled and she leapt to the most natural conclusion. Her mouth was so dry she had to swallow hard before she could level her accusation at him. "You knew what Aurora was doing all along, didn't you?"

Shocked by her insulting question, Luis straightened up abruptly. "How can you even imagine that?"

"Oh, it's a great deal more than imagination. I think you know all about the Gypsies' tricks, *Hokkano Baros,* if you will, because you participate in them. How much of the thousand francs did *you* receive?"

Luis had to grip the back of the chair to restrain himself. He had seldom been so angry as Michelle had just made him. He had no idea what she might have told Antoine about him but doubted it was anything incriminating. While he could not deny that he had led Aurora to Michelle's aunt's home, he had thought her only interest was in telling fortunes and selling love charms. It had not even occurred to him that Aurora might have more grandiose ambitions she had not shared with him. In that instant, he felt as used and cheated as he knew Magdalena and Michelle must feel.

"I admire the Gypsies' music, their love of dancing and fun," he readily admitted, "but that is all, Mademoiselle Minoux. I do not condone the way they prey on anyone who does not share their Gypsy blood, nor do I participate in their crimes."

"Is that merely another of your convenient lies?" Antoine asked pointedly. "Which is your real name, Luis or Augustín?"

Again Luis had to strive to control the fury of his temper. While he could understand Antoine's reasoning, he most certainly did not like it. "I am Luis Augustín Aragon y Bourbon," he said proudly. "And now that you've stated your business, albeit rudely, I'll thank you to leave."

"Not before you've told us where we can find Aurora," Michelle demanded quickly.

"I told you that I'd take care of it," Luis insisted darkly.

"No, you said that you'd see what you could do. That's no promise at all."

Stung by Michelle's lack of confidence in him, Luis decided that perhaps she and Antoine were well-suited after all. "Go home," he ordered firmly. "I'll find Aurora and recover your aunt's money. Is that clear enough for you to understand?"

"Tonight," Michelle repeated.

"You'll have the money before dawn," Luis promised. "Go home and wait for me." He turned away and, without bidding them a good night, left them to find their own way out.

Luis did not know which was worse, that Aurora would steal from an elderly woman or that Michelle would accuse him of being the brazen *gitana's* accomplice. Disgusted with both young women, his mood was exceedingly foul by the time he reached the ramshackle inn on the Callejon de Lavapies where the Gypsies made their home. It was near the *mercado*, the marketplace, where *gitanos* carried on a lively business selling the horses and other farm animals they had frequently gotten by less than honest means.

Despite the lateness of the hour, Luis found Aurora and Sergio seated outside in the courtyard sur-

139

rounded by more than a dozen family members who ranged in age from infants to old age. He recognized the young woman who had danced with Sergio at Antoine's party, but hers was the only other familiar face. Two young men were playing their guitars in an apparent competition his arrival had failed to interrupt. Knowing how jealous a man Sergio was, Luis bent down beside him rather than approach Aurora.

"I need to speak with you and Aurora," he whispered.

Flattered that Luis had sought him out, Sergio rose and extended his hand to help Aurora to her feet. He hesitated a moment, and then motioned for Luis to follow them into the barn behind the inn. He lit the lantern hanging just inside the door, and offered a barrel as a seat. "We don't get many guests here," he joked easily, "so our furniture is probably not as fine as yours."

Neither of the Gypsies had been to the house Luis was using in Madrid, but he let them believe whatever they liked about his furniture. He had changed into the casual clothes he always wore when he visited them, but his manner was far from the relaxed one they were used to seeing. Accepting Sergio's hospitality, he perched himself on the barrel and explained why he was there. He studied Aurora's expression as he described Michelle's anguish over her aunt's loss, and came to the sorry conclusion that the *gitana* was more elated than ashamed to have been caught.

"I told the old woman to wait until I returned to dig up the money. It's not my fault the spell didn't work. What can she expect when she didn't do as I said?"

"Aurora," Luis chided, "don't mistake me for a fool. There was no spell. You stole the woman's money and now you're going to repay it."

140

Aurora turned her back, then peered over her shoulder to strike a coquettish pose. "There is no money, Luis. When the spell is broken, the money disappears."

"Not even Magdalena would believe that lie," Luis scoffed. "I don't think you want to go to jail over this, do you?"

Sergio jammed his hands into his pockets. "You are taking the old woman's side rather than Aurora's?" he asked incredulously.

"Of course. The poor woman was deceived. Aurora would never have returned, and I doubt the coins she helped Magdalena bury were underground more than an hour. Your *Hokkano Baro* didn't work this time and the money must be repaid. Tonight."

Aurora faced him squarely this time. "What I earn with my wits, I keep, Luis. You will have to tell poor Mademoiselle Minoux that you couldn't find me. Tell her I'm so afraid of her that I've fled to Granada and am hiding in the caves!"

Luis had never noticed that Aurora's boisterous laughter was closer to a cackle than any woman's should be. He had already heard enough insults for one night, and in a single fluid motion rose to his feet and reached out to catch her wrist. He pulled her close and spoke in a threatening whisper.

"The money will be repaid tonight. Now where is it?"

Also capable of moving quickly, Sergio drew his knife. "Let her go, Luis. The money has already been spent. Whatever we earn supports us all."

Luis kept a firm grip on Aurora. "This money wasn't earned, it was stolen."

Sergio shrugged. "We earn our money differently than you do, that's all. You've known all along what we are. Why are you pretending that you didn't?"

Rather than taunt Sergio into using his knife, Luis released Aurora and quickly wiped his hands

141

on his pants as though touching her had dirtied them. "You're right, of course," he agreed with a deceptively innocent smile. "No one has anything complimentary to say about Gypsies. It was foolish of me to expect you to behave well simply out of regard for our friendship. I won't make the same mistake twice."

As Luis took a step toward the door, Sergio replaced his knife in its sheath on his belt and reached out to catch his arm. "Wait, your friendship does mean a great deal to us. We can't repay the old woman's money, but we do have something of value."

Luis doubted that. "What is it?"

Sergio nodded to Aurora. "Go get the map."

"But it's worth far more than I took!" she exclaimed.

"Go and get it anyway," Sergio ordered. "You are from Barcelona," he continued while they waited. "Do you know someone with a ship?"

"I might," was all Luis cared to admit.

Sergio pulled off his velvet cap and ran his fingers through his hair. "I swear that what I am about to tell you is true."

"And I've already said that you'll not trick me twice, Sergio."

"No! This is no trick," the *gitano* insisted. "When my grandmother died last year, a map was found among her things. She used to talk about it, but none of us had ever seen it until then. She had been a great beauty once with many admirers who had hoped to take her away from the Gypsy life. She refused to leave, though, even though many men were rich and gave her expensive gifts and offered far more if she would marry them. One such man gave her the map."

Skeptical of Sergio's story, Luis reserved his judgment until Aurora returned with the document in question. The parchment was old, the ink of the

142

drawing now badly faded, but Luis recognized the eastern coast of Spain, and in the Mediterranean, the islands of Ibiza, Mallorca, Menorca, and another isle too small to have a name.

"Look on the back," Aurora encouraged. "There's another drawing of the smallest island."

Luis turned the parchment over and studied the far more detailed map on the reverse. Someone had done a meticulous job of tracing the island's shore and at the northern tip, there was an X marked at the base of a grove of pine trees. Captain of his own ship while still in his teens, Luis had seen a great many treasure maps, none of them worth more than the parchment on which they were drawn. This map was more carefully executed than most, but he suspected it was also a hoax and no more valuable than any of the others.

"Did your grandmother ever mention what is supposed to be buried here?" he asked.

Aurora shook her head. "You're giving him too much," she insisted to Sergio.

"Hush!" Sergio scolded. "Gold, from the New World," he revealed in a conspiratorial whisper. "Treasure from a sunken ship that was hidden here and then never recovered. My grandmother said this was the only copy of the map and I want you to have it. We will never have a ship to follow it, but if it makes you a wealthy man, perhaps you will remember us and give us a share. Even if you keep all the money for yourself, you'll know how much your friendship means to us."

"You should make him promise to give us half of whatever he finds!" Aurora complained.

"No," Sergio refused. "The map is a gift. The treasure is his."

Anxious to be on his way, Luis had no interest in debating the value of the map. He carefully refolded the fragile parchment and slipped it into his pocket.

143

"Unlike some people," he offered pointedly, "I earn my living honestly. If this map does lead to a buried treasure, I'll be happy to share it with you."

Sergio pulled Aurora to his side. "I knew you were a generous man. By the time you return to Madrid, Aurora will be my wife," he bragged proudly.

Not surprised by that announcement, Luis nevertheless paused a moment to take a long look at their garish costumes and wicked grins. He wondered why he had ever thought the incredibly shallow couple were amusing companions when all he saw now was their selfishness and greed. They thought nothing of cheating elderly widows and he considered it likely the treasure map he had just been given was nothing more than another of their despicable tricks. He reacted with anger to again being taken for a fool.

"I wish I had known," he remarked easily. "I would have brought you a present. This will have to do."

Sergio didn't see the punch coming, and Luis's fist struck his chin with a force that dropped him in the straw and left him too dazed to rise. The angry Spaniard then reached out to catch Aurora before she could go to her fiancé's aid. "I would never have told you where Mademoiselle Minoux lived had I known what a heartless creature you truly are. You should be grateful that Sergio wants to marry you. No honest man would give you more time than it takes to spit in your face."

He released her then with a rude shove that sent her stumbling toward Sergio who was now holding his head and moaning pathetically. Revolted by them both, Luis extinguished the lantern on his way out of the barn and left them in the dark.

Tears flooded Aurora's eyes as she watched Luis depart. She had never expected him to learn about the money she had taken from Magdalena, but it had not been nearly enough to pay for the loss of his friendship. She knelt beside Sergio, pulled him into

her arms, and let him think she was weeping for
him rather than for the proud man she loved and
would never see again.

Nine

Seated in Magdalena's parlor, Antoine sipped brandy while Michelle fidgeted nervously. It had been more than an hour since they had left Luis and neither cared to speculate on what success the Spaniard might have had or what their next step would be should he fail to arrive with the thousand *francs* he promised.

Antoine listened to the clock on the mantel chime one-thirty and then rose to replenish his drink. Thoroughly bored, he began to pace in front of Michelle with the purposeful stride of a soldier on guard. Like all his motions, his measured step appeared carefully rehearsed to achieve the proper effect, for he was not a man who left anything within his control to chance.

Michelle watched him with a distracted glance, unwillingly comparing him to Luis, who was at least half a head taller and possessed of a more muscular build. Antoine was undeniably handsome, his features aristocratic, his manners courtly, and his apparel elegant. Everything about the sophisticated Frenchman contrasted sharply with Luis's challenging bravado and preference for simply tailored black garments.

Uncomfortable with such thoughts, Michelle toyed with the fan she had gripped tightly all evening and attempted to force Luis's darkly menacing image from her mind. She had not expected to have to see him twice that night and the agonizing wait was nearly unbearable. She just wanted to go home with her lovely memories of the royal wedding, a cherished proposal from Antoine, and forget everything else that had transpired in Madrid.

Antoine stopped suddenly and turned toward her. "Aragon told you to go home and that he'd meet us here later. How does the man know where you're staying?"

Appalled by what Luis had inadvertently revealed by that request, Michelle gestured helplessly. "I've no idea. Perhaps Aurora told him."

Antoine continued to regard her with a thoughtful stare. "Yes, that's certainly possible. He was fascinated with you at the party. Aurora supplied your aunt's address. He then came here the next morning and followed us to the Prado. Yes," he mused thoughtfully. "That's a logical explanation, but somehow I don't believe it's the truth."

Hoping to hide her blush, Michelle lowered her head and concentrated on repleating the folds of her fan. "The man is a consummate liar, Antoine. Why would anything he does be logical?"

"Exactly." Antoine resumed pacing, but this time more slowly. "His manner struck me as being overly familiar. If I didn't know better, I'd swear that you and he were acquainted."

Michelle was uncertain whether or not he expected a reply but she kept still rather than tell another lie. While her parents had been devoted to each other, she had overheard whispered innuendoes of romantic liaisons among their friends and she did not understand how any woman withstood such a strain. While her midnight meetings with Luis could not truly be described as liaisons, they were far from innocent and burdened her conscience badly. She knew she would never be tempted to betray her hus-

147

band's trust by flirting, let alone sharing her body with another man.

A loud knock at the front door startled her, but relieved their wait had finally come to an end, she gathered up her skirt and rose to her feet. Antoine signaled for her to wait while he admitted Luis. Left alone momentarily, Michelle eyed the decanter of brandy longingly, then decided liquor was the last thing she needed that night. She drew herself up to her full height, and hoped that by some miracle this meeting with Luis would go better than their first.

When Luis entered the room dressed in the black silk shirt, close-fitting pants, and boots she had frequently seen him wear, rather than the expensively tailored evening clothes he had been wearing earlier, Michelle was appalled. For him to arrive looking like her Gypsy lover rather than a wealthy Spanish gentleman was the ultimate insult. Only Antoine's presence kept her from saying so. Her glance swept over the dashing Spaniard in an insolent sweep that clearly conveyed her disapproval. Then she noticed that he was empty-handed.

"What happened?" she asked. "Couldn't you find Aurora?"

"I'll consider that a compliment," Luis replied, "since you obviously believe that I would have recovered your aunt's money had I found her."

Not amused by his uninformative reply, Michelle closed the distance between them and confronted him anew. "Just tell us the truth, if you're even capable of it."

Luis cocked his head slightly in a mock bow. "Is it really the truth you want spoken here tonight, mademoiselle?"

Because there was a great deal that she did not want discussed, Michelle reacted very badly to that taunt. Livid, she looked to Antoine for help, but he was eyeing her with a puzzled frown and she realized instantly that by speaking to Luis as boldly as she had, she had unintentionally fed Antoine's suspicions. She turned her back on both men and moved toward the unlit fireplace.

"Well," Antoine prompted. "Did you recover Magdalena's money or not?"

Luis's gaze remained focused on Michelle. He could not help but admire the pride with which she held herself. Clearly she was furious with him but dared not berate him as he felt certain she would like to within Antoine's hearing. That amused him. "Aurora claimed that the money had disappeared because Magdalena had broken the spell," he finally replied.

"That's absurd!" Michelle scoffed loudly.

"I agree. When I pressed her, she then insisted the money had all been spent to support her family. It appears to be rather large."

"There will be one fewer to feed with Aurora in jail," Antoine offered with a disgusted sneer.

"Talk of jail will get us nowhere," Luis counseled Antoine, but he directed his next remark to Michelle. "While I'm in no way responsible for Aurora's crime, mademoiselle, I have my own reasons for wanting to make good on your aunt's loss. I'll see that she receives the appropriate sum in gold tomorrow."

Antoine watched with growing dismay as Michelle turned to face Luis. Her expression mirrored not merely surprise but something far more revealing. Fearing it was awe mixed with admiration for a generous gesture he could not begin to match, he was not only jealous but also deeply resentful that he would be unable to collect the hoped-for reward.

"That's extremely considerate of you, Señor Aragon," Antoine admitted reluctantly. "I am certain that both my fiancée and her aunt will be most appreciative."

Startled by his choice of words, Luis sent Michelle a quizzical glance. "Are you now his fiancée?"

That the tall Spaniard would find such an announcement difficult to accept angered Antoine all the more. "Do you have some objection to our engagement?" he asked.

Again Luis concentrated his attention on Michelle. "Would you like me to object?"

The tremors of foreboding that had filled Michelle upon her arrival at Luis's house had been mild compared to the premonition of disaster that choked her now. Antoine was staring at her so intently she feared he could see her guilt, while Luis, obviously very proud of himself, wore a decidedly superior grin. She wanted to scream at him to get out, but she could not draw the breath to even whisper that command.

"One of you had better tell me what's happening here," Antoine demanded angrily. "I'm not blind and the unspoken messages passing between you are as plain as the banner headlines proclaiming the recent royal marriage. Have you been calling on my fiancée, Señor Aragon? Well, have you?"

Luis was still attempting to formulate an ambiguous response to that question when Michelle began to sway slightly. Fearing she was about to faint, he rushed forward and guided her to the settee. "Pour her some brandy," he called over his shoulder to Antoine.

Not eager to take orders from a man he so heartily disliked, Antoine hesitated to do so until he noted that Michelle's usually beautiful peaches-and-cream complexion had grown deathly pale. It was very late. The evening had begun with a joyous celebration of their engagement, but it had taken a grim turn when they had learned Magdalena had been taken in by a Gypsy's cunning tricks. Realizing that it was no wonder Michelle had become overwrought,

150

he hurried to bring her a snifter of brandy. Just as he knelt at her side with it, Luis released her pearl choker to allow her to breathe more easily.

The Spaniard brushed Michelle's cheek with a lover's caress as he drew away, but that shocking liberty did not enrage Antoine half as much as seeing the clear mark of another man's passion on his fiancée's throat. Michelle raised her hand to cover it, but she had been far too slow and Antoine's already smoldering temper burst into a consuming fury. He rose, and set the delicate brandy snifter aside rather than risk crushing it in his hand.

"Get up!" he ordered Luis hoarsely.

The hostility that filled Antoine's expression was enough to prompt Luis to obey. He dropped the choker in Michelle's lap, and then returned Antoine's murderous stare with a level gaze. "I'm afraid I've forgotten your question," he stated with a sly smirk. "Would you care to repeat it?"

Luis Aragon was too tall and strong for Antoine to attack with his fists or he would already have gone for his throat. "I asked if you'd been calling on my fiancée," he said again. "I should have asked if you had seduced her."

Horrified by that question, Michelle reached up to grab Antoine's sleeve, but he brushed her hand away. "I'm not blaming you, *chérie*," he offered in a tone that lacked any hint of forgiveness. "Aragon is the one who will answer for this disgrace."

Michelle still looked frightened to death, but Luis, with a reckless aplomb, unbuttoned his shirt and opened the collar wide. "Her mark is on me as well," he revealed proudly. "Perhaps I was the one who was seduced."

Beside herself now, Michelle had to fight dizzying waves of panic to speak. "He's lying, Antoine. He's lying again!"

"Shall I describe your bedroom, *chérie*, or perhaps

151

the exquisite lace that trims your silk nightgown?" Luis teased.

Antoine saw the horror fill Michelle's eyes and had the answer to Luis's question. "You are the most contemptible bastard ever born," he began, "clearly with fewer scruples than your Gypsy friends, but I'll not allow you to cast any further doubt on my fiancée's virtue. You have insulted us both for the last time. I demand satisfaction."

Huge tears began to pour down Michelle's cheeks, but her anguish failed to touch Luis. "Do you really feel that she's worth it?" he asked Antoine flippantly.

"I will see you at dawn," Antoine threatened. "Name the place, unless you are a coward as well as a habitual liar."

Luis reached out to stroke Michelle's curls, but she recoiled from his touch. "I've never lied to you," he stated simply, "and the only reason I lied to him was to protect you. Is this the way you show your gratitude?"

Her lifetime dreams had been dashed that night, and Michelle despised Luis for it. "You twist everything," she sobbed. "The truth, lies, they're all the same to you."

Luis doubted that he deserved Michelle's scorn, but she was obviously too distraught to see his side clearly. It had been an amusing week, and he did not want to see it end in a senseless duel. In his view, Michelle's virtue had scarcely been compromised by a few heated kisses, but it was plain Antoine did not agree.

"I'll meet you," he offered. "But if we're to duel over Michelle, then she has to agree to marry the winner."

"I would rather marry the devil himself than you!"

"Be quiet!" Antoine ordered. Clearly disillusioned with her, he pondered Luis's demand for only a few seconds before his decision was made. After all, if he won the duel, Michelle would marry him. If he died because of her sordid flirtation with a Spaniard who gloried in deception, then she deserved to have the type of husband Luis Augustín Aragon would surely be.

"She'll either be my bride or yours," Antoine announced. "It's agreed."

"It is not!" Michelle cried. "I won't have him!"

Luis merely laughed at her obvious revulsion to their plan. "Pack your belongings so you'll be able to leave Madrid as soon as the matter is settled. Dueling is no more popular with the local authorities here than it is in France so you'll not want to tarry. Come with me to the door, and I'll tell you where we'll meet."

As the two men left the room, Michelle buried her head in her hands and wept over the hideous fate that had overtaken her. When Antoine did not return in a few minutes, she fought back her tears, and, clinging to the pearl choker, followed him to the front door. When she looked out and found that his carriage was gone, she was all the more terrified that he had simply left her to prepare all alone for the possibly disastrous consequences of the morning.

Sheltered all her life, she had never experienced such a desolate feeling of abandonment. Sick with fear, she climbed the stairs with a weary step and returned to her room not knowing whether to spend the hours before dawn packing or in prayer. She closed her door, and rested her forehead against the cool oak while she tried to gather the strength to decide what to do.

With his usual stealth, Luis walked up behind her and placed his hands on her shoulders. "You mustn't carry on so," he cautioned softly. "I'll not kill the fool."

Luis was standing too close to permit Michelle to slap his face the instant she turned toward him, though that was her first impulse. She searched his face for some sign of emotion to match his words, but he merely looked amused and that was so dreadfully inappropriate it wasn't at all reassuring. "Antoine is no fool," she contradicted.

Luis responded to that ridiculous opinion with a kiss he found flavored with the salty taste of her tears. When he drew away, Michelle looked no less hurt and confused, but she had at least been stunned into silence. "Listen carefully," he said. "Your Antoine is too proud a man to back down, but the chances of either of us being wounded tomorrow, let alone killed, are slim. He'll be shaking so badly he won't be able to hit the side of my carriage let alone shoot me. I'm not worried about my aim, but you have my promise that my shot will go wide and that I'll not hurt your precious Antoine. I'll proclaim him the winner and you and he can return to France and grow old together."

When he kissed her a second time, it was with a gentle sweetness that again brought tears to her eyes and he wiped them away with his fingertips. "Your trunks are here. Wake your maid so you'll be packed and ready to leave tomorrow when Antoine arrives to tell you the duel ended in a draw."

Intending to leave, he released her, but Michelle grabbed his arm. "No, wait. Antoine left without telling me his plans, but I want to be there."

Luis was completely serious now. "You might think that you do, but believe me, you don't."

Infuriated that he would discount her feelings in the same cavalier manner Antoine did, Michelle became more insistent. "If you two insist upon dueling over me, then I have every right to be there. I'll lose my mind if I have to stay here and wait for word of what happened."

Luis sighed impatiently. "It will go exactly as I predict. I'll send Antoine back to you unharmed. Believe me, the last thing I want on my conscience is the death of some French dandy. Even a reputation as fine as mine might not survive such a scandal."

Michelle not only doubted that he had any reputation to save, she was also appalled by his attempt at humor. "This is no laughing matter!"

"I'm not laughing," Luis disputed, "but I can be more serious if you'd like."

"Please."

Luis glanced toward the bed. Yvette had turned down the covers for her mistress, creating an inviting scene. "I'd like to spend the night with you. You ought to know what lovemaking is meant to be since Antoine will never teach you."

That arrogant boast was not one Michelle wished to test. "Antoine is right. You are the most contemptible bastard ever born."

She looked so horribly disgusted, Luis had to laugh. "It was only a suggestion."

"Well, it was in very poor taste. Now I want to know where you're meeting Antoine in the morning. I've got to be there."

Luis sent another suggestive glance toward her bed. "And what will you give me if I tell?"

"Absolutely nothing!"

"Then you'll have to ask Antoine," Luis informed her with a sly wink. He crossed to the double doors and disappeared into the night before she could think of a way to stop him that wasn't worse than the prospect of witnessing a duel. She was still holding her pearl choker and she could not help but feel Luis had removed it not to assure her comfort but to bring about her disgrace.

Bastard is not nearly vile enough a word to describe him," she murmured to herself. Deciding against waking Yvette, she went to the wardrobe and began removing her gowns. In less than an hour she not only had everything packed, but knowing it

155

would be pointless to try to sleep, she had also changed into the tailored navy-blue suit she had saved to wear on the journey home. She doubted that Antoine would be any more likely to want her to attend the duel than Luis had been, but that did not mean she would not be there.

With an hour to spare, she awakened Magdalena's driver and told him to wake a footman to help him harness the team to the carriage and load her luggage. She tipped them so generously, neither man complained and they drove her to the Castillos' home where she had them wait in the shadows until Antoine and his cousin left in his carriage for his appointment at dawn.

"Don't let them see us!" she warned in an urgent whisper, and despite not having had a minute of sleep, as the first pale rays of dawn began to lighten the eastern sky, she had never felt more awake.

Luis and his second, Ramón Guerrero, were the first to arrive at the outskirts of town where the road to Valencia began. They had hidden Luis's carriage and a spare horse for Ramón to ride home in the adjacent olive grove and were keeping a close watch on the road. They had been up all night, but were freshly groomed and handsomely dressed in the somber shades they preferred.

"From what I saw of him the night we played faro, Monsieur Lareau does not lack for courage," Ramón mused thoughtfully, "but I do not think it runs deep."

"No, he is a man who deals in appearances rather than substance," Luis agreed. "He is a pretentious braggart, nothing more."

"Regardless of his faults, this is still a stupid thing to do."

Rather than argue with an opinion he shared, Luis measured out twenty paces. The dewy chill of the night still clung to the earth, drenching his boots with every step. "My stride is longer than his," Luis called out, "and I'll move as far away from him as I can."

"I still think you should have allowed me to bring a surgeon. There's always the slight possibility Lareau might hit you even if you've no intention of wounding him."

"The fewer witnesses to this charade the better," Luis reminded him.

"Perhaps he has already taken Mademoiselle Minoux and left for France," Ramón hoped aloud. "I wish that I had met her."

"I'm glad that you didn't." Luis rejoined his friend beside the road. "She's too hot-tempered for your tastes, but you would have fallen in love with her anyway."

"And you didn't?"

Luis clasped his hands behind his back and kept his gaze focused on the road. "I find it difficult to discuss an emotion as sweet as love and Mademoiselle Minoux in the same breath. She definitely stirred something within me, but I'd not describe it as love."

"Lust, perhaps?"

"Oh, yes, definitely lust, but something more, too." Yet Luis was unable to define it properly. The woman had simply appealed to him in ways that were impossible to describe. She was annoyingly independent and troublesome, but her kisses had been worth the struggle to win.

With Luis lost in memories of Michelle, Ramón was the first to see a carriage approaching. "Look!" he called excitedly. "There's someone coming."

Neither man made any attempt to feign work as though he truly belonged in an olive grove but stood shoulder to shoulder, waiting to see if the carriage would stop or continue on. When it rolled to a halt, they waited for Antoine and his second to approach them. Recognizing Francisco Castillo, Luis greeted him by name and suggested that he direct his driver to park his carriage out of sight.

It was not until the empty carriage rolled by that Luis realized he had been hoping that Michelle would be with Antoine. He had told her not to come, but had expected the exact opposite of her and was shocked by the depth of his disappointment. Damn the woman! She was distracting his thoughts again, and at the worst possible time.

Ramón held a rosewood case containing a set of dueling pistols and Francisco had also brought along a handsomely boxed pair. "Because you challenged me," Luis explained. "I believe the choice of weapons should be mine and I would prefer to use my own. They have brought me luck in the past, and I'll rely upon that same luck today."

Francisco had argued for hours in a vain attempt to persuade his headstrong cousin to flee immediately for France rather than face Augustín Aragon in what he feared would be a suicidal confrontation rather than a duel. He felt sick to his stomach and had to struggle not to whine pathetically as he spoke. "Do I understand you to mean that you've fought previous duels?"

Luis frowned slightly, as though such a question were too obvious to merit a response. "I had no idea Monsieur Lareau was inexperienced in such matters. If he wishes to withdraw his challenge, I will forgive him for making it in the first place."

"You will forgive me!" Antoine repeated incredulously. "No, sir, what you ask is impossible when you have insulted both Mademoiselle Minoux and me. If we use your pistols, then I am allowed first choice."

"Certainly." Luis nodded to Ramón who opened the case to reveal a handsome set of .50-caliber dueling pistols. The ornately decorated pair Francisco carried were designed more for presentation than firing, but Luis's sleek weapons, their lethal purpose clear, were unadorned.

Antoine was too angry to note that menacing difference and quickly chose one pistol. It was surprisingly heavy, but he was confident he could fire it accurately. He handed it to Francisco to load. The sun had barely begun to rise above the horizon, but he was impatient to have the duel over and done.

Not wanting to be seen and in all probability sent away, Michelle had directed her driver to stop far enough behind Antoine's carriage for her to remain unobserved. She got out and walked the last hundred yards, cautiously keeping a screen of trees between her and the scene of the duel. She saw Luis and Antoine take their places back to back. Their seconds were standing nearby, along with the drivers and footmen of both the hidden carriages. She moved close enough to hear the men counting as Antoine and Luis began to walk in opposite directions.

She crept closer still, anxiously awaiting the dreadful moment when the shots would be fired. Her heart in her throat, she stared at the men with a haunted gaze. In terror-filled fascination, she watched Luis turn. His stance held a matador's insolent pride as he lowered his arm to take aim at Antoine. In the next instant she was blinded by the rising sun and the equally blinding realization that she had put all her faith in a man who could not be trusted. Positive Luis was about to shoot her fiancé dead, she screamed Antoine's name.

His powers of concentration far deeper, Luis was so intent upon his task that he failed to hear Michelle's piercing shriek as he squeezed the trigger, but Antoine did. The Frenchman turned toward her as he fired, sending his shot wide of his mark but presenting Luis with his full chest as a target rather than a narrow profile. Luis watched in horror as instead of passing by Antoine with several inches to spare, his bullet knocked the young man off his feet. He heard Michelle then, but her hysterical screams were no worse than those echoing in his mind.

While the drivers and footmen hung back, Francisco and Ramón ran to the fallen man and knelt at his side. Blood was gushing from Antoine's left shoulder and spilling out over his clothes in ominous waves. Francisco ripped off his own coat and then pressed his waistcoat against Antoine's wound. Barely conscious, Antoine tried to reach out for his cousin, but he was too weak to raise his hand.

Eager to help, Luis joined them, but Ramón rose, wrenched the dueling pistol from his grasp and pushed him away. "No. Michelle was to be the prize. Take her and go. She's the one who killed him, not you. I'll handle everything. Now get out of here, go!"

Luis could hear Antoine's tortured gasps. Certain the Frenchman was about to draw his last breath, he did not bother to argue with Ramón but instead ran to Michelle. Horrified by what she had witnessed, she had fallen to her knees and, muffled by her hands, her screams were now hoarse sobs. Luis lifted her into his arms and called to his driver to bring his carriage.

"How did you get here?" he asked, but Michelle could neither hear his question nor give a response. He clutched her even more tightly and kissed her wet cheeks with trembling lips. "It's all right, my love. Everything will be all right."

When his carriage drew alongside them, he placed Michelle inside with great care. Then he looked back toward his friend, but Ramón shook his head. Believing Antoine was dead, Luis had no time to deal with that horror. He hurriedly located Magdalena's carriage and reloaded Michelle's luggage on his.

Magdalena's startled servants had heard the sound of gunfire, but had seen nothing and Luis saw no reason to lessen their ignorance. "Go home and tell your mistress that Mademoiselle Minoux has eloped with Augustín Aragon and will write to her when she can."

While both men were certain there was far more to the story than they had been told, they turned their carriage around and headed back into Madrid. They might know little of what had transpired that morning, but they recognized the name Augustín Aragon. Knowing he deserved their respect, they did not dream of disobeying him.

Once he was certain Magdalena's men were on their way, Luis climbed into his carriage and scooped Michelle up into his arms. While he had not been reduced to hysterical grief, his life had been as dramatically altered that morning as hers. He had planned to leave for Valencia immediately after the duel, but not with blood on his hands or a wife in his arms.

Francisco was sobbing like a frightened child which forced Ramón to take charge of the injured man. Antoine had lost consciousness and his breathing was growing increasingly faint. Ramón removed the dueling pistol from his hand and replaced it in the case along with the one Luis had used. He would later clean both weapons so thoroughly that no one would be able to prove they had ever been fired.

Francisco's driver had brought his coach within a few feet of them, and Ramón summoned the footman rather than rely upon Francisco to help him place Antoine inside. When that had been accomplished, he pulled Francisco to his feet. "If your cousin is still alive when you get back into town, he'll be in desperate need of medical attention. Do you know where to take him?"

Antoine's blood dripped from Francisco's hands and, horrified by the gore, his eyes were wild with fear. "A doctor?" he mumbled, the word apparently meaningless to him.

Ramón turned to the footman. "Take your master home and send for a physician."

Readily understanding the necessity for haste, the footman helped Francisco into the carriage and then thinking the bewildered man would never be able to care for Monsieur Lareau, he climbed in after him. As they started back toward town, he kept the makeshift bandage pressed to Antoine's shoulder.

"Hold on, sir, that's it. Just hold on." While he thought it was hopeless, he kept up a steady stream of encouragement and the badly injured man was still clinging to life when they reached Francisco's house.

While the footman's attentions were credited for saving Antoine's life, in truth, Antoine had heard none of his exhortations to take courage. It was not hope that kept him struggling to breathe but hatred for Augustín Aragon. He cried out in pain as he was lifted from the carriage and carried into the house, but he welcomed that torment. He focused on the excruciating pain, swam in its waves, and vowed with each anguished breath that he would live to see Augustín dead.

Ten

Michelle was wearing a small, dark-blue bonnet whose brim was liberally trimmed both inside and out with bright-pink ribbons and silk flowers. Luis loosened the bow under her chin, removed the charming hat, and, with a careless toss, threw it to the opposite seat. Her fair curls were scented with a seductive perfume, providing a fragrant resting place for his cheek, but he was far more concerned about her comfort than his own. He kept her hugged tightly in his arms and allowed her to weep undisturbed until she finally fell into an exhausted sleep.

When snuggled against him, the gentle contours of her lithe figure fit his embrace as perfectly as when they were standing. In fact, the pose felt so natural to Luis that Michelle's slight weight presented no burden. He supposed if he had to marry, then it was fortunate that it was to a young woman with such abundant physical charms. From what he knew of her disposition, however, he doubted that there was any hope that she would see a similar reason to appreciate him.

A man who preferred action over unproductive worry, Luis decided they ought to marry before the shock of Michelle's grief turned to hatred. He hoped that if he proved himself to be a considerate husband while her emotions were still in ragged turmoil, when she regained her composure there might

163

be a chance for them to fall in love. Not marrying her was not an option. Her reputation had been irrevocably compromised by Antoine's ridiculous challenge to a duel. Gentleman simply did not fight to the death over a woman and then walk away from her.

No, for better or worse, he would have to take Michelle Minoux as his bride.

The slow, rocking motion of the carriage had lulled Michelle into a deep, if troubled, sleep. Too heartbroken to dream, it was past noon before she stirred. Luis had fallen asleep long before then and his hold on her was relaxed rather than confining. She found it no less objectionable, however, but lacked the strength to move away. Immediately recalling why they were together, she began to cry all over again and her abundant tears soaked his coat for the second time.

Awakened by Michelle's sobs, Luis patted her curls lightly but none of his tender gestures or sympathetic words penetrated her heavy veil of grief. He had hoped to travel a great deal farther that day but now doubted the wisdom of keeping to his usually brisk-paced schedule. When Julio, his driver, stopped at the inn in the next village to rest and water their horses, Luis carried Michelle inside. His request for their finest room was met with startled stares, but he soon had a bed for his tearful companion and he was positive rest would help her more than his heartfelt, if unwanted, words of sympathy ever could.

He placed her on the bed, and with far more tenderness than Yvette had ever shown, removed her blue kid slippers before he began peeling away her clothes. Beneath her suit jacket she had on a delicately embroidered pink silk blouse which slipped off easily. He marveled at the narrowness of her waist as he unfastened her skirt, but that distraction was

164

swiftly forgotten in the chore of removing her numerous petticoats. He had disposed of a corset or two in his time, but again he thought Michelle's slender figure splendid without such a device to enhance it. When only her chemise, pantalets, and stockings remained, he hoped that she would be able to sleep more comfortably than was possible when she was fully dressed in his carriage.

She had watched him struggle with her maid's tasks but had not offered any help or uttered a single word of protest at having him so near. Preferring her indifference to open hostility, Luis patted the pillow. She lay down and closed her eyes with an unexpected obedience. He covered her with a light blanket and then, without thinking, leaned down to kiss her temple. She was already fast asleep before his lips touched her skin and he feared that sweet gesture, like all his others, had been futile.

Horribly depressed, Luis now took the time to look around the room and he found the Spartan decor as sad as their situation. He walked out onto the balcony and surveyed the small settlement with scant interest. It was a town through which he had traveled on many occasions, but this was the first time he had ever had need to stop. There was a church in the plaza, and while he would have preferred to join Michelle in the bed for an extended nap, he left to speak with the priest and make the preparations for their wedding. That they would undoubtedly never share a happy anniversary when the date would have such a gruesome connotation was something he could neither help nor avoid.

Night had fallen before Michelle awakened. Disoriented, she sat up slowly and tried to make out her surroundings but the single lamp on the nightstand illuminated little more than the bed where she lay.

While clean and pressed, the linens were coarsely woven and the blanket threadbare. Puzzled to find herself in such humble circumstances, she tried to remember how she had come to be there, but her head ached too badly to make concentration on such a difficult question possible.

"Ah, you're finally awake," Luis called from the balcony.

In the darkness, his voice provided a chilling reminder of the grim outcome of the day. Michelle strained to see him, but her throbbing headache as well as the darkness prevented her from doing so. Frightened, she called out to him. "Where are we?"

"Nowhere of any consequence," Luis replied.

"This isn't your house then?"

"My house?"

"We called at your home in Madrid," Michelle reminded him and a fresh flood of tears filled her eyes, for that was the last visit she and Antoine would every pay anyone.

To make conversation less difficult, Luis stepped off the shadowed balcony and came to the foot of her bed. He was dressed in the same black evening clothes he had been wearing on the night in question. The strain of the day was evident in his every gesture despite the handsomeness of his attire.

"That house belongs to a business associate," he explained. "It wasn't mine."

That the impressive residence had not actually belonged to him fit the strange pattern of their relationship all too well. Everything about the man had been a sham. Even as distressed as she was, Michelle knew that was too hostile a comment to make aloud. "Then where are we now?" she persisted.

"We're on the way to Valencia. My ship, the *California*, is moored there for the time being, but my home is in Barcelona. I intend to take you there."

Now that she could see Luis, Michelle felt no

more secure, and the very last place she wanted to visit was his home. "Could I please have something to drink?" she asked in a tentative whisper. Luis went to the table placed near the windows and in a moment approached her side with a glass of freshly squeezed orange juice. Michelle's hands were trembling so badly, she had to use both to guide the glass to her lips.

"You need something to eat, too," Luis remarked.

Michelle took several sips of juice and, strengthened, began to argue. "I couldn't possibly eat anything."

"I don't want you to fall ill."

"I can't believe that you have any concern for my welfare," Michelle countered with bitter bravado. "If you had, you would have kept your promise. Antoine would be alive and I'd be with him now instead of you!"

Her blue eyes now glowed with such smoldering hatred that Luis had an extremely difficult time not pointing out that rather than a failure on his part to keep his word, it was her sudden scream that had caused Antoine to turn into the bullet that had killed him. Had he been as angry with her as she was with him, he would have done it, but fortunately, the painful consequences of Antoine's death were weighing too heavily on him for that to occur.

He did not want to increase her burden of sorrow with guilt. Thinking it better for her to hate him rather than herself, he ignored her insult. "If you're not hungry, I won't force you to eat. I've unpacked a few of your things. I'll arrange for a bath and when you're dressed and ready, we'll walk over to the church. The priest is expecting us."

Surprised that he had not responded in kind to her taunt, and touched by his unexpected thoughtfulness, Michelle's expression softened. "Thank you. I didn't realize you'd want to pray for Antoine."

167

"Finish your juice," Luis directed first, and when she had, he took the glass. "While we're at the church, you may pray for Antoine as long as you wish, but you'll do it after we're married."

Shocked by how completely she had misinterpreted his motives, Michelle shrank back into her pillows. They were stuffed with feathers, but not the fine goose down to which she was accustomed and were uncomfortably lumpy. "No, I never agreed to marry you," she insisted fiercely. "That was something between you and Antoine, but I took no part in it. You can't hold me a bargain you made with him when you failed to keep yours with me."

This time, Luis had to defend himself. "I kept my word," he informed her coldly. "But Antoine shifted position at the last instant. Had he remained where he stood, my shot would have missed him. He could just as easily have killed me, which obviously would not have concerned you in the least.

"I don't find that thought flattering, but it's nothing compared to what will be said of you if we don't marry. While you're getting dressed, why don't you consider the gossip that will undoubtedly surround you for the rest of your life? Then perhaps by the time we leave for the church, you'll be more than willing to call me husband. If you can't do it for your own sake, then have some regard for your family's feelings."

Luis slammed the door on his way out with a force that jarred every piece of furniture in the room, but Michelle was shaking with rage. "How dare he threaten me with malicious gossip when he has never bothered to show a second's regard for my reputation!" she cursed.

She left the bed so hurriedly she nearly fell, but caught herself before she had to suffer that additional indignity. Hoping to find something to throw, she looked around the room, but it contained so little that desire went unmet. "Damn the man!" she shouted instead, but it was not in the least bit satisfying.

She was still seething with frustrated rage when two maids arrived with a small copper tub, several pails of hot water, soap, and towels. Michelle opened her mouth, intending to send them away, but instantly realized that she would only be punishing herself rather than Luis if she declined to bathe. She stood aside and watched them work.

The two young women giggled constantly as they filled the tub and Michelle wondered if it was because she was in her lingerie or if Luis had made some amusing remark about her. Fearing it was the latter, when they came forward to assist her in disrobing, she shook her head and hurriedly showed them out the door. She had not thought of Yvette until then, but now alone she looked down at her beautiful and nearly transparent silk lingerie and dimly recalled Luis removing her clothes. She had been too anguished to protest, but now she took the precaution of locking the door before she stepped out of her remaining apparel and entered the tub.

She had expected to return to her aunt's home with Antoine. She had meant to thank Magdalena for her hospitality and pick up Yvette for the trip home then. That Yvette had been stranded at her aunt's house was a pity, but scarcely tragic compared to the predicament in which she found herself. Or, dear God, her beloved Antoine's tragic fate!

Would Francisco accompany his slain cousin's body home, or would he trust that grim duty to servants? From what she had seen of Francisco, he was a good man, but not a forceful one who would think it imperative that he be the one to make the trip. The thought of Antoine's coffin being callously transported by servants as though it were no more than a trunk filled with old clothes broke her heart and she began to cry.

She wept the whole time she washed herself clean and, when finished, she was again so emotionally drained that she lacked the energy to stand. Devastated by her loss, she remained in the tub while the bath water cooled. She knew she shouldn't be on her way to Valencia with the man who had murdered her fiancé, but she lacked the strength to dry her tears, let alone escape him.

She knew Luis's prediction about gossip had been painfully accurate. She would undoubtedly be the subject of fascinated whispers for as long as she lived. She would always be the woman Antoine Lareau had given his life for, and the speculation over whether or not she was worth it would never cease. Her own heart held the answer to that question, for she doubted any woman was worth such a sacrifice.

Michelle wished that she had never taken a wrong turn while shopping, had never met Aurora, had never spoken to Luis. She had foolishly become involved with people whose only interest was in hurting her and those she loved. She would pay for that costly mistake the rest of her life.

In addition to his three younger brothers, Luis had also been raised with two sisters and was well aware of how long it took for a woman to dress. He had unpacked fresh clothing to save Michelle that chore, but out of consideration, did not rush her. He waited an hour, and then an additional thirty minutes before returning to her room. He rapped lightly on the door and called her name, but she failed to respond.

No fool, he had been seated where he had a clear view of the foot of the stairs and he had also taken the precaution of stationing Julio and the footman, Tomás, outside to catch her should she attempt to

170

climb down from the balcony. He was not surprised to find her door locked, but having expected as much, he removed the room's second key from his pocket.

Still hesitating to intrude, he again called her name. The silence that greeted him was alarmingly deep and this time he felt justified in unlocking the door and striding through it. When he found Michelle still seated in the tub, staring off into space, looking so miserably unhappy that she was apparently completely unaware of the water's chill, he lost patience with her.

"Have you again fallen asleep?" he scolded, but Michelle gave no sign that she either saw or heard him. Perplexed, Luis picked up a towel and tried to decide how best to lift her from the tub. He had expected her slender body to be as superbly lovely as her face and he was not disappointed, but knew this was a most inappropriate time to pay her lavish compliments. Instead, he reached for her hands and coaxed her to her feet. He then wrapped the towel around her and lifted her out of the tub.

She looked away rather than meet his gaze and he could not recall ever seeing a more vivid portrayal of heartbreak. He knew she was not faking her despair, either, and regretted having greeted her so rudely. "I shouldn't have left you alone with your memories," he whispered.

He had certainly been tortured by his, but her reaction was far more extreme than he had anticipated after her spirited refusal to marry him. He used another towel to pat her dry and attempted to lift the blackness of her mood with teasing.

"Is it the thought of marriage to me that has caused you to collapse in this speechless panic? You needn't be afraid of me, precious. I'll be in no mood for passion tonight, either, and I may not be for a good long while."

171

Still, Michelle did not even glance his way, let alone reply. After sleeping all day, her upswept curls had become a scrambled mess that Luis knew would only increase her unhappiness should she get a glimpse of herself in the mirror. He left her momentarily to fetch her brush and then slowly brushed out her hair. After the first couple of strokes, he realized he had forgotten to remove the combs from it and he quickly laid them aside.

"From the pale shade of your hair, I'd say that you have Norse blood. Am I right?"

Michelle did not speak, but Luis did not allow her reticence to communicate with him to stifle his conversation. "Danish Vikings invaded France nearly a thousand years ago and a great many took up residence there. You certainly look like one of their legacies, and if you'll forgive me, you sound like one, too. I admire spirit in a woman, but not if it's directed toward her husband."

Luis debated the wisdom of putting her back to bed, and swiftly decided against it. The priest would surely think his intended bride alarmingly distracted, but Luis knew that was preferable to walking into church with Michelle shrieking curses at him. That he was about to marry a woman who was so withdrawn she appeared to be mentally unbalanced frightened him, but she had not shown any instability in the few days he had known her. He was counting on her true temperament being the fiery one he knew rather than the pathetic, if understandable, mood she had displayed for most of the day.

He had laid out lingerie as well as the stunningly beautiful white gown Michelle had worn to the royal wedding. While he found getting her into clean clothing far more taxing than removing her previous apparel, he kept up a steady stream of conversation as he worked. It was no more than inconsequential comments on his difficulties with hooks and ribbons,

172

but it served to ease his tension if not hers.

He was quite pleased with himself when he finally succeeded in getting her dressed, but the challenge of re-creating her usual hairstyle was completely beyond his abilities. Rather than make such an attempt, he pulled her curls back, secured them with combs, then covered her head with the white mantilla she had been wearing when they met. He stepped back to admire his handiwork and was startled to find Michelle was now regarding him with a curious stare. Relieved that she had not permanently retreated from reality, he slipped his arm around her waist and led her toward the door.

"The church isn't far," he assured her, "and Julio and Tomás are waiting to go with us. What you deserve is a wedding celebration as splendid as that given for La Infanta, but the result of a simple ceremony will be just the same: we'll be legally wed."

Nearly blinded by the worst headache of her life, Michelle leaned against Luis as they made their way down the stairs. She had not realized he was such a talkative individual, but as they left the hotel the sound of his whispered encouragement was surprisingly reassuring. He was the last person she would ever trust, and yet she knew he was right about their having to marry.

The placid course of her life had been altered so drastically that she no longer had a clear vision of what her future would be. She had no dreams at all now, no hopes other than to live out the day without disgracing herself any further. As they started toward the church, Luis's driver and footman fell in behind them. They were both tall and lean, handsome young men like their master and she wondered if they knew how much Luis enjoyed pretending to be a Gypsy.

"You mustn't do it again," she warned Luis suddenly.

"Dear God, do you think I search for men to duel?"

"That wasn't what I meant," Michelle told him. "I was referring to your facility for acting the part of a Gypsy. I don't want you to do it ever again."

Luis shook his head in dismay. They were not yet married but Michelle was already giving him orders and he couldn't abide that. Rather than say so in words so rude she could not help but understand, he drew in a deep breath and let it out slowly in a vain attempt to rein in his temper.

"I am fully capable of running my own life without any help from you," he stated firmly. "I'll make you my wife, Michelle, but I'll not allow you to order me about like a servant."

Michelle did not really feel well enough to argue, but this matter was too important to her to keep still. "Had I not become involved with Gypsies, Antoine would be alive. I don't want to even imagine what further tragedy might occur should you continue to emulate their lying, thieving ways."

Embarrassed by what they overheard, Julio and Tomás dropped back several paces, but Luis reached out to pull Michelle closer still. "I do not lie and steal, mademoiselle. Do not ever again make the mistake of accusing me of those crimes."

Not surprised by the hostility of his response, Michelle continued undaunted. "There is still the matter of the thousand francs Aurora stole from my aunt. What happened to your offer to replace it?"

"It was sent to her home this morning," Luis insisted. "I keep my promises."

Michelle refused to dignify such a vile lie with a response. She pulled away from his confining grasp and entered the church on her own. The interior was dark, several degrees cooler than the night, lit by flickering candles, and filled with the haunting scent of incense. The atmosphere was not the joyous one of hope and light that greeted wedding parties in daylight hours, but instead a gloomy, oppressively dark funereal one. Michelle could not help but shudder and glanced back over her shoulder at Luis.

The small church had not seemed so terribly depressing when Luis had been there that afternoon, and he felt the very same chill wave of alarm that was reflected in Michelle's eyes. He searched his mind for words to console her, but none came to him before the priest appeared. A short, rotund man with gray hair and thick spectacles, he had spent his whole career ministering to the needs of the simple folk who made up his congregation. He had been so profoundly impressed by Luis's visit that he was eager to serve him in whatever way he could. That Luis had made the largest donation the church had ever received was also most inspiring.

Luis greeted the priest, and introduced Michelle as well as Julio and Tomás, who would serve as witnesses. As they took their places in front of the altar, he could not help but wonder what he could possibly put in a letter to his parents that would make any sense. He had been intrigued by Michelle at their first meeting and had pursued her expecting no more than a brief, playful flirtation. That it had ended in the very worst of consequences was appalling and he doubted that he would ever be able to make his parents understand how innocent his original intentions had been.

With her face hidden by her lacy mantilla, Luis could only guess at Michelle's expression, but he knew it could not possibly be any less strained than his own. He took her hand and gave her fingers an encouraging squeeze as the priest began to read the marriage ceremony. Luis had attended enough weddings to know the words by heart, but now that they were directed at him, they carried a far deeper meaning than he had ever imagined. Marriage was

175

sacred, meant to last for a lifetime, and he was about to wed a stranger.

Michelle saw the priest's lips move, but she couldn't hear his voice over the pounding of her heart and the agonizing drumming in her head. She felt sick to her stomach and fearing she might faint, she leaned against Luis for support. Thoughtfully, he again slipped his arm around her waist and she was grateful for that show of kindness if little else.

She was only nineteen and already her life was ruined. She would never know a husband's love, never be introduced without fear vicious rumors of how she and Luis had come to marry would have preceded her. She would never be a respected member of any community, but instead a subject of scorn. Her only comfort was that she was marrying a Spaniard and would never have to return home where the disgrace she had brought upon herself would taint her family's lives as well.

There would certainly be speculation in Lyon as to how Antoine had died, but without her constant presence on the scene to inspire gossip, it would soon fade. Her mother and sisters would be safe from the scandalous rumors that might otherwise abound. She hoped that her extended absence would soon erase all memory of her in Lyon and the fine name of Minoux would remain untarnished.

Luis was greatly relieved when Michelle managed to repeat her vows with minimal prompting. He could feel her trembling all over and knew this was not the wedding she must have dreamed of someday having. Not only were the time and place wrong, he was the wrong man and that had to be causing her the most pain. The only ring he had been able to find in the little town was a plain gold band. He slipped it on her finger and was surprised by how perfectly it fit, since nothing else had gone right for them.

When the priest pronounced them man and wife, Luis made no attempt to kiss his reluctant bride. Instead, he thanked the clergyman for dispensing with the reading of the banns and performing the ceremony on such short notice. After they had all signed the necessary documents, he dismissed Julio and Tomás and then half led, half carried Michelle back to the hotel. When she again declined his offer of food with a vigorous shake of her head, he escorted her upstairs to her room. The tub had been removed, but it was still far from the expensively furnished honeymoon suite he would have liked to have provided.

In what he feared was a move to get as far away from him as possible, Michelle went to the balcony and stepped out. While toasting their marriage struck him as being wildly inappropriate, Luis did not want to leave her alone to again brood over the sorrow of the day. Instead, he walked up behind her and slipped his arms around her waist.

"Everything will be easier for us if we face it together," he mused aloud.

"I don't feel well," Michelle confessed softly. "Please don't ask me to make any plans now."

"You haven't eaten all day. I'm sure that's the problem. At least let me get you some soup."

"No, I don't want anything. It would just make me feel worse than I already do."

With a sudden dark shiver of foreboding, Luis feared he knew what was wrong with his bride. She was a passionate woman, and despite appearances to the contrary, perhaps Antoine had sampled those passions. He had had ample opportunity to appreciate the perfection of her figure that day. If she were pregnant, it was by no more than a few weeks, but she would not be able to hide her condition indefinitely. He prayed his suspicions were unfounded.

"Michelle," he encouraged in a persuasive whisper.

"I want you to tell me the truth. I won't be angry with you no matter what your answer might be, but if you're carrying Antoine's babe, don't try and fool me into believing it's mine."

Aghast by what his question implied about her morals, Michelle turned to face him. When she found his expression a thoughtful one rather than the obnoxious smirk she had expected, she swallowed the harsh reply that had sprung to her lips. "Antoine and I loved each other dearly," she informed him, "but we weren't lovers. He had far too much respect for me for that."

While she had not raised a hand to him, Luis felt as though he had just been slapped, for his midnight visits to her had certainly not demonstrated the respect she clearly felt she deserved. That had been his fault rather than hers, but he refused to admit it. He responded as though her words had not carried a double meaning.

"I'm sorry, I didn't mean to offend you. I simply hoped to begin our marriage with the honesty we'll need." She greeted that announcement with too skeptical a gaze to overlook and Luis tried again to make himself understood. "Had our first child been Antoine's rather than mine, I'd still have raised him as my own and made him my principal heir. You must never be afraid to confide in me, Michelle. We might not have married out of choice, but that doesn't mean that we can't learn to care for each other and be happy. I know tonight isn't the time to voice such hopes, but I do have them."

Luis had not behaved that day like the cocky Gypsy she had known and Michelle was merely confused rather than reassured. Suspecting his kindness was another deceitful ploy, she preferred to be alone. "You're right about one thing. This isn't the time for a discussion on any topic. Please go."

All day, Luis had tried to be considerate to Michelle, but she had shown such little regard for his feelings that he had absolutely no desire to grant her request. He had intended to sleep in the next room, but now decided to spend his wedding night right there with her. "I understand, but let me help you with your gown," he offered with a slight smile.

Oblivious to her attire, Michelle had to glance down to see what she was wearing. Because Luis had already helped her to both undress and dress that day, she removed her mantilla and turned so that he could again assist her. "I wore this to the royal wedding," she recalled wistfully.

"I'm sure you looked even more beautiful than La Infanta. I wish I'd seen you there."

"We . . . I saw you," Michelle revealed.

"Did you?" Now Luis was really disappointed that he had failed to notice her in the crowd. "What did you think?"

"I thought you were very well dressed for a Gypsy, but Antoine said it wasn't you."

Luis helped her to ease out of the exquisite gown and then leaned down to kiss her bare shoulder. "We agreed to talk another time," he reminded her.

Content to simply prepare for bed, Michelle fell silent. She stepped out of her slippers and this time as they peeled away her petticoats, she was the one to undo the ties. Luis proved to be quite helpful, though, and laid her clothes aside in neat stacks. He went to the bed to turn down the covers as she slipped off the last of her lingerie and donned her nightgown. When she climbed into bed, he covered her and reached for the lamp.

"No," Michelle said. "Leave it on."

"Do you always sleep with a light?"

"No, but tonight I don't want to be in the dark."

"Whatever you wish."

Luis sat down on the side of the bed and yanked

off his right boot. Before he could remove the left one, Michelle had sat up and leaned toward him.

"Just what do you think you're doing?"

"If you're afraid of the dark, Señora Aragon, I dare not leave you alone."

That he had never intended to leave her was Michelle's first thought. She tried to recall what he had said so she could point out that he had just told her another lie, but she could not remember him actually promising to leave. He had simply given her the impression, clearly false, that he would.

"My head hurts so badly that I'm sick to my stomach," she reminded him. "If you force yourself on me, I'm going to be sick all over you."

"My, what a disgusting thought," Luis agreed with a theatrical shudder. "I'm sorry to disappoint you, but I told you earlier that I had no interest in passion tonight and I still don't. Still, a husband and wife ought to spend their wedding night in the same bed, if not in each other's arms. You might as well get used to my company tonight, because you'll share my bed for the rest of your life."

"I want my own room!"

"You may have it," Luis readily conceded. "But you'll sleep in my bed."

Michelle glared at him as he rose to remove his coat. Rather than demonstrating the same care he had taken with her garments, he simply tossed his this way and that. When he had removed his shirt, it was not his well-muscled arms and chest that impressed her, but the still-visible print of her lips on his throat. Filled with shame, she could not bear to see anymore. She turned away from him and lay down on her side.

She agonized how such a handsome man could be so insufferably mean. At that moment, she did not care what he did to her that night because it could not possibly be any more painful than the blame she had heaped on herself all day. Antoine was dead and she was married to the man who had killed him. Why hadn't she had the courage to kill herself instead?

When he was completely undressed, Luis joined Michelle in the bed. "Come here," he ordered, but he did no more than slip his arm around her waist to pull her close. She felt soft and sweet, and the perfume clinging to her fair curls teased his senses in a way he had not thought possible. Too late he realized passion was not going to be a stranger that night, but he had given her his word that he expected to do no more than sleep and he knew he dared not break it.

"Buenas noches, Señora Aragon," he whispered, but Michelle chose not to wish him the same.

Eleven

Francisco and Maria Lourdes Castillo stood at the foot of Antoine's bed, their expressions as anguished as their hearts as they watched Dr. Armando Tejada hover over the cousin they believed to be mortally wounded. They had been preparing themselves all day for the painful eventuality of Antoine's death and that endless torture had created a nearly unbearable anxiety. For the last two hours, Antoine had passed in and out of consciousness communicating little other than tormented moans, but they continued to watch and listen, expecting his last words to be imminent and profound.

"How long?" Francisco finally found the courage to ask.

"The bullet passed through his shoulder just below the collarbone," the elderly physician murmured in the hushed tone he reserved for sickrooms. "His lungs are undamaged. If he survives the night, he'll live."

"But he lost so much blood, Dr. Tejada," Francisco reminded him.

"What? Are you disappointed to learn he might survive?"

"No, of course not, I just don't understand how it's possible."

"I have been practicing medicine for nearly fifty

years," Armando stated proudly, as though his gaunt and bent frame alone did not attest to his lengthy career, "and I've learned that miracles are more common than most people believe. This is a strong young man and he is struggling mightily to live."

"Can he hear us?" Lourdes asked.

"Perhaps, perhaps not. Go on to bed. I will sit with him tonight."

Eager to go, and yet fearfully reluctant to leave, Francisco remained where he stood. "I should never have permitted him to take such a dangerous risk. His family will never forgive me if he dies. He was like a younger brother to me. I should never have allowed him to become involved with—"

"Francisco!" Maria Lourdes scolded. "You've said enough."

Dr. Tejada waited, but Francisco obeyed his wife and did not identify the man with whom Antoine had been dueling. "Maintain your silence," he counseled. "I am an old man and can't be expected to remember everything I hear, but it is better if I do not hear the name of a man involved in a duel in the first place."

Francisco nodded. He had called on Armando Tejada precisely because of his age. He no longer had a regular practice but was known for his success in tending unfortunate victims of scandalous accidents. He was also known for having a memory so poor that he could never provide the name of a patient after he had affected a cure. In truth, his memory was as sharp as his medical skill, but he pretended to be senile whenever it suited his purpose.

"Go on to bed," he encouraged. "I'll watch him tonight."

Maria Lourdes took her husband's hand and pulled him away from the bed. "You'll call us if, well, if we're needed?"

"I will summon you if there's any change," the

183

doctor assured them. When the couple had left the room, he pulled a chair close to the bed and sat down. He then leaned forward and began to talk to Antoine in an encouraging whisper. "You're a very handsome young man," he began. "Women must adore you. I don't think you're tired of the earth just yet, not when there are so many beautiful women left to love. That's a damn good reason to live. Sleep. Dream. Feel the hands of your lover caress you and you'll be filled with the strength to survive. Dream of love, and live."

Antoine responded more to the soft, undulating rhythm of Dr. Tejada's voice than to his words, but he had been filled with the determination to survive from the moment he had been shot. He had to live. Had to see Augustín Aragon dead. He could smell his own blood clotting beneath the bandage that wrapped his shoulder and longed to savor the scent of Augustín's as it flowed from his broken body into the dirt.

In fitful dreams he recalled the bullfight he had attended with Michelle and saw himself as the matador in a glittering costume and Augustín as the doomed beast. He heard the wildly delirious shouts of the crowd as the arrogant Spaniard fell dead and exulted in the sweet sense of victory that was finally his. In a matador's traditional tribute to the woman he loved, he had slain Augustín in front of Michelle and won her love forever.

"Michelle," he whispered. He had waited all day to feel the gentle sweetness of her touch, her kiss. Even half dead he longed for Michelle and could not understand why she had deserted him when he needed her most.

Having no idea who Michelle might be, or where she was, Armando nevertheless patted Antoine's hand and assured him Michelle would soon arrive.

* * *

After having slept all day, Michelle awoke repeatedly during the night, and each time she found herself more firmly entangled in Luis's embrace. At first, she had not realized he was wearing no clothes, and that discovery terrified her, for there seemed to be no way to elude his grasp without placing her hands somewhere she would rather not touch. Each time she tried to simply roll out of his arms he shifted his position without waking and captured her anew.

He had also bathed and shaved before their wedding with a spicy soap whose appealingly masculine scent clung to his deeply tanned skin. The light at the bedside sculpted his even features with flattering shadows, creating as delicious a sight as the fragrance that enveloped him. His hair fell across his forehead in a boyish wave, making him appear far younger than his actual years. The total effect was one of such sensuous appeal that Michelle was not merely embarrassed but horribly ashamed of the direction of her thoughts. She despised the man, and yet the heat of his muscular body warmed her clear through. Disgusted with herself, she made another attempt to break free.

Luis opened his eyes. "Stop your incessant squirming," he ordered gruffly. "If you can't sleep, then sit up and read, but stop wiggling all over the bed and waking me. Unless, of course, you deliberately wanted me awake."

Startled, Michelle shrank away from him. "Why would I want you awake?" she asked as though such a possibility were truly preposterous.

"Shall I show you?"

"No!"

"Then you do know," Luis teased with a deep chuckle.

"I just want to be left alone."

"So do I," Luis pointed out. "You're the one who's jumping all over the bed."

"I am not!"

"Oh yes you are." Luis raised up slightly, and after observing her obstinate expression for no more than two seconds, leaned across her and with a possessive flourish endeavored to renew his mark on her neck. Outraged, she pounded his shoulders, but her blows were totally ineffective. Nearly a foot taller, and outweighing her by one hundred pounds, he had little trouble subduing her resistance and continued to savor the taste of her tender flesh until he was certain he had succeeded in branding her with his kiss.

"Do you want more?" he asked as he released her.

"More of you? Never!" Michelle shouted, but that he could still work the same magic on her senses had shaken her badly. He was no Gypsy, cast no spells, and yet when his lips brushed her skin she felt an uncontrollable desire her years with Antoine had not conditioned her to expect. Too ashamed to admit how strongly he affected her emotions, she placed her hands on his chest to keep him away. The instant her fingertips brushed the crisp black curls that covered the broad expanse she regretted touching him and pulled back.

"You promised to leave me alone," she reminded him.

"You started it."

"I did not."

"Then why did you wake me?"

"I didn't wake you." His defiant stare said he thought otherwise and she rephrased her denial. "I didn't deliberately wake you."

"Do you always flop around like a fish out of water when you sleep?"

Michelle did not think so, but then, she had had a bed of her own her whole life. "Yes," she claimed with sudden inspiration. "Neither of my sisters will sleep with me because I bother them so. I'll need a separate bed or you'll never get any sleep."

Her eyes looked enormous in the dim light and gave her expression an innocent sweetness Luis was positive she did not deserve. "You'll learn to sleep with me in time," he assured her, "and after we make love for several hours, you'll have no trouble sleeping. Now close your eyes and do the best you can to rest without the benefit of my affection tonight."

Michelle turned her back toward him and promptly realized her mistake when Luis cuddled up behind her and again encircled her waist. She could feel the warmth of his breath against her cheek and wished with all her heart she were anywhere but in his bed. It was *her* bed, she reminded herself, but not truly hers as long as he was in it.

She had expended so much energy hoping for a proposal from Antoine she had not thought as far as their wedding night, but she knew it would have had nothing in common with this one. She and Antoine would have been married in the company of all their family and friends. They would have had a wonderful party with music and dancing, toasted each other with his most delicious champagne, and then, finally alone, would have made love until dawn. She closed her eyes and tried to imagine that she was lying in Antoine's embrace rather than Luis's, but the Spaniard's presence was too strong for such a pretense to take hold in her imagination.

She could not overcome the guilty sensation that she was betraying her first love, and she lay quietly in her husband's arms, dreading what the new day would bring. Surely it could be no worse than what she had already suffered, but as Luis shifted his weight slightly, she realized how wrong that conclusion had been. She did not want to make love with him, not ever, but if the rest of his affection was as

187

intoxicating as his kiss, she knew she would never be able to refuse.

Luis could feel Michelle's every twitch and wondered if she could possibly exhibit such nervousness every night. He usually did not spend the whole night with a woman and on the rare occasions that he had, he did not recall a single one who was anything other than a delightful companion. If he and his bride were unable to sleep together, it would definitely prove to be a problem, but it was insignificant at the moment and he ceased to worry over it and fell asleep.

The aroma of freshly baked rolls and steaming-hot chocolate coaxed Michelle from the last of her dreams, but the sight of Luis up and dressed spoiled her appetite completely. She eased herself into a sitting position and pushed her tangled hair out of her eyes. Her headache was only slightly less painful and she still doubted that she ought to eat.

"I'm assuming that you'd rather not have my company while you have breakfast," Luis said as he headed toward the door. "I'll come back in half an hour to help you dress."

He left the room before Michelle uttered a word, but grateful for the privacy he had afforded her, she felt somewhat better and decided a cup of hot chocolate might not upset her stomach too badly. She left the bed, sat down at the table, poured herself a cup from a quaint little pot, and when her first sip proved surprisingly good, took another. The rolls were warm, and accompanied by butter and jam, looked tasty as well. Assuming Luis would wish to continue their journey, and that it might be a long while before she had another chance to eat, Michelle reached for one of the rolls and its flaky crust crumbled at her touch.

By the time Luis returned, there was no more than a single spoonful of chocolate left in the pot and a few scattered crumbs on the plate where the rolls had been stacked. Amused to find his slender bride had such a robust appetite, he was about to tease her and then thought better of it. He had sworn to be the best of husbands and did not want to embarrass her about her appetite. He made no comment whatsoever on the disappearance of the food and instead shook out one of the gowns he had unpacked the night before. It was a pale-apricot shade he thought most attractive.

"Would you like to wear this?" he asked.

Michelle had put her time alone to good use and had an answer ready. "I'll wear the same suit I did yesterday with another blouse. Navy-blue is as close as I have to mourning attire."

That she would prefer mourning for Antoine to being on a honeymoon with him did not surprise Luis, but he was hurt nonetheless. "Do you really need my help, or can you dress on your own today?"

"I can manage by myself, thank you. I don't suppose you'd consider returning to my aunt's home to fetch my maid?"

"No, I most certainly wouldn't. We'll leave as soon as you're ready. Don't keep us waiting long."

Again he left her room without waiting for a reply and Michelle was surprised by how badly his rebuff made her feel. They barely knew each other, and what they did know they had not learned under the best of circumstances. Fearing every move she made was the wrong one, she brushed out her hair and dressed with trembling fingers. Luis had brought the smallest of her trunks up to the room, and she carefully repacked her belongings before stepping out on the balcony.

Luis was standing in the courtyard below her room talking with his men. His hair glowed in the morning light with a coppery sheen she had not had a previous opportunity to appreciate. When he glanced up at her, she was embarrassed to have been caught watching him and waved as though she had been attempting to catch his attention.

"I'm ready to go," she called to him.

She looked as prim and proper as she had the previous day, and Luis could not help but notice the confused glances that passed between Julio and Tomás. Both men were aware of how much he enjoyed the company of beautiful women, but Michelle certainly did not look as though his efforts to entertain her on their wedding night had met with any success. Luis was not about to provide excuses to his driver and footman, however.

"Go up and get her trunk," he ordered instead. He was impatient to continue their journey, but when Michelle came downstairs, she had a request he had not foreseen.

She waited until her trunk had been loaded on the carriage and then shied away slightly from Luis. "I'd like to stop at the church if I may," she asked politely.

Somewhat surprised that she would ask his permission rather than simply say where she was going, Luis stepped up to her side and took her elbow. "I promised you'd have all the time you wished to pray, but you didn't seem up to remaining in church last night."

"No, I wasn't, but I am now and you needn't come with me."

That he might have prayers of his own he wished to say obviously had not occurred to her and Luis refrained from pointing that out. He nodded, and watched her walk away, but the instant she entered the church he followed her. He was not really afraid that she would flee out the door on the opposite side, but he wanted to keep an eye on her just the same. She slipped into a pew near the front and knelt, and he took his place in the last row.

He was not a religious man, but he did manage to say a prayer for the repose of Antoine's soul. Having gotten that far, he asked God's blessing for his marriage, and most especially for his lovely bride who had come to him in such a tragic way. He then sat back and watched Michelle's silent meditations for what seemed like an eternity. When she finally rose, he got to his feet and hurried out the door before being seen. He waited for her just outside and when she appeared, he tried to look as though he had been enjoying the beauty of the morning rather than worrying about their future.

Respecting her sorrow, Luis remained silent for the first hour of their journey. Then the uncompromising rigidity of Michelle's posture began to annoy him. He was doing his damnedest to make the best of a disastrous situation and he thought she should be gracious enough to do the same. "We have more in common than you might believe," he announced suddenly. "My mother is French. She was little more than a child at the time of the Revolution and fled to Spain with her mother when her father was slain."

Lost in thought, it took a moment for Michelle to take in what Luis had said and respond to it. She had thought his command of the French language excellent, and now understood why. "Was your grandfather sent to the guillotine?" she asked with a shudder.

"No, but he was a Bourbon, if only distantly related to the king, so he might very well have been condemned to death. Apparently he sympathized with the ideals of the Revolution and was killed in the early rioting. That was enough to terrify my grandmother so greatly that she and my mother escaped to Spain with little more than the clothes on their backs, elegant though they must have been.

191

They stayed with a succession of relatives and friends. When she met my father's father, who was a widower, they went to live with him. That's how my mother and father met. After they had married, her mother and his father also married, so we had only one set of grandparents."

In spite of her best efforts to remain disinterested, that was such an intriguing story Michelle got caught up in it before she realized what had happened. "I see. That is rather complicated, but if your parents weren't stepbrother and stepsister when they wed, there shouldn't have been any objection."

"Perhaps not, but their marriage did create considerable strife, although we never heard any of the details, and they soon sailed for Mexico. My father managed to kill a particularly troublesome pirate on the way and was rewarded with a land grant in California. That's where I was born."

Michelle regarded her new husband with a fascinated glance. "You speak of your parents as though escaping death during the Revolution or slaying pirates were minor incidents in their lives. Is that true?"

"You'll have to ask them. I hope that you'll meet them someday. Your fair coloring resembles my mother's. My two sisters and two of my brothers are blond. Only my brother Daniel and I look like my father."

That Luis might have a brother who was as darkly handsome as he was an unnerving possibility. "Do you and Daniel look very much alike?"

"No, he's considered quite handsome," Luis replied with mock seriousness.

"And you're not?"

Amused by her shocked expression, Luis had to laugh. "I suppose there are some people who regard me as handsome. Do you?"

Embarrassed by how foolish her question must

have sounded, Michelle concentrated on the passing scenery for a moment. Luis was far more than merely handsome, but she did not know how to state that in words that would not make him more insufferably conceited than he already was. "Do you expect compliments on your looks from everyone you meet?" she finally asked.

"No, but I wouldn't mind hearing them from my wife."

Michelle was startled by that reminder. She had said the words, signed the papers, but the bond that ought to exist between a husband and wife was sadly missing in their case. How could it be otherwise? she asked herself. Unwilling to dwell on the unfortunate circumstances of their marriage, she urged Luis to continue.

"Tell me more about your family. Where do they all live? What do they do?"

Because he had been striving to engage her in conversation in the first place, Luis was glad to indulge her curiosity. "My sisters, Marie and Magdelena, live with their husbands and families on ranches in Mexico. Esteban, who is the horseman of the family, runs my parents' ranch in Monterey. Daniel is a physician. He trained here in Spain, but returned home to practice medicine. Marc has his captain's papers just as I do, but from what I understand from the letters I receive from home, he's gone off to fight for the Americans in their war against Mexico."

"But if he was born in California, then he's a Mexican citizen, isn't he?"

"Yes, and so am I."

That the man she had thought a dashing Gypsy was in fact a Mexican citizen born in California of Spanish and French heritage left Michelle feeling completely dismayed. Nothing about the man was as it seemed, except for his astonishingly attractive appearance. She had to force herself to explore his brother's actions. "Isn't that treason?"

Again Luis made no effort to stifle an amused chuckle. "Yes, it certainly is. Marc believes the Americans will win the war. He's hoping that will greatly improve the situation in California as it will become a valuable part of the United States rather than remain a remote province of Mexico."

"Do you agree?"

"No, I'd like to see California become an independent nation."

"What are the chances of that happening?"

"They are probably extremely remote, but because I make my home in Barcelona, I don't give it a great deal of thought. I concentrate on our ships, and the transporting of goods between profitable markets. Perhaps that isn't nearly as exciting as fighting in a war as Marc is doing, but it's not nearly as dangerous, either."

In Michelle's opinion, Luis's gaze was too direct, as though he were daring her to mention the dangers inherent in a duel. Not about to fall prey to any such verbal trap, Michelle issued a challenge of her own. "You've already proven to me just how greatly you love danger," she assured him calmly. "You led people to believe you were a Gypsy. You called on me repeatedly at hours that were calculated to cause a scandal. You used the truth interchangeably with lies. I think danger is what you love best."

She looked very proud of herself for drawing that conclusion, so Luis did not dispute her word. Instead, he moved close, slipped his hand around her slender neck, and drew her into a kiss he savored until she stopped struggling to break free. At that precise instant, he released her. *"That's* what I like best," he informed her with a mischievous wink.

His kiss frightened Michelle not because she was

revolted by his touch, but because she could not seem to stop craving such a delicious thrill. She moved along the padded leather seat to the end and clenched her hands tightly in her lap. "Is that why you've been exiled to Spain? Because you can't control your desires where women are concerned?"

Luis had discovered Michelle had a delightful array of expressions which ranged from despair through dazed confusion to furious anger. He had not realized until then that he had not had the opportunity to study her face when she was free of care. He wondered how she looked when she was happy and hoped that it would not be too much longer before he caught a glimpse of unabashed joy lighting her delicate features. She was a rare beauty with her face in repose. With a smile, he was positive she would be incomparable. He made a mental note to have her portrait painted as soon as she felt up to smiling for the artist.

"I wasn't 'exiled,' as you put it. As the eldest son, the task of managing our European operation quite naturally fell to me. I've done very well with it, too. I've acquired ships, arranged for lucrative shipping contracts, and improved the lot of the merchant seamen who work for us. When I arrived in Spain, there were several captains in our employ who were more suited to the profession of butcher than life at sea. I saw that they had the opportunity to make that change."

"That sounds like a very good way to make enemies."

"It was," Luis agreed, "but any man who'll cripple a sailor with savage floggings doesn't deserve to have his own command. The threat of creating an enemy didn't deter me from making the Aragon Line a fine one of which my whole family can be proud."

That Luis had championed the cause of merchant seamen over captains surprised Michelle. She had expected him to be so utterly ruthless that he would stop at nothing to achieve his goals. Apparently the welfare of his crews was a genuine concern and she was very favorably impressed. Then she wondered if he might not be lying again in a deliberate attempt to paint a flattering picture of himself.

"Do you recall the names of any of the captains you fired?"

Puzzled by that request, Luis nonetheless nodded, and after a brief hesitation supplied some names. "There was José de la Torre, who expected several of his crew to die from maltreatment each time he set sail. Miguel Villa was so careless in the way he maintained his ship that men often fell to their deaths from rotten rigging. Then there was the Englishman, Boris Ryde. He was the worst of the lot. He'd flog men for infractions so small they would be overlooked by even the most conscientious captain. He was simply a brutal man whose greatest pleasure was in inflicting pain. Now do you mind if we discuss a less gruesome subject?"

Satisfied by the detail he had supplied that the men he listed were real, Michelle nodded. "Certainly not."

"Good. There's a nice place to stop just ahead. I had the inn pack something for us to eat. We can have lunch, take a walk if you like, and you can tell me all about *your* family."

He had been so open with her, Michelle hated to disappoint him. "My story isn't nearly as exciting as yours."

"I still want to hear it," Luis insisted. "It isn't every day that I am presented with a set of in-laws, and I'd like to know who they are."

He smiled at her then. It was the relaxed, lazy smile of the Gypsy who had plagued her dreams and Michelle had to look away rather than respond with a smile of her own that would reveal far more than she wished to about her frustratingly contradictory feelings for him.

They were swinging south across the highlands on their way to Valencia and the countryside was especially pretty. When Luis asked Julio to stop, Michelle was actually looking forward to resting a while and having something to eat. She still felt Antoine's loss as a dull, aching pain that encircled her heart and numbed her thoughts, but made her best effort to reflect a mature calm rather than the hysteria of the previous day. All the tears she had shed had failed to ease her grief or lighten her guilt and she knew weeping forever would not bring Antoine back to life.

Luis helped Michelle from the carriage and, taking from it one of the blankets he kept for cool weather and the basket of food, led her down a winding path that extended from the road to a peaceful glen split by a rippling brook. He set the basket aside, unfurled the blanket, and then gestured for her to make herself comfortable. He had asked the cook to pack rolls, slices of ham and cheese, wine, cakes, oranges, and nuts. As he took two pewter mugs from the basket, he was pleased by Michelle's obvious delight.

"Is there something you'd like to have to eat tomorrow?" he asked. "I'll send Julio and Tomás out to find it as soon as we stop for the night."

"No, this is more than enough," Michelle assured him. The setting had such a tranquil beauty that she was about to ask if he went there often, but thinking he might have done so with other women she went to the brook instead. She washed her hands and, after setting her beribboned bonnet aside, splashed water on her face to refresh herself more completely. She was certain he must know a great many women, but she did not want to hear about any of them. It would only add to her pain to learn she had good reason to be jealous.

"How are you feeling?" Luis knelt by her side to wash his hands, too.

"Not very good," Michelle confessed shyly. "Though hunger isn't the problem, I do want something to eat." She waited for him to finish and walked the few steps to the blanket ahead of him. When she sat down, she discovered that it was woven of wool as soft as cashmere, but it was as gray as her mood. She reached for an orange and began to peel it.

Luis could see by Michelle's downcast expression that she was again lost in her grief. While that was to be expected, he was sorry the light mood they had shared briefly in the carriage had disappeared. Something must have happened to remind her of her sorrow, but Luis did not understand what it had been. He poured them both some wine and then cut several slices of ham and half a dozen wedges of cheese to go with the rolls.

"You promised to tell me about your family," he reminded her.

Finding it easier to concentrate on dividing the orange into sections than face her inquisitive companion, Michelle spoke without looking up at him. "I'm from Lyon. My father died suddenly four years ago and my mother still misses him terribly. We all do. I have two sisters. Nicole is fourteen and Denise is seventeen."

"Are they as lovely as you?"

His voice had been honey-smooth, and the sweetness of his compliment caressed her ravaged emotions. "Thank you. Yes, they are very pretty. Nicole has the more serious nature, but that might be because she was only ten when our father died. She enjoys writing poetry, and we think it's quite good. Denise is, well, she's very

198

charming but not given to literary pursuits."

"She's a flirt, you mean."

"Well . . ." Michelle tried to find a less derisive word to describe her sister, but there didn't seem to be one. "Yes, she enjoys flirting more than anything. She's done it since she was a small child. It's as natural to her as breathing."

"And not to you?"

"I never had any reason to flirt. Antoine and I, well, from the time we were children, we knew we belonged together."

Luis watched a bright film of tears fill Michelle's eyes and feared it was going to be another very long afternoon. He reached over to pat her hand. "It's all right, Michelle. Cry as much as you want. I want you to feel better and perhaps crying will help."

Michelle doubted it. She just felt so terribly lost. She knew she ought not to be sharing lunch in a pretty glade when Antoine would never again feel the warmth of the sun on his skin. She remembered how they had all cried when her darling father had died, and Antoine's death had hurt her just as badly. It had taken months for her to recover from the loss of her father, but she did not think she would ever stop missing Antoine.

Luis had little appetite either then, but he forced himself to eat. He gave up on the effort to learn more about Michelle's family and kept still rather than pester her with annoying questions. When she returned to the stream to wash the sticky juice of the orange from her hands, he gathered up the remains of their picnic. He tossed out the wine she had not tasted and replaced everything in the basket. Michelle refolded the blanket and, carrying it and her bonnet, preceded him up the path.

Julio and Tomás had already eaten their lunch and appeared to be anxious to get under way. Luis handed them the picnic basket to store away and climbed into the carriage after his new but hopelessly distant bride. She again huddled in the corner and covered a wide yawn.

"I'm sorry," she apologized. "I hope you won't mind if I sleep."

"No, not at all, but my lap is much more comfortable than that chilly corner." Knowing she would never approach him on her own, he reached for her before she could object and lifted her onto his knees. "See, isn't this better?"

Michelle agreed, but wouldn't admit it. Instead, she lay her head against his shoulder and closed her eyes. Her bonnet still dangled from her fingertips and Luis removed it from her grasp so it would not be crushed while she slept. Another considerate gesture she thought to herself, but the memory of his part in Antoine's death never left her mind. When everything was wrong, she had no idea how to put it right, but she knew she ought not to be sitting on a handsome murderer's lap even if he *was* her husband.

Twelve

Late in the afternoon of the day following the duel, Antoine opened his eyes and, although he had to fight to remain awake, he was determined not to sink back into unconsciousness. He felt completely drained, as though he had not just emerged from two days of sleep but from the grave. Frightened that he had no energy at all, he looked up at the elderly gentleman who was peering down at him and tried to find the breath to ask just who he might be and why he was staring at him so rudely.

Dr. Tejada broke into a gleeful grin and then, exhibiting his usual discretion, introduced himself only as a physician. "Don't try to speak," he warned Antoine. "Continue to rest and I'll give you some broth. You nearly bled to death, and it will take you several weeks to regain your vigor. A young body heals more rapidly than an aged one, but still, it will take time before you are fully recovered."

Antoine had always spoken a passable Spanish, but now the chore of comprehending the doctor's message was completely beyond him. He understood only that he was in the man's care, but little else. He recognized the room he had been given at Francisco's home and felt safe there, but he sensed something was dreadfully amiss. His shoulder throbbed with an agonizing burst of pain with every heartbeat, but he could recall being shot only dimly. What he did remember vividly was the blood pooling up all around him.

Armando excused himself and left the room to call Francisco and fetch the bowl of broth. When he had first arrived, he had instructed the cook to prepare the nourishing soup in hopes his patient would live to consume it. He was a firm believer in the power of lean meat to invigorate victims of severe blood loss, but unfortunately they had to possess the strength to chew properly, which Antoine obviously did not. When Francisco followed him back into the sickroom, he proceeded to share his views on nutrition while he fed Antoine all the broth the Frenchman could swallow.

"Encourage your cousin," the physician instructed, "but do not tire him."

Francisco waited until Dr. Tejada had left the room to speak. "Thank God you've survived this horrible misfortune." He slid into the doctor's chair and hoped the strain of the last two days was not evident in his expression. He was grateful that Antoine, who had always been so fastidious in his appearance, could not see how unkempt he looked now.

"I know you had planned to return home, but you are welcome to remain with us for as long as it takes for your wound to heal. I'll write to your mother and provide a believable excuse, relating to business perhaps, so that she won't worry. You're going to be fine, Antoine. I know that you will. Maria Lourdes was awake most of the night and is resting now, but she'll come in to see you as soon as she wakes."

Antoine noted not only the dark circles beneath his cousin's eyes but also his nervousness and desperate words and gathered that he had escaped death by an exceedingly narrow margin. He *had* escaped, however, and that was all that mattered. Lacking the energy to speak above a hoarse whisper, he mouthed his question. "Where is Michelle?"

Stunned that Antoine did not know, Francisco sat back slightly. He did not know what to say when the truth would undoubtedly be as painful as Antoine's wound. What if he told him and Antoine died of a broken heart? Flustered, he glanced toward the door, hoping Dr. Tejada or his wife might appear, but no one arrived to distract Antoine from his question or offer Francisco help in answering it.

"Tell me," Antoine urged.

Francisco took out his handkerchief and wiped his suddenly perspiring brow. "You're alive, Antoine. We must rejoice in that miracle for the time being, for surely it *is* a miracle. Thank God that you have been spared and forget Michelle. She's gone."

Antoine failed to grasp the meaning of Francisco's words. His cousin was so greatly disturbed that he feared the worst. "Not dead?" he rasped.

"Oh, no, forgive me. I didn't mean to frighten you so badly." That he had just terrified the injured man was plain in Antoine's panicked expression and he had not meant to add to his poor cousin's woes. He leaned close and took care that his words could not be overheard by servants passing by out in the hall. "You and Aragon agreed that Michelle was to wed the winner. She is with him."

Shocked by so unlikely an event, Antoine felt as though the last bit of his life were fading away. He had been infuriated with Augustín when he had made that bargain, and Michelle had been so outraged to be used as a prize that he had never expected her to go through with it. Filled with despair, he closed his eyes inspiring Francisco to grow frantic when he did not respond to his urgent calls.

Michelle had been Antoine's devoted companion for as long as he could remember. How could Augustín Aragon have seduced her? The man was undeniably handsome, and wealthy as well, but had his beloved Michelle been no more than a faithless harlot who would have strayed with any rogue who approached her?

Responding to the urgency in Francisco's voice, Dr.

Tejada returned to Antoine's room. "What's the matter here?" he asked crossly before closing the door. His patient had been doing so well when he had left that he could not believe that he might have taken a sudden turn for the worse.

Already on his feet, Francisco gestured helplessly. "We were talking, and he just, well, he just left me."

Armando leaned over Antoine and observed him closely. He then grew exasperated with Francisco. "He's just fallen asleep is all. He's exhausted and he won't be able to keep from lapsing off at times. You mustn't become hysterical over it. Think nothing of it. Now I'm going home. Each time he wakes, give him more broth. I'll stop by in the morning to see how he's doing."

Still desperately frightened, Francisco walked him to the door. "Do you really think it's safe to go?"

"Yes," Armando assured him. "He's very weak, but not feverish. The danger's past. He'll recover completely in time."

Dr. Tejada had not only an exuberant confidence but a long string of successful cases with which to document his optimism. Trusting in the physician's prediction, Francisco thanked him profusely and wished him a good afternoon. He then went to wake his wife, tell her the good news about Antoine's expected recovery, and draw upon her expertise in affairs of the heart.

When Luis and Michelle stopped for the night, it was at an inn where he was well known. He presented his bride to the owner and his wife with a great show of pride, but Michelle knew he could not possibly be pleased to have married her and was again fabricating a convenient lie. Rather than share her pessimistic views on their marriage with the staff of the inn, however, she kept still until they had been shown upstairs to the establishment's only suite.

This inn was larger than the one in which they had spent their wedding night and the accommodations were far more luxurious. Apparently willing to provide the privilege of separate lodgings, Luis had his luggage placed in one room of the suite and hers in the other. Michelle waited until the porters had left before she went to the open doorway between their rooms.

"You're a gifted storyteller," she called to him, "but I see absolutely no reason to pretend we're an ecstatically happy newly wed couple when we're not. You needn't introduce me with an enthusiasm that you can't possibly feel."

Wanting to clean up before supper, Luis had already removed his coat and waistcoat and unbuttoned his shirt as he came toward her. "Believe me, Señora Aragon, I'm not faking my enthusiasm. I'm very proud of you."

His graceful stride held more than the hint of a predator and Michelle stepped back when he got too near. His glance was taunting rather than appreciative and she did not feel complimented despite his praise. "That's impossible."

"No it isn't," Luis countered. "You've both beauty and depth. What more could any man want in a wife?"

"To have wed under less harrowing circumstances surely."

Luis nodded. "I'll concede that point. But don't forget that I'm the one who insisted you marry the winner of Antoine's absurd challenge. You know I didn't expect it to turn out as it did, but now that it has, I think that was a brilliant bit of foresight. I do want you, Michelle, and don't pretend that I haven't made my desire abundantly clear."

Michelle knew exactly what he was about to do when he inclined his head but her feet stubbornly refused to carry her away. Her body would not turn from him, nor would her lips maintain their firm line when his tongue caressed them. She felt foolish and weak, and at the same time so eager for his affection she was frightened that he would sense it, too. She did not want to respond to him as wantonly as she previously had, and yet her body betrayed her as it did each time he touched her. With no weapons to fight his immense physical charm, she relaxed in his arms as though becoming his wife had been her fondest dream.

To maintain his balance, Luis leaned back against the doorjamb and enfolded Michelle in a rapturous embrace. While she had slept in the carriage, he had fought the painful stirrings of desire that had filled him, but her taunting denials of the sensual magic that had always existed between them had inspired him to kiss her again. He could no longer keep his distance, and lost the last of his reserve.

He kissed her as deeply and aggressively as he would have any woman he wanted as badly as he wanted her. He lost himself in her taste, loosed the combs from her hair, and slid his fingers through her tawny curls. She was a woman made for loving. How could she even imagine that he did not want her! he cried out in his mind. He had never wanted any woman more. If only she weren't wearing so damn many layers of clothes! Wanting her completely *un*-clothed, he peeled off her jacket and hurriedly unbuttoned her blouse but he did not end his first kiss until he was ready to begin another.

Cradled in his arms, Michelle was equally lost in Luis. She slipped her hands inside his shirt and traced the sleek planes of his well-muscled back with a newly discovered joy. He had the superbly proportioned body of a god and just touching him flooded her with desire.

She was only dimly aware of the shouts drifting up to her open window until she recognized Julio's voice as he called to Tomás. The two men were unhitching the team from the carriage and carrying on an animated conversation filled with jests and hearty laughter. They had seen the duel, and watched Antoine die. How could they be in such high spirits when they had witnessed something so awful? Fearing that she was behaving just as badly, Michelle was overcome with shame and finally found the resolve to break free of Luis's grasp.

"Please," she whispered as she backed away. She raised her hands, intending to fend him off if he followed her, but he remained standing in the doorway observing her with an incredulous stare.

It wasn't until then that Luis heard Julio and Tomás's playful though crude banter. He doubted Michelle understood their words, but clearly she had made an accurate interpretation of their tone. It was a simple matter to deduce how she had been distracted momentarily and then overwhelmed with guilt. After all, she was reacting strongly to a man other than her dear, dead Antoine. Discouraged, he crossed her room and slammed the window shut.

"They weren't talking about you," he assured her, but even as he spoke he could see that possibility had not even occurred to her. He had intended to let her set their pace and lead him into intimacy. While in some respects he thought that was what had just happened, he could see that she was upset by the passion they had shared. He considered that as tragic a happenstance as Antoine's untimely demise.

"You're amazingly loyal, *querida*. That's also an admirable quality in a wife. I didn't mean to rush you into giving more than you wish." Luis walked to the doorway, and then turned back to add another thought.

"I'm not a patient man, however, so don't keep me waiting too long or we may both regret the consequences. The food here is excellent. We'll dine in an hour."

He smiled before closing the door, but it was a smile meant to convey his displeasure more than his fondness for her and Michelle felt utterly defeated. After having had only an orange at midday, she was hungry but she did not think she could eat with him seated at the same table. She knew better than to suggest she remain in her room, however, and rather than upset him again, hurried to unpack the apricot gown he had admired that morning.

The rare roast beef was as delicious as Luis had promised, but Michelle found it difficult to swallow more than a few tiny bites. She toyed with a roll and butter and the delicately seasoned rice, but had consumed very little by the time Luis had finished his whole meal. Other than a few complimentary remarks on the food, he had made no attempt at amusing conversation and she feared when they returned to their rooms the situation would again be beyond her control.

Desperate to avoid such a disastrous eventuality, she seized the initiative. "I can't stop thinking about Antoine," she blurted out. "If only I hadn't spoken to Aurora that first time, you'd not have followed me to my aunt's home. The paths of our lives would have forever remained separate and Antoine would be alive today."

Luis leaned forward and delivered his response in a hushed whisper, but his words stung with the hostility he could no longer hide. "Antoine is dead because he didn't stand still! We wouldn't have been dueling in the first place had he not issued that stupid challenge. The man knew what he was risking and he paid the price. I won't allow you to ruin both our lives brooding over a tragedy that Antoine brought on himself. Now, if you've finished eating, I'd like to show you the gardens here. They're worth visiting even in the dark."

Michelle had no objection to touring the gardens, but she would much rather have avoided her new husband and done so alone. He gave her no opportunity to decline his invitation, however. He simply rose, helped her from her chair, took her hand, and led her outside with the same dispassionate determination he would have shown an unruly child. He started off down the path that wound through the trees and flowering shrubs with such a brisk stride Michelle could appreciate little other than the fragrance of what they passed, but gradually he slowed to a more leisurely pace.

"I didn't mean to badger you," he finally apologized, "but I don't want to discuss personal topics in a public place. They are our private concern and I don't want anyone to overhear something which might be used against us later on. I mentioned Captain Ryde. He's not the only man who would like to see me suffer. If you and I are observed having words, the news will swiftly reach those who can make the most of it.

"I'm referring to shipping rivals rather than personal enemies for the most part. My father inherited the shipping line from his father and he is still the owner of record. He's also a Spaniard, which I am not. Here they dismiss me as a *criollo*, but my father is still respected, as well he should be, and I conduct business in his name. I try my best not to damage his reputation as well as my own. That's why our private life has to remain private, Michelle. Perhaps you enjoyed an idyllic existence in Lyon where no one ever raised his voice or conspired against a neighbor, but intrigues are quite common here in Spain."

Michelle had confessed her feelings of guilt in an attempt to win Luis's sympathy for her reticence in returning his affection. Not that she had ever actually displayed any such reticence, but she knew that she should and found the attendant shame that she had not nearly unbearable. That she had failed miserably in her effort to reach him also pained her deeply.

Apparently he was more concerned about possible danger to himself or his family's shipping line than her peace of mind. That realization compounded her already heavy burden of sorrow. He was treating her just as Antoine had. Her feelings mattered not at all when compared with his own.

"Can we speak freely out here?" she asked flippantly. "Or do you suspect someone might be lurking in the bushes hoping to hear a tantalizing secret they can sell to your competition?"

"Had my itinerary been announced, that would be a very real possibility. Fortunately, I wasn't expected here, so you needn't worry. Say whatever you wish."

Michelle intended to, but she took her time with it. The garden paths were lit by wrought-iron lanterns placed at convenient intervals. She thought this must make a wonderful place for a child to pretend he was exploring a forest. It felt good to walk after riding in the carriage all day and she had such long legs she had no real difficulty keeping up with Luis.

"Thank you for suggesting a walk," she began. "The grounds here are truly lovely."

Luis glanced down at her, certain that was not all she wanted to say. "I live in my grandfather's house in Barcelona. The garden is not nearly as large as this one, but I like to think it's every bit as relaxing a place to be."

"I'm sure that it is." Now that she had his attention and his encouragement to speak her mind, Michelle did not want to make the mistake of stumbling into their previous arguments. She hoped by being more specific in her comments she could make her point without angering him.

"We've been thrown together by fate, and that's precisely how I feel, as though I've been tossed into a situation that's totally beyond my control. I need an opportunity to adjust to the abrupt changes in my life. I believe what I need most is time to sort out my feelings, but that's impossible to do when I'm with you."

"If you'd rather have Julio's company, I could drive the team tomorrow."

Michelle halted abruptly and yanked her hand from his. If she had needed proof of how little value he placed on her needs, he had just provided it. "Don't you dare laugh at me. What's happened to us isn't in the least bit funny and I'll not have you making jokes about it. This is the very worst of situations and we can't simply pretend that it doesn't exist."

As always, Michelle's eyes sparkled brightly when she was angry, but Luis knew better than to mention how pretty she looked when her mood was so foul. He was struck then with the blinding insight that had the duel ended in a draw as he had intended, he would never have been able to watch Michelle leave Madrid with Antoine Lareau. He would have done his damnedest to convince her to stay with him. It was his turn then to choose his words with care.

"I wish Antoine were alive, too," he told her. "Then when you left him for me, you wouldn't have felt so guilty about it."

"Left him for you?" Michelle repeated in an astonished gasp.

Luis took a step closer. "Yes, although I didn't realize it then, I would never have been able to watch you leave for France with Antoine. That would have been condemning you to a tedious life of such unrelieved boredom that you would have had to have at least a dozen children just to keep yourself busy. Don't forget that I followed you through the Prado. Antoine talked incessantly, but his conversation was about himself rather than the museum's treasures. Wasn't that his usual habit? I doubt that he ever loved anyone but himself. He would have made a very poor husband for you, or any sensitive woman for that matter."

Both shocked and hurt by Luis's denigrating comments, Michelle put her hands over her ears and shook her head. "Stop it!" she begged. "I won't listen to you speak badly of Antoine."

Disappointed that she shut out the truth so consistently, Luis pulled her into his arms but gave up his effort to make her see her lost love for the totally self-absorbed man he had surely been. He rubbed her

211

back and waited for her to regain her composure. "Build a shrine to Antoine," he exclaimed. "I won't object, but what we truly need is the opportunity to forge a life together, not to go our separate ways. Don't bother asking for time to be by yourself again, because I'll never agree. Now it's getting late. Let's go inside."

Michelle was not only angered by how swiftly he had refused her request, but badly frightened as well. Was anything Luis said ever the truth? she agonized. Had he wanted her so badly that he had goaded Antoine into a duel with her as the prize, and then killed Antoine to have her? That was the most diabolical plan she could imagine and yet it did not seem past Luis's capabilities to conceive and carry out.

She tried to recall what had happened. Antoine had been livid, *outraged* over the attention Luis had shown her. Feeling both his honor and hers had been compromised, he had insisted upon a duel, and Luis had calmly agreed. He had displayed that same calm demeanor when he had come to her room and assured her no harm would befall Antoine. He had again been composed the next morning while poor Antoine had undoubtedly still been consumed with a blind rage. She looked up at her husband, and was chilled clear to the marrow by how ruthless a man he had just revealed himself to be.

"You make a very powerful enemy yourself, don't you?" she asked.

Surprised by that question, Luis frowned. "Boris Ryde would say so, among a few others. I'm not despised by multitudes if that's what you mean, but every powerful man has enemies, my pet, and I'm no exception."

But Michelle was positive he was exceptional in every way. He had toyed with her life, and destroyed Antoine's. He had shown little in the way of remorse, and tonight he had revealed his intention to keep her regardless of the outcome of the duel. It terrified her to think he might have killed Antoine out of some twisted desire to possess her. That was positively evil.

She remained silent as they entered the inn and climbed the stairs. When they reached their rooms, Luis unlocked her door, but after she crossed the threshold, he excused himself.

"I want to check on our team. I think it might be a good idea to pick up our pace tomorrow and I want to make certain the horses are up to it."

Relieved that she would be able to prepare for bed undisturbed, Michelle nodded and closed her door. Her headache had returned and she undressed at a lethargic pace. She had too many questions to consider, too many horrible possibilities to explore, but her mind refused to subdue the pain and think. When she finally climbed into bed, it was to escape her shameful thoughts rather than to pursue sleep. She wished she could go home and talk with her mother. Her mother had always been able to separate the truth from lies, but Michelle knew she had not inherited her talent.

"I want to go home," she murmured softly into her pillow, and yet at the same time, she was too ashamed that she had married Luis to have the courage to face her family again.

When Luis found their four ebony thoroughbreds well fed and handsomely groomed, he took another stroll through the garden and then sipped a brandy in the common room of the inn. He did not know what had gotten into him that night, but he had never behaved so foolishly with a woman. What had possessed him to admit that he would have done his best to prevent Michelle from going back to Lyon to wed Antoine? He might just as well have admitted that he had shot the Frenchman in cold blood, which could not be further from the truth. He had been even more horrified than Michelle when Antoine had fallen.

When he finally grew weary, he hoped that he had given his morbid bride time enough to fall asleep and climbed the stairs with a defeated step. After entering

213

his room, he looked into hers and was pleased to find her sleeping soundly for a change. He was not even tempted to allow her to sleep alone, however, and after removing his clothes, joined her in bed. Again lured near by her enticing perfume, he inched close to her, but he refrained from touching her that night. He was tired, too, and content to share her bed even if she refused to sleep in his arms.

Each time Antoine awakened, Francisco and Maria Lourdes took turns feeding him the nourishing broth Dr. Tejada had prescribed. Antoine had no appetite, but desperate to recover, he swallowed each spoonful they brought to his lips without hesitation. He hated being so helpless, despised being dependent on his cousins for all his needs. His drive to recover was so intense that Francisco feared he might attempt to leave his bed and injure himself.

"Relax," he cajoled. "Rest. If you force your body to exceed its present limits you'll only reopen your wound and you mustn't do that. You can't afford to lose another drop of blood, Antoine, not even a single drop. Should you prick your finger on a thorn, I fear it would be the end of you."

Antoine could feel the truth of Francisco's words each time he tried to lift his head from the pillow. His body responded so sluggishly to his commands it felt as though it were made of lead and he feared he would not be able to walk for several weeks. That Michelle and Augustín Aragon would spend that time celebrating their marriage was intolerable to him. He thought of nothing but recovering his strength and punishing them both. Each day they spent together would be a hideous torment to him.

"I want Aragon dead," he confided in his cousin.

Francisco shrugged. "So do I, but the duel was a fair one, and you can't challenge him again. Nor would I allow you to make such a foolish mistake a second time. No, Antoine, the matter is settled. Put any thought of another duel out of your mind."

Annoyed that he had not made himself clear, Antoine closed his eyes for a moment to gather what little strength he had. "I want you to find someone," he said.

"Who? Dr. Tejada does not want you having visitors other than Lourdes and me just yet. It would be far too great a strain on your limited resources. If there's someone you really must see, then I'll invite them to come for a brief visit next week. If Dr. Tejada allows it, of course."

"No," Antoine mouthed silently. "Find someone to kill Aragon."

Francisco had just finished feeding Antoine some broth and he was so shocked by that request that the empty bowl and spoon slipped from his hands and clattered to the floor. Embarrassed, he scrambled to pick them up before his wife came in and asked what had made him so clumsy. He turned the bowl over, and was relieved to find that it had not been cracked.

"Oh, Antoine, please," he begged with genuine horror. "You can't mean that. A duel is meant to settle a dispute between gentlemen. The question has been decided. You can't follow it with a quest for revenge."

"Find someone who hates Aragon," Antoine insisted. "He must have enemies. Find them."

Horrified by his cousin's train of thought, Francisco sat back in his chair. This time he spoke in a voice as quiet as Antoine's. "What are you suggesting, that we find someone who also has good reason to want Augustín dead and inspire him to carry out the deed?"

Antoine was able to affect a slight smile to show his pleasure at Francisco's cleverness. "Find them," he whispered and, hoping Francisco would do just that, he drifted back to sleep.

Francisco had grown accustomed to Antoine's frequent naps, but he doubted that he would ever find such a fiendish plan as his French cousin had just suggested easy to carry out. It was not impossible, of course. There were men who would do anything for a price, and doubtless men who despised Augustín Aragon. The challenge would be to find a single man who combined both qualities and Francisco did not even want to look, let alone find such a frightening individual.

Praying that when Antoine next awoke he would have completely forgotten about making such a gruesome request, he returned the bowl and spoon to the kitchen and then went to his own room for a much-needed nap. To have been Antoine's second at a duel had been the most terrifying experience of his life, and he considered arranging for a murder a thousand times worse.

Thirteen

Michelle sensed Luis's presence in the bed even before she opened her eyes. He wasn't all snuggled against her that morning, but she could feel the weight of his body on the mattress and the heat of his gaze. Both sensations made her feel horribly uncomfortable. She had never met anyone who could dominate even the silence in a room as pervasively as he did and it was most unnerving. Unwilling to acknowledge this second intrusion into her bed, she feigned sleep until he apparently grew bored with watching her and got up.

She heard him cross the room and open the window. Certain he would again be without clothes she kept her eyes closed. He would have been a handsome sight to behold, but she had enough trouble resisting his looks when he was fully clothed. Her imagination supplied the only distracting image she cared to see of him for the moment. When he opened the wardrobe and sifted through the few things she had placed in it, she thought perhaps he meant to offer another suggestion for her attire. He had not remarked on her choice of the apricot gown for dinner, but she had to assume that he had been pleased to have her wear it.

She waited until he had gone into his room to sit up, but she did not relax until she saw that he had closed their connecting door. Relieved, she lay back down, but she was no longer sleepy. She was amazed that she had slept the whole night without waking when she had been so troubled upon retiring. Thinking Luis must have taken great care to remain on his side of the bed, she hoped that he would continue to be as thoughtful. Then she recalled the reference he had made to consequences and began to wonder.

Unsure of his meaning, she rose and removed her dressing gown from the wardrobe. She noted the absence of her blue suit and assumed Luis had taken it. She supposed it must have been badly wrinkled and was embarrassed that he had taken the initiative to do something about it before she had. She was so preoccupied with his puzzling comment, however, the state of her clothing was of slight consequence.

She was tempted to go ask Luis for a clarification, but because she did not want him in her room, she dared not enter his. Hoping that he would again bring her some breakfast, she picked up her brush and began to brush out her hair. She considered it fortunate that she was used to styling her hair herself or she would have sorely missed Yvette by now. She supposed Luis must have a full staff at his home, but doubted he would employ a lady's maid. She was going to have to make a greater effort to master Spanish if she wished to run his household without confusion.

Luis knocked lightly before again carrying in a breakfast tray. "I hope I didn't wake you when I got up."

Pretending complete ignorance of what had transpired during the night, Michelle glanced toward the unmade bed. "Why, no, I had no idea that you'd shared it again."

"Really? Perhaps I should strive to be a more amusing bedmate."

"You needn't bother." The rolls he had brought that morning were dripping with honey and looked absolutely delicious. The aroma of the hot chocolate also made her mouth water, but Michelle had a couple of questions she wished answered before she sampled the morning meal.

"What did you mean yesterday when you talked of consequences we might both regret if I tried your patience before I decided to accept your affection? Were you threatening to harm me, or to turn to other women?"

"Neither," Luis responded. He had placed the tray on a small table, and now that he had both hands free, he placed them on Michelle's shoulders to prevent her from bolting as he ended her confusion. "I meant that I might not be able to control my passions where you're concerned and then the choice of time and place would be mine rather than yours. I take my wedding vows seriously, Michelle. I would no more take a mistress than you would a lover. Now is there anything else I can clarify for you?"

He was in his shirtsleeves, and his casual dress reminded her all too vividly of the time she had believed him to be a Gypsy. Despite the seriousness of his words, she thought he was teasing her again and she did not like that at all. "Yes, please," she replied. "Where's my blue suit? Did you give it to a maid to press?"

Luis released her then, stepped back, and, striking a relaxed pose, clasped his hands behind his back. "Yes, I did indeed give the blue suit to a maid. I gave her the bonnet, too, and told her to keep them both. It has to be considered very poor etiquette for a married woman to mourn the death of a former fiancé. As you mentioned, that suit was your only passable mourning attire. Find something else to wear today."

Michelle had already had ample evidence of how arrogantly he disregarded her welfare in favor of his own, but this was too much. "How dare you!" she shrieked, but she was more appalled by the fact that since waking she had not had a single thought of Antoine until Luis had just mentioned him. That lapse of memory disturbed her just as greatly as his willful discarding of her clothes.

"You had no right to give my things away. Absolutely none," she continued, her disgust with herself compounding her anger with him tenfold.

"I obviously disagreed," Luis replied with a calm he considered more than admirable when she was again behaving like a shrew. Actually he was quite pleased that she was showing her former fiery nature rather than weeping. "You'll find me an extremely generous husband, *querida*, and I'll be happy to replace that suit a dozen times over with garments in whatever bright, colorful shades you'd enjoy wearing. Because you had no opportunity to shop for a trousseau before our wedding, I'll provide for your every need. My mother and sisters always had extensive wardrobes, so I'm well aware that a beautiful woman can never have too many flattering gowns."

It was not the size of her wardrobe that concerned Michelle but his wanton intrusion in her life. "You are not to touch my things ever again!"

Luis could not help thinking she was absolutely adorable when she lost her temper and started screaming at him. Color flooded her cheeks and her eyes flashed with sparks of bright blue. What he really wanted to do was take her back to bed and replace the anger in her gaze with passion, but knowing that was not the tender introduction to lovemaking she deserved, he walked over to her trunk and began pulling out her lingerie instead.

"Are you forbidding me to merely touch your garments like this? Or is it giving them away that you'll not allow?"

He took a handful of silk stockings and tossed them into the air. Several pairs of gloves followed, but his next grab for items to throw contained Aurora's charm in the neatly tied handkerchief. Weighted by the pearl earrings, it fell to the floor with a dull thud. Ignoring the other things he was strewing right and left, Michelle scurried to retrieve the token-filled handkerchief

220

before Luis could discover what it was. She then grasped it tightly behind her and began to back away.

Intrigued, Luis stopped pulling the lacy feminine apparel out of her trunk. "What do you have?" he asked. His smile grew sly as he extended his hand. "Show me."

"It's nothing of any interest to you."

"Oh but you're wrong. Anything you'd hurry to hide is of interest to me. Now let me see what it is."

"No." Michelle backed away. She was near the open window and for an instant considered tossing the handkerchief through it, but she knew Luis would just run downstairs, circle the inn, and search through the bushes until he found it. She dared not take the risk of that happening. "I'm sure you must have things you'd like to keep private from me. I'll never demand to see them."

Luis raised his hands in a broad gesture of innocence. "A man shouldn't keep secrets from his wife, and I have no intention of doing so. Nor should a woman keep secrets from her husband. Now let me see what you have."

"No."

Luis needed to look no farther than the stubborn set of her jaw to know she would never willing give in to him on anything. That would definitely make for a very exciting marriage, but he wanted an unshakable trust to exist between them as well. Sadly, he knew that Michelle did not trust him. Why would she after he had posed as a Gypsy, and, in her distorted view of what had happened, deliberately shot and killed Antoine? Winning her trust was going to be a true challenge, but he considered a woman of her spirit worth such a tremendous effort. He just hoped it would not take his entire lifetime to accomplish.

"As you wish," he conceded politely. "Keep whatever trinkets Antoine gave you since that's undoubtedly what you're hiding, but as I mentioned before, the sooner you forget him and start behaving like my wife, the better off we'll both be."

Michelle did not draw a breath until Luis had closed the door between their rooms on his way out. She then eased herself into the chair at the table and poured herself a cup of hot chocolate. Their argument had taken such little time, it was still steaming, but she felt as drained as though they had fought all day. She was very proud of herself for standing up to Luis but hated the fact that she had again had to do so.

Luis expected Michelle to request some time to stop at a church that morning, but she walked straight to the carriage and climbed in without even acknowledging his presence, let alone mentioning taking the time to say a prayer. Julio and Tomás tried to hide their laughter but failed, and Luis chastised them both in such forceful terms they did not dare even smile for the remainder of the morning.

Annoyed that his generosity was being repaid so rudely, Luis toyed briefly with the idea of actually driving the team himself that day. The strength needed to maintain control of the four high-spirited horses would have kept him occupied physically, if not mentally, and that was an appealing prospect. Michelle had just made it embarrassingly plain that she would prefer to do without his company, and that was a deciding factor. He'd be damned if he would allow the blackness of her moods to influence his decisions. Determined to spend another entire day with his feisty bride, he got into the carriage and signaled for Julio to get under way.

Preferring to confront rather than avoid their problems, Luis chose the seat opposite Michelle's that day. He had never enjoyed riding facing backward, but when his traveling companion was as bewitching a young woman as Michelle it was a small sacrifice. She was dressed in a mauve gown, and while it was perhaps a melancholy shade, it was a great improvement over the dreary navy-blue suit. The sweet, pink-toned lavender enhanced her fair skin, making it glow with a

222

delicate blush that was so lovely he found it difficult to take his eyes off her.

He waited with diminishing patience for her to be the first to speak, but when after an hour she had paid more attention to the scenery than to him, he finally realized that she might never feel the need to speak with him ever again. "Do you like to ride?" he asked.

Michelle glanced toward him only briefly and then looked away. "I enjoy it very much with an agreeable mount and an equally agreeable companion."

"May I assume that you would regard a well-trained horse who responded readily to gentle commands as an agreeable mount?"

"Yes, you may."

"Good. Now tell me what makes for an agreeable companion in your view?" Luis knew it was dangerous to push her for an opinion because she could easily criticize him again, but he considered that risk preferable to her prolonged, obstinate silence.

Michelle drew in a deep breath and let it out slowly as she considered his question. She doubted that anything she said would make much of an impression on him when nothing had in the past. "We are talking about a riding companion and nothing more?" she asked first.

"Yes. Pretend that you have a few hours, an obedient mount, and lovely countryside to explore. What sort of person would you like to take with you?"

Still not convinced this was merely a hypothetical question, Michelle nevertheless described precisely the respect she had always wanted but had never received from Antoine. "I'd like someone who gave my feelings, my hopes, my desires, as much weight as his own. Someone who would listen and really hear what I have to say. Someone who would not dismiss my comments as ridiculous or unimportant merely because I'm a woman and he's a man."

Her voice had been soft rather than strident, her expression one of relaxed interest rather than fury, but

223

Luis was still stung by what she had said. She had told him plainly and repeatedly to leave her alone. Rather than respect her wishes, he had paid no attention to her objections to his serenade, or impromptu visits, or, even now that they were married, to her request for time to adjust to being his wife.

Clearly his behavior was inexcusable in her view and he was now sorry that he had given away her navy-blue suit and bonnet. He was embarrassed by what a bully that action had shown him to be. It was a continuation of a regrettable pattern he had not recognized until she had just pointed it out. He knew he was handsome and rich, and had assumed from long experience that that was all a woman would ever expect from him. Now he knew that was not going to be nearly enough for Michelle, but could he change the habits of a lifetime, he wondered, or should he?

Rather than repeat his mistake of the previous evening and say too much, Luis made his response brief. "You're describing the courtesy and consideration a gentleman quite naturally owes a lady. I'm sorry if I've failed in that regard. I promise to do better in the future."

Michelle was absolutely flabbergasted by the obvious sincerity of her husband's apology. Coming from a man as proud as he, she knew it was an enormous concession. She was so touched, tears came to her eyes. She was tempted to confess that what she had refused to show him that morning was the love charm Aurora had instructed her to make. Then she grew fearful any mention of the Gypsy might remind both of them of things better left unsaid, and did not.

"Thank you," she replied simply, and resumed her study of the roadside through a shimmering veil of tears.

When he awakened that day, Antoine had not forgotten his plan to get revenge. On the contrary, he was more insistent than ever that Francisco pursue his quest to locate some unscrupulous person to carry it out. "Go to your club," he encouraged between sips of broth. "Mention Aragon and listen to the gossip. I'd go with you myself, but I can't even sit up let alone stand. You must do this for me."

Francisco opened his mouth to argue, then realized that he could go to his club, play faro, never mention Augustín Aragon, and then return home and report to Antoine that the Spaniard he despised had no enemies. He gave his cousin another spoonful of broth and, with a pretended reluctance, hesitantly agreed to visit his club that very night.

"I'll do my best," he promised, but he was still too frightened by what Antoine wished to do to fully consider becoming a part of it.

Ramón Guerrero was shocked when Francisco Castillo entered the club that night. He was still badly shaken by the duel and had come there hoping to distract himself, but he found it difficult to believe that Francisco, who had lost a cousin, would feel up to playing cards so soon after such a terrible loss. He had not heard even a faint reference to the duel in the three days since it had occurred and had to admire the discretion Francisco had shown.

Ramón hastened to speak with him before he sat down at one of the gaming tables. "I want to offer my sincerest sympathies," he whispered softly so as not to attract the attention of the club's other members. "Although you and I have never been friends, I hope that Antoine's death won't make it impossible for us both to remain members here."

Francisco knew Antoine had certainly appeared to be dying when Ramón had last seen him, but he was nevertheless shocked to learn Ramón had simply assumed he *had* died rather than coming to his house to inquire about him. He was about to correct the man's misconception when he suddenly realized it was to his cousin's advantage to have Augustín Aragon believe

225

him dead. After all, dead men did not hire assassins to stalk their enemies.

Rather than tell an outright lie, Francisco pretended to be overcome with grief and responded only to Ramón's last comment. "Let's continue to be strangers and never speak again, here or anywhere else."

While that was not the gracious response for which Ramón had hoped, he nodded and turned away, content to let that brief conversation be their last. He had lost interest in cards, though, and returned home rather than seek to be amused in simple pastimes in such sad times.

Francisco, however, was filled with unexpected exhilaration. That Antoine was considered dead put a whole new perspective on his actions that night. He sat down at a faro table with renewed enthusiasm for his favorite game. To anyone who inquired about his French cousin, he replied that Antoine, as planned, had returned to Lyon after the royal wedding. Then, as the game progressed, he bemoaned the money he had lost when last at the club. He had only to mention the name of Augustín Aragon in passing to elicit a wealth of information.

Then, with a cleverness Francisco knew Antoine would admire, he gently nudged the conversation toward men who might hold grudges against such a powerful man. One of the players familiar with the shipping trade mentioned Boris Ryde's name almost immediately. Pretending only mild interest, Francisco soon learned that after being dismissed from the Aragon Line for cruelty and incompetence, Ryde had somehow managed to purchase his own ship and made Valencia his home port.

"I've never met Captain Ryde," the fellow explained, "but from what I've heard he's a despicable sort who's probably turned smuggler. Any other enemies Aragon might have could not possibly compare to that bastard."

The conversation then drifted into a discussion of

226

smuggling that held little interest to Francisco, but he continued to play faro until the others at the table grew weary and ended the game. He then rose and stretched lazily. Surprisingly, despite being distracted by thoughts of the grim deed he and Antoine were plotting, he had won more than he usually did. He was actually quite pleased with himself until he returned home and was greeted by his wife.

"How could you have left Antoine alone the whole evening?" Maria Lourdes scolded. "I did my best to keep him company, but I know he would have much preferred to have spent his time with you. It isn't like you to be so thoughtless, Francisco. Now go in and sit with him a while. He's been waiting up for you."

Francisco only laughed at his wife's complaint. "It was Antoine himself who sent me off to my club. I didn't want to go, but he feared he was a burden to us and that I was growing bored with him. He was wrong, of course, but it was easier to go to the club than tire him by arguing about it. Now here. Take my winnings and buy yourself something extravagant."

Appeased by her husband's gift, Lourdes ceased to complain. She kissed him good night and went on to bed thinking herself very lucky to have such a thoughtful and generous husband.

When Francisco first entered Antoine's room, he thought his cousin was asleep, but as he approached the bed, the Frenchman turned toward him and smiled. He was relieved to find him awake. He first explained Ramón Guerrero's remarks and assured him Augustín Aragon must also believe him to be dead.

"Things could not have worked more to your advantage had you planned them," he assured Antoine. "I think I have the name of a man who will avenge the wrong done you. I don't dare meet with him myself, but I have contacts in Valencia whom I can trust to deliver a confidential letter. We'll have to offer a reward of some kind. How much can you afford?"

227

"Not all that much," Antoine admitted, "but I can send it as a first payment and promise five times as much when Aragon is dead."

"Will you be able to provide the larger sum?"

Antoine almost laughed, but the resulting pain sobered his mood instantly. "No, but the killer won't know that, will he? Now, sit down and tell me what you learned."

Francisco did precisely that, and after Antoine had heard that Captain Ryde was a man of apparently no virtue, he told his cousin to fetch pen and paper so that they could compose a letter to him that very night and dispatch it the next morning. For the first time since he had been shot, Antoine felt certain that he would be the eventual winner of the duel.

"I don't want Michelle left a wealthy widow," he confided suddenly.

"Don't be too hasty," Francisco advised. "You would naturally be the one to console her, and as her second husband, would inherit whatever she received of her late husband's estate."

"I don't want the faithless harlot now that she's been with Aragon, nor do I want his money," Antoine explained in the harsh whisper which was all the voice he could muster to communicate the rage he felt each time he thought of Michelle. "Add to the letter that I'll pay double what I've offered for Aragon if he kills them both."

Shaken that Antoine would want such a lovely creature as Michelle Minoux dead, Francisco hesitated to put the request in writing. "I fear killing her, too, will tie you to the crime and you don't want to incriminate yourself."

That was certainly true, but after a moment's thought Antoine had the perfect suggestion. "Tell him to make it appear to be an accident rather than murder. I can't hold the pen to sign the letter, so you must do that for me, too. Use only Antoine. That, along with the first payment, will be enough to convince

Captain Ryde that I am a real person, but it will not be enough for him to identify me. Tell him I have my own sources of information, and will forward his final payment upon learning of the deaths of Aragon and his bride."

Due to the gruesome nature of his task, Francisco was so nervous that he had to make several drafts of the letter. When he finally succeeded in creating a legible copy, he burned his previous attempts and read the message to Antoine. "Well, what do you think?" he then asked anxiously. "Is it what you wanted said?"

"Perfect," Antoine assured him. "In the morning, send it along with the money I'll give you to your friends in Valencia. After they have passed it along to Captain Ryde, it will be up to him to do the rest."

"Do you think we can trust him?"

"No, but the prospect of earning a reward for killing a man he must despise should be enough to inspire him to carry out the deed. After all, we're appealing to both his greed and his desire for revenge. How can he possibly refuse such a tempting offer?"

Francisco nodded. It was not his idea of temptation, and although it pained his conscience, he was willing to put his cousin's plan in motion and leave it up to Captain Ryde to carry out.

Neither Michelle nor Luis felt much like talking after their initial discussion that morning. They had again shared a picnic lunch, but her polite replies to his questions on what she would care to eat had not led to further conversation. She stayed awake all afternoon, but again she and Luis exchanged little more than casual comments on the terrain.

While it had at first seemed unlikely, after Luis had remained subdued all day, Michelle could not help but feel that he had been hurt by her request for respect. That left her feeling equally anguished and confused. She had not made unreasonable demands nor vile threats. She had merely voiced the heartfelt desire to be considered an equal. Perhaps it was impossible for him to understand why she would wish to be treated as a grown woman rather than endlessly pampered like a pretty child.

As Luis had announced, that day they had traveled an extended distance and did not stop for the evening until after dark. In a downcast mood, Michelle had bathed and dressed for dinner expecting the same morose partner who had shared her day, but Luis surprised her by making every effort to be charming.

"The English are attempting to create a new breed of horse by crossing Arabian stallions and English mares. The result is a handsome horse with great speed. I'm using four as a team to test their endurance, and they seem to be holding up. In my opinion a horse which can't be ridden long distances or used in harness isn't of much value regardless of how beautiful it might be. What do you think?"

Michelle studied Luis's expression carefully before answering. When she decided he was completely serious in seeking her opinion, she endeavored to give him an equally serious reply. "I think you're right. A horse ought to be of some practical use. They're too big to be pets."

Pleased with her response, Luis flashed a wide grin. "I'm glad you agree. I'm hoping to send a few Arabians to California soon. I told you Esteban is a fine horseman and he can get the best from any breed."

"My father also had a gift with horses," Michelle revealed rather shyly. "He used to talk to them, and I swear they understood."

"His horses spoke French?" Luis teased.

"No, of course not. They couldn't speak any language other than that common to the horse, but they understood his French."

"Thank you, that's ever so much more clear."

Michelle tried not to smile, but couldn't help herself. Luis had always been able to enchant her with his smiles, but she had not expected to feel relaxed enough to respond after the ordeal they had been through. She ate very slowly to make the time they spent at dinner last as long as possible. She was not attempting to delay the hour they went to bed, although that was a consideration, as much as she was extending the pleasant nature of the meal.

Luis had not really expected Michelle to be such an enjoyable companion that night, but he was delighted and in no hurry to rush through their meal, either. He consumed every scrap he had been served and sipped his wine to prolong the evening as long as he could. Each time Michelle glanced toward him he smiled, which was no trouble at all to do.

"I'm sorry there are no gardens here," he said when they no longer had any excuse to remain at their table. "But it's been a tiring day, and perhaps we ought to go upstairs to bed."

Embarrassed by his suggestion since it implied far more than she cared to consider, Michelle was sorry they couldn't go for a stroll first. Luis had been so thoughtful that evening that she could not help but wonder what the night might bring. He did not look like a man who was at the end of his patience with his bride's reluctance to consummate their marriage, but she thought he might attempt to rely on his abundant charm to overcome her objections and that brought back feelings of helplessness she didn't want to explore.

He helped her from her chair and escorted her to their rooms. They again had a suite, but that did not make her feel secure. She hesitated at the door, not knowing whether she should wish him a good night or expect him to again join her in bed later. Fearing he might mistakenly believe she was eager for his company, she did not want to ask him what he planned to do, either.

Luis read both the confusion and fear in Michelle's expression and felt very badly that he was responsible

231

for them both. The passion of their first kisses had made him confident that he could please her, but when she was still so obviously frightened of him, he knew better than to try.

"I want to check on the team again," he told her, but he leaned down to brush her cheek with a light kiss before he turned away.

Gripping the door, Michelle watched him walk toward the stairs. It wasn't until he had disappeared from sight that she realized that she had not told him good night. She shut the door and, uncertain whether or when he might return, hurried to prepare for bed. She felt better that evening than she had since Antoine had died, but she knew she wasn't up to a passionate encounter with the man who had killed him.

"God, what a horrible situation," she moaned, and then thought it was fortunate that her father had not lived to see her married to Luis. The two men might have shared a common interest in horses, but her father had been such a gentle soul that surely the difference in their morals and values would have placed them at odds on everything else.

She had just climbed into bed when she heard Luis return to his room. She knew then the day had not been nearly tiring enough for her to fall asleep with him in her bed. Dreading another sleepless night when his warmth would cruelly tease her senses, she stretched out and prayed that he would stay away. When he began to strum the first chords of one of the love songs he had played beneath her balcony in Madrid, she was grateful that he had not been bold enough to stand beneath her window that night where he would have undoubtedly drawn encouragement from the inn's other guests.

He did not sing for her this time, but it was a lovely serenade all the same. He had a large repertoire and one song flowed effortlessly into the next without a noticeable pause. He played each tune beautifully, and chose such haunting melodies that before Michelle was aware of what was happening, the music had lulled her to sleep.

Luis played for more than an hour before he got up and went to the door that separated their rooms. Michelle had left it unlocked, which he considered a good sign, but when he found her sleeping soundly, he decided it was probably due to an oversight on her part rather than as an intentional invitation for him to join her. He touched her tousled curls with a fond caress, and then returned to his room to sleep alone. He had never missed a woman's company until that night, but now he ached to have his lovely bride by his side and there was no one to serenade him to sleep.

Fourteen

It took another two days for Luis and Michelle to reach Valencia. Luis continued to be quietly attentive during the days and at night slept in a separate room. Michelle appreciated the privacy he accorded her, and yet she could sense his disappointment in her in his every gesture and expression. That he would state he wished to be understanding and yet unwittingly show himself to be as deeply troubled as she left her constantly feeling confused and disheartened.

As soon as they had checked into an inn with a magnificent view of the Mediterranean Sea, Luis brought her to a window and pointed out where his ship was moored in the harbor. "That's the *California* with the bright red pennants flying from the tops of all three masts. Can you see her?"

"Yes." Impressed, Michelle was anxious to go on board. "Are we sailing for Barcelona in the morning?"

Luis was in no particular hurry to return home where he would have to introduce Michelle to all his friends and add another layer of pretense to the one at which they were both rapidly becoming adept. "No, most of the crew is on leave for another couple of days. I was uncertain just when I'd return from Madrid and there's no reason to rush home anyway.

Valencia is such a pretty place, you'll find plenty of things to keep you amused."

Puzzled by that remark, Michelle nevertheless kept her attention focused on the triangular Aragon flags rather than meet her husband's gaze. "What will you be doing?"

Not daring to hope that she would miss him, Luis shrugged slightly. "I've neglected my business affairs since going up to Madrid for the wedding. It's time I ended my vacation and got back to work. A great deal of produce is shipped from Valencia and I want to make certain ships flying the Aragon flag are carrying most of it."

"Do you take lengthy voyages?"

"No, I seldom leave Barcelona. The *California* is the flagship of our line and is constantly in use, but she is under the command of other captains."

Luis was beginning to wonder if he ought not to seriously consider returning to sea. If things did not improve between them soon, he knew commanding the *California* on a regular basis might be a far more tempting prospect than remaining in Barcelona with a wife who shared nothing but her unhappiness. His only consolation was that they had been married less than a week and he still had hopes that they might not only remain together, but be happy with each other.

"We can plan a trip to Lyon if you like," he offered with what he realized was an inconsiderate delay for such an obvious suggestion. "I'm looking forward to meeting your mother and sisters."

Rather than respond with the delight Luis had anticipated, Michelle shuddered and gave her head an emphatic shake. "No, that wouldn't be at all wise. Antoine was very well liked. He'll be widely mourned. You'd receive the very worst of receptions and I can't even bear to imagine the insulting names I'd be called. No, I'll never be able to go home again. Thank you for making such an offer, but it's impossible to accept."

Luis was shocked by the vehemence of her tone. "Are Antoine's parents living? Does he have brothers who might feel they have to avenge his death?"

"Antoine's parents were much older than mine. His father died a dozen years ago and his mother is quite frail. She'll probably not survive long after learning her only child is dead. He had some cousins in addition to Francisco Castillo, but none who will pose any threat to you. That doesn't mean that we'd not be shunned by everyone and I'd rather avoid being the object of the scorn we'd undoubtedly receive. The wisest course will be to avoid Lyon forever."

Luis could readily understand why she might not wish to return home until her memories of Antoine had begun to fade, but he was outraged by the shame she had just revealed. "Are you certain that you wouldn't just rather avoid *me?*"

His dark eyes had narrowed to menacing slits and Michelle regretted confiding her feelings so openly. It had been a serious mistake. She had not realized how tactless her comments must have sounded to him. "I meant to spare you the pain a visit to Lyon would surely be, not insult you," she assured him. "Please, you mustn't think that I, well, that I—"

"What? That you're not inordinately proud to be my wife? You've just made it plain that you'd prefer any title to that of Señora Aragon," Luis taunted. "You needn't worry. If you're ashamed to introduce me to your relatives, I won't insist that you undertake such a loathsome ordeal."

Michelle raised her hand to her temple. Her head had begun to throb with the painful rhythm she recognized all too well and she feared she would soon be ill. "Please, Luis, don't do this."

"Do what? Speak the truth for a change?"

The only truth Michelle knew was that Antoine was dead and they were alive. "I don't feel well," she announced softly. "I'd like to rest and I doubt that I'll want any dinner."

"Believe me, madam, I feel just as sick as you and I'll be happy to spend the evening in my own company."

Michelle turned away rather than watch him walk out on her, but she had had ample opportunity to observe how his stride lengthened when he was angry and knew by the echo of his footsteps that he was furious indeed. Her parents had had such a happy marriage and she couldn't believe she and Luis were doomed to a lifetime of bitter arguments.

Her family's estate was on the Rhône River. Homesick, she was soothed by the sight of the sea. She drew a chair close to the window and watched the tranquil scene in the harbor until it grew too dark to see, but her heart was still filled with anguish rather than peace.

Traveling on horseback, Francisco's messenger rode into Valencia the evening of that same day. He delivered the package he had been given and then sought out the nearest tavern to quench his thirst and ease his weariness. He had not known what he had carried nor did he care since he had been well paid, but he had made the fastest time possible and planned a far more relaxing return trip to Madrid.

The man to whom the package was addressed removed the letter tied to the top and read it through twice. He had no idea who Captain Boris Ryde might be, but he owed Francisco Castillo a favor. Not realizing he was taking part in a deadly conspiracy, he summoned one of his young footmen and instructed him to carry the package to the port and find Captain Ryde.

237

"Shall I wait for a reply, sir?"

"No. It's from a friend, undoubtedly concerning business. Just place it in the captain's hands and come home." The man handed over the neatly wrapped package and promptly forgot it.

The second messenger knew his way around the port and although his inquiries as to the whereabouts of Captain Ryde's ship brought disgusted sneers, once named, he found the *Salamander* easily enough. It was an ancient schooner that looked none too seaworthy, but he was a conscientious sort, gathered his courage, and climbed the gangplank to ask for Captain Ryde.

"Who wants him?" came a booming voice from the shadowed deck.

"I've a parcel for him, sir," the messenger announced.

"A parcel, is it now?" A heavyset man with an upwardly curving white mustache stepped forward to receive it. "I'm Captain Ryde," he announced in a voice that rang with an authority that carried far out over the water.

A suspicious sort, he first studied the messenger and finding him neatly groomed and expensively dressed decided the parcel was worth investigating and took it. "Who sent this?" he asked.

"I don't know, Captain. I was just told to deliver it."

Ryde gave the package a vigorous shake, and, intrigued by its weight, he did not bother to offer the young man a tip for his trouble before going below to his cabin to open it.

Not impressed by Captain Ryde's rude dismissal and thinking the whole errand odd, the footman returned home. Enamored of the newest scullery maid, he also promptly forgot it.

Boris placed the package on the table and drew his knife to cut the string. Pulled very tight, there

238

was a popping sound as each strand was severed. He removed the wrapping paper, crushed it into a tight little ball, and, not caring where it landed, tossed it over his shoulder. Now faced with a curious wooden box, he backed away and used the tip of his knife blade to flip open the lid. A letter lay on top, but knowing there had to be something underneath, he levered it aside to reveal three small bags.

Hoping they were filled with gold coins, he grabbed for the first and dumped its contents on the table. When what spilled out was the gold for which he had just wished, he poured out the second and third. Astonished to have come into such unexpected wealth, he collapsed into a chair and hurriedly read the letter. Long fluent in Spanish, he followed Francisco's flowery script easily, but understanding the words and accepting the proposition they presented were two entirely different things.

He got up and poured himself a whiskey, but he was shaking so badly that he spilled as much as splashed into his glass. How many nights had he lain awake plotting Augustín Aragon's murder? he asked himself between sloppy sips. It had to have been thousands, and now to be offered money, and a princely sum it was, too, for carrying out the best of his fantasies unnerved him completely.

While it was no secret that he and Augustín despised each other, to have a stranger, and a French one at that, suggest he end the bastard's life made him shiver. He felt as though Antoine, whoever he was, had read his mind, looked into his ugliest thoughts, and then offered the gold he needed so desperately.

Returning to the table, he examined the stationery for an identifying crest, but it bore none. The coin bags were unmarked muslin, and the box of simple construction. He recalled the well-dressed messenger and, after locking his cabin door, raced up on deck

to look for him. He had not really expected to find
him lounging against the rail, but he was infuriated
with himself for not making him wait until he had
viewed the contents of the box.

"Did you see where the lad went?" he called to his
mate.

"What lad is that, Captain?"

Disgusted that his mate was so unobservant, Ryde
waved him off and returned to his cabin. He fondled
each of the gold coins with a more loving touch than
he had ever shown a woman. They were undeniably
real and, while he would have preferred to feast his
eyes on them all night, he returned them to their
bags, placed the bags inside the box, and then
searched his cabin for a good place to store it. His
mate knew where he hid what little money he had.

They had been in port two weeks and he had
spent the whole time attempting to arrange for a
cargo to transport, but so many lies had been told
about him that no honest merchant would hire him.
He knew exactly who had spread those lies, too:
Augustín Aragon. Boris doubted that he had been
any more strict than many of the other captains who
had once worked for the Aragon Line. A captain
had to have discipline or he was no captain at all in
Boris Ryde's view. Augustín had taken exception to
his methods, and not content to fire him, had blackened his name with hideous lies. While it was true
that more than one man had lost his life while serving with him, Boris knew each and every one had
brought that tragedy on himself.

As he prowled through the cupboards and drawers
built into his teak-paneled cabin seeking a place to
conceal his unexpected treasure, Boris continued to
mumble his grievances against Augustín. He had
mouthed them so often they rang with the monoto-
nous rhythm of a litany, but every other word was
obscene. "Kill Augustín," he chanted. He could kill

240

him a thousand times over and it would still not make up for what the arrogant Spaniard had done to him.

He had enjoyed considerable respect and prestige with the Aragon Line. He'd had a fine ship and industrious crews, but when Augustín had finished with him, he had lost everything but his captain's papers. He had soon learned how little *they* were worth. When no one would hire him, he had been forced to use the money he had saved for his retirement to purchase the *Salamander*. The profit from the few cargos he had then been able to get barely kept him out of debt.

With the gold he had just been given, he could make the much-needed repairs to his ship, outfit her with new sails, and paint her up to look as fine as she once had. He could have a new uniform tailored and buy meals that he would not be ashamed to eat. Merchants would think the sudden improvement in his lot due to hard work, forget the rumors about him, and be eager to provide him with profitable cargos. In time he would not only be able to replenish his savings so that he could retire in England one day, he might even save enough to purchase a larger ship. With the increased revenue it would generate, he could retire a wealthy man rather than a poor one.

When he finally came upon an overlooked cranny that suited him, he slipped the gold-filled box inside. He then poured himself another drink and sat down to again study the letter from the mysterious Antoine. He did not really care who the Frenchman might be. Antoine had shown himself to be a kindred soul: he also despised Augustín Aragon, and that fact alone made Boris want to be his friend.

He was pleased to learn Augustín had married, and hoped he might earn the double bounty Antoine offered for killing his wife as well. It would be a

241

challenge to arrange such a dreadful accident that both Augustín and his undoubtedly lovely bride would both perish, but he felt equal to the task. Yes, years in which he had endured enforced idleness while awaiting cargos had provided him with a great many opportunities to plot Augustín's death, and it would be a joy to finally implement them. He threw back his head and laughed as he had not laughed in years, but the evening had taken such a bright turn he simply could not contain his mirth.

By the time Luis had walked down to the docks, his temper had cooled sufficiently for him to be thoroughly ashamed of the way he had lashed out at Michelle. He might be positive that they were a far better match than she and Antoine could ever have been, but she was still reeling from the loss of her childhood sweetheart and unable to see past her sorrow. Disgusted with himself for promising to be more thoughtful and kind and then failing miserably in that regard, he considered returning to the inn and apologizing. He turned back, in fact, but had taken only a few steps before deciding Michelle would already be asleep and he did not want to disturb her rest.

Badly discouraged, he wished he could ask his father's advice. He could recall his parents having arguments, and heated ones at that, but they had usually ended with the outspoken pair collapsed in each other's arms laughing over which of them was the greater fool. He had expected to combine the very same mixture of passion and laughter in his marriage. Perhaps that was the problem. He had just assumed the happiness he had seen his parents enjoy to be his right, but for all he knew, they had struggled for years to achieve harmony when he had been too young to observe or analyze their actions.

Anxious to communicate with his family, even though it would take months to receive a reply to a letter, Luis boarded the *California* intending to write to them that very night. After a personal word of encouragement for each of the men on board, he attended to a more pressing need first and took his first mate, Encario Vega, below to his cabin.

"Sit down," he ordered.

Fearing from the seriousness of Luis's tone that he had found something amiss, Encario began to defend himself. "There's not so much as a speck of dust anywhere and —"

Luis pointed to one of the chairs at his table and waited until Encario had dropped into it. "I'm not criticizing the way you've run the ship in my absence," he assured him. "I just don't want you to faint from the shock when you learn that I've taken a wife."

"You've done *what?*" Every bit as astonished as Luis had expected, Encario gaped like a witless fool. A muscular young man with sandy hair and green eyes, he had been with the Aragon Line for ten years and was Luis's close friend as well as first mate.

Luis waited a moment for Encario to digest his announcement before he continued. "I'd like to say that I was so inspired by the royal wedding that I couldn't resist the temptation to wed. Unfortunately, nothing could be further from the truth."

Over the next half-hour, Luis provided Encario with all the detail that he cared to admit. He explained that he had won Michelle in a duel, but little else. "I don't want to take her home to Barcelona just yet. She's a rare beauty, but quite naturally, her mood is subdued rather than joyous, and I'd not want anyone to draw the wrong impression of her. I want everyone to meet her when she's at her best."

Encario knew Luis to be a man of daring, but he was shocked to hear him calmly discuss his part in a fatal duel. "I don't know whether to offer my congratulations or condolences," he apologized. "Are you planning to take Michelle on an extended honeymoon cruise?"

Because it implied a celebration of the love he and Michelle might never have, the word *honeymoon* made Luis wince. "No. I realize recently married couples don't usually wish to be apart, but she's repeatedly asked for time to adjust to our marriage and I've come to the sad conclusion that the only way I'll be able to provide it is by leaving her for a week or two."

"If she's as lovely as you claim, that might be a serious error."

Luis knew he had made a great many grievous mistakes where Michelle was concerned, but he couldn't agree with Encario. "Things ended so badly with me that she'll not grow fond of another man while I'm away. I doubt that she would even deign to speak to one."

"When can I meet her?"

Luis shrugged. "You'll have to be patient." He asked Encario to suggest a voyage that might take no more than ten days to two weeks, but nothing the mate proposed appealed to him. Then he recalled the treasure map Sergio the Gypsy had given him. It had been in his coat pocket the entire trip, but he had had too much on his mind to give it any thought. He withdrew it now, and unfolded it on the table. He still doubted it led to anything but sand, but it would provide a much needed excuse to set sail.

"Perhaps this is the answer," he mused aloud.

Encario turned the map around, and after a moment's study, looked up at Luis. "Did you get this from your bride?"

"No. It came from a man I know in Madrid."

"I've seen a dozen such maps over the years. None was ever worth the trouble it took to follow."

"That's the beauty of this," Luis revealed with a sly grin. "I don't care whether it produces a single gold coin or exquisite jewel. I just want to leave Valencia. I'll tell Michelle the map is authentic and too valuable to ignore or allow to fall into another's hands. She'll be so grateful for the time alone, she'll never guess why I'm really leaving.

"Tell the crew we'll be sailing in search of treasure as soon as everyone is on board, but don't mention that I've wed. I don't want any comments about my marriage yet, not even good-natured ones."

Encario pursed his lips thoughtfully. "Your bride might not understand your reticence to admit she exists."

"I don't plan to keep her hidden forever, just for a couple of weeks. Believe me, she'd be unable to accept congratulations graciously, and I want to spare her that anguish."

"All right, I'll trust your judgment as always, but what about the men? They'll think we're actually looking for treasure and expect shares."

"Of course," Luis agreed. "There's always a chance the map might actually lead to riches. If it does, they will all share in it equally. Now please excuse me, I want to have a letter ready to send to my parents before we sail."

Encario left his chair immediately and went to the door, but he hesitated to leave just yet. "I hate to think of you wed to a woman you don't love."

"Did I say that I didn't love her?"

"No, but you didn't say that you did, either."

"As long as Michelle does not complain about that omission, I really don't believe it is any business of yours."

Struck by the truth of that opinion as well as by

the belligerent tone of Luis's voice, Encario kept his thoughts to himself. He returned to his duties on deck and announced Luis's intended plan, which the crew greeted with hearty enthusiasm. Not one of his men had ever been on a voyage to recover treasure, but they were all eager to try.

Luis refolded the map and slipped it back into his pocket to show Michelle later. He then took out his writing supplies, and began a letter to his parents. In many ways it was the most difficult letter he had ever written, and yet just being able to put his feelings into words provided a much-welcome release. It wasn't until he had filled an entire page describing Michelle's beauty that he realized just how smitten he truly was. He might not love her yet, but he knew it would take only slight encouragement on her part for him to make such a declaration, and mean it.

He spent the night on board the *California,* but the next morning he returned to the inn in time to again take Michelle her breakfast. He apologized as he carried the tray through the door. "I hope that you're feeling better. I never should have said what I did. Can you forgive me?"

Michelle had not really expected Luis to return before noon, if then. She looked up slowly, steeling herself for the confrontation she felt was certain to come. Even that precaution was insufficient to prepare her for the dazzling warmth of his smile. With too much to forget and nothing to which to look forward, she had slept poorly and failed to respond in kind.

The wistfulness of Michelle's expression broke Luis's heart and he couldn't bear to leave her alone again. "May I join you?" he asked. He had had the foresight to double her usual breakfast order in the hope that she might consent to having his company.

"If you wish."

While that was not the enthusiastic invitation Luis would have preferred, he sat down before she could change her mind and poured two cups of hot chocolate. "I've happened upon a curious map. It might prove to be a hoax, but I'd like to investigate it all the same. Spain brought a great deal of gold and treasure out of the New World but not all of it reached these shores. Ships were sunk in terrible storms. Pirates took their share and often buried it on uncharted islands. They always intended to retrieve it later, of course, but a pirate's life was an extremely hazardous one and not all lived to enjoy their ill-gotten booty.

"Often the lone survivor of a pirate's crew would draw a map. That's probably how the one I have came into existence. Would you like to see it?"

"Yes, please," Michelle replied, greatly intrigued.

Delighted by her interest, Luis handed her the map. "Take care with it. It's quite old and the parchment has grown brittle."

Michelle unfolded the Gypsy's treasure map with the reverence she would have shown a holy relic. She recognized the coast of Spain and with only a little effort made out the faded outline of Mallorca. "This is very close, isn't it?"

"Yes. I'll only be gone a week or so, and who knows? I may bring back some exquisite jewels for you."

Caught up in his tale of pirates and buried treasure, Michelle's hopes for adventure soared, but then died when he said that she was not to be included. She didn't like the idea of being left behind, not at all. She didn't know a soul in Valencia, and after her disastrous encounter with Aurora and Luis in Madrid, she dared not leave the inn on her on to explore the town. Her spirits plummeting, she refolded the map and handed it back to him.

"I hope that you have a pleasant voyage."

Looking at her woebegone expression, Luis doubted that she was sincere. "I'll not be leaving for a couple of days. Would you like to see something of Valencia after we've finished breakfast?"

Feeling more like an object of pity than she cared to admit, Michelle was nevertheless too restless to refuse whatever invitations he offered. "Yes, thank you, I would like that very much."

Luis recalled Encario's words and knew he ought not to escort his beautiful bride around town without first stopping by his ship. There was too great a chance he would meet someone he knew, and once Michelle had been presented as his bride to one person, the gossip would travel so fast, all of Valencia would soon learn that he was married. He had never intended to hide Michelle, however.

"Do you feel up to stopping by the *California* and meeting a few of my crew? If not, we can delay it until my return. Whatever you wish."

Michelle debated with herself only briefly. Being introduced as Señora Aragon was never going to be easy and she saw no reason to allow her dread to mount by delaying it. "No, I want very much to see your ship. I'm sure that it's as splendid a vessel as it looks from here."

"That, my dear, is an understatement. The *California* is magnificent."

As Luis beamed with pride, Michelle tried her best to smile. The day was warm, the sky clear, her companion utterly charming. Yet seeking happiness with him meant shutting the door to all that had gone before. It meant giving up the dreams of her childhood to embark on a voyage whose discoveries might only be further pain. Still, she managed to smile, even though her thoughts remained dark indeed.

* * *

When Luis brought Michelle on board the *California,* Encario nearly had to resort to threats of flogging to keep the crew from crowding too close. Awed himself, Encario thought Luis had done a very poor job of describing his bride. She was not merely a classic beauty with the blue eyes and blond hair men admired, she also possessed the elegance and grace of a princess. Despite the fact that she apparently spoke only French, none of the men dared make anything other than excruciatingly polite remarks within her hearing, and when Luis took her below to his cabin, an audible sigh of envy rippled clear across the deck.

While Michelle was as impressed by the *California* as Luis had hoped, she eyed the narrow bunk in his cabin and wondered where she would sleep when they sailed to Barcelona as it did not seem wide enough for two. Embarrassed by the prospect of again having to sleep in his arms, she quickly turned away and scanned the cleverly designed cupboards and drawers the cabin contained. The teak paneling was as beautifully carved as the wood in a cathedral and she could not help but think that the *California* was not only a swift ship but also a very expensive one.

"You're right, *magnificent* is precisely the word to describe your ship."

"I'm glad you agree." Luis seldom invited women on board, and now that he and Michelle were sharing the close confines of his cabin, he could not recall the name of a single one of his previous female visitors. All he saw was Michelle, but when he stepped close and pulled her into his arms, she stiffened in his embrace. Rather than hug and kiss such an unwilling woman, he pretended to have had no such intention. He trailed his fingertips down her arms and took her hand.

"There's lots more to see. The cathedral is not

nearly as impressive as those in France, but perhaps you'd like to visit it anyway."

"Yes, of course." Suddenly feeling trapped in his cabin, Michelle would have agreed to go anywhere. It was not at all easy to traverse the narrow passageways and climb ladders in her full skirts, but she was so eager to return to the deck, she scarcely noted the difficulties she encountered.

Luis, on the other hand, was greatly amused by her haste. There was absolutely no reason for Michelle to display the demure sweetness of a new bride, but she projected it so beautifully he was sorry that it wasn't real.

Rather than embark on an exhausting walk, they took his carriage and commenced a leisurely tour that lasted the whole day. Luis related every interesting bit of Spanish history he could remember. He took Michelle to Sagunto, which boasted a Roman theater large enough to seat eight thousand spectators and told her something of its history.

"In the third century, the people of Sagunto defended themselves so vigorously that rather than surrender to Hannibal during the Punic Wars, they resorted to eating their own dead. Then, with defeat imminent, they set the town ablaze and threw themselves into the flames. Quite a heroic end, don't you think?" Luis regretted having asked that question the instant it passed his lips, but Michelle did not draw the implication he had feared.

"Why no, I think that's ghastly, but I know Spaniards have a much darker nature than the French, so I can understand why you'd regard them as heroes rather than martyrs."

"What do you think of my nature since I am both Spanish and French?"

Luis was teasing her, but Michelle had never had her sister Denise's facility for flirting and had no ready response. "I really don't know you well enough to make an accurate judgment of your nature," she explained.

"You'll be sure and tell me when we've become better acquainted?"

"If you remind me."

"I'll make a point of it."

Luis helped her back into their carriage and recounted the tale of how El Cid had freed the city from the Moors in 1094. "Unfortunately, it was lost again after he was killed in battle seven years later."

"I've heard of him."

"That's good. I'll try and find you an interesting book on Spanish history to read while I'm away."

Despite Michelle's enduring shyness, Luis had had a far better time that day than he had anticipated. He and his bride dined together that night and shared a delicious paella, the saffron-flavored rice and seafood dish that is Valencia's specialty. When he bid her good night, it was with sincere regret that they would not be spending the entire night together.

The next day, Luis spent most of his time on board the *California*, but when he returned to their inn that night, he had remembered to bring a book of Spanish history for Michelle. "It was a challenge to find such a volume published in French," he admitted with a broad grin as he presented it to her. "I do hope that you find it informative."

"I'm sure that I will." Despite her earlier fears, after having been driven around the city the previous day, Michelle had gone out for a brief walk on her own. She had found some shops with goods which interested her, but had not made any purchases that day. After all, if she was to have a week or more with nothing to do, she would spread out her shopping over several days.

Luis waited until they had finished dinner and returned to their rooms before he revealed his plans. Even though he believed leaving her for a few days was his best option, he knew he would miss her terribly. "The last of my crew returned to the ship today, so we'll be sailing first thing in the morning. I'll stay here at the inn tonight, but I'll be gone before you're awake. Julio and Tomás will be here so you'll have the carriage whenever you wish. Ask for whatever you want and the staff here will provide it. I'll leave you some money, but you needn't spend it. Just tell the clerks in whatever shops you patronize to send the bills here to me. I'll settle them all before we leave for Barcelona. That way you won't have to worry about running out of money."

"I'm not extravagant," Michelle denied. "Truly I'm not."

"I didn't say that you were, *querida,* but believe me, even if you were, it wouldn't bother me. I can well afford to indulge an extravagant wife."

"Yes, I'm sure that you can."

Whenever she was so astonishingly agreeable Luis had a difficult time remembering the passionate nature of their initial meetings. He hoped that by the time he returned, she would again be the woman he had first admired. He kissed her cheek, and bid her good night, but once in his own room, he wasn't at all pleased with the way the evening had ended. He picked up his guitar and let music convey the longing he could not express in words, but he could not stop wishing that Michelle had wanted to at least return his kiss that night, if not much, much more.

Equally restless, Michelle placed her gown and petticoats in the wardrobe, donned her nightgown, and brushed out her hair with long, anxious strokes. She was having an increasingly difficult time reconciling Luis's current consideration with the string of lies he had told in Madrid. Now he was a model of respect and his frequent smiles looked so sincere. How could the man who had shot Antoine have such a disarming smile? she asked herself.

She had done her best to suppress her memories of the duel, but when Luis's sweet serenade failed to help her sleep, those forbidden images poured forth in vivid detail. Even stretched out on the bed with her arm flung across her eyes, her mind was filled with the mist-shrouded olive grove where Antoine had died. She had been watching Luis. The aggressiveness of his stance had alarmed her and she had screamed.

She could hear that scream echoing still, and for the first time, her attention swung to Antoine. She saw him turn toward her in response to her call. That's when he had been hit, in that precise instant, not before. She covered her mouth to choke off her cry, but it was now plain to her that Luis had been telling the truth. If only she had not called out to Antoine, he would not have turned and Luis's bullet would have missed him with several inches to spare.

The horror of watching Antoine fall dead did not compare to the wretched anguish that now tore Michelle's soul. She was the one who had killed Antoine, not Luis, and, weeping hysterically, she struggled to stand and tell him so.

Fifteen

Still idly strumming his guitar, Luis was stretched out across his bed. The headboard made a comfortable backrest and the wide mattress provided ample room for his legs. When Michelle suddenly burst in on him, she looked so terribly distressed that he instantly set his guitar aside and rolled off the bed. Before he had taken more than one step toward her, she rushed into his arms.

"Michelle? What's happened?" he asked, but her unintelligible sobs failed to provide the slightest clue as to the cause of her despair. With the question left to his imagination, he assumed that she must have again been dwelling on Antoine's death. Hoping to restore her composure, he lifted her into his arms and laid her on the bed, but when he tried to sit back, she clung to him so tightly that he had no choice but to stretch out beside her.

He could not dry her abundant tears with his fingertips, although he tried, but the softness of her skin was so inviting, he leaned close in an attempt to kiss away the salty droplets. Too late he realized what a grave error that had been, for once his lips brushed the velvet smoothness of her cheeks, he was overwhelmed with desire. He wanted her too badly to care why she was crying and longed to turn her heartbreaking sobs to soft sighs of surrender. He gathered her into his arms and kissed her with the same desperate urgency with which he had once bid her farewell.

Michelle had been crying so hard she feared she had not made any sense, but she was well aware that she no longer had any reason to blame Luis for Antoine's death. He was not the guilty party. She was, and that knowledge dissolved the once insurmountable barrier her bitter accusations had formed between them. She returned his kiss with a shamelessness that shocked her, but Luis responded as she had known he would. He deepened his kiss until she felt as though she were drowning in the sweetness of his affection, but she craved still more.

Thrilled to have rekindled Michelle's responsiveness, Luis began to caress her with a knowing touch, hoping to ignite her passions with the fiery desire that consumed him. He caught her hand, and kissed her fingertips with playful nibbles. When that seemed to please her, he grew more bold and circled her breasts with a gently adoring flourish.

Abandoning herself to a moment she hoped would last forever, Michelle pressed against him. She slid her hands under his shirt to enjoy the warmth of his bare skin and again exulted in the sheer joy of holding him near. When he began to nuzzle her throat, she was amused that he would still want to leave evidence of his kiss and made absolutely no objection to his doing so.

Luis drew back for a moment, but only long enough to pull off his shirt and toss it over his shoulder. Michelle greeted his next kiss as though those few seconds apart had been an eternity, she had missed him so. Late at night, there were no men in the courtyard whose voices would distract her. With several hours remaining before dawn, there would be no interruptions of any kind, but Michelle wanted to go on kissing Luis long past sunrise. Not only was his taste delicious, his caress was seductively sweet. She had always wanted far more than she had ever dared admit and finally there was no longer any need to deny how attractive she found him.

She ran her fingers through his hair. It was very thick, but fine in texture rather than coarse and invited her fond touch. Its inky blackness reminded her of the vast contrasts between them. She was very fair, her hair and skin tinged with the subtle golden shadings of sunshine while his bronze skin and ebony hair conveyed the dark mood of midnight. As opposite as mirth and sorrow, or perhaps because of their inherent differences, their need to become one grew increasingly acute.

While Michelle had readily acknowledged her inexperience in flirting, lovemaking involved no such artful pretense. When Luis grew impatient with the soft but confining folds of her nightgown, she slipped out of it without feeling any more shyness than he had felt when discarding his shirt. Before meeting Luis, she had not known a woman could find such incredible pleasure in a man's arms and would have been content had there been nothing more to lovemaking than what he had already shown her. She knew there *was* more, however, and continued to follow his entrancing lead toward total surrender.

Lost in the passion Michelle had so easily aroused within him, Luis was past caring about anything other than their mutual pleasure. He knew precisely how to kiss a woman, and how to bestow an intimate caress that created sensations of indescribable beauty. The most considerate of lovers, he shed the last of his clothes between kisses, never giving Michelle more than an instant's respite from his affectionate attention, and even that was the worst of deprivations for them both.

Her flesh seemed to hum beneath his fingertips,

warm and pliant. Had he been making love to a goddess he could have been no more adoring. He waited until he was certain her whole body throbbed with the ecstasy he had taken such tender care to bring forth before he sought his own release deep within her. That she was a virgin echoed dimly in his mind, but it wasn't until she recoiled in pain from his first forceful thrust that he fully understood what that meant.

Even if hurting her had been unavoidable, he feared he had been unforgivably clumsy. He did not withdraw, but instead lay still and kissed her again and again until finally all trace of the sudden tension he had caused left her lithe body and her embrace again became a welcoming one. He took far more care this time, and moved slowly until his body's own heated demands took the choice of pace beyond his control. The strength of the rapture that swept through him left him lying breathless in her arms. Despite being a man of considerable experience, he had learned far more that night than his lovely bride, and had he been able to gather the energy to speak, he would have told her so and thanked her.

Unable to make that effort, he remained silent as he basked in the warm afterglow of her loving. Sleep soon overtook him, but when he awakened before dawn Michelle was still clasped in his arms and she was even more beautiful than he had recalled. The wondrous joy they had shared had convinced him that they were meant to be together, but a moment's reflection made him thoroughly ashamed of the way he had gone about it.

Grief-stricken, Michelle had turned to him for comfort and he had provided it in abundance, but it now seemed as though what he had really done was take selfish advantage of her sorrow. As with her requests for patience and understanding, he had again

257

appeared to agree, but had just as swiftly proved that he thought only of himself. He had gotten what he wanted last night, but had she?

He eased out of the bed and agonized over what he ought to do while he got dressed. He was due on board the *California* and hoped by the time he returned from the fanciful voyage for buried treasure, Michelle would have had enough time to put what had happened between them into perspective. They were married, after all. He had committed no crime in making love to her, but heavily burdened with guilt, that was precisely how he felt.

He used a piece of the stationery the inn provided for its guests and wrote a single sentence: Please forgive me. He signed his name and left the note on the nightstand where Michelle would be sure to see it upon waking. Praying that what he had done would not prove to be an unpardonable sin in her view, he placed a light kiss on her tangled curls and left her to enjoy her dreams.

Bereft of his comforting warmth, Michelle soon sensed that Luis was no longer by her side. She awakened within a few minutes of his departure, sat up, and looked around the room. When she discovered she had been left alone, her reaction was a wholly predictable one. Badly frightened, her first thought was that she must have disappointed Luis somehow, although his eagerness during their lovemaking had masked whatever failings she might have had. She had thought it had been absolutely glorious, but obviously Luis had not or he would not have left without waking her to say goodbye.

While it had not really been their wedding night, it had held the same magical sweetness for her and she was positive no bride ought to awaken on the first morning of her marriage alone. Suddenly chilled, she reached for her nightgown which Luis had thoughtfully placed across the foot of the bed. His note caught her eye then, though its meaning escaped her entirely.

Forgive him for what? she wondered, but a few moment's reflection provided a plausible answer. She had been weeping so pitifully when she had entered his room that he apparently had not understood a word she had said. He must still believe that she blamed him for Antoine's death. Not wanting him to be tortured by suspicions she no longer held, she hurriedly left his bed and returned to her own room.

Fearful that the *California* would sail before she reached it, she used the water in the pitcher on the washstand to rinse away the evidence of their passionate union and dressed as quickly as she could. Wanting to look pretty despite her haste, she slipped on the apricot gown, left her long curls flowing loose, and covered them with the lacy white *mantilla*. There was no time to wake Julio and Tomás and ask them to hitch up the team, but she remembered the route they had taken to the port, hiked up her gown, and walked with a step so brisk it bordered on a run.

To her immense relief, the *California* was still at the dock. Men were moving about the deck, but they were preoccupied making the preparations for an imminent departure. In the gloomy half-light before dawn, no one noticed her. Having come this far, she gathered her courage and ran up the gangplank. She saw Luis in the stern talking with Encario, and feared her impromptu appearance would embarrass him in front of his crew. Because that would only complicate an already difficult situation, she darted for the unguarded companionway and made her way to his cabin unseen.

259

It wasn't until she had closed the door behind her and drawn a deep breath that the possibility of stowing away occurred to her, but it was such an incredibly appealing idea that she hoped Luis would not enter his cabin until they had been at sea for several hours. For now, she looked around for somewhere to hide, but the cabin had been designed to make the best possible use of the limited space and every square inch served a specific purpose or provided storage. Cleverly designed lockers contained Luis's belongings, but none was spacious enough for her to slip inside.

She supposed that she could crawl under the table, but that struck her as much too silly. What if Encario or a steward were to enter the cabin rather than Luis? If they caught her in such an unbecoming pose they would undoubtedly think her extremely foolish and she wished to avoid giving anyone such a sorry and, she hoped, incorrect impression.

For the time being, she stepped behind the door, so should anyone merely peer into the cabin, her presence would go undetected. She took a deep breath and hoped that they would soon be under way but as the wait grew uncomfortably long, Luis's bunk began to look increasingly inviting.

Captain Boris Ryde was also eager for the *California* to set sail. He had been observing her for the last hour from a perch atop a nearby tavern. Spy glass in hand, he had noted Michelle's arrival although he could only speculate on who she might be. That she went below rather than approach Augustín confused him, but when she did not reappear, he soon became convinced that she must be Augustín's bride. He was then ecstatic that fate had provided him with this unexpected means to earn Antoine's bonus.

Because Boris had had but a limited amount of time to put a plan into effect, he feared his strategy was somewhat crude. Among his crew, Pablo Herrera and Norberto Macias were the two men he trusted most. Neither had ever served with Augustín Aragon, but they despised the handsome *criollo* simply because he had been born rich while they had barely survived the grinding poverty of their youth. The Aragon name alone filled them with such virulent envy that Captain Ryde had only to inquire if they might not enjoy doing Augustín some grievous harm to inspire them to volunteer for just such a mission.

Knowing the men well, Boris had stressed the danger involved rather than minimized it. He had outlined his plan and watched with growing satisfaction as Pablo and Norberto had nodded their enthusiastic approval. Once the loyal pair had been hired by Encario Vega, the rest had been surprisingly easy. The *Salamander* was not nearly as swift a ship as the *California,* but serving as Boris Ryde's spies, Pablo and Norberto had solved that problem by providing him with their approximate destination. That Augustín Aragon would trifle with a treasure map amused the English captain, but the more he considered it, the more likely he thought it was that Augustín would actually find some long forgotten pirate's cache of riches.

He was far too clever to scuttle a ship filled with treasure, and had given Pablo and Norberto specific directions in that regard. When at last the *California* set sail, Boris Ryde climbed down off the tavern roof and hurried back to his ship. In a matter of minutes, the *Salamander* also sailed out of the harbor to begin what her captain hoped would be an extremely profitable pursuit. His only regret was that if everything went according to his plan, the *California* and all hands would be counted as lost at sea. Only Antoine would credit him with ending the lives of Augustín Aragon and his wife. As long as he received the money he had been promised, as well as the satisfaction of knowing Augustín was dead, Boris had decided not to complain.

Luis was confident he had done the right thing in leaving Michelle in Valencia, but that knowledge failed to overcome the uncomfortable sensation of guilt he felt about the way he had left her. He had provided her with sufficient funds not only to keep herself amused but also to pay her way home should she be angry enough to leave him. As he watched the coast of Spain recede into the distance, he wondered if her disgust with him would outweigh the disgrace she had anticipated receiving in Lyon. Somehow he thought that it would. He would then be faced with the agonizing decision of whether or not to follow.

Encario joined Luis at the rail, but one look at his captain's menacing expression was enough to warn him to be discreet in his comments. "Do you miss her so much already?" he asked.

Luis rubbed the back of his neck. He doubted he had gotten more than an hour's sleep, but fatigue was a small problem in his present mood. "Of course I miss her. Any man would."

"The *California* is capable of far greater speed than we're making now. We can easily visit the island and return to Valencia in less than a week. Perhaps you'd like to surprise your bride by returning early."

"Have you always pried into my life so shamelessly?"

"I'm not prying, merely making a suggestion."

"Spread your advice elsewhere." Luis turned away from the rail and leaned back against it. "I don't care if we have to drop anchor at Palma de Mallorca, and simply relax for a couple of days, I want Michelle to have a week to herself."

Still thinking Luis daft, Encario made no more suggestions, discreet or otherwise. He simply scanned the horizon, and because they were in a well-traveled shipping lane, he took no particular notice of the schooner trailing them in the distance. He thought the reason for their voyage frivolous in the extreme, but like the crew, he could not help holding the slim hope that they might really find buried treasure.

Luis was already rich, but Encario was not and he could not stop daydreaming about what he might do should he suddenly become wealthy. It was a pleasant pastime, and from the darkness of Luis's expression, he knew it had to be far more enjoyable than the thoughts that filled the captain's mind. Remembering something he ought to have confided, he cleared his throat noisily.

"I hired a couple of new men yesterday when it didn't look like everyone was going to make it back on board by the time we sailed. They've proven to be such an industrious pair that I'll probably keep them on when we return to Barcelona."

Luis was paying scant attention to Encario's comments. "Are they experienced seamen?"

"From the quality of their work they definitely are, but I had no time to check their stories. They claim to have worked aboard several Portuguese ships, but none was in the harbor."

"Let this be a trial cruise for them then. If you're satisfied with their work, keep them on. If not, dismiss them. Now I'm going below," Luis announced

263

suddenly and he started for his cabin. He meant to lie down and sleep all day but when he entered his quarters and discovered Michelle sound asleep on his bunk he swiftly changed his mind. A cursory glance around the cabin revealed no sign of any luggage. What had she intended to do, merely tell him good-bye? Had she wanted to vent her rage on him again, he was positive she would have done it up on deck in front of his entire crew.

A slow smile dispelled the last trace of worry from Luis's features and he turned and left his cabin without making a sound. He really didn't care why Michelle had come on board, but he wasn't going to disturb her rest until it was far too late to turn back to Valencia. Encario looked surprised when he approached him, but Luis chose to ignore his obvious puzzlement.

"You're absolutely right," he began. "We can make much swifter time than this. Let's see what the *California* can do this morning under full sail."

Encario stared at Luis for a moment, and then saluted. "Aye, aye, Captain." He put his astonishment aside and relayed Luis's orders, but he wished he dared ask what had turned the captain's mood so quickly from dark preoccupation to a triumphant grin.

When the *California* disappeared over the horizon, Boris Ryde began to swear. Even knowing where the ship was bound would be of no help if she traveled so fast Luis was able to recover the treasure and begin the return voyage for Valencia before Boris sighted her again. "Damn!" he screamed, but the rest of his obscene utterings were unintelligible.

Startled by the captain's rude shout, the crew jumped in alarm. Captain Ryde was a hard man to serve on his best days, and clearly this was not going to be one of them. The merchant seamen exchanged worried glances, but none had an encouraging word to share with his mates.

In Madrid that morning, Antoine sat up for the first time and struggled to feed himself a poached egg. That he was still so feeble brought tears to his eyes, but he forced them away before Francisco noticed. "I want to go home," he revealed between tiny bites. "The very day that Dr. Tejada says I may travel, I'm leaving for home."

Fearing Antoine was becoming bored with his company, Francisco attempted to lift his spirits. "If there's anything you wish, books, or any amusements that we might provide, we'll be happy to get them for you."

Antoine shot him an evil glance. "You know all I really want is to hear that Augustín Aragon and the faithless bitch he married are dead."

Francisco shrugged helplessly. "Not knowing Aragon's plans makes it difficult to judge when Captain Ryde might have moved against him. I doubt that we'll hear anything for several weeks, although news of a tragedy involving the Aragons might reach us much sooner."

"Weeks!" Antoine cursed. Having lost interest in eating, he motioned for Francisco to take his tray and then tried to wiggle the fingers on his left hand. His shoulder began to throb painfully and, badly frustrated, he instantly gave up the effort to exercise his hand.

"Aragon has crippled me!"

From dawn to dusk, Francisco heard nothing but bitter complaints from Antoine now, and he was as desperately sorry as his cousin that he had been so badly injured. "Dr. Tejada has assured you repeatedly that you'll eventually regain the use of your hand."

"Eventually!" Antoine mocked. "It's not his hand, nor yours. How would either of you understand how it feels to be maimed?"

"You're not maimed, Antoine."

Convinced the opposite was true, Antoine rearranged his pillows with his right hand and eased himself down into them. He had done nothing more strenuous than eat an egg and he was exhausted. "Please, I need my rest."

Delighted to be dismissed, Francisco picked up the tray and started for the door. Before this visit, he had always enjoyed Antoine's company, but now his fair-haired cousin struck him as being so dreadfully self-absorbed that Francisco was ashamed he had failed to notice that failing in the past. He smiled as he backed out of the room and swung the door closed, but he was looking forward to the day Antoine returned home even more than the injured Frenchman himself was.

Satisfied with their increase in speed, and exhilarated by the hope Michelle's presence on board meant something good, at noon Luis returned to his cabin in high spirits. He had left orders that he was not to be disturbed and that he would send for his meals if and when he wanted them. He closed the door as carefully as he had earlier, and this time took the precaution of locking it.

Michelle had changed positions only slightly and there was no trace of tears on her cheeks. He sat down on the narrow space left beside her on the bunk and began to comb the ends of her long curls through his fingers. He was amusing himself rather

266

than trying to wake her, but she soon stirred. She opened her eyes and rewarded him with the sweetest smile he had ever seen.

"I knew you'd have a beautiful smile," Luis revealed with surprising candor, "but I despaired of ever seeing it."

Luis looked far too pleased with himself for Michelle to believe he was ever heavily burdened with despair. Before she could think of a witty reply, he leaned down to kiss her and words no longer held any significance for her. All she wanted was to lose herself in him again, and when he was so eager to oblige, she had no need to voice such a request.

Luis had hoped they would be able to talk and finally reach an accord, but the first kiss he had meant merely as a greeting soon blurred into a dozen with an increasingly seductive intent. The undulating motion of the ship as she plunged through the Mediterranean Sea encouraged the erotic nature of his mood until he could no longer aspire to any other. He fumbled with the buttons on Michelle's bodice. Knowing she had nothing else to wear, and unwilling to parade her on deck in a dress he had torn to shreds, he tried to undress her with the utmost care.

Noting her husband's scowl, Michelle took pity on him. She brushed his hands aside and unfastened the tiny covered buttons herself, but she hesitated to remove her gown while he was still fully clothed. A raised brow was all the encouragement Luis required to stand and fling his coat aside. Michelle could not help but giggle then.

"I've nowhere to go," she reminded him. "I can't possibly escape you. Why are you in such a rush?"

Luis wanted her too badly to explain with more than another exchange of convincingly heated kisses. Michelle did not tease him again, but peeled away his clothes with the same joyous abandon he had shown her. She had seen the naked bodies of small boys if not full-grown men, but she thought Luis's powerful build was magnificent rather than frightening. It did not even occur to her to demurely divert her gaze as he removed his pants, nor did he make any effort to shield her with a gallant display of modesty. He met her gaze and, pleased that she was not hiding her eyes or blushing, he laughed and gave her bottom a playful swat to encourage her to move over so there would be room for him to join her in the bunk.

Michelle had originally come to the *California* intending only to apologize to Luis, but she was very glad she had decided to stow away. His enthusiasm for her company made serious conversation totally unimportant for the moment. Content to talk later, she edged over as far as she could and welcomed him to the bunk with open arms.

"I doubt that we'll ever be able to sleep together here when we found it so difficult to rest in a real bed."

"We didn't last night," Luis whispered between lingering kisses. "Besides, I'm not tired and it won't bother me if we never sleep."

Michelle slid her fingertips down his spine in a sensuous sweep before hugging him tightly. She had always dreamed lovemaking would be as exciting as Luis made it, but there was still a forbidden flavor to his kiss. In her mind's eye, a sudden vision of Antoine made her shiver. For an instant she felt as though she had no right to enjoy the pleasure Luis bestowed with such masterful ease when it had come at such a terrible price.

Luis felt as well as saw Michelle withdraw slightly and this time he was correct in his assumption that thoughts of Antoine were to blame. "Look at me," he encouraged. "All that matters is what happens between us. And when it is so good, you mustn't let anything spoil it."

He smothered whatever reply Michelle might have cared to make with a lengthy kiss. He ran his hand down her ribs, caressed the smooth flatness of her stomach, and then delved lower to create the first tinglings of ecstasy. He shifted his position slightly and licked the pale-pink crests of her breasts. Then, timing the slow circular motion of his tongue and fingertips, he played with her senses until her whole body was coiled around him as tightly as a snake embraces her prey. That she wanted him so desperately fed Luis's passions until he could no longer think only of her and had to satisfy his own aching need.

This time, however, he entered her very slowly to spare her any additional pain. Her fiery inner heat enveloped him as before, and he felt her muscles contract around him with waves of rapture that washed over him as well. She moved with him, inviting, urging, demanding all he could give and, when he had, he rolled over and pulled her atop him. He kept her wrapped in his arms, but, despite his earlier boast, he could not stifle a wide yawn.

He brushed Michelle's hair out of his eyes, but as he looked up, he saw not only the blue of the sky through the skylight above his cabin but the face of a curious stranger. Having been caught, the man instantly ducked out of sight, but Luis had gotten a good look at him. The two new men were the only strangers on board and Luis was shocked to think one of them would stop his work to gawk at Michelle and him in the throes of passion. He was positive that breach of manners ought to bring swift and severe punishment, but he could not discipline the man without making a fool of himself.

269

He then realized that he was damn lucky the entire crew had not been lined up around the skylight and made a mental note to close the shutters that covered it as soon as he returned to deck. For now, he reached down to pull the blanket up over them, and gave Michelle another grateful squeeze.

Norberto Macias had learned all that he knew about passion from whores. He had never even dreamed that respectable women, and he assumed that Captain Aragon's wife must be considered such, ever behaved in the wanton manner he had just observed. He had been both repulsed and intrigued by the sight of the Aragons' mutual eagerness, but he had been even more badly startled than the captain when he had been caught spying on the pair. Confident he had not been recognized, he went on with his work as though he had seen nothing more exciting than the reflection of the sky and clouds in the skylight's glass panes.

He had been swabbing the deck when he had noticed the erotic antics going on below in the captain's cabin. A single glance at the unclothed couple had fascinated him too completely to turn away, but he now scanned the deck to make certain no one else had observed him watching the captain and his wife. Relieved that his actions had not drawn any notice from the others, he continued mopping the deck, but he could hardly wait until he had a chance to tell Pablo what he had seen.

He then thought it a shame that the voyage would be such a brief one. He had never expected their participation in Captain Ryde's plan would prove to be so wildly entertaining. He wondered what else the agile couple did together and if Señora Aragon always behaved like a whore. If so, why would she

270

object to having both Pablo and him before they set fire to the *California?*

Continuing to be industrious, Norberto moved on down the deck to put as much distance between himself and the skylight as he could before Captain Aragon reappeared. When ten minutes passed, and then twenty, he relaxed his pace. The captain had seen someone, but obviously he did not know who the man was or he would have been up on deck long before this to chastise the seaman for playing a Peeping Tom. Because that would be the least of his crimes, Norberto could not help laughing, but it was a quiet laugh he kept to himself just as he had the real reason he was on board.

Sixteen

Luis was so completely relaxed he had no desire to ever move. Michelle was draped over him with the same sensual grace with which her provocative scent clung to the air and it was an indescribably sweet sensation. He could tell she wasn't asleep, but he hated to speak and risk spoiling such a perfect moment. He stroked her hair, massaged her back, and waited for her to tell him why she had decided to join him. Knowing Michelle as he did, he was positive she must have had an excellent reason.

Michelle could not recall ever being so blissfully content. The hollow of Luis's shoulder provided the ideal pillow and she snuggled against him wishing that there was nothing more to the world than the space enclosed by his cabin. The slow rocking motion of the ship and the steady beat of her husband's heart would have lulled her to sleep if she had not been so eager to talk. Even then, she delayed voicing her concerns until she could no longer contain them.

She looked up at Luis. That he was every bit as handsome a man as she had thought upon first seeing him always amazed her. She kept expecting to detect a flaw she had previously overlooked, but, if anything, his attractiveness continually grew in her mind rather than diminished.

"I had something important to tell you," she confided hesitantly. "That's why I went into your room last night. I'd not have disturbed you otherwise."

Luis tried not to laugh, but it was difficult to stop with no more than a wide grin. "You may disturb me whenever you wish, *querida*. I'll never complain. As you must recall, you're the only one who wanted to sleep alone."

"Well, yes, I did say that, and I meant it, too," Michelle had to admit. Her reason had been genuine at the time, but not now. She hastened to explain before he distracted her again. "I didn't mean to stay with you last night. I'd only wanted to tell you that I had remembered more clearly what I'd seen at the duel. You've repeatedly insisted that Antoine was shot because he didn't stand still. I realized last night that he turned in answer to my call. If only I hadn't shouted his name, he'd be alive. It was my fault that he was killed, not yours."

Astonished that she had reached the conclusion on her own, Luis needed a moment to provide a suitably evasive reply. Then he decided that since she had discovered the truth on her own, there was no need for him to deny it. He reached up to caress her cheek lightly with the back of his fingers.

"I told you that my brother Daniel is a physician. Although he's very competent, sometimes his best efforts fail to save a patient. At first he was as devastated as the deceased's family when that occurred, but gradually he came to believe that each person's fate is in God's hands. I happen to think Daniel's right. Don't blame yourself. Antoine's fate was the one God chose for him."

Thinking he was merely parroting a bit of philosophy he hoped would prove comforting, Michelle could not accept her husband's view. She opened her mouth to debate the issue, and then thought better of it. She had wanted to tell him that she no longer

273

blamed him for Antoine's death and she had succeeded. She would stop there rather than belabor the point with irrelevant arguments.

"Regardless of what your brother believes, it's difficult for me to hope that you and I can ever be happy when our marriage had such a tragic beginning."

Luis laced his fingers in her hair so she could not avoid his kiss. He made it long and deep. "I'd never have let you go back to France," he then reassured her in a husky whisper. "Regardless of what Antoine might have done to stop me, you'd still have become my wife rather than his. What we have is very precious and rare. We should enjoy every minute of it."

All that Michelle knew for certain was that the joy of her lovemaking with Luis surpassed all her dreams and expectations. He filled her life with an excitement that had been frightening at first in its intensity; now she accepted it as a vital part of his masculine charm. "I just wish—"

When she fell silent, Luis prompted her. "Whatever it is, if it's humanly possible to achieve, I'll do it for you."

Michelle shook her head. "I just wish that we'd met under better circumstances so I'd known who you really were."

Luis enveloped her in a fond hug. "So do I!"

Michelle's stomach responded with a noisy rumble that embarrassed her terribly. "I didn't realize how hungry I was," she apologized.

"You're not half as hungry as I am, but for some reason, until you mentioned it, I hadn't noticed, either." Luis rolled over with Michelle still clasped in his arms, and then propped himself on his elbows to spare her his weight. "I always make stowaways work for their passage, but I'll make an exception in your case and share my quarters and food with you without expecting anything in return."

274

The teasing sparkle in his eyes conveyed a far different message, but pleased by that silent promise, Michelle kissed him rather than argue. When he broke away, she looked up and noticed the skylight provided an excellent view of his bunk to anyone who cared to look. "Oh, no!" she cried. "Someone could have been watching us the whole time!"

Luis glanced over his shoulder as though he had not already been fully aware of that possibility. "My crew have too much to do to stand around watching what goes on in my cabin. Besides, no one knows you're on board, so why would they glance down here in the first place?"

Relieved by his words, as well as the fact she hadn't seen anyone peering down at them, Michelle relaxed slightly. "You don't plan to keep me hidden down here, do you?"

"No, of course not, but I can slant the shutters over the skylight to provide privacy as well as light, and I'll do it before I see what the cook has prepared. I must warn you that he's considered very fine for a ship's cook, but we seldom carry passengers and the crew is satisfied with very plain fare."

"I'll not complain if he provides nothing more than porridge, as long as it's hot. But I would like to have some soon."

Luis gave her another kiss and then left the bunk to get dressed. "Perhaps you better stay put until I close the shutters."

Michelle yanked the blanket up to her chin. "I shall be happy to. It would be awful if your men began taking turns spying on us. I should have thought about what they'd say before I decided to stay on board, but I hadn't meant to do that at first. I was only going to talk with you."

Luis paused at the door. "You said the same thing about it last night. Whatever your excuse, I'm glad you're here. Any time you want to talk, or do any-

275

thing else you find amusing, be sure and let me know."

Embarrassed by his suggestive comment, Michelle yanked the blanket up over her head, but as Luis pulled the door shut, she was laughing just as hard as he was. She knew that had to be wicked, but she could not help herself any more than she had been able to resist Luis's enchanting affection. She knew she was falling in love with her husband. She had heard that in arranged marriages couples often came to love each other, but she did not believe it was supposed to occur this rapidly.

She felt as though she had been caught in a whirlwind, spun until she was dizzy, and then flung into a calm so delightful she feared it could not possibly last. That distressing thought proved to be her undoing and, without Luis's teasing presence, her joyous mood began to ebb. She and Antoine had been together so long. It was unconscionable that she should have played such a crucial role in the events leading to his death and then lose herself in another man's arms. Even alone in the cabin she felt the heat of the scornful looks she knew she deserved and could not suppress a shudder of remorse.

The sunlight filling the cabin dimmed slightly as Luis changed the angle on the shutters overhead and, assured of her privacy, Michelle sat up. The direction of her thoughts had grown too painful and she deliberately forced herself to instead consider the practical matters she had overlooked before boarding the *California*. She was disappointed she had not been clever enough to bring along some extra clothes, but Luis's incomparable affection made the prospect of spending the whole voyage lying naked in his bunk incredibly appealing.

Luis would not have argued with that, but when he returned to his cabin and found that Michelle had not moved, he was somewhat surprised. He set the tray with their lunch on the table and turned toward her. "You're going to need more clothes, aren't you?"

"Not if I'm careful not to spill anything on my gown and I can rinse out my lingerie each night. I'd really like to bathe before I put on my clothes, though. If that's not possible, a pail of warm water will do."

"I'm sorry. I should have thought of that myself." Luis opened one of his lockers and withdrew a neatly folded shirt. He shook it out and handed it to her. "Why don't you put this on for now. When we're finished eating, I'll fetch some hot water for you."

Michelle slipped the shirt on over her head and rolled up the sleeves. It was made of a fine linen which was wonderfully soft, but it was much too large to flatter her slender proportions. She laughed as she climbed out of bed, for not only were the shoulder seams close to her elbows but the hem reached her knees.

"I fear I must look like some poor waif who's clothed in hand-me-downs."

Luis disagreed. Even in an ill-fitting shirt she was strikingly beautiful. He usually paid women compliments as easily as he remarked on the weather, but as Michelle took her place at his table, he found himself searching for the words to adequately do her justice. Embarrassed when none came to him, he brushed her complaint aside.

"You look fine to me. Besides, aren't you more interested in food than your appearance for the moment? Fortunately the cook makes a delicious baked chicken, so you've the opportunity to sample one of his best recipes."

Still convinced she resembled a child dressed in her father's shirt, Michelle nevertheless ceased to complain. "I think it's the company more than the food that makes a meal memorable. Don't you?"

277

Again, Luis felt an uncharacteristic burst of shyness. "Yes, I do." He served her plate and then his before filling two silver goblets with a cool white wine. After handing her one, he raised his in a silent toast. He would have liked to have made an elegant tribute to their prospects for a long and happy marriage, but, despite the current levity of his bride's mood, he feared she might consider it inappropriate. He felt very close to her, and yet somehow still estranged. Those were not feelings he could give recognizable form, let alone express in coherent words.

"We can visit Palma de Mallorca, on our way to the island if you'd like to supplement your wardrobe," he said instead. Choosing such a safe topic was cowardly, he supposed, but he didn't want to say or do anything that would upset Michelle and spoil their newly forged accord. "Or, if you'd rather, we can search the island first. There's always the chance we'll discover such fabulous wealth that you will no longer wish to wear whatever we might find for you in Palma."

"Do you really think so?"

Luis shook his head. "No, not really. I didn't mean to give you false hopes. I doubt that we'll find anything at all, but I do believe the map is worth investigating."

Michelle took several bites of the chicken before she paused to consider his question. "I think I'd like to visit the island first."

"Fine, that's what we'll do then. We're making such good time we should be there before noon tomorrow."

Intrigued by that possibility, Michelle looked up and waited for him to elaborate on his plans, but he was too preoccupied with eating to speak. She had previously noted that his hands were as handsome as the rest of him, but now that he had touched her so

278

intimately, as she observed the way he held his knife and fork, she could almost feel his tantalizing caress. She hurriedly looked down at her plate before he caught her staring at him with what she knew had to have been a lustful glance.

But it never had been lust and it wasn't now, she scolded herself. It was closer to *love* from the instant he had appeared in her life. She again wished that she had had the opportunity to quietly contemplate that possibility, instead of hating both herself and him for being unable to resist a charming Gypsy's cunning lies.

"None of this seems real," she blurted out suddenly. "We met just over two weeks ago, and now—"

"Michelle." Luis spoke softly. "Stop berating yourself for what's happened. It's what was meant to be."

"Obviously, or we'd not be together, but—"

This time Luis waited for her to finish her sentence, but she failed to do so. "But this, but that," he replied more crossly than he had intended. "Granted we went about everything wrong, but that doesn't mean what we're doing now isn't right."

"I'm sorry. I didn't mean to offend you."

"You didn't."

While he sounded sincere, the darkness of his expression chilled her clear through. "I should have left well enough alone and remained in Valencia, shouldn't I?"

"No!" Luis argued. He reached out and took her hand. "You belong with me now, Michelle. Naturally it will take a while for us to grow accustomed to each other's ways, but that's to be expected. I don't want you to constantly be worrying that you've done something wrong. Just be yourself and give me the same privilege. Now stop fretting and finish your chicken before it gets cold."

When he released her hand, Michelle obediently picked up her fork. Luis was being so kind to her that she had to fight back tears, but she took several deep breaths and managed to eat the remainder of her lunch without weeping. As promised, he provided warm water for her to bathe and then escorted her up on deck where the crew's startled glances made it plain they were as shocked to see her on board as Luis had been.

Having lived on the Rhône River, she had frequently ridden in boats, but this was the first time she had traveled on the open sea and it was much more exciting. Luis took care to place himself between her and the wind so she was not buffeted as cruelly as the sails, but with no more than a mantilla for a wrap, she soon grew chilled and asked to return to his cabin.

"I'll have to provide you with another set of clothes to wear while we explore the island tomorrow. Mine are obviously too large, but there are smaller men on board who might be persuaded to loan you some of their things."

"I didn't mean to cause so much trouble."

Luis wrapped her in an enthusiastic hug and lifted her clear off her feet. "I don't want to hear another apology from you, woman. Not ever."

"I just hope that I'll not have any reason to apologize in the future."

Until Antoine had been killed, Luis had not suspected Michelle possessed such a vulnerable nature. While it was endearing, he preferred the stubbornly defiant mood she had continually shown him in Madrid. It was very nice to see her smile, though. He gave her a final loving squeeze and placed her on her feet.

"I should have had the presence of mind to take your measurements before you got dressed," he revealed with mock seriousness. "Now you'll have to remove your clothes all over again so that I can judge your size and make certain that the garments I find for you will fit properly."

"Remove my clothes?" Michelle asked as though she did not know precisely where this conversation was leading.

Luis broke into a wicked grin. "I don't want you tripping over your pant legs, or otherwise hampered by shirts and sweaters that are much too large. This is for your benefit, after all. I'd not ask it otherwise."

Michelle raised her hands to the top button on her bodice. "If I go through all the bother of getting undressed again, I'll be much too tired to try on the clothes you've promised to provide before tomorrow."

"What a shame," Luis sighed, but his laughter swiftly convinced her that regardless of her need for a change of clothes, he much preferred to have her *un*clothed.

They passed the rest of the afternoon in each other's arms, and while Luis did succeed in finding Michelle several garments and a pair of boots close enough to her size to be comfortable, he did it while the cook prepared their supper so that he had to leave his cabin only once. He knew the whole crew was undoubtedly envying him his good fortune in having his wife aboard, but he was enjoying himself too much to care if the remarks passing between them weren't concentrated solely on their duties. He told Encario to keep a closer eye on the two new men, but chose not to reveal the reason why.

That night, Luis told Michelle more about the ranch where he had been born and raised, and with his gentle encouragement, she also talked openly about her family. While Luis did not press the issue now, he had already made up his mind to accompany her to Lyon to meet her mother and sisters. They would pass the winter quietly in Barcelona and then visit France in the spring. By then, he hoped that their marriage would win acceptance rather than cause the scandal Michelle anticipated. Luis

281

could not help himself, but having met Antoine Lareau, he simply could not believe anyone other than his mother would truly miss him.

Putting all thought of future conflicts aside, Luis again made love to Michelle, displaying all the tenderness and strength she had come to expect. He had never been so taken with a woman, but it had not yet occurred to him as it had to her that he had already fallen in love with her.

Until Michelle had to scramble down the rope ladder to reach the lifeboat waiting to take them ashore, she felt very foolish to be dressed in men's clothing. After that frightening ordeal, however, she appreciated the practicality of male attire and ceased to worry over the attractiveness of her appearance. In truth, her unlikely assortment of apparel merely enhanced her beauty rather than detracted from it.

Love had given her delicate features a captivating radiance that was undimmed by her makeshift garb. Holding Luis's hand in the lifeboat, she looked as pretty as she did when dressed in her finest gown. Thinking the search for buried treasure a great adventure, she looked toward the island they intended to explore with an eager gaze. Six of the crew had come along with them, but Michelle was too curious to worry about having their conversation overheard.

"How can you be sure we've found the right island?" she asked.

"My navigation skills are sufficiently fine to permit me to sail from Spain to California without becoming hopelessly lost. Finding an island, even one as small as this, was no great challenge when I had an accurate map."

Fearing that her question had sounded as though she had no faith in his ability as a captain, Michelle was prompted to apologize, but at the last instant remembered Luis's stern warning that she need not apologize to him ever again. Still, she felt as though she had done something wrong. "I didn't realize a pirate's map would be all that accurate," she mumbled softly.

Seeing by her averted glance that his arrogant boast had hurt her feelings, Luis was sorry that he had made it. He wanted Michelle to feel comfortable with him, and not merely when they shared a bed. That he had not answered her question more politely disappointed him. He withdrew the old map from his pocket and made a more considerate effort to answer her question.

"Mallorca is correctly placed. As are the smaller of the Balearic Islands: Menorca, Cabrera, Ibiza, and Formentera. There are additional islands, like the one we've found, which are little more than dots on a detailed navigational chart. They are too small to sustain a settlement of any kind, but would make a fine place for a pirate to hide his booty. Because it's not terribly remote, however, it's highly probable that whatever treasure this map revealed was found long ago."

"Still, you said it was worth the time to look for it."

"That I did," Luis agreed. He returned the map to his pocket for later reference. He had wanted something useful to do other than cruise the harbor for a week while she mourned Antoine's loss alone, but he was delighted she had come with him even if it was on a wild-goose chase. She was smiling again and, grateful that he been able to lift her spirits so easily, he made a mental note not to be so careless with his comments in the future.

When they neared the shore and the water became too shallow for the men to continue rowing the lifeboat, Luis went over the side with them. He then told Michelle to stay seated while his men towed the boat through the breakers. After they had hauled it up onto the narrow border of white sand along the rocky shoreline, he reached in, grasped her around the waist, and lifted her out.

"If this tiny island has no name, I think it should be called Michelle, after you," he suggested.

"That's a flattering tribute," she replied in the same teasing tone he had used. "But perhaps I should insist on your waiting until you discover a more impressive isle to use my name."

"That's a very good point. We could probably walk all the way around this island in less than an hour and you certainly deserve better."

Embarrassed by the couple's playful banter, one of the seamen coughed noisily to remind the captain and his bride of their presence. Luis took note of the man's impatience, but he was amused rather than annoyed. They had brought along plenty of food for the men, and a picnic lunch for Michelle and Luis. Luis picked up their portion of the refreshments, tossed those intended for the men to one of them to carry, and then led the way toward the northern end of the island.

Just as it was depicted on the map, the small cove on the west, where they had landed, formed an inward curve, giving the rocky island a beanlike, irregular shape. Pine trees grew in profusion along the limestone cliffs rising toward the center of the island. Though the cliffs were jagged, the walk along the gently sloping shore was an easy one.

Michelle had never set foot on an island before and thought that despite its diminutive size, this one was remarkable. Sea gulls flew in noisy profusion overhead, and she strained to see what might be lurking among the pines. "Are there likely to be wild animals here?" she asked.

Luis could not resist teasing her. "Are you thinking of jungle beasts, like tigers?"

Instantly apprehensive, Michelle tightened her grasp on his hand. "Tigers come from Asia, don't they? That's a very long way from here."

"Yes, it is," Luis assured her. "You needn't worry. "Nothing is going to come galloping out of the shrubbery and eat you up. At least not as long as I'm here to protect you."

A single glance at Luis's confident grin was enough to restore Michelle's courage and she nearly skipped as she walked along beside him. The men were following, carrying shovels slung over their shoulders, and she hoped, even with Luis's repeated skepticism, they would not have to dig too deep before they discovered a cache of riches equal to a king's ransom. It would make a marvelous story if they did, but even if they didn't, she was very grateful that she was there with Luis rather than back in Valencia brooding.

The rocky shoreline became more treacherous as they neared the island's northern tip and Luis slowed their pace to give Michelle ample time to make her way across the rocks safely. When they reached the grove of pines illustrated on his map, he stopped to study the neatly penned drawing more closely. If the map was truly as old as Sergio and Aurora had insisted, then the steady erosion caused by wind and surf would have made some changes in the rugged shoreline that might make it difficult to judge where the treasure, if it existed, had originally been buried.

"Do you feel ready to do a bit of climbing?" he asked Michelle.

Unwilling to be left behind, Michelle assured him that she did. "Are we going all the way to the top of the cliffs?" she then inquired bravely.

"No, just high enough to judge whether or not the map still accurately illustrates the coastline. If it doesn't, we'll have to make some adjustments so we don't waste our time digging in the wrong place."

"I understand." Determined to keep up with him, Michelle gave the wool cap that covered her curls a fierce tug and followed right on Luis's heels. They entered the trees, and using the gnarled roots peeking above the surface of the rocky soil for footholds, moved up the steep incline until they came to a ledge where they could stand comfortably while they viewed the shore.

Luis scanned both the map and the waves breaking against the rocks below for several minutes before handing the map to Michelle. "Well, what do you think? This appears to have been the vantage point from which the map was drawn. Has the shoreline changed any since then?"

Michelle traced the line drawn on the map then looked down at the shore. "No, the outcropping of rocks to our right is identical, and the dip on the left has precisely the same curve. What does that mean?"

Luis reached for the map, folded it carefully, and returned it to his pocket. "It means someone took great care to draw the map accurately, but they sure as hell didn't do it fifty years ago. The map is a fake."

Michelle's heart fell. "Then there's no treasure?"

Luis hated to disillusion Michelle further. "Probably not a single coin, but since we've come this far, shall we have the men dig a few feet just to make certain?"

Michelle looked down toward the six men who had come with them. They were seated on the rocks, laughing among themselves. "Wouldn't they mind doing such hard work for nothing?"

"We won't know if it's for nothing unless we do it," Luis pointed out.

"Well, if you think it's worth a try, then I think so, too."

"Why haven't you always been this agreeable?"

"Perhaps I had no reason to be," Michelle replied smugly, and delighted with Luis's charming grin, she followed him down the steep incline. While it was more difficult to keep her balance going down than climbing up, she nevertheless displayed commendable agility.

Luis pointed out precisely where he wanted his men to dig, and then picked up the basket that held their lunch. "Let's see just how long it really takes to walk all the way around this island."

Michelle was surprised he didn't want to stay and watch the men work even if there was only a slight hope that they would unearth anything valuable. The sandy soil at the base of the pine trees didn't present an impenetrable barrier, but she still felt rather guilty about leaving the men to work while they went for a stroll. Then she realized that if they remained, they would be watching the men rather than working themselves, and she saw no reason to stay. Again, she took Luis's hand and, with a happy smile, continued on around the islet.

Luis stopped as soon as they came to a stretch of dry sand that he thought would make a good place to eat. He laid out a lunch similar to the ones he had served Michelle on the trip from Madrid to Valencia and hoped she would have a bigger appetite today. As they ate, the innocent sweetness of her smiles made him uncomfortably aware that he had failed to tell her the truth about the treasure map. There was a lot more he knew he ought to have revealed as well.

"I am trivialized as a *criollo* by a great many Spaniards. There are others, however, who are eager to befriend me because of my wealth. Thus I am constantly surrounded by people I don't really trust, although I do have a few close friends. I'll readily admit to missing my family and I think it's because

I've never really felt completely at home in Spain that I enjoyed spending my time with Gypsies, who are also outcasts—"

"Please," Michelle interrupted. "I'd rather not hear about your Gypsy friends."

She began to tear huge chucks out of the roll she had been consuming with dainty bites, and Luis realized he should have waited until they finished eating to speak. "Just listen to me for a minute, please. The night I went to see Aurora in an attempt to get your aunt's money back, she and Sergio—he was the other man who played the guitar at Antoine's party—gave me the treasure map."

Michelle could not believe her ears. "Then how could you have ever imagined that it was genuine?"

"I didn't really believe that it was," Luis admitted. "But I'm trying to tell you that you needn't worry about me posing as a Gypsy, or having anything to do with them ever again. I was their friend when it suited them, but Aurora and Sergio lied to me about the map just as smoothly as Aurora must have lied to your aunt. They view the world differently than we do. They consider themselves a family, and everyone else in the world is an easy target for their mischief. The word *scruples* has no meaning to them."

When Luis fell silent, Michelle thought she saw something in his expression that he had failed to admit aloud. "You're hurt that they lied to you, aren't you?"

Luis nodded. "I mistook their interest in me for friendship, but obviously it was never that. Perhaps they expected to get money from me someday. Who knows what devious plan they might have had? As it was, they got nothing at all from me but scorn."

While she was sorry to learn Luis had been hurt by Aurora and Sergio's deception, Michelle dared not allow her thoughts to drift back to the days she had spent in Madrid. She wanted the door to those memories kept not only closed but locked as well. She tossed the remainder of her lunch on the sand for the gulls, stood up, and brushed the crumbs from her borrowed clothes.

"Let's go back and tell the men there's no point in their digging another inch deeper. Rather than keep the map as a souvenir, I hope you'll burn it. I also hope that you'll finally stop telling me lies."

Luis watched as Michelle walked down to the water to rinse her hands. He had seen that same defiant posture too often not to know she was totally infuriated with him. He had made a sincere attempt to confide in her, but rather than appreciate his honesty about the map, she had chosen to focus on the fact that he had not been truthful about it all along. He rose to his feet with a weary sigh. More than anything in the world he wanted to make Michelle happy, but that seemed like a completely impossible task.

Seventeen

When Michelle and Luis returned to the northern
tip of the island, they found the six men they had
left working had excavated a hole approximately five
feet square to a depth of four feet. All they had
found was an old bottle filled with sand and a rusted
key. With water now rapidly seeping into the bottom
of the hole, the last man to have been working
climbed out with the aid of his mates.

"We can't dig much deeper without shoring up the
sides and constantly bailing, Captain, but none of us
thought to bring a saw to cut down a tree for wood
or buckets."

So they would not feel that their efforts had been
wasted, Luis peered down into the hole before he
spoke, but he had lost interest in the project. "Pirates would have had the same problem and they
wouldn't have buried anything below the water
table," he told them. "If there had been something
here, you should have found it before now. Rest a
while, and then fill in the hole."

"Smugglers hide their loot in caves on Mallorca,
Captain. Shouldn't we search for caves here? If I
were a pirate, I'd rather leave my booty in a cave
where I could recover it quickly than buried here on
the beach where anyone might come along and see
me digging it up."

Luis glanced toward Michelle to see if she cared

to offer an opinion, but she was looking away, clearly lost in her own thoughts rather than listening to him and his men. "That's an excellent idea. Fill in the hole, and then circle the island. If you find anything interesting, come and get me. My wife and I will be waiting at the lifeboat."

Shifting the picnic basket to his left hand, Luis grasped Michelle's hand and again took special care to see that she did not trip and fall while they traversed the rocky shoreline near the point. When they reached dry sand, she pulled free and walked ahead of him. Exasperated with her, Luis came to an abrupt halt. At her request, he had left Valencia to provide her with ample time alone, but rather than mourn in private, she had come after him. It was a great pity she had forgotten the reason why.

"This is getting to be extremely tiresome!" he called after her. When she paused and turned to face him, he strode right up to her. "I'll gladly agree that your anger with me is justified, but you can't just ignore me as though I don't exist."

Offended by his combative tone, Michelle nevertheless replied calmly. "I'm not angry at you. *Disappointed* is a better word."

Luis gestured back toward the way they had come. "I only followed that silly map as an excuse to leave Valencia after you'd made it plain you preferred your own company to mine."

Michelle placed her hands on her narrow hips. Without several petticoats and the folds of a lavish gown, her figure looked as boyish as her makeshift garb. "Are you saying that I forced you to lie to me, that it's all my fault?"

"No!" Luis didn't understand how she could have twisted an apology into an insult, but she had done it with amazing ease. "I was just trying to salvage my own pride, rather than slink away with nowhere to go."

Rather than wait for another of Michelle's barbed responses, Luis brushed by her and hurriedly crossed the remaining distance to the lifeboat. He tossed the picnic basket into the stern, and then, unable to suppress the rage boiling within him, he kicked the side in an attempt to expiate the frustration his darling bride continually caused him. His only reward for that foolishness was a stinging burst of pain. Disgusted with himself, he looked out toward the *California.* Several men waved to him and he hoped they hadn't seen him behaving like a spoiled brat who took out his anger on his toys.

Having also witnessed Luis's temperamental display, Michelle waited several minutes before joining him. Even after the intimacy they had shared, it was difficult for her to think of him as her husband. He might know how to make love with the skill of the Greek god Eros, but he was equally adept at inflicting emotional pain. It was the weight of that burden that prompted her to speak.

"Can't you understand why your constant deceptions hurt me?" she asked. "If I can't trust you to tell me the truth, then I'll be forever lost, unable to comprehend who you really are and what you truly think of me."

That poignant question was almost more than Luis could bear, but Michelle had asked it so sweetly, he wanted to give her a considerate reply despite the blackness of his mood. Again, he failed. "I don't want to have this same wretched argument every day for the rest of our lives. I do not routinely lie rather than speak the truth. If a man were to make that same accusation, I'd—"

"You'd what?" Michelle interrupted to ask. "Challenge him to a duel?"

"No, I'd thrash him with my bare hands." Luis looked down at his bride, his dark gaze icy. "We have to be on the same side, Michelle. I can't bear to think my own wife would want to destroy me."

"How in God's name could I possibly destroy someone with your magnificence?" Michelle sarcastically shot back at him.

Luis had already opened his mouth to reply when one of his crew shouted his name from atop the nearby cliff. He turned toward him and quickly interpreted the man's excited gestures. Grateful to have another of their senseless arguments interrupted before it got any worse, he relaxed visibly.

"It looks like they found something. Do you want to come with me or stay here?"

What Michelle would have really liked would have been to magically transport herself to her family's tranquil estate in Lyon, but because that was not an option, she announced her second choice. "I want to go with you. If they've actually found a smuggler's cave, I don't want to be left out."

The bright splashes of color filling Michelle's cheeks jarred Luis into recalling that he had actually lamented the absence of the fiery side of her nature while she had been so distraught over Antoine's death. Now that he again had that proud beauty by his side, he felt like a fool complaining about how poorly they got along. He extended his hand, and after a slight hesitation, Michelle took it. She had a fine lady's beautifully manicured nails and the contrast with her mannish attire brought a smile to his lips.

"If smugglers did or do use this island as a hiding place, it's unlikely they left anything here for long. I hope that you won't again be disappointed if we fail to find something of value."

The way Luis stressed the word *disappointed* made Michelle wince, but she forced herself to smile. "I'd just like to be able to say that I'd explored a cave. I don't care whether or not we find anything."

"Good." Luis studied the sloping face of the limestone cliff framing the cove for a moment and decided it would be no more strenuous to scale than the northern face of the isle where they had gone up to the ledge to compare the map to the shoreline. At least it wouldn't be for him. "Do you feel up to another climb?" he asked Michelle.

Michelle followed the direction of his glance and decided she would rather not. "Wouldn't it be easier to walk around the island than climb over it?"

"Yes, but not nearly as much fun." Luis pulled a pair of gloves from his hip pocket and handed them to her. "I should have given these to you earlier. Put them on and you won't scratch your hands on the rocks."

That was a clear challenge, and while Michelle rebelled inwardly, she took the gloves and yanked them on. Apparently he thought she could not keep up with him, so she would have to prove him wrong. "Lead the way," she offered, but her tone held more contempt than she had meant to show. When Luis did not respond with an angry retort, she was relieved to have gotten away with it and trudged along after him across the sand.

Luis started making his way up to the bluff and, following his example, Michelle took every advantage of the craggy surface of the limestone to ease her way. He was moving slowly, deliberately choosing secure footholds but his legs were so much longer than hers that she had to seek additional indentations between the toeholds he used. While his gloves did serve to protect her hands from being cut on the sharp edges of the rocks, they were so large they made her clumsy and badly hampered her ability to hold on. By the time she crawled up onto the pine-covered bluff, she was breathing heavily and hoped Luis would also want to sit and rest now that they had reached level ground.

Luis did not even look back to check on her, however. He just headed into the trees and left her gasping for breath on her own. Michelle looked back down at the beach from where they had started and was surprised it was still so close when she felt as though she had climbed clear up into the clouds. Reaching the bluff had not been terribly difficult, but it wasn't the type of activity a well-born young lady was trained to do, so it was no wonder that she was fatigued.

She wondered if Luis would continue to expect her to keep up with him. If so, he wasn't being at all fair. His powerful build proved he was used to strenuous physical activity, while she had never done anything more taxing than dancing, or riding a favorite mare. She had friends who weren't nearly as active as she, but thoughts of how poorly they would do brought little comfort when she was there and they were not.

Lack of stamina was only one of her problems, however. Although it was impossible to become lost on such a small island, she didn't appreciate being left behind on her own. As soon as she caught her breath, she hauled herself to her feet and started after Luis. The air beneath the stand of pines was cooler than that on the sun-drenched shore, but she was too upset to feel refreshed. Used to the company of family or servants, she surveyed the small forest with an apprehensive glance. She didn't like being alone in a strange place, even one that wasn't particularly forbidding.

She trusted Luis enough to feel confident that he would not leave her stranded there, but even when they returned to the *California,* he would be her only friend on board. Could she even consider him a friend? she wondered. Tears welled up in her eyes, and, despite her earlier bravado, she lost heart, sat down and hugged her knees.

The grove shielded her from the breeze coming off

the sea, but she did not feel protected. Other than the constant screeching of the gulls, the island echoed with an eerie silence that served to depress her mood even further. She felt horribly out of place and as isolated as the rocky island. It had looked so inviting from a distance, but now that she had seen it up close, all she wanted to do was leave.

Luis had not gone far before he sensed Michelle was no longer following right behind him. He stopped, leaned back against a conveniently placed pine, and folded his arms across his chest. As he waited for her in that peaceful setting, the last traces of his anger slipped away. He had to admire Michelle's spirit for even trying to match his pace and swore to himself that he would not tease her for failing in the attempt.

He started to chuckle to himself, and growing too impatient for Michelle to appear to wait any longer, he turned back and went to find her. When he saw her seated in a dejected heap, his first thought was that she must have tripped and fallen. He rushed to her and knelt by her side.

"Are you hurt?"

Embarrassed by the pitiful sight she knew she must make, Michelle hurriedly brushed away her tears. She *was* hurt, but only inside where it didn't show. She reached out to use his shoulder for leverage and rose to her feet. "No, I'm fine," she stated unconvincingly. "Let's continue."

Luis straightened up and caught her arm before she could take the first step away. "Michelle, you were sitting here crying. Tell me what happened."

Unable to express the pain of her doubts in words, Michelle just shook her head.

"Do you want me to carry you?"

"No, I can walk. See?"

All Luis saw was a woman who looked so desperately unhappy she could not wait to get away from him. He let her go, but he matched his stride to hers this time, and when she did not draw away from him, he took her hand. "If you insist you're all right, then I'll assume that you are," he stated matter-of-factly. When she again failed to respond, he abruptly changed the subject.

"Because the Balearic Islands are formed of limestone, caves were created by the constant ebb and flow of the tide. I should have remembered that when Sergio gave me the map. Why would anyone bury anything on an island when caves provide a much better hiding place?"

Michelle had to admire him for trying so hard to draw her into a less personal conversation. She gave the best reply she could. "Maybe there was a pirate or two who didn't know about the caves."

"That's possible, there could have been." Luis was so grateful that she was at least speaking to him, even it if wasn't about anything important, that he continued to talk about the islands until they had reached the opposite side. Here on the east the slope down to the shore was more gentle than it was on the west, but as they made their way down to the beach, he still kept a close watch on Michelle to be certain she was in no danger of falling.

"We found what looks like the entrance to a cave, Captain," two of the seamen announced in an excited chorus. They led the way through the rocky tidepools to a portion of the cliff that projected out into the water. "You have to bend down to see more than just a sliver of the opening, but it's there."

Intrigued, Luis hunkered down to peer into the narrow crevice his men had found. At high tide, it would be completely under water. He had seen a few of the caverns on Mallorca. They were spacious enough to hide almost anything valuable enough to smuggle. Most of the goods came from Tangiers and found their way from Mallorca to other Mediterranean ports. A tradition carried on by successive generations of fishermen, smuggling had brought a great many families considerable wealth.

His curiosity satisfied for the moment, he rose and walked back to the sandy shore where Michelle was waiting. He then began to unbutton his shirt. "I'll go in first, but if there's anything worth seeing, I'll take you down with me."

Each time a wave struck the rocks jutting out from the cliff spray it shot up high into the air and Michelle quickly reconsidered her wish to explore a cave. "I didn't realize we'd have to get in the water. I can't swim."

"This is as good a day to learn as any," Luis advised with a sly wink. Once he had removed his shirt, he sat down to pull off his boots and socks. "Of course, you'll have to shed some of your clothes."

Two of the men understood French and began to snicker. Michelle bit her lip rather than complain in front of them, but she could not help but wonder just how much of her apparel Luis would ask her to discard. In front of men who were as easily amused as these, she would not feel comfortable removing more than the gloves he had loaned her.

"It's October. Isn't the water too cold for swimming? I think next summer would be a much better time to learn how to swim. I don't want to worry about catching a chill."

Luis rose to his feet and brushed the sand from the seat of his pants. "I'll look forward to next summer then," he offered agreeably. He turned to his men. "Take off your boots and jackets. If I'm not back in a two minutes, I expect every last one of you to come in after me."

One of the men hopped around while he pulled off his boots, but the others sat down in the sand to tackle that chore. As soon as they were ready, Luis again ventured out onto the rocks. When he reached the entrance of the cave, he eased himself down into the surf. "The water's still plenty warm!" he called out to Michelle.

"Good luck!" she replied, knowing she had to say something and unable to come up with more inspiring words. It frightened her to think how eager Luis was to swim into the cavern. He didn't appear in the least bit apprehensive, but *she* certainly was. She turned and glanced at the pine-covered bluff above them. The island was still a picturesque spot, but she was growing increasingly anxious to leave. She held her breath as Luis dove beneath the water and began to count slowly in her mind. When she got to sixty, she focused her attention on the seamen, but unlike her, none seemed concerned.

Once out of sight, Luis moved slowly through the narrow opening, twisting sideways to speed his progress. The channel into the subterranean cave was longer than he had anticipated but he still had sufficient air not to have to gasp hungrily when he surfaced inside. Extending back under the bluff, the cave was long and narrow, the sides steep. Filtered through the water, what little light reached it had an eerie green glow.

It took Luis a moment to be able to see clearly. Then he wished that he had had the good sense to remain outside on the beach, for dangling just above his right shoulder was a skeleton whose vacant eyes had clearly kept a lengthy vigil. An iron collar and cuffs fastened to the uneven wall of the watery cave had prevented the skull, arms, and ribs from floating out to sea with the tide, but the pelvis and legs were gone.

The old metal was nearly rusted through, but Luis was sure the poor soul had been alive when he had been imprisoned there and left to either drown or starve. That was too hideous a fate to wish on any man and Luis crossed himself before he ducked under the water. Hurriedly leaving his gruesome discovery, he swam out to the open sea. He broke through the surface, climbed out onto the rocks, and made his way back to the beach.

Thoroughly sickened, he described the cave as being too small to be of any use to smugglers, but he did so without giving away the ghastly secret it contained. He was lying again for Michelle's benefit, but he was positive it was justified in this case. He flipped the hair out of his eyes and picked up the clothes that he left piled on the sand.

"Why don't we try your suggestion and walk around the southern end of the island to return to the lifeboat rather than again making the trek through the forest?" Luis asked Michelle.

Michelle had been around Luis long enough to recognize the sudden change in his mood. He had been in high spirits before exploring the cave, but now his manner was subdued. She could not help but wonder why. He had reappeared just seconds before his two minutes were up, but he had not been breathing heavily as though he had barely escaped being trapped. He had not cut himself on the rocks. Something had happened, though, and she wished that he would confide in her. Again, she thought better of questioning him in front of his men.

Luis turned his back to Michelle as he pulled on his shirt and spoke in hushed Spanish to his crew, telling them of the skeleton in the cave. "Bury it and then catch up with us," he instructed. The men's eyes widened in alarm, but Luis nodded toward Michelle and they swiftly adopted his nonchalance. When he turned back to face her, Luis was smiling.

"This has been quite a day, hasn't it? You'll find our stay in Palma far more entertaining."

Hoping that touring Palma would not also provide mysteries he would not explain, Michelle waited patiently while Luis pulled on his boots. Once he was ready to go, she took his hand and they made their way over the slippery rocks surrounding the entrance to the cave. Luis shielded her body with his so that she was not drenched by the waves. When she glanced back and saw that his men weren't following, she drew his attention to it.

"Aren't they coming with us?"

"I told them to give us a minute," Luis hastened to explain. "Would you rather have their company than mine?"

Michelle waited until they had reached a stretch of sand where they could walk side by side to reply. "I wish that you'd stop teasing me like that. It isn't in the least bit amusing for you to suggest I might prefer the company of other men. It sounds as though you would be grateful if I did."

Luis laughed rather than take offense. "Forgive me," he begged. "I enjoy teasing you because it upsets you so, but that isn't very nice of me, is it?"

"No, it isn't nice at all."

"Then I'll try not to do it in the future."

"Can't you do better than to merely try?"

"No, that's all I can promise."

Exasperated with him, Michelle made the mistake of turning to look up at him and his smile was so charming that she could not even recall why she was miffed with him, let alone continue to complain. He had warned her that it would take time for them to become accustomed to each other. A formal courtship was designed to provide that time, but they had not had one. Less than a week had elapsed between the day they had met and the night they had married. Michelle took a deep breath and made a promise to herself to be more patient with Luis.

Luis was pleased by Michelle's shy smile and endeavored to keep the mood light by pointing out how the topography of the island had changed. Here

301

the bluff tapered down to the sea in a gentle incline and the sandy soil was dotted with dwarf palms whose stubby trunks supported graceful bursts of fronds. It was too late in the year for the wildflowers that blanketed Mallorca each spring to be in evidence, but there were aloe vera and other plants which remained green all year.

"My mother always had an aloe or two growing in our garden to use on cuts and burns," Luis explained. "She cultivates herbs for cooking rather than medicines, but she swears by the juice of the aloe. It's an attractive succulent, but I think our cuts and scrapes would have healed just as rapidly without her rubbing bits of aloe leaves on them."

"Oh but you're wrong," Michelle insisted, for her own mother had also believed in the plant's value. "The juice of the aloe vera really does hasten healing. What about your brother Daniel. Does he use it, too?"

Luis shrugged. "I've no idea. The next time I write to my family I'll make a point of asking for the physician's view if you like."

"Yes, please do." Michelle fell silent for a long moment, and then spoke her worries aloud. "I'll have to send a letter to my family as soon as we return to Valencia, but I don't know how I'll explain what's happened."

"I've already written to my parents, and while it wasn't easy, I'm relieved that it's done."

"What did you say?"

After a slight hesitation, Luis paraphrased the letter. "I said I'd gone to Madrid for La Infanta's wedding, met a very beautiful Frenchwoman, fought a duel for the privilege of marrying her, and had made her my wife."

Michelle just shook her head. "Thank you for the compliment, but while that's all true, it doesn't begin to tell the whole story."

302

"Are you in the habit of telling your mother everything you think and feel?"

"No, but—"

"It was the truth, Michelle. I may have put it more bluntly than you would, but it was still the truth."

"Yes, I'll not deny that, but perhaps there's a great deal more to my side of the story than yours."

"As long as you notify your family of our marriage, I'll not complain of the words you choose."

"How very generous of you."

"Yes, you'll find me a very generous husband."

Luis again flashed the disarming smile Michelle found so captivating. Her thoughts instantly turned to how they would spend the night rather than how she would communicate his presence in her life to her family. Embarrassed as well as excited by the direction her mind had taken, Michelle looked out to the sea.

They had reached the western side of the island where they had an excellent view of the *California* lying at anchor. The impressive ship was home for the time being and Michelle was surprised by how happy she was to see the vessel. Her spirits lifting, she revising her opinion and decided their visit to the island hadn't been nearly as disappointing as she had first thought.

"It's a shame there wasn't any treasure," she remarked wistfully.

Luis pulled her into his arms, and lifted her off her feet in an enthusiastic hug. "I've already got the only treasure I'll ever want right here."

Michelle knew he was just teasing her again, but it was still a wonderful sentiment to hear.

Luis's mood had merely been playful, but when Michelle relaxed in his embrace, he, too, began to wish that they were back on board the *California* where he could take the desire she aroused within him to its natural conclusion. For now, he had to settle for a lingering kiss, but its intoxicating sweetness held the promise of so much more.

Pablo Herrera and Norberto Macias had spent a far from diverting day polishing brass fittings and by the time the shore party returned they were looking forward to nightfall even more eagerly than Luis and Michelle. While the others on board had focused their attention on the island all day, they had kept a sharp watch for the *Salamander*'s sails. True to his word, Captain Ryde's vessel had appeared in late afternoon. After sailing close enough to identify the *California*, the ship had disappeared over the horizon, but neither Pablo nor Norberto doubted the sincerity of Captain Ryde's promise to rescue them.

To provide everyone with the opportunity to enjoy a leisurely dinner, Luis waited to give the order to get under way for Palma until the last of his crew had finished eating. The night was clear, the voyage an easy one, and he returned to his cabin confident he would awaken with Mallorca in sight. The fact that he would also have Michelle in his arms was an even better thought.

Rather than remain in borrowed clothing, Michelle had bathed before dinner and donned her only gown. She watched her husband closely as they dined, thinking each of his expressions provided its own special glimpse into his character. She became all the more convinced that something had occurred while he had investigated the cave, but she did not want to pry into matters he had chosen not to share.

Instead, she encouraged him to relate what he knew of the Balearic Islands' history and he proved to be surprisingly knowledgeable for a man born and raised in the New World. He traced successive occupations beginning with the Phoenicians. Hannibal had been born on Ibiza, but the Romans had taken over the islands from the Carthaginians. They were followed by the Vandals, a Germanic tribe, and then Arabs before Jaime I, of the kingdom of Aragon made them part of Spain. For most of the eighteenth century the islands, which were prized for their superb natural harbors, had belonged to England, but in 1802 a treaty had returned them to Spain.

"I'm afraid history is not something I've studied as carefully as I should," Michelle admitted.

"I had little choice," Luis revealed. "Despite the fact we have French blood, my father considers all his children Spaniards and he did not want anyone to consider us insufferably ignorant when we visited Spain."

"He sounds strict."

"Yes, he is, but he's also very wise." Luis kept glancing toward his bunk with a longing he hoped was not obvious, but once their dishes had been cleared away and they had taken a brief stroll around the deck, he could no longer keep his need for Michelle a secret. The visit to the island had not gone nearly as smoothly as he had planned, but as long as she was responding to him sweetly now, he vowed simply to make the best use of the night rather than fret over the problems they had encountered during the day.

Luis tempted Michelle with seductive kisses and she soon found herself lying naked in his arms. Convinced thought was unnecessary when he created such marvelous sensations with every touch and kiss, she ran her hands down his sides and then slowly up his back.

If it was wrong to have fallen in love with him so quickly, then she knew she would gladly pay the price . . . but she could never have imagined how high it would be.

Unmindful of how the amorous couple was passing the night, Pablo and Norberto were also busy. As soon as the last man not on duty had fallen asleep, they returned to the deck, drew their knives, and silently despatched each of the men standing watch. The helmsman was last, and they hurriedly tied down the wheel to keep the ship on a steady course rather than allow it to weave about wildly while they carried out the rest of Captain Ryde's plans. Next they closed each of the hatches so the smoke from the fires they were about to set on deck would not awaken anyone in time to extinguish them.

They used liberal amounts of the whale oil carried on board to fuel the lamps to ignite fires in the rigging. Shooting up the masts, flames had consumed the canvas sails within minutes and set the entire superstructure of the ship ablaze. The evil pair paused only long enough to set two of the lifeboats afire, and then they lowered the third over the side and began rowing with all their might. Confident Captain Ryde would see the glow in the night sky from the burning ship and come to their rescue, they were convulsed with laughter at how easily they had destroyed the *California* and ended the lives of all on board.

Eighteen

Her spirit borne aloft on passion's wings, Michelle
arched against Luis, drawing him ever deeper into
the spell of her fervent loving. She was a temptress
who fulfilled her every unspoken promise with seductive grace, deliberately provoking the most primitive of emotions and unleashing the wildness at the
core of his being. Responding eagerly, Luis became
possessive rather than gently adoring, and she rev-
eled in his ardor. This fierce loving was what she
had always craved and that Luis gave it so willingly
thrilled her clear to her soul.

The narrow bunk provided the perfect cocoon for
the amorous pair and neither strayed from the
other's arms. Time had dissolved into a meaningless
stream and went unnoticed in their desperate need
to join not only their physical beings but also their
immortal souls. Striving toward that sublime union,
their bodies throbbed with the beat of life, and their
devouring kisses were flavored with madness.

Lost in the rapture they created with such spectacular ease, their inner fire threatened to consume
them long before the rising temperature from the in-
ferno raging on deck finally caught their notice.
Norberto Macias had secured the shutters above the
skylight so that no trace of the bright blaze overhead
lit the cabin, but the fire was now blackening the
wooden slats and radiating its scorching heat

307

through the glass. Alarmed by the suddenly oppressive heat, Luis rolled over Michelle and left the bunk. He pulled on his pants and shoved his feet into his boots, but did not waste the time to don other apparel.

"Something's wrong!" he shouted as he rushed to the door. When the metal handle burned his hand, he knew there would be no time to investigate the trouble and return for Michelle. Fearing the worst, he removed the *California's* log from his desk.

"Get up, Michelle!" he instructed. "Put on the clothes you wore to the island and hurry."

Terrified as much by his manner as the unusual heat, Michelle leapt off the end of the bunk, fell, and then scrambled to her feet. The lamp burning near the door provided light enough for her to find the pants and shirt and she yanked them on without bothering with her silk lingerie. Because Luis thought boots necessary, she slipped into her borrowed pair before going to him.

Luis handed Michelle the ship's log to free his hands. He had wrapped a sock around the handle to protect himself from another burn, but the instant he gave it a turn the door was whipped out of his hand by a blistering wave of heat. Thrown back, he and Michelle fought to recover their balance, but in the next instant the overheated skylight shattered showering them both with jagged shards of glass. Michelle's shirt protected her skin, but Luis's bare shoulders were streaked with blood.

With no time to tend his numerous cuts, Luis shook off the glass splinters and took Michelle's hand in a desperate grasp. The companionway was filled with thick black smoke, but it was their only way out and he pulled her into it. He knew every inch of the *California* and it was that store of knowledge that served him well now. He prayed that when they reached the deck what appeared to be a hellish fire would not have already engulfed the entire ship.

Just as they reached the smoldering hatch, Encario Vega pulled it open. The noise as well as the heat of the fire rolled over them in a sickening wave, and while they could not hear the mate's frantic shouts above the din of the blaze, they already understood the dire nature of their plight. As they made their way out onto the deck, the flaming debris from the burning sails came raining down on them and Luis pulled Michelle close as he dodged it. He lost all hope of fighting the fire and, devastated by the fiery destruction of the beautiful ship, he dragged both Michelle and Encario toward the rail.

Twenty men were already in the water, while others were flinging themselves into the sea on the port side. Panicked by the fire, most had been unable to think past the point of fleeing it with all possible haste, but a few had had the presence of mind to heave overboard the wooden barrels stored on deck. Using them to remain afloat, they were slowly swimming in circles and calling out to their mates.

Luis looked back over his shoulder, saw the two lifeboats in flames, and grasped the slim hope the third might have been lowered over the side. Encario understood Luis's questioning glance and shook his head. He had been among the first to be awakened by the fire but that it had been deliberately set was a horror almost beyond his imagining.

"Gone!" he yelled. "Stolen by the bastards who did this! We found all the men on watch dead, and the two new men missing."

The mystery of how the *California* could have caught fire with such rapidity solved, Luis was still confounded as to *why.* Before he could question Encario, however, another flaming mass of canvas broke lose from the mizzenmast. Weighted by a

piece of the yard that had supported it, it struck
Luis a cruel blow on the right shoulder and whipped
across his face. His vision obscured, he had to fight
his way out from under the suffocating piece of fiery
sail. Although he freed himself in a matter of seconds, he had been badly burned before he could
fling it aside.

The situation now far too dangerous to risk remaining on board, Luis nonetheless asked for Encario's assurance that the crew had all abandoned ship.
When the mate gave it, Luis directed Michelle to remove her boots and he hurriedly yanked off his. Michelle was shaking so hard she could scarcely obey
her husband, but as soon as she had flung her boots
aside, he picked her up, and holding her clasped
tightly in his arms, leapt over the side.

Their plunge into the sea had been accomplished
before Michelle had had time to argue that she
could not swim, but the instant the water billowed
up over their heads she knew escaping a burning
ship only to drown in the Mediterranean was the
cruelest of all fates. Fighting to break free of Luis's
confining grasp, she battered him with the logbook,
but he stubbornly refused to release her.

A powerful swimmer, Luis burst through to the
surface with Michelle still clutched in his arms. He
hurriedly switched his hold to allow him to tread water with one arm as well as both legs, but her frightened squirming continued to undermine his valiant
efforts to save her. Encario dove into the water right
beside them, and as soon as he came to the surface,
Luis shouted to him to knock out the hysterical
young woman.

Although greatly hampered by the water, Encario
smacked the hardest punch he could throw into Michelle's chin. Her head snapped back and she went
limp, easing Luis's task considerably, and the mate

grabbed for the log before it slipped from her grasp. Holding it above the water, he swam toward a barrel floating by unattended and towed it back to Luis.

"Drape yourselves over this," he encouraged.

Grateful for Encario's help, Luis lifted Michelle onto the barrel first, then drew himself up by her side. Only their heads, shoulders, and arms were out of the water, but it was enough to ensure their survival for the time being. He and Encario steered the barrel toward the cluster of men bobbing about nearby, but desperate to float far enough away from the burning ship not to be sucked under when it went down, they were rapidly drifting away. One man saw them and pushed the barrel he had commandeered close enough for Encario to join him. The mate grabbed for the barrel, but turned back in a vain attempt to keep hold of Luis's makeshift raft.

A sudden shout went up from the embattled crew as, through the darkness, they spotted the gleam of white sails in the distance. Believing help was on the way and that they would soon be rescued, they waved and called excitedly. As naive as the others, Encario let go of Luis's barrel and turned his attention to the approaching ship. It wasn't until he glimpsed the faint outline of the missing lifeboat that he realized the danger to them wasn't past.

Luis saw the lifeboat, too, and while it served as incontrovertible proof that the two men in it must have set the fire, he strained to recognize the larger vessel. Seamen did not sabotage the ships on which they served without reason, and Luis strove to comprehend what that reason might be. The ship was now close enough to be identified as a schooner, and as Boris Ryde's name leapt to mind, Luis let out an anguished cry. Obviously the two new men had lied about serving aboard Portuguese ships, for they were nothing more than Boris Ryde's hired assassins.

Caring little what they might be called, Pablo and Norberto were elated when they reached the *Salamander*. They climbed up the rope ladder that had been lowered for them and left the desperately needed lifeboat from the *California* to drift free. Expecting praise, they were dismayed when Captain Ryde greeted them with an insolent sneer.

"Where's the treasure?" he demanded gruffly.

Pablo and Norberto drew closer together. "Nothing was found, so there was nothing to steal," Norberto explained with a helpless shrug.

Boris Ryde nodded, but clearly he was not pleased. He stepped to the rail, and kept watch with his crew until the *California*, still sending up bright plumes of flame, sank into the sea. "Well, at least you've done one thing well," he offered begrudgingly before issuing a crudely barked command changing their course. As soon as his crew had dispersed to their stations, he threw his arms around Pablo and Norberto.

"Is Augustín Aragon dead? Did you see him die?" he asked.

The two culprits exchanged a worried glance, but dared not lie. "He must have burned to death in his cabin," they proposed eagerly.

"But you're not sure?"

"You said only to set the ship ablaze while all on board slept, Captain. If Aragon and his wife did not burn to death, then they will soon drown."

Boris nodded as though he agreed, but he was anything but pleased. He hoped that Augustín and his bride had been reduced to powdery cinders floating in the air, or were choking on seawater at that very instant. But if by some miracle they survived the sinking of the *California*, he did not want them to be able to tie Pablo and Norberto's mischief to him.

He drew the villainous pair to the rail, and

pointed toward the spot where the pride of the Aragon Line had vanished. Waiting for further questions, the two seamen peered out into the darkness. They didn't hear Captain Ryde draw his knife, and before they realized their lives were in danger, he had slit their throats and tossed their bodies over the side.

Boris wiped the bloody blade on his pant leg, and looked up and down the deck. If any of his crew had seen what he had done, he knew they would not dare complain for fear of receiving the very same treatment themselves. He waited a moment, but relaxed when the challenge he had not really expected anyone to make went uncalled. Satisfied everything had gone as well as he could have hoped, he went to his cabin where he spent his most restful night in years.

Luis watched the *Salamander* disappear over the horizon and made a silent vow to see that Boris Ryde paid with his miserable life for what he had done. To sink the *California* and endanger the lives of all on board when Ryde's quarrel had been solely with him was such a cowardly act, Luis found it difficult to believe even Boris Ryde could sink to such abysmal depths. Luis had several incentives prodding him to survive, his lovely bride, a hardworking crew, and family honor being among them, but to take revenge on Boris Ryde would have been a sufficient inducement in itself.

Encario called to him, urging him to swim toward the others, but with the weight of Michelle's limp body creating a constant drag on the left side of the barrel and weakened by the wounds he had suffered, Luis was unable to reach them. He kept them in sight for a while and then struggled to remain within earshot, but gradually the others drifted away. All he could do then was pray that before sinking they had sailed far enough to be within the shipping lane between Ibiza and Mallorca and would be rescued shortly after dawn. Until then, all he could do was hang on and keep praying.

When Michelle first regained consciousness, the solidity of the barrel gave her courage, but she was completely disoriented, for it was impossible to discern where the horizon lay in the unbroken darkness. For all she knew, she and Luis could have been floating in the sky rather than the sparkling sea. She tried to touch down, to find solid ground she could follow to the shore, but the sea was much too deep to permit such an easy escape from their peril. Terrified anew, Michelle began to cry, but her husband had her hand tightly clasped in his and spoke as soon as he felt her stir.

"I know this isn't the way we'd have chosen to travel, but if you relax and just float, you'll save your strength and we can hang on until we're rescued."

Michelle dared not contemplate what would happen should they be unable to survive that long. She was gripping the barrel with a desperate clutch and did not understand how Luis could tell her to relax. As far as she was concerned, if they relaxed, they would soon be dead. "I had hoped for a happy life," she revealed between choked sobs.

"So did I," Luis agreed. "Now pretend that you're as light as a leaf being whisked along by a stream and just float. We might sight land at dawn. Don't lose hope. Now let's save our energy and stop talking."

Michelle understood the need to conserve energy, but she would have preferred to go on listening to the reassuring sound of Luis's voice. He was so con-

fident about their chances for rescue that she fought
to show the same courage. Her hair and clothes
soaked, she felt thoroughly miserable, but not nearly
so discouraged that she would abandon the effort to
survive. With the buoyant barrel doing most of the
work, she knew she could float indefinitely, but she
prayed they would be sighted and rescued just as
soon as the sun broke over the horizon.

Her jaw ached where Encario had hit her. While
she understood she had been too frightened to think
rationally and follow Luis's commands, she did not
believe she had deserved to be treated that harshly.
"We're going to die, aren't we?" she asked in a plaintive whisper.

"No, we're not," Luis insisted bravely. "Now, hush.
Just float and conserve your strength. Don't waste a
bit of it in worry."

Hungry for his warmth, Michelle drew closer to
Luis. The barrel was rough, while the sea was slick
and cool. Surrounded by strange sensations, it was
the darkness which terrified her most. She told herself again and again that she could hold on until
dawn. That's all she had to do, just float like a cork
until the sun lit the sky with its reassuring light.

"How long have we been in the water?" she asked.

"Too long," Luis replied. He was a strong swimmer and did not doubt that he could hang on until
help arrived, but he was deeply concerned about her.
She could not even swim and now her life depended
on her ability to remain calm enough to float until
they were rescued. "Try and sleep."

"Sleep? How?"

"Just rest your head against my shoulder and close
your eyes. It will help to make the night pass
quickly."

Michelle wasn't about to close her eyes when the
likelihood of drowning was so great. Instead, she

struggled to catch sight of the men, but other than the gentle lapping of the sea against their barrel, there wasn't so much as a whisper that she could have attributed to a human being. Luis's many years at sea might have prepared him for the horror of that night, but *she* felt totally defenseless.

"Have you ever been shipwrecked before?" she asked.

"No, and I don't intend to be ever again, either."

Luis had lost none of his cocky self-assurance and Michelle's admiration for him grew. *Just hold on,* she kept telling herself, *just hold on,* but it became increasingly difficult. By the time dawn began to lighten the eastern sky, her arms ached and her hands were cramped and cold. She raised up slightly, desperately eager to sight a ship coming their way, but they were surrounded by nothing more substantial than a blanket of mist and she lost the last bit of her optimism.

Luis had dozed fitfully during the night, but he was no more rested than Michelle. The right side of his face felt as though it had been burned to the bone and the saltwater stung his cuts. Without fresh water they would live no more than a day or two, and he scanned the sky hoping for rainclouds but saw only the fog that had confounded Michelle's gaze. He strained to hear the sound of waves crashing against an island shore, but the pervasive silence was unbroken.

"No one's coming," Michelle uttered fretfully.

"We'll all be drifting in the same direction," Luis explained. "The first men rescued will make certain the rest are found. All we have to do is hold on until that time comes."

Even with their arms entwined, Michelle doubted she could cling to the barrel much longer. Her legs were numb, her body sore, and her will to survive at a dangerously low ebb. The thought that both she and Antoine should die in such senseless fashions made their tragic love story complete, but she prayed that Luis would live to fulfill his destiny. She closed her eyes for what seemed like only an instant, but when she opened them, the sun was high overhead, the fog had all been burned away, and the sky was a taunting, crystal-clear blue.

Luis's eyes were closed, and for a few terrifying seconds she feared he was dead, but the pulse throbbing steadily in his throat allayed that suspicion. Surviving until dawn had been a hard-won goal, but now the sunny morning had arrived and there was still no hope of rescue, Michelle lost heart. What was the point of clinging to life for a few more hours, a day perhaps, another miserable night, if death was inescapable?

To simply let go of the barrel and spare herself that needless suffering became increasingly tempting. Sinking into the oblivion of the cool blue-green sea would be painless, and whatever struggle her weary body might attempt to make mercifully brief. All that was needed was the conscious decision to let go now, before fatigue made it impossible to endure another minute of this senseless torture.

Luis's fingers were laced in hers, so she could not slip away without his noticing, nor could she bear to bid him farewell. She knew he would not let her drown if he could possibly prevent it, but how long would he possess the strength to save them both? And didn't her survival endanger his? Noble questions came easily, but floating listlessly, Michelle was unable to choose death over life, and continued to drift wherever fate would take them.

Luis's thoughts were no less desperate, and only slightly more coherent than Michelle's. While mentally he was determined to survive, his body proved

317

far less staunch in its resolve. His face and shoulders ached with an unrelenting agony that kept him from sleeping for more than a few minutes at a time. He had also expected to see something at dawn, a tiny island like the one they had explored, a ship, at the very least some of his men who had also managed to survive the wretchedly long night.

To be mocked by the indifferent dawn was the final insult and he gritted his teeth and fought to hang on. One hour passed in silent torment, perhaps two, and Luis began to fear his mind would fail him before his body lost the ability to cling to life. He began to see strange creatures floating by. They were hideous monsters with mouths agape showing angled rows of razor-sharp teeth. He flinched as one unfurled a snakelike neck and snapped at him. He knew only his imagination could conjure up such dreadful beasts, but that comforting thought made them no less terrifying.

Michelle saw nothing but the endless expanse of sea until the sun dipped low in the sky. Then she caught sight of a lifeboat drifting parallel to them. She raised up slightly, longing to see someone waving, but the boat was as empty as her store of hopes. Dazed, she could see no value in sighting an empty boat, but thought the occurrence merited mentioning to Luis. She squeezed his hand to get his attention.

"There's a boat!" she called.

The word *boat* tore Luis from his frightening daydreams and he turned to survey the sea. When he saw the lifeboat, he let out a hoarse whoop of joy. It was no more than ten yards away, and offered far more in the way of comfort and shelter than their barrel. The question was, did he still possess the strength to swim to it? Michelle's wan smile was enough to inspire him to try.

"Stay here," he urged. "I'll get the boat and come back for you."

"No, don't leave me," Michelle begged. "Please don't."

"I won't be gone more than a few minutes," Luis coaxed. "You'll be fine."

Michelle felt as bedraggled as she knew she must look. "No, you mustn't leave me."

"We can rest in the boat," Luis argued persuasively. "Now keep your eyes on me. Watch me swim over to the boat and then I'll come right back to get you."

"No," Michelle whimpered.

Unwilling to waste what little strength he had in arguing with her, Luis leaned over to give her a kiss. Her lips were icy cold, and knowing that he was only hours away from kissing a corpse, he gathered the courage to fight for both their lives. "This is our only chance," he assured her, and then before she could reach out and grab ahold of him, he pushed away from the barrel and started swimming for the boat. A powerful swimmer, he should have been able to reach it in a dozen strokes, but he was so tired and slow that the distance separating them from the lifeboat seemed to stretch on into eternity.

Finally he had to roll over on his back and just float in an effort to catch his breath. When he looked up, he was alarmed that the lifeboat was no closer than when he had begun, and worse yet, he saw Michelle and the barrel drifting away. She was just watching him, too terrified to call out to him or cry but still he felt her fear in the constant pain of his weary muscles. He couldn't leave Michelle, not like this, and he began to swim again with the long, lazy stroke that was all he could manage.

When his outstretched fingers finally scraped against the boat, he shook the water from his hair and grabbed for the side. As weak as he was, he needed several tries before he succeeded in hauling himself out of the water, but once inside the boat, he knew the exertion had been worth it. He waved to Michelle, and picking up the oars neither Pablo nor Norberto had thought to pitch overboard, he began to row the lifeboat back to his bride.

Exhausted, Michelle wept when Luis pulled her into the lifeboat. He eased himself off the center seat, and using it for a backrest, sat in the bottom of the boat and cradled Michelle in his lap. He patted her tangled hair and mumbled a string of encouraging, if unconvincing thoughts. There was some water in the bottom of the boat, but they were still far drier than they had been when hanging on to the barrel.

"Go to sleep," Luis suggested in a soothing whisper. "Next time you wake, we'll be out of danger."

Michelle let her head flop against his shoulder as though she believed his comforting lies, but she had lost all hope of rescue and doubted that either of them would ever awaken again. She had not had the opportunity to live the tranquil life she had planned, but even with death near, she loved Luis with all her heart and did not regret a moment they had shared.

They slept the rest of that day and well into the next when a squall overtook them and drenched them with warm rain. Aroused from their stupor, they sat up and drank in the moisture eagerly until neither could swallow another drop of it. The sky remained dark even after the squall had passed and, unsure of how long they had been adrift, they again fell asleep with nothing more than hope to sustain them.

The next time Michelle awoke she was stiff and

sore. Blinded by the brightness of the new day she sat up and shielded her eyes with her hand. Something had changed, but it was not until she saw the breakers in the distance that she recognized their welcome sound. She grabbed ahold of Luis and shook him hard.

"Wake up! There's land ahead!"

Luis's head rolled loose on his shoulders and, terrified that he had died while she slept, Michelle lay her head on his chest. She heard his heart beating steadily, but it sounded faint and slow. "Wake up!" she screamed and this time her shrill cry prompted him to open his eyes though there was no glimmer of recognition in his glance.

"Look, there's an island just ahead. We've got to reach it!"

Luis tried to sit up, but his arms were not equal to the task and he slid right back down into the bottom of the boat. He was drained of all energy and he could not comprehend how Michelle had retained the stamina to shriek at him. He flopped a hand over his ear in a futile attempt to shut out the strident sound of her voice.

Michelle had been on Luis's left while they had floated on the barrel, and even after they had entered the boat she had been too weak to notice his burns. Now he was stretched out on his left side and what she saw turned her stomach. Not only had his eyebrow and lashes been singed, the whole right side of his face had been marked by the flames. If that were not enough, he had so many deep cuts on his shoulders that he appeared to have been flayed by some demented torturer.

Michelle had not dreamed that he had been hurt so badly and, ashamed of that oversight, she made no further attempt to wake him. Instead, she grabbed ahold of the sides of the lifeboat and prayed it would float up on the beach rather than glide by the island refuge. They were so close, and she couldn't bear to think they might miss their chance for survival because of a fickle change in current. When it appeared that was precisely what was going to happen, she grabbed the oars and struggled to make them work in unison.

Her efforts were so clumsy that the boat lurched and spun rather than following a straight course for the shore. Tears poured down her cheeks as she called upon the last of her resources to steer the boat. When it finally broke through the breakers, she had been adrift too long to worry about drowning and climbed over the side into the surf. She pushed and shoved the lifeboat, fell facedown into the water more than once but finally succeeded in bringing it up on the beach.

She turned her attentions to Luis then. "Come," she coaxed. "You've got to get out of the boat. If we leave it here, it will surely float out with the next high tide. Come, please."

More annoyed than inspired by her insistent prodding, Luis finally gathered himself up into a crouch. He looked over the side of the lifeboat with a vacant gaze, but gradually his mind cleared enough for him to make out the dwarf palms growing near the cliffs. Trees meant land, and he dimly recalled that they had been searching for land. This was good news then, but his face refused to display the smile he felt inside.

He reached out a shaking hand for Michelle and with her help pulled himself out of the boat, but then his legs gave way and he collapsed on the sand. The waves were still lapping at his feet and he tried to crawl out of the sea's reach. He could hear Michelle pleading with him to get up, but he was spent, unable to move. He just wanted to be left alone to die in peace, but Michelle had never made his life easy, and his last thought before he slipped into unconsciousness was that she had fought him all the way to the grave.

Nineteen

Michelle knelt by Luis's side, cajoling, coaxing, urging, pleading, finally tearfully begging him to wake, but all to no avail. She feared Luis was going to remain unconscious for a long while. She hurriedly scanned the beach, searching for something, anything, she might use to enable her to move him. All she saw were the dwarf palms. Their wide fronds were waving gently in the breeze and, presented with no other alternative, she withdrew the knife from the sheath at Luis's belt and went to cut some of them.

Thinking it fortunate the palms were stubby rather than of majestic height, she hacked away three of the broad, fan-shaped leaves and returned to Luis. She stuck the knife in the sand, then spread out the fronds beside him. She knew he was much too heavy for her to be able to lift and carry him away from the water's edge, but she thought with his weight cushioned by the smooth fronds she just might be able to tow him to higher ground.

Taking care not to grind sand into the cuts on his shoulders, she eased him over onto the fronds. Apparently lost in peaceful dreams, Luis looked perfectly content to be treated like an oversize doll, but Michelle cursed and hissed as she tugged on the ends of the fronds and scooted him inch by tortuous inch all the way up to the curving line of palms where he could sleep in the shade. She then sat down beside him and rested her elbows on her knees while she caught her breath. Her arms and back ached with the strain of moving him, but she considered herself in excellent condition when compared to Luis.

Just looking at him hurt. He was such a handsome man that she could not bear the thought his looks might be permanently marred. She glanced up and down the beach, hoping there might be some aloes growing nearby, but the dwarf palms provided the only foliage in sight. Michelle pushed herself to her feet. She placed her hands in the small of her back and massaged it lightly as she turned to look up at the bluff. This island was remarkably similar to the one she and Luis had explored, but it wasn't that same small isle.

There were pine trees atop the bluff, and she realized it could be reached by walking up a gradual incline. Michelle left Luis to his dreams and made her way up to the plateau in search of the medicinal plant. From there she had a clear view for miles in all directions but the vastness of the sea was unbroken. If ships routinely passed that way, none was en route now. Desperately disappointed to find their isolation unbroken, Michelle turned her attention to the island. From her vantage point, it appeared long and narrow, with a dense stand of pine in the center. Both sandy beaches and rocky coves dotted the perimeter.

It wasn't topography that interested her, however. All she wanted were a few aloe plants whose leaves could be used to soothe Luis's wounds. Positive the valuable succulent had to be growing wild somewhere up there, she returned to the beach and picked up Luis's knife. Before leaving him, she tried to think of everything they could possibly need so she would not thoughtlessly walk right past something she would have to fetch later. A glance at the surf brought fresh water to mind, but she had scant hope of finding a spring. Even if she did, she would be unable to carry the water back to Luis.

"Am I being very foolish?" she asked the sleeping man. "Is it water we need rather than aloes?"

Not really expecting a response from Luis, Michelle turned away without waiting for one. She started off toward the southern end of the island and said a brief prayer of thanksgiving each time her feet touched the sand. They were out of the water, which was the first step toward rescue, and she tried to be grateful for that fact rather than feel bitter that they had washed up on a remote isle where surviving would call for not only strength but vast amounts of resourcefulness. More tired than she had realized, she had to stop often to rest, but the knowledge that there was no one but her to aid Luis kept her searching long after she might have quit.

By the time she finally located a clump of the medicinal plant, she felt completely drained and had to stretch out in the sand for a brief nap to gather the strength to return to Luis. Her need for fresh water was becoming acute. While they had clung to the barrel, she had been too badly frightened to be hungry, but now her stomach was rumbling noisily and she knew food was another necessity she would have to provide. Surrounded by the sea, fish ought to be plentiful, but how was she to catch any? Even if she did, how could she cook them with no way to build a fire?

There was simply far too much to do and with no one to do it all but her, Michelle grew horribly discouraged. She was positive Luis would know exactly how to survive on the island indefinitely, but he was unable to even moan, much less provide the practical advice she so desperately needed. She felt guilty taking even a minute of her time for a nap, but when she awakened, the sun was low in the sky and she feared she had slept the whole day away.

She cut several of the aloe's long, tapering leaves, and walking at a slow but steady pace, returned to Luis before nightfall. He did not appear to have moved in her absence. As Michelle slit the aloe and rubbed the juicy pulp on his cuts and burns, she doubted that he would thank her for preserving his looks if she allowed him to perish from thirst or hunger. Certain she had wasted too many valuable hours, she began to cry, but just as quickly convinced herself she had no time for such silly regrets and dried her tears.

The tide was coming in, and worried the lifeboat might be lost, she did her best to drag it farther up on the beach. She had watched six men carry an identical boat as though its weight were slight, but on her own, it was a cumbersome chore to shove it even a foot. Feeling very small and weak, she returned to Luis's side, lay down beside him, and took his hand.

"You'll be fine tomorrow," she told him. "You can help me find water and something good to eat. We can get through this together. I just know that we can." Her words sounded convincing, but Michelle did not really believe such optimism was warranted. She fell into a fitful sleep and dreamed their island sanctuary was flooded at high tide and they were again adrift on the brutally unforgiving sea.

Luis awakened first the next morning. His mouth was uncomfortably dry, but he was so thrilled to discover they were on dry land, he discounted that

327

complaint as minor. Michelle was snuggled against him, her expression one of childlike sweetness and he reached out to caress her cheek.

"Querida?" he whispered.

Michelle fought her way up through successive waves of exhaustion to respond. She opened her eyes, and did her best to smile. "We need to find fresh water," she announced as though she had dozed off in midsentence before making that point in conversation.

"Good plan," Luis agreed, but he did not really feel up to making such a search. "Is this our island?"

"No, this one is smaller," Michelle explained. "It has the same pine-covered bluff and rocky coves, but it's not the same one."

She pushed herself into a sitting position and swept her hair out of her eyes. Her usually glossy curls were stiff and dull from the salty sea but she was too distraught to care. "We'll need to catch fish for food. We can cut poles from tree limbs, perhaps tie bits of cloth from my shirt together for a line, but what can we use for hooks?"

Luis had not suspected Michelle possessed such a practical nature, but he was grateful that she was thinking about how to help them survive rather than weeping dejectedly over that challenge. Her chin was bruised where Encario had struck her. While he was sincerely sorry about that, he chose to follow her conversational lead rather than apologize.

"We won't need hooks," he contradicted. "We can sharpen the ends of some branches to make spears and catch fish." But when he attempted to sit up, he was so dizzy he knew he would not be able to stand, let alone fish. Michelle reached out to help him, but he waved her away.

"Just let me rest a little longer. I'll be fine."

Luis could not see how bad he looked, but Michelle certainly could and doubted he would be feeling better anytime soon. "I'll put some more aloe on your cuts and burns. Then I'll fashion that spear and fetch something for breakfast. You needn't do anything but rest while I'm gone."

Unwilling to depend on a small, slight woman, Luis started to argue, but he swiftly discovered he lacked the energy to raise his voice sufficiently to sound convincing. "I'll be fine in a while," he promised weakly.

"Of course you will," Michelle agreed. She took special care to smear a thick coating of aloe on his face before she treated his shoulder and arm. "Later you can help me with the boat. We could use it to form one side of a house, or we could simply leave it as it is to catch rainwater whenever it falls."

"We'll not need a house," Luis murmured. "We'll be rescued soon."

"Yes, I hope so, too," Michelle agreed, but she still thought they ought to take good care of themselves while they were waiting. She rubbed the last of the aloe into Luis's skin and then picked up his knife. "I'm taking this to make a spear. Is there some trick to catching fish this way?"

"Yes," Luis struggled to reveal. "Go out into the water, stand very still, and before long the fish will swim right up to you. You must spear them in one quick thrust or they'll be gone. Don't try and chase them through the tide pools. Just stand and wait for them to come to you."

Michelle bent down to kiss him goodbye, and she hurried away before he saw the tears in her eyes. She had expected him to have regained his strength when he awakened. To see him still in such a pathetic state unnerved her completely. She knew he would never get better if she didn't provide them with something to eat, but it was difficult to concentrate on that goal when she was so worried about her new husband

Luis's knife was very sharp, so after Michelle had mounted the bluff and broken a dead limb from a pine, it did not take her long to whittle the tip into a sharp point. She then made a few practice jabs, and swiftly discovered how easily she might lunge for a fish and stab herself in the foot. With poor Luis too weak to stand, she dared not allow that to happen, but it was a frightening prospect all the same.

Determined to provide a meal for them, she returned to the beach, and after trying several locations without success, walked out on a rocky point. Here she could see down into the water without standing in it, and, encouraged, she bent down and waited for a fish to appear. After a few minutes, a flash of silvery scales caught her eye, but rather than stretch beyond what she could comfortably reach, she followed Luis's advice and remained still. Unmindful of the danger overhead, the fish continued its languid perusal of the rocky shore until with one quick stroke Michelle brought its life to an abrupt end.

Elated by her success, she carried the fish back to Luis. "We'll need to build a fire," she suggested.

"There's very little difference between the taste of fish that is cooked and that eaten raw," Luis explained. "Clean and fillet it, and we'll eat it just as it is."

Michelle could not imagine a more nauseating thought. "You can't mean that!"

Luis squinted against the sun. "I'll build a fire for you tomorrow, or the next day at the latest, but right now, we'll have to eat the fish raw. It will contain more moisture that way anyway and that's precisely what we need."

Michelle had impaled the fish with a primitive

hunter's jubilant delight, but gutting it and preparing fillets presented another challenge entirely. "Could *you* possibly clean the fish?" she asked shyly.

"I would do it gladly if I could walk down to the water, but I can't. You'll have to do it yourself, Michelle. Just slit the belly from the tail to the gills and rinse it out."

Thoroughly disgusted by that prospect, Michelle nevertheless walked down to the water. After a brief hesitation in which she told herself she would either learn how to clean fish or starve to death, she bravely yanked the dead fish off the tip of the spear and followed Luis's directions. The instant that disagreeable chore was finished, she walked back to him.

"You'll have to fillet it. I'm afraid I'll just cut it to ribbons."

Luis tried to sit up, failed, and then compromised by turning on his left side and propping himself up on his elbow. "Get me a palm frond to use as a platter and I'll do my best," he offered.

Michelle provided the frond, but she couldn't watch him work on the fish. She knew she was being impossibly foolish, but telling herself that didn't stop the queasiness she had felt ever since he had made it plain they would have to eat the fish raw. "Perhaps I should try and catch more."

"Yes, you should, but first let's eat this one."

"I wish there were some fruit trees on this island," she mused wistfully, longing for anything other than raw fish.

"We'll have to come back and plant some."

"Once we get off this island, I'm never coming back!"

While it wasn't polite, Luis was certain he would have to take the first bite of fish, and did so. "This is delicious. Sit down and have some."

331

Michelle bent down on one knee, ready to bolt at the slightest provocation. She wondered what other indignities they would have to suffer and feared nothing could be worse than this. "Maybe I just didn't look hard enough," she blurted out suddenly. "Maybe there's something good to eat growing here and I just didn't see it."

"Close your eyes and open your mouth," Luis ordered. When she complied with a terrified grimace, he plopped a tiny bite of fish into her mouth. "Now, chew."

Michelle gave only a tentative munch, but surprised by the mild taste of the fish, she opened her eyes and swallowed it without gagging. "That wasn't nearly as awful as I'd thought it would be."

"It's a lot like being married to me then, isn't it?"

That he would tease her about such an important thing dismayed Michelle, but delighted that he felt well enough to make jokes, she rose to her feet. "You finish that one. I'll go and get us a few more."

"Wait!" Luis called. "Take what we can't eat and toss it out to sea. It will help to keep our camp clean."

Embarrassed that she had neglected such an obvious chore, Michelle waited while Luis tore off a piece of palm frond to wrap the fish's head, bones, and tail. He made a neat package of it, and when she reached the water, she flung it out as far as she could where the scraps would nourish the creatures who lived in the deep.

Luis remained on his side so he could watch Michelle fish. Dressed in men's clothes she still looked ridiculous to him, and yet for some inexplicable reason, she had never been more alluring. Too weak to act on the impulses the mere sight of her brought, Luis concentrated on eating the fish, but he was in a great hurry to get well. It wasn't until he had taken the edge off his hunger with the last bite of fish that he noticed his arm and he was sickened by the gruesome sight of the red and blistered flesh. He was certain his face must look even worse.

Beginning with his throat, he traced the growth of his beard upward toward his right cheek, but when that became too painful he let his hand drop. He was glad there was still some skin left on his face, but he had seen people who had been severely burned and feared he would suffer the same disfiguring scars.

Unlike Antoine Lareau, he had never dwelt on the fact he was handsome. It was simply a fact, like having brown eyes. What if his burns were so severe that now all he could expect were mournful, pitying glances rather than boldly admiring ones? he worried. He raised his hand to his temple and combed his fingers through his hair. While he could feel a few frizzled ends where the flames had licked at his scalp, he was relieved to discover he still had a full head of hair, but that wasn't nearly enough to lift his spirits.

Slumping back down on the sand, he let his imagination entertain him for a few minutes, conjuring up tortures for Boris Ryde that would truly punish him for the agony he had caused him and his crew. There was also Michelle to consider. She was a delicate beauty who could easily have succumbed to the horrors of being lost at sea. Perhaps setting Boris adrift would be the most appropriate punishment, but that image failed to provide Luis with the satisfaction he sought by witnessing the villain's final agony.

When Michelle returned with two more fish, which she had cleaned without prompting from him, Luis provided her with a brief lesson in how to fillet them as he worked. He then cut the fillets into bite-size pieces. He waited until she had taken several bites before he broached the painful subject of his appearance.

"If my face is burned as badly as my arm, I'm surprised that you can bear to eat with me," he remarked in a deceptively offhand manner.

"Neither of us is at our best," Michelle assured him. "But we've too many truly desperate problems to worry over something as trivial as our respective appearances."

"Trivial!" Luis gasped. "I've been horribly disfigured and you regard it as trivial?"

Astonished by his outburst, Michelle stared at him for a long moment before replying. "I'm sorry. You tease me so often that I didn't realize you were serious when you mentioned your appearance. Your burns will soon heal. You've not been disfigured. Don't even imagine that's what's happened."

While her calm manner was persuasive, Luis didn't believe a word she said. "Well, perhaps it is too early to judge how I'll look," he offered grudgingly, "but I doubt anyone will describe me as handsome ever again."

"I will," Michelle insisted.

Luis's glance turned insolent. "Don't patronize me, Michelle. Things are bad enough without your resorting to flattering lies."

Deeply insulted, Michelle reached for the knife before she got to her feet. "Take a nap," she suggested flippantly. "Better yet, sleep until you can be better company for me. I'm going to go look for fresh water."

"Michelle, come back here!" Luis called, but the proud French beauty kept right on walking, making him feel all the more helpless and abused. He watched her make her way up to the bluff and cursed the fact he could not even crawl across the sand, let alone follow her.

"Damn!" He lay back down, frustrated that he could not do his share of the work. Michelle wasn't used to such primitive conditions and that he had gotten her into such a dreadful mess pained him deeply. It would be up to him to see that she did not suffer one second longer than necessary before they were rescued.

He wondered what had happened to Encario and the others. Were they scattered about on islands no bigger than this one? If so, how many days might pass before the first rescue led to others? Tortured by dark thoughts, Luis fell asleep, but when he awakened, Michelle had not returned and he could not blame her for staying away if he looked even half as disfigured as he feared.

Michelle lost track of time as she combed the island for fresh water. The presence of the pine trees provided ample evidence of its existence, but she feared underground springs might run too deep for her to reach them without digging a well. She knew she wasn't nearly strong enough to attempt such an ambitious project and kept looking for any sign of moisture that might indicate a subterranean spring.

It was midafternoon before she noticed a thick bed of grass bordering the cliffs on the southern end of the island.

She bent down and looked over, hoping for a glimpse of a spectacular waterfall, but only a thin stream of water dripped down the limestone. It *was* water, however, but it could not have been in a more inaccessible location. Discouraged rather than elated, Michelle moved away from the cliff to the pines. She broke off a dead bough, sharpened the end with the knife to fashion a digging stick identical to her fishing spear, and began to dig at the edge of the grass.

The rocky soil was muddy, and she did not have to dig deeply before the hole began to fill with water.

She waited patiently for the silt to settle to the bottom and then leaned down to take a sip of the water. It was colder than she had expected, but quite good. She then stepped back and tried to judge how wide and deep an area she would have to excavate to provide them with sufficient water. A bubbling stream was what she had hoped to find, not merely a trickle of water that would provide a week's worth of backbreaking work to tap.

Recalling the hole the men had dug in their attempt to find buried treasure, Michelle decided that if she was going to have to dig for water, she would be smart to do it in the sand rather than on this rocky bluff. Water was water, after all, and a well on the beach would be far handier than one here. Disgusted that the day had passed without her providing any water at all, Michelle carried the digging stick along with Luis's knife and returned to the beach.

"I'll try and catch more fish for supper," Michelle called out as she walked past Luis.

Gathering all his strength, Luis managed to sit up, but he took no pleasure in such a feeble accomplishment. Michelle had been gone so long he had begun to fear she was never coming back. Now that she had, he was at a loss as to what to say. There were so many things that they needed and lacked that he scarcely knew where to begin. He had promised to build a fire, and while that was not an impossible task, he did not feel ready for that yet. Thinking that Michelle might not feel ready for what she was doing, either, he tried to stand, but the same dizziness that had wrecked that plan the last time he had tried it struck again.

Thoroughly dejected, he sat and waited for Michelle to bring him some more fish for supper. He wasn't hungry, but knew he had to eat if he ever wanted to get better. This was not the first time he had faced life-threatening difficulties, but in the past, he had been at the peak of his abilities. Now he was as weak as a newborn babe.

When Michelle finally brought him five fish to fillet, he tried to smile. "At least the fish are plentiful here," he commented slyly, "but they don't provide much in the way of variety. Maybe I can catch us some crabs in a day or two."

"I'm not eating a raw crab, Luis. That's completely out of the question."

"No, I told you I'd build us a fire and I will. We can steam the crabs. They'll be as delicious as they are in Valencia."

Michelle sank into a cross-legged pose as she watched Luis fillet the fish. Because he seemed bent on ignoring their earlier argument, she did, too. She described the one pitiful source of water that she had found and asked his advice about digging a well on the beach. "Was it fresh water that seeped into the hole your men dug on the other island?" she asked.

"I doubt it."

"Well then, there's no point in digging a well if all we'll hit is the sea."

"I agree. Give me another day or two and I'll help you look. We might find a cave with a source of fresh water. That's a possibility."

Michelle didn't want to think about caves, which she imagined as being as damp and forbidding as death. "Maybe you ought to teach me to swim before we explore any caves. Not that I've seen any, but I spent the day up on the bluff. Tomorrow I'll follow the beach all the way around the island and search for caves."

Luis finished slicing the fish and slid half over to

337

Michelle. *"Bon appétit,"* he teased. "That's a good idea. We'll know this lump of limestone better than the gulls in a few days. If there's anything here, we're sure to find it."

Michelle wondered at his choice of pronoun since she was the one doing all the work. At least he seemed in better spirits. It was not his fault that he had been burned, but she did think he was to blame for the way he was taking it. With no mirrors on the island to confirm her reports, she wondered if he would continue to doubt her word. She certainly hoped not, but knowing what a stubborn man Luis could be, she feared she might never overcome his doubts. She did believe they would be rescued some-day, but until then, she feared she and Luis might not get along any better than they had in Madrid.

Unwilling to risk being called a liar again, she made no comment at all on his injuries. She insisted upon smoothing a fresh aloe leaf over his burns be-fore he went to sleep, but she could tell by his skep-tical glance that he had no faith in her remedy. Too tired to praise its beneficial properties, she again lay down beside him and fell asleep worrying that she had merely wasted the day.

While Michelle had ignored the shrill cries of the gulls that slowly circled the island the previous day, their frenzied calls startled her awake shortly after dawn. The birds dipped and dived over the water, snatching up fish with an enviable ease. Michelle could not help but wonder if seagulls tasted as good as chicken. She decided quickly she did not care how they tasted. They would provide a welcome change from raw fish even if they were tough and stringy.

The ambitious birds had not disturbed Luis's

sleep, and Michelle saw no reason to wake him, either. Fearing it would be several days before he could help her search for caves containing fresh water, she decided to do some preliminary scouting on her own. If water trickled down the southern face of the cliffs, that would be a good place to start, she concluded, and, taking only her digging stick, she headed off in that direction.

Then she wondered if she shouldn't have first gone up on the bluff to look for a ship. But what if she actually saw one? she agonized. How would she be able to signal their plight? Luis had promised to build a fire, but as yet they did not have wood gathered to ignite as a beacon. That was another chore to which she would have to attend.

Frantic with worry, Michelle missed the narrow opening to the cave the first time she passed it. It wasn't until she made a more diligent search of the rocky face of the cliff that she noticed a suspicious shadow. Intrigued, she climbed over the rocks to scale the steep incline. When she reached the cleft, she hung back, not eager to explore on her own. Then she heard something. At first she feared it was only the echo of the sea bouncing off the rocks, but what if it were fresh water bubbling just inside the cave's eerie entrance?

Michelle took a deep breath and then squeezed between the rocks and peered into the darkness. The sound of water rushing by was much too loud now to be no more than an echo and, driven by thirst, Michelle inched her way into what she hoped would be a massive cavern overflowing with the most delicious water she had ever tasted. Desperate for a drink, she took another step, and when the limestone beneath her feet crumbled away, she was plunged into a deep pool that contained enough fresh water to see to her needs for a lifetime.

She fought her way to the surface and reached out for the rocks that she knew had to surround her, but in the darkness her fingertips missed them by mere inches. She thought of Luis sleeping on the beach. He would awaken to find her gone and, too weak to care for himself, he might also perish. Infuriated by that terrifying possibility, she kicked her feet and flailed her arms with sufficient force to propel herself into the rocks she had missed just seconds before.

Their edges had been worn smooth by the water, but she held on with a frantic grasp and knew if she just remained calm, she could survive long enough to find a way to escape the cave's watery grip. The narrow beam of light coming from the entrance gave her courage, but it seemed an awfully long way away. She forced herself to breathe deeply and prayed that when her eyes adjusted to the darkness, she would be able to get herself out of this predicament. This time, Luis was not there to help her.

Twenty

A cloud of persistent gnats teased Luis awake, and infuriated by their annoying presence, he batted them away with a fierce swipe. His blow parted the thick stream of tiny insects, but they immediately regrouped and continued to circle his head in close formation. Outraged at having his sleep disturbed by such insignificant bugs it took a score of them to be noticed, Luis continued to swing at them until he had dispersed them so many times they grew bored with their assault and flew on down the beach.

He was then too wide awake to get back to sleep, and looking up at the sun, judged the time as midmorning. He was embarrassed to have slept so late. He looked around for Michelle, and when he did not see her down by the water fishing for their breakfast, he was at first perplexed and then concerned.

He had made an attempt, though perhaps a halfhearted one, to be more cheerful at supper, but he could not blame her if she was still angry with him. Although he thought she should be more understanding, he honestly did not know what his reaction would be had she been the one to have sustained the burn. Thinking he might have been just as quick to reassure her that she would soon look her best, he knew he should not have criticized her so harshly, since she was just trying to make him feel better.

341

None of her encouraging words would lessen the severity of his scars, however. He wanted her to realize that right now so she would not waste any more of his time and her breath providing optimistic assurances that would only aggravate his eventual disappointment when he got off the island and found her observations weren't true.

Lost in his own despair, a long while passed before Luis noticed that the spear Michelle had used for fishing was lying right where she had left it. His knife was there, too. Where had the woman gone? She knew he was too weak to fish for himself. How could she have gone off and left him without a morsel of food? Was she even more angry with him than he had imagined? Did she intend to ignore him all day just for spite?

He had not thought Michelle would stoop to such a childish ploy, but as the day wore on and she did not appear, that seemed like the most likely possibility.

Finally Luis's hunger prompted him to attempt to go fishing on his own. He was lying close enough to a palm to use its trunk to help him rise, but then he was so far from steady that he had to ease himself back down into the sand.

If he didn't eat, he wouldn't regain the strength required to stand, but if he couldn't stand, how could he catch something to eat? Clamping the fishing spear between his teeth, he started off for the water on his hands and knees. He felt absolutely ridiculous, but eventually he reached the shore. Then he realized how foolish he had been, for he couldn't wade out into the water, and the fish were unlikely to flop up on the dry sand.

He sent a longing glance toward the rocky point where Michelle had had such success, but he doubted he could reach it. It would be agonizing to attempt to crawl over the rocks, and walking was out of the question. Even if he did succeed in pulling himself upright, the sea made the rocks treacherous for a sure-footed man. For him, they would swiftly prove disastrous and he dared not risk a serious fall.

Discouraged, he watched the gulls circling overhead. He had never tasted seagull, and felt certain that if they were at all palatable, he would have been served one at some point. There was an enormous difference between savoring a food and escaping starvation, however.

Luis reached into his hip pocket and withdrew his handkerchief. He folded it in half on the diagonal and then knotted the two opposite ends to form a slingshot. He crawled over to the rocks to find stones of the appropriate size, and once armed, let a stone fly toward the ever-present gulls. The stone arched high into the air but only ruffled the tail feathers on one gull before falling harmlessly into the sea.

Luis now realized he was going to have to take more careful aim. He needed not only to hit a gull, but to do so over the sand so the bird would not plunge into the water and float away out of reach. He grabbed another stone and waited for a gull to glide by overhead. While killing seagulls with stones might prove damn near impossible to do, he was positive it was preferable to waiting for Michelle to reappear and having nothing to show for his time.

When Michelle's eyes first adjusted to the darkness, the slippery walls of the cave looked too sheer to scale, but she refused to accept that preliminary observation as the final one. She moved her left hand over the rocks seeking a new place to hold while still hanging on with her right. When that tactic failed to produce a way out of the water, she held on with her left hand and felt along the adjoining rocks with her right. She had better luck on that side, and pulling herself over, attempted to convince herself that moving sideways was almost as good as moving up.

Trying not to think of the sea creatures that might be occupying the indentations in the rocks, she felt for toeholds, too. Determined to get out, she pulled herself over the rocks, exploring each dip and recess in the cave until she finally found a ledge that did not extend so far out over the water that she could not pull herself up on it. From there, the entrance to the cave could be reached by a precarious stretch that very nearly landed her back in the water before she got a good hold on a solid piece of limestone.

Now aware of how easily the porous rock could crumble, she drew herself up slowly. Each torturous inch was a hard-won victory, and when she finally lurched out into the sunshine, she was too tired to be pleased by her accomplishment. She sat outside the cave for a long while, gathering her composure and waiting for her hair and clothes to dry before making the short trek back to Luis. She did not know how many hours she had been imprisoned in the cave, but she at least had the satisfaction of knowing she had found a plentiful source of fresh water.

What she needed now was a bucket to carry some back to her husband, but she had no idea how to go about making one. Wood was in abundant supply, but what could they use to hold pieces of wood together, or to make them watertight? Animal skins could be used to carry water, but she had not seen even so much as a mouse in all her travels about the island, let alone a beast of sufficient size to justify killing for its hide.

Tired and hungry, she forced herself to her feet

and started walking back to the small camp she shared with Luis. What she needed was to be held and reassured the desolate island would not be their home for long. She knew that Luis would not feel well enough for lovemaking, but that did not stop her from craving his affection. All alone, she was afraid he might have spent as miserable a day as she had, but his greeting made it plain that he had been able to amuse himself quite well. Luis had always surprised her, but never more than he did now.

While it had taken him more than an hour, Luis had managed to kill two gulls with his slingshot. Once he got them plucked and cleaned, he had crawled around the beach gathering bits of driftwood dry enough to start a fire. Next he had been presented with the challenge of building the fire he had promised Michelle. The blade of his knife was steel, but without flint, he could not create the necessary sparks. As a child, he and his brothers had learned how to ignite a fire by rubbing two sticks together. It had been fun then; now it was a tedious process that threatened to sap what little energy he had before the first tiny puff of smoke appeared.

He was determined to succeed, however, and kept working until what began as one faint flickering flame grew to a fire over which he could roast the gulls. Skewering them on Michelle's fishing spear, he leaned back against a palm and kept a close watch so that he could turn them before they began to burn. When he finally saw Michelle approaching, he waved and called out to her.

"You're just in time for supper. I hope you're hungry."

Luis looked so pleased with himself that Michelle decided against relating the embarrassing details of how she had been trapped in a cave for most of the day. Convinced that the harrowing ordeal did not merit mentioning now that it was over, she sat down next to Luis and watched the gulls sizzle with the same rapt gaze as her husband. She ached with the need to touch him, but fearful of causing him pain, she refrained from doing so. She hoped having something to eat and then the luxury of a long nap would make her feel better, but it did not compare to the tenderness she longed to receive.

Luis waited patiently for Michelle to recount how she had spent the day, and when she showed not the slightest desire to do so, he found it difficult to be civil. "With just the two of us here," he scolded, "we ought to work together rather than each selfishly going our own way."

Bone-weary, Michelle did not feel strong enough to defend herself. If Luis believed she had abandoned him to rest in the shade on the opposite side of the island, then she was willing to let him harbor that delusion. She continued to stare at the roasting gulls. "I found a cave with plenty of fresh water, but we'll need buckets to haul it back here and I've no idea how to make one. Do you?"

Surprised that she would choose to change the subject rather than respond to his critical observation, Luis took a closer look at Michelle. She had washed her hair, and it fell in pretty waves that caught the sunlight each time she turned her head. Her expression, however, was one of such unconcealed despair that he instantly regretted being sharp with her. It was a mistake he had vowed to avoid and he was annoyed with himself for doing it again.

"You'll have to fetch me the wood, but yes, I can make a bucket without too much trouble." When Michelle simply nodded, Luis's imagination painted her feelings in vivid shades of blue. It appeared that she had taken his request to heart and had ceased to expect him to regain his good looks. He had not been her first choice for a mate, and now she must surely feel trapped in a loveless marriage with a man whose burn-ravaged features would repel everyone he met. That was a ghastly fate for such a young and pretty woman and he could not blame her for looking as sad as she did.

That he was equally distraught only compounded their problems in his view and he kept quiet about them. He checked the gulls, and deciding they were ready to eat, he slid them off the skewer. He hacked off a drumstick and gave it to Michelle. "Tell me how it tastes while I attempt to carve the breast."

There wasn't much meat on the piece he had handed her, and Michelle consumed it in one bite. She then grimaced slightly. "It's rather tough," she described thoughtfully, "although I'm certain that's no fault of the cook. The taste isn't too bad, but I think it's obvious why gulls aren't roasted by anyone who has another choice."

Luis tasted a sliver of meat from the breast and had to agree. "I was hoping they would taste as good as pheasant," he offered regretfully. "Would you rather catch us some fish instead? The fire's still hot enough to cook them."

"No, this is a nice change," Michelle assured him. She took a piece of the breast and tried not to count how many times she had to chew it before she swallowed.

That she would even attempt to eat what was essentially an inedible meal amazed Luis and he was inspired to follow her example. "What we need are some well-seasoned vegetables," he exclaimed.

"Freshly baked bread would be nice, too," Michelle added.

"Oh, yes, it would, with plenty of butter and berries for dessert. It's a shame this island is so terribly lacking in that regard."

347

While Michelle preferred Luis's teasing to hostility, she wondered how long they would be able to survive there on a diet of fish and water. The prospects for a brief stay did not look good, but she tried to smile as though talking about the foods they missed would somehow make the dry, stringy gull more flavorful.

When they had eaten all they could, she again tossed their trash into the sea, but she stepped back hurriedly before the onrushing water lapped over her feet. She was proud that she had escaped the cave on her own but no less worried about what perils the next day might bring. She walked back to where Luis sat, and exhausted, she stretched out on a freshly cut frond and instantly feel asleep.

Luis was worn out, too, but he had hoped for more in the way of conversation from Michelle before they went to sleep. It was not yet dark, and after spending the day alone, he could not shake off the uneasiness her long absence had created. People could go crazy when left all alone and he did not want either of them to suffer any more mental anguish than they already had. He did not attempt to wake Michelle, though, he just lay down beside her and hoped his confident boast that he could make a bucket did not prove impossible to fulfill.

Antoine straightened up slowly. He still favored his left shoulder and probably always would, but he was determined not to waste another day convalescing when he felt well enough to leave for Lyon. He was still far from strong and he did not really look well, but he had convinced himself it was time to go. He turned sideways to study his far too slim silhouette in the long mirror and then complained to his cousin.

"I look half starved. Oh, I'll readily admit that the loss in weight helps to accentuate the bone structure in my face, but what's the point of being such a handsome man when I now have this spindly body?"

"As soon as your appetite returns, you'll regain the weight you lost. Besides, I think being thinner makes you appear taller."

"Taller?" Antoine again studied his reflection. "Yes, my proportions *are* more elegant, but all a man need do is stand next to me to see that I've not gained any height."

"Why concern yourself with what men think, when women admire you so highly? Women are taken in by appearances far more easily than men. If you appear tall to them, they will assume that you are just that."

"Your flattery is contemptible, Francisco, but I think in this case you may be right. Women are greatly influenced by things men barely notice. Look at how swiftly my darling Michelle fell in love with another man. Is there any news of Aragon's ship?"

"Not yet, but you must be more patient. I'll write to you the instant I hear something. The Aragons have so much influence that if Augustín's ship is lost, all of Spain will go into mourning. The news of the tragedy might reach France before my letter does."

Antoine frowned petulantly. "Let's hope that we don't have to wait much longer. I'm thoroughly bored with the whole affair now." As if to prove the truth of his words, he changed the subject abruptly. "Where are you taking me for supper? Even if I don't eat much, I am desperate for a change in scene."

"We shall go to a marvelous new café," Francisco exclaimed. "The cuisine there is superb. There are separate rooms for each party, so we needn't worry anyone will see you."

"I really don't care whether or not I'm seen," Antoine contradicted as he moved away from the mirror. "It may have been convenient to allow Ramón Guerrero to believe I died of my wounds, but I don't plan to avoid Madrid for the rest of my life."

"No, of course not," Francisco agreed, "but you will be cautious for a year or two, won't you? Only a few people know that you quarreled with Augustín, but we don't want them to ever suspect that you had anything to do with his, shall we say, *disappearance?*"

Antoine understood the need for caution, but he was too delighted to finally be leaving the confines of his cousin's home for an evening of splendid food that he could not be concerned about it. In the morning he would be leaving for home, and he savored that thought all the way to the café.

Señora Maria Elena Dolores Verdugo was a great beauty with ebony hair and light-brown eyes that shone with the rich golden glow of topaz. She was also still in mourning for her late husband, a man twenty years her senior whom she had not loved a whit. A respectable young woman who would not flaunt the strict conventions of Spanish society, she nevertheless had a natural desire for entertaining company.

More than willing to provide all the amusing company Maria Elena could possibly want, Ramón Guerrero did not infringe upon the exemplary way she mourned her late husband in public. He never called at her home where his presence would draw criticism. He did not pester mutual friends for news of her welfare. If they should chance to meet on the street, he offered no more than a polite greeting before continuing on his way. That was all a clever ruse, however, for Maria Elena and he frequently met at exclusive inns and fine restaurants where their desire for discretion was accommodated.

They arrived in separate carriages, used private entrances, and even more private rooms. They left several minutes apart so that no one passing by would imagine that they had been together. This was no brief flirtation that would soon run its course, however, since the pair intended to wed just as soon as Maria Elena had completed a proper period of mourning and could remarry without being censored for merely being young and in love.

To ensure their privacy, Ramón made a point of arriving first for their trysts. That night, they were visiting a new café that had come highly recommended, and he wanted things to run smoothly as they always had and arrived several minutes early. He had yet to alight from his carriage when Francisco and Maria Lourdes Castillo strolled by with Antoine Lareau. While the Frenchman had lost weight, Ramón recognized Antoine immediately, and, astonished, called out to him as he left his carriage.

"Monsieur Lareau! What miracle is this? Your cousin led me to believe that you had succumbed to your wounds. It's most gratifying to see that I was misinformed."

Francisco had not expected to encounter anyone they knew at the café, and he was completely flustered by Ramón's greeting. Merely annoyed, Antoine reacted with his customary icy charm. "Señor Guerrero, wasn't it?" he asked. "How nice to see you again."

Antoine looked anything but pleased, and Ramón readily understood why. The Frenchman, though alive, was pale and thin, and had obviously suffered a great deal of distress. Ramón gestured toward the café's private entrance. "Please don't let me detain you. Perhaps we'll have an opportunity to talk at another time."

"I doubt it. I'm leaving for France in the morning."

"Have a pleasant journey then," Ramón wished him with a jubilant smile. He was overjoyed to discover Antoine was alive and he knew Luis would be even more ecstatic. He watched the small party enter the café, and then remained outside until Maria Elena's carriage arrived. Unwilling to dine there now that he had been seen, he gave her driver another address and left to meet her there. He was tired of their intrigues, and eager for the day they could wed, but he could not shake the suspicion that Francisco Castillo had had a good reason for allowing him to believe Antoine was dead.

Positive he did not know half as much about intrigues as that pair, he vowed to write to Luis just as soon as he returned home. He began to chuckle then, for usually Maria Elena left him too tired to even hold a pen, let alone compose a letter.

The next morning, Michelle caught some fish for their breakfast, and then brought Luis several of the dead pine boughs she had found laying on the ground up on the bluff. "I suppose we could make a stone axe," she proposed, "if you need freshly cut wood for the buckets."

"Michelle, really," Luis responded with deep amusement, "we're not setting out to build a new civilization. All we have to do is satisfy our basic needs for a few days. We're bound to be rescued soon."

Michelle glanced out toward the sea she had scanned thoroughly from the bluff. As before, there

352

was no sign of a ship. "Maybe we're the only ones who made it to land," she mused darkly.

"No, there were too many of the crew cast adrift for none of them to have survived. They may have been picked up by a ship before they reached land. If so, then we won't be here more than a few days before someone comes searching for us."

"Shouldn't I gather more wood for a signal beacon? A ship might pass by that hasn't heard about the *California* being lost. We don't want to miss an opportunity to be rescued."

"No, we certainly don't, but I hate to ask you to gather more wood."

"It's not that disagreeable a chore."

"Perhaps not, but it's not what you're used to, either."

Michelle thought his comment absurd. "No, I'm used to wearing silks and satins rather than a man's castoff clothing. I'm also used to taking hot baths, sleeping in a feather bed, and eating superbly prepared meals. None of that matters here, though, does it?"

Luis was not certain whether or not that flash of temper was a good sign. Despite his hopes for an imminent rescue, they might be stranded on the island for several weeks, and if Michelle was already tired of the primitive conditions, then she was going to be very unhappy indeed. That scarcely compared to the pain his burns had caused him, though, and he tried to make light of her complaint.

"You're right. It doesn't matter and the less we moan about what we don't have, and the more we make good use what we do, the better off we'll be."

"That was precisely my point," Michelle explained. "We have to get along as best we can. Whether or not I'm used to physical labor does not matter when I'm the only one strong enough to do it."

353

She might have been stating the obvious, but Luis was deeply hurt all the same. He did not need to be reminded that he could not provide for his wife when that failing could scarcely have escaped his notice. "I'll be stronger in a day or two," he promised through clenched teeth. "You won't be stuck with all the work for long."

"I'm not complaining about the work!" Exasperated with him for being so dense, Michelle got up and walked down to the water, but the vast expanse of the cool blue Mediterranean did little to soothe her mood. They were marooned on a godforsaken island barely able to provide for their most basic needs and Luis was so confident that they would soon be rescued he did not appear to be taking the desperate nature of their situation seriously. Well, Michelle certainly was!

The terror of the fire followed by their ordeal at sea had dulled her memory of the sinking of the *California,* but as she watched the waves roll in, she suddenly recalled Encario's words. He had said the fire had been set and that the culprits had taken one of the lifeboats. *"Mon Dieu!"* she exclaimed.

She hurried back to Luis. "Undoubtedly because Encario struck me so hard, I must have forgotten, but didn't he say that the fire had been set?"

Luis looked up, his gaze as ominous as his words. "Yes. Encario had hired two new men. They'd appeared to be an industrious pair. Apparently they were even more industrious than we'd first realized. I think they were Boris Ryde's men. We caught sight of a schooner that night, probably rendezvousing with them. You and the crew were merely unfortunate bystanders who got caught up in his plot to kill me. As soon as we're rescued, I'm going after him."

Michelle knelt in front of Luis. "You saw Ryde's ship the night of the fire?"

Luis shrugged. "Encario and I both saw a ship. It picked up the men in the lifeboat. I can't think of anyone who wants me dead badly enough to set fire to my ship except Boris Ryde."

Michelle felt very foolish, for she had not once questioned the source of the abandoned lifeboat they had found. Now it seemed as though she had failed to ask a great many important questions. "If Ryde despises you, why did he sail away? Why didn't he shoot all of us while we were in the water and unable to defend ourselves?"

Luis was appalled by that possibility. "Perhaps he thought drowning was sufficient punishment for us, or he may have been afraid that his crew would mutiny if he went that far. Who knows why the man did what he did?"

"He is that unpredictable?"

"Obviously! Had I even suspected that he might come after me, I'd have called him out years ago."

"Another duel?" Michelle shuddered.

"Yes, but it would have been a damn sight better than putting you and my crew at risk as I did."

"But you couldn't have known what Ryde was planning."

"No, I had no idea. It's been several years since I fired him. When I learned that he had his own ship, I assumed he was doing well enough on his own."

"Then why would he have tried to kill you now?"

"Maybe his hatred just festered until he couldn't bear it anymore."

Michelle rose and glanced out at the sea. "What if he begins to suspect that you might have survived the sinking of the *California?* What if his is the first ship that we sight?"

Shocked that she could even imagine such a horrendous possibility, Luis stared up at his bride with his mouth agape. "He just sailed away, Michelle."

"Where would he go—to Palma, Valencia, Barcelona? You had planned to be away only a week. Won't the authorities at the port, or the office of the Aragon Line, become concerned when the ship is overdue?"

"Well yes, but—"

"There would be a reward offered for anyone who sighted wreckage from the *Californian* or rescued some of her crew, wouldn't there?"

"Yes, of course."

"Then Ryde could set sail again." When Michelle turned to look down at Luis, she saw him nodding. "We ought not to be sitting here on the beach. We ought to move up to the bluff where we can recognize any ship that comes near and choose whether or not we wish to set a signal fire to announce our presence."

"Boris Ryde won't come back, Michelle."

"You didn't expect him the first time, did you?"

Luis could not dispute the logic of that statement and, convinced her plan was a wise one, looked around at their camp. "We'll need to hide the boat, but we can just push it up against the bluff and cover it with palm fronds. We can carry some of the coals with us to start another fire." Luis set the beginnings of his first bucket aside, and again using the adjacent palm, pulled himself to his feet. He was still somewhat unsteady, but far better than he had been the previous day.

"See, I told you I was getting stronger."

What Michelle noticed was that while his burns were healing nicely, his ribs were growing more prominent. "You must eat more."

"More *what?*"

"More of whatever we can find. Do you feel strong enough to help me move the lifeboat?"

"No, but I'll do it anyway." Luis had not appreciated how difficult it had been for Michelle to pull the lifeboat out of the surf by herself until he attempted to help her. They struggled, fell, got up, and after half an hour of the most exhausting work he had ever done, succeeded in moving the boat well up on the beach where it could be hidden. He then collapsed beside it and watched as, without his having to suggest it, Michelle whisked a palm frond across the sand to obliterate both the deep groove the passage of the boat had left and their footprints.

"You're a very strong woman," he complimented, "and I don't mean just physical strength. I think I'm very lucky to have you here with me."

Surprised by his unexpected praise, Michelle blushed and looked away. She hadn't felt strong when they had been adrift at sea. Nor had she felt confident when it had taken her all day to escape the water-filled cave. She did not want to even imagine what new challenges might still await them before they made a safe return to civilization. She brushed her hair off her face and walked back toward her husband.

"Let's not congratulate ourselves until we're off this blasted island."

As Luis looked up at her, he was filled with a bittersweet longing. Knowing just how unattractive he must look to the disheveled yet still ravishing beauty, he nodded and hauled himself to his feet.

"Whatever you say, Señora Aragon, whatever you say."

Michelle saw the anguish in his glance, and afraid he was in pain, she gestured toward the trees. "You just rest. I'll go up on the bluff and find us another campsite."

Luis was too tired to argue. "Fine," he snapped. "Just don't be gone the whole damn day."

"No, I'll be back soon." Michelle waved as she

started up to the top of the bluff, but when she had reached the trees rather than search for a likely spot for a camp, she sat down and cried. She knew Luis wanted to leave the island as badly as she did, but the thought that he would then seek to avenge the wrong Boris Ryde had done them meant that they would not be out of danger even then.

Twenty-one

When Michelle returned to the beach, there was no sign in either her manner or appearance to suggest how many tears she had wept. "The terrain of the bluff is all the same," she told Luis. "I don't think it matters much where we make the camp as long as we choose a protected place with a good view of the sea."

Luis was not satisfied with his efforts to make a bucket, but it was complete enough to carry a few coals up to the bluff to ignite another fire. He used the end of the fishing spear to gather up the coals and then handed his crude wooden container to Michelle. "If you'll carry the coals, I think I can make it on my own."

Michelle watched with a wary glance as Luis pulled himself up to his feet. She feared moving the boat had sapped too much of his strength, but he seemed so determined to walk unassisted, she turned away and concentrated on carrying the smoldering coals without dropping them or burning herself. "The way isn't steep. You can stop and rest as often as you like."

"I'm not an invalid," Luis complained, but he certainly felt like one. He rubbed his hand over the left side of his face and frowned at the coarseness he felt. He had grown beards upon occasion, but had never cared for either the feel or look of them. He was already dark enough without the addition of a menacing black beard. He imagined his current stubble must make his burns look all the more gruesome.

He then grew disgusted with himself for again dwelling on his appearance when he ought to be concentrating on creating a shelter for Michelle. He bent down to pick up the fishing spear and nearly toppled over. He caught himself at the last instant and then hurriedly straightened up, hoping that Michelle had not noticed that pathetic slip. Fortunately, she was already halfway up the slope and had not observed his near accident. Making a greater effort to be careful, Luis clutched the spear tightly, and using it as a walking stick, slowly crossed the sand.

As he began the climb, he leaned toward the face of the bluff and followed Michelle with slow, shuffling steps. He dared not look down for fear of falling, but when he glanced up ahead, Michelle had already disappeared from sight. That he could not keep up with her embarrassed him so, he was grateful there was no one else on the island to laugh while he doddered along like an elderly man, and a frail one at that.

He had to stop several times to catch his breath, but finally fought his way on up the gradual incline Michelle had climbed without the slightest difficulty. He wanted to lie down and sleep the rest of the day, but first had to pretend an interest in where they set up camp. Michelle was waiting for him to offer an opinion.

"Where is the fresh water?" he asked.

Michelle nodded toward the southern end of the island. "It's in a cave that can be entered from the beach. The cliff is too steep to climb there, though."

"Well then, if we'll have to use this same path down to the beach, let's make our camp as near to this cliff as is safe."

"It will be winter soon," Michelle reminded him.

360

"We ought to find a place well protected by trees. With neither warm clothes nor blankets I'm afraid we'll suffer terribly."

"The winters are very mild in the Balearics," Luis argued. "We'll not suffer at all. Besides, we'll be rescued soon."

Michelle straightened proudly. "On the off chance that this is the worst winter these islands have ever seen and that we're stranded here for several months, let's choose our campsite wisely."

Despite thinking her reasoning daft, Luis surveyed the closest stand of pines and gestured with the fishing spear. "For now, that looks like a fine place."

Michelle followed his glance to where half a dozen closely spaced pine trees grew in a gentle curve. "Yes, that will do," she agreed. She set the coals down for a few minutes while she gathered up dry wood for a fire. She had watched servants tend fires her whole life, and using the glowing coals, soon coaxed another blaze to life. "I'm going to collect all the dry wood I can. I'll stack some for a signal beacon and pile the rest against the trees to make a wall to shut out the wind."

That Michelle felt so energetic while he had difficulty remaining on his feet saddened Luis, but he caught himself before he made what she would surely interpret as a critical remark. "That's a good idea. I'll keep working on the bucket."

"We'll need some sort of a rope, too," Michelle realized suddenly. "There's plenty of water, but it's rather difficult to reach."

"Cut some palm fronds. They'll tear into long strips we can braid into a rope. I know that for sure. I've done it before," he added when she appeared to be skeptical.

"I'll do that first then so I can bring you some water. I know you must be thirsty."

While Luis was looking forward to a drink, he

361

wasn't desperate for one. The fish they had eaten for breakfast had been moist enough to satisfy his thirst. He sat down among the trees he had chosen for their camp and picked up the partially finished bucket. He was merely hollowing out a length of wood Michelle had found for him, but even with alternating burning and carving, it was slow and tedious work.

She sat down beside him to plait a rope, and when she had finished, he handed her the bucket. "That will hold a cup or two. Why don't you try it?"

Michelle dared not criticize his efforts, but she could not help but think that if he fulfilled all his confident promises with such crudely fashioned implements they were going to have an even worse time surviving than she had feared. He had carved an indentation around the lip to provide a secure hold for the rope and she wrapped it around and tied it carefully. "I wouldn't want to lose this."

"You *can't* lose it. It will float."

"Oh, yes, of course it will. How silly of me to have forgotten that. I'll be back just as soon as I can."

"Take your time."

Michelle carried the bucket back down to the beach and then hurried to the cliff where she had discovered the cave. She had not expected to be frightened now that she knew there was a way out, but when she got near, she began shaking in spite of herself. She had to draw on all her reserves of courage just to climb up to the opening in the cliff. Afraid to step inside for fear the limestone would again crumble and catapult her into the water, she flung the bucket out into the darkness. She heard it bounce off the rocky inner wall of the cave and then splash into the water.

All she had to do now was draw in the palm rope slowly, but it wasn't until she had the bucket sitting

362

in the sunshine that she felt safe. Thinking she ought to assuage her own thirst here, she raised the bucket to her lips and drank deeply. The water was as cold and delicious as she had remembered and she hurriedly refilled the bucket and carried it back to Luis. Quite a bit sloshed over the rim until she slowed her pace, but she did manage to arrive at their camp with enough left for him to have a drink.

"I'll go and get some more," she quickly volunteered. "What we really need is a larger container, something I can fill each morning so we'll have water for the whole day."

"We're going to need that stone axe after all, aren't we?" Luis joked. "I can use it to fell one of these trees. Then I can hollow it out to make a trough that will also catch any rain that falls. We could use some platters and cups. What more would you like?"

Michelle snatched up the bucket and left without dignifying his teasing question with the surly response it deserved. When she reached the beach, she made a lengthy search for large shells that could serve as cups. The ones she found were no bigger than demitasses, but she shoved them into her pockets and fetched another pail of water. She set it down beside Luis and handed him the shells, telling him how they might be used.

"And there's plenty of sand," she added. If we could get the fire hot enough, we could make glassware. Since you're so knowledgeable about everything, you must know how to do that, don't you?"

Luis reached out in an attempt to catch her ankle and pull her down onto the ground beside him but she was too agile to be caught and easily avoided his grasp. "I've watched glassblowers in Venice, but I've not mastered their art. If it's glassware you want, you'll have to wait until we're rescued."

"There's no sign of a ship again today," Michelle said sadly.

"There might be one tomorrow."

"We'll need that signal beacon then."

"Must you rush around so? Can't you just sit down and talk with me for a while?"

"Talk? About what?" When there was so much to do, Michelle did not understand how he could ask her to simply sit.

"All right, go on. Gather up all the wood you want and we'll talk later."

Luis looked disappointed in her, but Michelle couldn't help the way she felt. "I need to get some more aloe leaves for your burns, too."

Luis couldn't bear to look at his arm. All the aloes in the world wouldn't be enough to treat his burns and he did not respond to her offer. "We could use a few more palm fronds to cover the ground when we sleep," he said instead.

Michelle left to gather the aloes and fronds and Luis wondered if she had always been so helpful. He could easily imagine her as a lovely child who ran to fetch whatever her mama needed, but it was far more difficult to accept her current helpfulness as anything other than evidence of sheer panic. Just reaching the island had been enough to satisfy his need for security, but it was becoming increasingly plain that Michelle needed a great deal more.

No longer able to remain awake, Luis lay down and slept until early afternoon. Michelle had an enormous pile of wood assembled by then. He wondered whether the blaze might not be sighted on Mallorca if it was lit. Wisely, he did not pose that question aloud, but instead showed Michelle how to wrap the fish she had caught in palm fronds and then bake them over the coals for supper.

This was the best day they had spent so far, and Luis was confident their situation would improve

364

each day until they were finally rescued. It wasn't until Michelle snuggled against him that night that he began to worry about their future. Clearly Michelle was terrified, as any gently bred young woman in her position surely would be. It was only natural for her to cling to him while they slept, but what would her reaction to him be once they left the island? He doubted that she would feel any need to cling to him then.

What if his scars made him so repulsive she could not bear to occupy the same room with him, let alone the same bed? What if all she felt for him was pity? He then realized that he had had no idea how his bride felt about him *before* his burns. Perhaps pity was the very best he could hope to receive from her. Michelle had fallen asleep quickly, but he studied the stars for hours before dozing off and, by then, he had begun to wonder if he wouldn't be better off remaining on that deserted island forever. At least it would spare him the pain of watching others flinch when they looked his way.

Luis felt much stronger the next day, and while Michelle went to the cave for water, he did the fishing himself. Pleased that he was again surefooted enough to walk out over the rocks and successfully spear fish, he caught more than they could eat at one sitting. "I can't believe we have too much to eat rather than too little."

Michelle laughed with Luis, but it was a small comfort to have a surfeit of fish. "How long can we live on fish and water?" She posed aloud the question she had previously asked only herself.

"Long enough," Luis assured her, but he was sorry her thinking had again taken such a dark turn. "I think we ought to establish a patrol," he suggested the instant the idea occurred to him.

"What sort of patrol?"

"We look out to the sea here often, but we really need to cross the woods to be able to see a ship coming from the east. I'm not saying we should separate and spend our whole day watching for sign of a ship, but it wouldn't hurt to check the horizon every hour or two."

Michelle nodded thoughtfully. "Should we have two signal beacons?"

"No, the one will send up enough smoke to arouse curiosity, but you've got to let me decide when it's to be lit. I sincerely doubt that Boris Ryde is clever enough to come looking for us, but there are other men I'd just as soon not meet. That's why I've got to be the one to decide whether or not we'll signal to a passing ship."

"You mentioned firing some other captains. Are those the men you mean?"

"Yes, them certainly, but it's possible smugglers might have a base here."

"I've only seen the one cave and it's flooded."

"Good, then maybe any ship that we sight will be friendly. Don't fret about it, though. We'll be safe if we're careful."

"Do you feel strong enough to go exploring?" Michelle asked.

Luis swept his hair off his forehead. He was sure he could manage a little exploring, and fortunately the island wouldn't require more than that. "Yes. Why don't you show me where you get the water?"

"All right." Michelle rose, and brushed the pine needles from her seat. "I wish that we had a change of clothes. I realize that we'd need soap to wash them, but—"

Luis interrupted her quickly. "We're the only ones here. We don't even need to wear clothes if we don't want to."

Michelle's eyes widened in alarm. "You wouldn't!"

Luis glanced down at his faded pants. "I'm half naked now, Michelle."

Michelle was already well aware of that, but in her view there was an enormous difference between his displaying a bare chest and going completely unclothed. "I prefer to think of your being half clothed." She shoved her sleeves up her arms and gestured defensively. "I say the more clothes the better. Look at how tanned I'm getting. I can imagine what my face must look like. Is it completely covered with freckles?"

The once peaches-and-cream tones of her complexion had darkened while they had been adrift, but he thought her newly acquired golden tan made her all the more beautiful. "I haven't noticed any freckles."

He rose and gestured for her to come near and she stood so close their toes were touching. While there was a light dusting of freckles across her cheeks, he thought them a charming accent to her beauty. She was looking up at him with a completely innocent gaze, awaiting his comment without the slightest sense of what havoc her nearness was playing with his senses.

Choking on desire, Luis took a step back. "Your freckles are endearing. Now come show me where you've been getting the water."

Michelle turned away to pick up the bucket without noticing how flustered her husband was. She followed him down to the beach and then walked beside him to the cave. She had made enough trips to have grown confident that she would not topple into the water again. "I just stand there by the entrance and toss in the bucket."

Luis made his way over the rocks to the narrow entrance and bent down to peer inside. "I should have thought to bring a torch. I can't see a bloody thing."

367

"There's nothing to see. It's some kind of an underground spring whose water collects here. Step back and look up at the face of the cliff. Can you see how the water trickles over the rocks at the top? That's where I first noticed it."

Luis nodded. "Give me the bucket." When she handed it to him, he lowered it into the cave, taking care to measure how much of the palm rope he had to let out. He then coiled it up carefully as he withdrew the bucket of water. He figured the water level was at least six feet, if not slightly more, below the cave's entrance. He was not only curious, but alarmed.

"How did you wash your hair the first day you came here? Were you inside the cave?"

Michelle was not even tempted to lie to him, but she made it sound as though it had been a brief stay rather than a near day-long ordeal. "Yes. After a while my eyes adjusted to the dark."

"I'll just bet they did! Tell me what really happened."

"I just did."

"There's more to it than that, Michelle. Even hanging by your toes you couldn't have reached the water to wash your hair. How did you do it?"

Michelle swallowed hard. "All right, if you must know, I fell in."

"Is the pool shallow?"

"No." Embarrassed, Michelle looked away and to her utter delight and amazement, she saw a ship on the horizon. She grabbed Luis's left arm and pointed. "Look! There's a ship!" she screamed excitedly.

Luis was surprised she had noticed it, for it was some distance from shore. "Hush!" he cautioned sharply. He pulled her back against the rocks.

One look at Luis's dark scowl was enough to terrify Michelle. "Is it Captain Ryde's ship?"

"No, it's a much smaller vessel, lateen rigged, probably no more than half a dozen men, most likely smugglers. Now we're going back up on the bluff, where we're going to be very quiet."

Michelle's heart leapt to her throat. "Smugglers?" she whispered.

"I doubt anyone would come here to chop firewood." He took her hand and hoped whoever was on the ship did not have a spyglass trained their way.

Michelle kept looking back over her shoulder. "Our tracks are all over the beach again." She slipped her hand from Luis's and dashed ahead to yank a frond from the closest palm. She ran back to cover their trail with broad strokes of the wide leaf, but she still felt as though their presence would be felt by the strangers.

Luis hurried her up the incline to the bluff. He emptied the bucket of water on the coals remaining from their breakfast fire and then kicked dirt over the puddle. Still not satisfied that the evidence of a fire had been sufficiently disguised, he broke off a small pine bough and laid it atop the damp mound. "There. Unless someone trips over it, that won't be noticed."

Michelle gestured toward the pile of wood she had amassed for use as a signal beacon. "What about the wood? Doesn't that look suspicious, too?"

"It certainly does, but we haven't time to disperse it all over the bluff. Let's just pray no one comes up here." Luis bent down to pick up the palm fronds that served as their carpet and sleeping mats. He rolled them up and hid them between closely spaced boughs of one of the pines. The area looked as though it might have been occupied, but it was now impossible to determine when. He kicked the pine needles that littered the ground to put them in disarray and then found a low limb behind which to conceal the bucket. After all the work he had put into its construction, he didn't want to lose it.

"Let's cross the bluff so we can keep an eye on the ship," he suggested. "I want you to stay well behind me, though. That white shirt will be too easily seen, and I know you don't want to remove it."

"How can you tease me at a time like this?"

"It's the best time. Now come on." Luis reached for her hand and they made their way through the trees to the eastern bluff. Luis found a place for Michelle to stand where she would be hidden by the trees, but he stretched out right at the cliff's edge. The ship was about a hundred yards off shore now and steering straight for them.

"It's a good thing we were getting water," Luis called over his shoulder. "We'd not have seen them otherwise."

Michelle was every bit as frightened as she had been in the cave. In her mind, smugglers were the same as pirates and she just knew each and every man on board the ship would be wanted for a string of gruesome crimes. Luis might finally be strong enough to fish or walk a short way, but how could he defend them if they were caught? Smugglers would want their hiding place to remain a secret, so they would never show any compassion toward anyone who had discovered it.

Hurling herself off the bluff was always an option, but it was an extremely poor one as her resulting death would be no different than if some smuggler had slit her throat. Gagging on that grisly thought, she had to cover her mouth with both hands for a moment. She tried to calm herself by remembering something pleasant, but since the day she had met Luis, her luck had been exceedingly bad.

"They'll try and kill us, won't they?" she whispered.

"No! Don't forget I'm an Aragon. I can offer them such a splendid reward for taking us to Mallorca that they'll want to see us arrive there safely."

"Then why are we hiding?"

Luis found her question painfully amusing. "Because I'd rather not have to bargain with smugglers if I've any other choice. Right now the choice is to keep quiet, watch, and wait."

"What if they decide to stay? We've no water, no food here."

"This island won't appear any more hospitable to them than it does to us. Now hush."

Michelle knew their voices couldn't possibly be heard above the noise of the surf and the abundant gull population, but she understood that Luis did not want to be distracted and did not argue. The ship was nearing the breakers and she tried to count how many men were aboard. It looked like only a few to her, and she was somewhat cheered that they were not as badly outnumbered as it had first appeared.

Luis was also elated by the fact there were only four men in the ship. It was riding high in the water, so they had to be picking up goods rather than hiding them. As the four brought their small vessel close to shore, he tried to see their faces but recognized none. Not that he knew any smugglers, he didn't, because they were usually fishermen rather than merchant seamen, but he wanted to know exactly what they were up against. These men were nervously looking out to sea as though they were being pursued and that gladdened Luis's heart as well.

"They look to be in a hurry," he called to Michelle, but to his dismay, when the men reached the beach, they sat down and began to pass around a bottle of whiskey. Disappointed to find them not nearly as rushed as he had hoped, Luis rested his forehead on his crossed arms.

"What's wrong?"

Luis waved at Michelle to be still. He wanted the

men to hurry up with their business and leave, but two broke into song and their companions accompanied them by clapping in time. One fellow got up to dance, but having had a little too much to drink, soon toppled over and sat laughing as loudly as his friends at his clumsy antics. Luis feared it was going to be a long afternoon, but even if the smugglers kept up their antics all day, it would at least keep them from exploring the island and discovering their presence.

Peering through the boughs, the pine needles tickled terribly and when Michelle could no longer stand their prickly itch, she inched away from the tree. Kneeling, she crawled up behind Luis, but stopped well back of the edge of the bluff. "What are they doing?" she asked. "It sounds like singing."

Luis glanced back toward her. "Yes, they *are* singing, but you still need to stay out of sight." Michelle responded by resting her cheek against his calf, filling him with an unexpectedly sharp torment. She had apparently made herself comfortable for a long stay, without realizing how the intimacy of her gesture would affect him. He kept telling himself that she was just frightened and that the seductiveness of her pose was unintentional, but that explanation did not cool the heat of his response.

He longed to send her away, but knowing she would defy him and stay, he did not give such an order. He just kept watching the smugglers' revel and tried not to think about his beautiful bride, nor, about how ugly his burns had surely made him. Two hours passed before the men on the beach roused themselves. They then moved some twenty yards south and set about moving what appeared to be an accumulation of rocks at the base of a landslide. They were working in an easy rhythm, still laughing as they uncovered the mouth of a cave.

When Luis relayed that information to Michelle,

372

she scooted up beside him. She took one look at the four men shifting chunks of limestone, and then gazed at the ship they had left lying at anchor. "Could we sail their ship ourselves if we stole it?"

Luis's eyes widened in astonishment. If he had been stranded with another man, they would already have sailed away in the smuggler's ship, but he would not endanger Michelle's life with such an audacious plan. "No," he said. "They'd see us swimming toward the ship and overtake us before we could raise the anchor and sail away. Besides, you can't swim!"

Michelle pursed her lips thoughtfully. "When they enter the cave, we could wait just outside and use a stone to knock out each man as he emerges. Then we could sail away without any interference from them."

Again, had Luis been with another man, he would have thought her idea inspired. Coming from a delicate woman, it simply sounded absurd. "No. There's no cover near the cave, so we couldn't reach it without being seen. They probably won't stay inside more than a few minutes and I'll bet one of them remains outside as a lookout. It wouldn't work, Michelle."

Michelle fixed him with a steady stare. "You killed the gulls with stones, didn't you?"

"Yes, but I'm not nearly good enough with a slingshot to incapacitate a man, let alone four of them, and in rapid succession."

"If we moved to the spot just above them, we could throw stones down at them. You can throw accurately enough, can't you?"

"Look! Each man has a pistol shoved under his belt. I might be able to strike one man or two with stones before one of the others shot me. Then what would you do, continue to pelt them with stones, or tend me?"

"There's got to be a way to steal their ship!"

Michelle appeared to be thoroughly incensed with him for not coming up with a realistic plan, but he just wasn't strong enough yet to take on four smugglers alone and he thought she ought to realize that. "There's too great a chance that one, or both, of us would die in the attempt. That's not a risk I'm willing to take. Are you?"

Rather than reply, Michelle moved back to the trees. She sat down, hugged her legs tightly, and rested her cheek on her knees. She was absolutely positive a man as dashing as Luis Aragon could steal a smuggler's ship if he wanted to. The question was, why didn't he want to? "Do you actually like being here?" she asked.

"It's a damn sight better than being dead!" Luis ignored her then and concentrated on the smugglers. Just as he had expected, they entered the cave singly, or in two's. At no time were all four inside. They removed a few wooden crates from the cave, then restacked the rocks to cover the entrance. They floated the crates out to the ship, loaded them on board, and set sail before Luis again spoke to Michelle.

"They're gone. We can search their cave tomorrow, but I doubt they left anything behind." He rose to his feet and started a lazy stretch which he halted when the burns across his shoulder caused him pain. He reached out his hand to help Michelle rise, but she got up without accepting his assistance. "I'm sorry if I disappointed you, but odds of four to one just didn't appeal to me."

"Two to one," Michelle contradicted. "You could have counted on me to help."

"No thank you, I won't ever need a woman's help in a fight."

Michelle's eyes filled with the light of a murderous rage. He was standing close to the edge of the bluff

374

and for an instant she was sorely tempted to give him such a mighty shove that he would go careening right on over. Then she caught herself. "We already have a fight to survive here and you haven't once rejected my help. When you were too weak to stand, I was the one to catch the fish, gather the wood, and search for water, which you recall, I found. If it wounded your pride to depend on me, you certainly haven't shown it by refusing my help before now. Do you want to change your mind? Shall I just spend my days lounging in the shade while you do all the work from now on? Is that what you want?"

"What I want," Luis explained through clenched teeth, "is for none of this to have happened!"

He brushed on by her and headed for their camp. It would take him a while to kindle another fire, and that was only one of the many tasks to which he was not looking forward. As he saw it, he had failed Michelle in every possible way. He had been so captivated with her that he had not kept a close enough eye on the new crewmen to prevent them from setting the *California* on fire. Thanks to him she had been lost at sea and marooned on an island with such scant resources they could barely provide for their most basic needs.

"Some husband I am!" he muttered under his breath, but he honestly could not understand how Michelle could have expected him to ask her to help him kill four men. He most certainly would not ask his wife to be an accomplice to murder. An eerie shiver ran down his spine as he remembered Antoine. Perhaps they were already guilty of murder.

Luis tried to force that horrendous thought aside, but it plagued him unmercifully for the remainder of the day.

Twenty-two

The bitterness in Luis's voice hit Michelle with the force of a painful backhanded slap. As she interpreted his remark, he was referring to the horrible burden of having her for a wife. Rather than follow him, she turned to gaze out at the sea. Even blurred by tears she could make out its calm, predictable rhythm, but like her husband's moods, she knew the sea could swiftly turn violent.

"*Husband,*" she murmured as though the word were a curse. She wrapped her arms around herself to hold in the heartache that threatened to tear her in two. She just knew another ship would never come to their miserable little island. They had had only one chance to escape and Luis had refused to seize it. They were doomed to spend the rest of their lives — and she doubted they would be long ones — in a place where the seagulls provided better company for them than they apparently did for each other.

When the sea view brought no sense of peace, she entered the woods. Not anxious for more of Luis's depressing tirades, she meandered down to the southern tip of the island rather than following his path straight back to their camp. When she finally rejoined him, he already had a fire burning and was down on the rocks fishing for their supper. She stood on the bluff, watching him the whole time, but he did not once turn and notice her longing glance.

They ate his catch in silence, and when they went to sleep Michelle chose a spot well away from him rather than cuddling up close. She was not isolating herself as much as giving him the distance she thought he had made it plain he craved. She was so confused, but hurting too badly to know what to do to end her torment.

Not about to beg Michelle to stop what he considered a childish pout, Luis did not bother to bid her good night. He slept poorly and awoke in no better mood than when he had fallen asleep. Michelle was still sleeping, all curled up in a ball as though she were cold. His first reaction was to cover her and then brush her tangled tresses aside to give her the good-night kiss she had missed, but he had no blanket or heavy coat to share. The sun would soon lend the island a pleasant warmth, but until then, all he could do was add wood to their fire and that hurt more than her sullen silence had. He left their camp and once down on the beach, felt strong enough to swim. He was used to living an active, vigorous life and intended to do so again just as soon as humanly possible. After tossing his only pair of pants aside, he walked out into the waves and dove beneath them.

As he broke through the surface, the saltwater no longer stung his cuts and burns as it had while they had been adrift. Thinking perhaps Michelle's constant applications of aloe were doing him some good, he swam for half an hour before leaving the water to get dressed and fish. He took care that morning not to spear more than they could eat at one meal and when he returned to their camp, he found Michelle was awake and had built up the fire.

Not wanting their awkward estrangement to continue, he greeted her warmly and then began talking about the day as though nothing had ever been

377

amiss between them. "I still think starting a patrol is a good idea. There are several ways we can arrange it. We can take turns checking the eastern shore, or we can divide the island and each be responsible for half."

Luis was smiling, but his suggestion chilled Michelle clear through. "Are you saying we ought to have two camps?"

"No, we'll still share this one."

Michelle had had little appetite to begin with, and by the time Luis had roasted the fish, she had none. She picked the flaky white meat apart with her fingers, but took only a tiny bite. "I'll take the other side," she volunteered, thinking he was about to banish her there anyway. "I want to see what's in the smugglers' cave."

Recalling the skeleton dangling in the cave he had entered, Luis immediately lay his fish aside. "We'll both go. I don't want you exploring any more caves alone. It's far too dangerous. We got interrupted yesterday, but there's plenty of time now. Tell me how you got out of the cave after you fell in the water."

Michelle shrugged as though it had been a simple matter rather than a lengthy challenge to make her way to safety. "The rocks inside the cave are as easy to climb over as those on the outside. I just climbed out."

The fact Michelle didn't look at him, but toyed with the fish she was pretending to eat while she spoke convinced Luis there was far more to tell. He did not want to badger her into confiding in him, though, if she would not do it willingly. He finished his breakfast and waited for her to complete what little she cared to of hers.

They took the remnants of their meal down to the beach to scatter for the gulls, and then, carrying the bucket, headed around toward the opposite side of

378

the island. Michelle made a great show of rolling up her sleeves as an excuse to avoid taking Luis's hand and then shoved her hands into her pockets. She didn't enjoy living in the same clothes, and again wished for a change.

"Is there any chance the smugglers left bolts of materials in the cave?"

Understanding her question, Luis broke into a wide grin. He still found her appealing in her borrowed garb even if she hated wearing it. "The object of smuggling is to avoid paying the duties required by customs laws. While expensive fabrics might be profitable to smuggle, I doubt the men had any material in those crates we saw yesterday since they made no attempt to keep them dry."

Michelle shook her head sadly. "Is there any way to make garments from palm fronds?"

"I suppose it's possible to weave the long fibers into cloth, but it would probably take every frond on the island to make a yard of material. And then I doubt it would be comfortable to wear. Stop worrying so about your clothes, Michelle. They'll do just fine until we're rescued."

"They shall have to, won't they?"

"I'm sorry I didn't grab a shirt the night of the fire. Of course, it would probably have burned when the sail fell on me, so I'd not have it now to lend to you anyway."

"Your burns would have been much more severe had you been wearing a shirt," Michelle hastened to argue. "The fabric would have held in the heat and you'd not have been able to just flip a shirt aside as you did the sail."

Luis shot her an incredulous glance. "How could my burns have been any more severe?"

Michelle did not want to have this argument again. His burns were not nearly as awful as he

379

imagined, but she had learned quickly that he would not accept her word for it. "I forgot to use the aloe on you last night," she complained instead. "We can get a few leaves now."

"If you think it's still worth the trouble."

"It's no trouble."

Luis had never felt awkward around women, but he felt anything but secure with Michelle now. At least she was talking with him in a reasonable tone, though, and he was grateful for that. After stopping to drink at the cave, they left the bucket by the entrance to retrieve later and made their way along the eastern beach to the cave. The drunken smugglers had done such a poor job of concealing the entrance that they would have found it the first time they came that way.

"The rocks are much too heavy for you to lift. Just rest a minute while I move them aside," Luis directed, anxious to do at least this small thing for her.

Believing he was again dismissing her as though she were too frail to lift a stone larger than her fist and rebelling, Michelle walked down to the shore and stood where the waves would just tickle her toes as they curled up onto the sand. One minute Luis was telling her to take the responsibility for patrolling half the island. In the next, he was shooing her away as too weak to be of any help to him. Perhaps he saw no conflict in his statements, but she most assuredly did. A married couple were either partners or they were not, and she was sadly afraid that in his view they were not and never would be.

She waited until Luis called to her to walk back to the cave. He had uncovered only a portion of the entrance, just enough to allow them to squeeze through. "I'll go first," he said, and noting the disapproval in Michelle's gaze, he rephrased his comment.

380

"Just in case there's anything we'd rather not see. I can spare you that fright."

Michelle frowned. "What do you mean? Some sort of sea monster?"

"No, we both know they don't exist. I'm just worried we might find the remains of a smuggler who didn't make it off the island on his last visit." When Michelle shuddered, Luis leaned down to kiss her cheek, but it was a hasty gesture rather than a prelude to something more. "It won't take me but a few seconds to look around," he promised, and then, ducking his head, he entered the cave.

He had made the opening large enough to let in sufficient light to illuminate the interior, but discovered a small antechamber led into a much larger cavern and he would need a torch to see what it contained. He left to tell Michelle what he had found, and then backed away from the cliff to look for a way to reach the bluff.

"I think I can climb up this way. That will be a shortcut back to camp."

The uneven face of the rocky bluff provided a rugged surface to scale, and Michelle wondered if Luis felt up to such a rigorous climb. "It will be hard work," she pointed out.

"I'm feeling better every day, and if I slip, the sand will cushion my fall."

As Michelle saw it, Luis was again making a joke out of a possibility that wasn't in the least bit humorous. "Well go on then. The sooner you leave, the sooner you'll be back."

Michelle had chosen to occupy herself kicking the sand with her toe rather than watch him climb, but Luis did not need to see her expression to hear the disapproval in her voice. "I won't fall," he promised.

"I'm sure no one ever intends to fall, but that doesn't mean that accidents don't happen."

She had not pulled away from his light kiss and Luis now longed to give her a reassuring hug, but she had again become so distant that he thought better of making a gesture that she might easily regard as an uninvited liberty. Instead, he turned away, and after choosing what looked to him like the easiest route to climb, he started up the cliff. As Michelle had predicted, it was a more arduous task than he had anticipated, but he forced himself to keep moving and reached the bluff without mishap. Michelle was still kicking sand this way and that and rather than call down to her and gloat rudely, he started through the woods to their camp.

Michelle had expected Luis to present a rebuttal to her dire warning, and when he did not immediately do so, she waited patiently for him to speak. Finally she grew bored and turned around. When she discovered Luis had vanished from sight, she at first assumed he must have gone back into the cave. Still eager to see it, she followed him inside.

As Luis had reported, the small antechamber held nothing of interest, but still thinking he was just up ahead, Michelle peered into the adjoining chamber. "Luis!" she called, and his name reverberated all around her with a taunting echo, but there was no answer. Wary, she took a tentative step to judge the firmness of the ground before moving forward. Feeling solid rock, she ventured into the cool, dark cavern. She reached out her hands to search for unseen dangers, but her fingertips struck only stagnant air.

Thinking the cavern must be immense, she took several small steps and again called Luis's name only to be mocked by another distant rumbling echo. It was so dark here that Michelle knew Luis would not have come that way. She felt very foolish for not considering that he might have succeeded in climbing the cliff while she had had her back turned. She hurried to leave before he arrived with the torch and found her stumbling around in the dark. Meaning to simply retrace her path, she took a step backward but rather than retreating into the antechamber as she had expected, she collided with the wall of rock at her back.

Startled, she spun around and, again relying on her hands to guide her, tried to find the opening she had stepped through only moments ago. "This can't be happening," she cried out. She had entered the cavern and taken only one step, or had it been two? she agonized. Still, even if it had been a few, she couldn't be more than two steps away from the antechamber.

Her worst fear was not of being lost, because she knew that she couldn't be, but of falling. The entrance to the antechamber had to still be within reach, but if she began flailing about wildly she might carelessly step onto another piece of limestone that wouldn't support her weight. If she wasn't killed in the fall, she could still be badly injured, and how would Luis ever be able to rescue her?

She bit her lower lip and forced herself to be calm. She was in absolutely no peril whatsoever that wouldn't be swiftly alleviated when Luis returned with the torch. She kept repeating those comforting words until her breathing resumed its normal, steady pace. All she had to do was stay right where she was and wait for him.

Michelle eased herself down against the wall and crossed her legs to get comfortable. She was alone in a dark, dank cave, but as she considered her predicament, it was trivial compared to her other recent adventures. She wiped the tears from her eyes, and leaned her head back against the rocky wall. All she had to do was wait for Luis to arrive and they would explore the cave together. Patience had never been one of her virtues, but she was confident Luis would not leave her stranded in the dark for long.

Unaware of Michelle's dilemma, Luis nonetheless hurried back to the eastern side of the island. He had brought several handy lengths of dry wood, as well as one branch that he had lit from the coals of their fire. It had burned down to where he could use it to light another and when he did so, it would be tossed aside. He was puzzled only briefly when he didn't see Michelle, then her whereabouts seemed obvious. Disgusted that she had not waited for him to explore the cave, he muttered several of the more colorful expressions he had learned at sea and went to find her. He crossed the antechamber in two long strides and called her name as he burst into the cavern beyond.

"You needn't yell. I'm right here," Michelle greeted him cheerfully. She stood up and brushed off her clothes before smiling sweetly.

Luis might have been fooled by her smile had there not been streaks on her cheeks where she had wiped away her tears. During his absence she must have been upset about something, but he assumed that she had come into the cave for the solitude it provided, rather than considering it might have been the cave itself that had caused her tears. "I might have known you'd not wait for me."

The torch that he held cast enough light for Michelle to see how she had gotten lost so easily. The entrance to the cavern was at an angle, so it had been slightly to her right when she had tried to back through it. She had missed finding it by inches. That question answered, she chose to look around rather than respond to her husband's sarcastic greeting.

"Look, there's a lantern," she pointed out.

Clearly left by the entrance deliberately, it was only two steps away. Luis knelt beside it, found that it contained enough oil to light, and did so with the torch he then laid aside with the wood he would no longer need. He raised the old wrought-iron lantern and turned to study the smugglers' lair. The chamber had a high ceiling which had given them both an erroneous impression of great size, but in reality it was no more than twenty feet deep. There was an empty crate, similar to those they had seen the smugglers move, lying on its side nearby, but nothing else.

"I'm sorry. I was hoping they might have left something you could use to supplement your wardrobe."

"And yours," Michelle added. Feeling brave now that they had the lantern to light their way, she stepped past Luis. "Could there be another room?"

Luis reached out to catch her arm. "Wait. Stay behind me and we'll look together."

The cavern had been formed by water eroding the limestone, and the irregular walls could indeed conceal the entrance to another chamber. Luis walked along slowly, carefully testing the stones beneath his feet as Michelle had done. Three-quarters of the way around the cavern, they found a wide crevice that beckoned invitingly. Hidden by the shadows, they would have missed it had they failed to examine the cavern closely.

Luis glanced back at Michelle. "Are you frightened, or would you like to explore a little farther?"

She wasn't afraid now that he was with her. "We have so little. If we could find anything at all, it would surely prove useful."

If she wished to justify further exploration on that basis, Luis wouldn't object. He moved into the next chamber and blocked the entrance with his body to keep her out until he had quickly surveyed it. He then reached back and drew her inside. This room was smaller than the previous one. The floor slanted down toward an oval opening in the corner that would require them to get down on their hands and knees to go through. There was nothing to show anyone had ever passed that way, let alone stored smuggled goods there.

"Listen," Michelle cautioned. "It sounds like water."

Alerted, Luis heard it now, too. It was distant, faint, but unmistakably the rushing sound of a rapidly flowing stream. "Do you suppose these caves connect with the one where you fetch the water?"

"Perhaps. Could the whole island be honeycombed with caves?"

"Yes." Intrigued, Luis crossed to the low crevice. He knelt and extended the lantern into the next chamber. It appeared to be as immense as they had imagined the first one to be. "What do you think?" he turned to ask Michelle.

"I think we should have been unrolling a ball of twine to leave a trail."

"Do you want to stop here?"

"Would you come back later by yourself?"

Her perceptiveness didn't surprise him. "Yes."

"Then we might as well continue."

That was precisely the answer he had wanted. "Come and hold the lantern while I crawl through, then you can pass it to me and I'll light your way."

Michelle did as he asked, but when she got ready to follow him, the drop was much steeper than she anticipated and she would have fallen had Luis not caught her with one hand. He had to juggle her and the lantern for a few terrible seconds, but he managed to set both of them down safely.

"Are you all right?" he asked.

Although shaken, Michelle swiftly assured him that she was fine. She turned away, and after her first startled glance, gazed in rapt fascination at the large chamber. The lantern did not begin to illuminate the whole area, but what she could see looked to her like the delicate stonework on a Gothic cathedral. "This is magnificent," she whispered.

Equally awed, Luis agreed. He took her hand and they walked out into the middle of the cavern. Now the sound of the underground stream echoed all around them. The limestone beneath Luis's feet felt damp and he recognized what that meant mere seconds before the porous rock buckled. He leapt backward, scrambling for secure rock for them both, but like partially frozen ice on the surface of a lake, the floor of the cavern continued to slip away beneath their feet and crash into the stream below.

The resulting noise and its thunderous echo was deafening. The whole cavern shook with a mighty shudder. Knocked off balance, the lantern flew out of Luis's hand and rolled into the widening tear in the rock, instantly engulfing them in darkness. He clung to Michelle, though, pulling her along with him as he fought to remain upright and regain solid footing. He was almost there when a huge piece of the floor disintegrated under Michelle. The end of the world could not have been more terrifying, but Luis refused to release her to save himself, and the abyss that had sucked her under swallowed him as well.

The ten-foot drop felt like a hundred to the plummeting couple. Then, caught up in the stream's swirling current, their senses had no time to recover from that horrifying plunge. Luis gulped in huge breaths of air each time he was able and prayed that Michelle was doing the same. In the darkness it was impossible to discern if they were about to be dashed against overhanging rocks or swept down into a tunnel so deep and narrow that they would swiftly drown.

Luis was a brave man, but he had never faced a challenge as torturous as the underground stream. It curved, dipped, and flung them against slippery walls where they had no chance to cling and save themselves. The biting chill of the water combined with a current as fierce as any undertow made the hope for survival ridiculous and yet Luis refused to let go of either Michelle's hand, or whatever was left of his life.

When he saw a glimmer of light ahead, he dove for it, still drawing his exhausted bride along with him. He felt the stream veering the other way. It tugged on them, fighting to wrench the last bit of strength from their limbs, but he kicked against it, and with a final burst of energy, broke through the surface of the water to find they were in a cave whose narrow opening let in a bright beam of sunshine.

He swam toward the light, grabbed ahold of a ledge to steady himself, and pulled Michelle around to face him. For one terrible instant he thought all he had saved was her lifeless body, but then she began to cough and gasp for air. Relieved beyond words, he hugged her tightly until she had finally caught her breath.

"There are rivers in California where riding the rapids is almost that perilous, but no one does it in the dark. God but that was awful."

"Awful?" Michelle repeated in a hoarse whisper. She had not realized how loudly she had been screaming, but the pain in her throat attested to it. "Awful does not begin to describe what it was like." She was still shaking all over and it wasn't because of the water's icy chill. "Let's get out of here."

"Is this where we draw the water?"

Michelle saw at a glance that it was and nodded. "I climbed out over there." She pointed weakly. "But I don't think I can do it now without your help."

"I don't expect you to." Being taller, Luis had a far easier time of it than she had had and he had her outside on the sand in less than a minute. He pushed the hair off her forehead to satisfy himself that she had not suffered any cuts, but when he drew his hand away, it was covered with blood. Not wanting to alarm her, he turned her head slightly and found a deep gash near her crown.

"You must have hit a rock. Does your head hurt?"

"No worse than the rest of me."

Luis sat down. "I want you to just lie down here in the sand and rest your head on my knee. If I keep some pressure on the cut, it should stop bleeding soon." At least he hoped it would. Amazingly, his knife was still in its sheath, and he eyed her shirt. "If it doesn't, I'll use one of your sleeves as a bandage."

"You will not," Michelle contradicted sharply, but she stretched out as he had asked, got comfortable, and closed her eyes.

Luis had propped her head up intentionally to send her blood flowing away from the cut rather than toward it, but he wished that he could think of something more to do. "I had a medical book on board the *California* that Daniel gave me. It had suggestions for treating almost any emergency. It's a shame we haven't got it with us."

Michelle opened one eye and peered up at him. "Yes, it would be nice to have something to read, but I don't think a little cut is much of an emergency. You needn't bother to set aside any time to teach me to swim next summer. After today, any-

389

thing more than a bathtub full of water will be too much for me."

She closed her eyes again, but Luis was delighted that she could make jokes about water after nearly drowning. He turned to look out toward the sea and wondered where the stream emerged. That was certainly not a question he would ever investigate.

He had thought he was leading an adventuresome life before he had met Michelle. Now, after their series of narrow escapes, he could not help but wonder what would present the next threat to their safety. Surely they would not encounter any more trouble on the island, but what about when they left?

He raised his hand slightly, and was pleased to see his prompt attention to Michelle's wound appeared to be working successfully. He kept up the pressure a while longer, and when he next checked the cut, it had stopped bleeding. He was about to suggest they return to their camp when he realized Michelle had fallen asleep. Knowing he could also use the rest, he took care not to disturb her as he lay back in the sand. It was warm, but the fact it was dry was what cheered him most as he drifted off to sleep.

The weary couple slept until sundown. Stiff and sore, they made their way back to their camp where Luis barely had light enough to catch fish for their supper. As they ate, Michelle kept thinking about how easily they could have died and it was all she could do to look at Luis without crying. He also seemed to be preoccupied, and she could easily understand why.

Because she had slept all afternoon, Michelle wasn't tired. Rather than make any preparations for bed, she continued to sit by the fire with Luis after their meal. The flickering flames cast his features in

390

high relief and, even with the addition of a beard, she thought him extraordinarily handsome. The sweet longings of desire that filled her were impossible to ignore and she reached out to touch his arm.

Startled, Luis straightened up. "I'm sorry, did you say something?"

"No, but I should have. Thank you for again saving my life. You've done it rather often, and it's always appreciated."

"I'd not have abandoned you," Luis scoffed.

Michelle had not meant to suggest such a thing had even occurred to him, and his rebuff prompted her to be even more gracious. "I should have been more willing to see your side of things yesterday, but after what we survived today, I think we really would have been able to steal the smugglers' ship."

"That incident is better left forgotten, but what I did today was incredibly stupid," Luis argued. "I was so careful to test the floor of the first two chambers of the cave. Leading you out into the middle of the third was the biggest mistake I could have made. If only I'd realized that just a couple of seconds sooner, we would have walked out unharmed."

Unwilling to listen to him blame himself for their latest brush with death, Michelle moved closer and laced her fingers in his. "We're alive and well," she reminded him. "Let's be grateful for those blessings." When Luis turned toward her, she did not hesitate to kiss him, but he broke away instantly.

"You needn't be that grateful." Luis not only pulled his hand from hers, he also stood up and added more wood to their fire. Apparently deeply concerned about the blaze, he then remained on the opposite side from her.

Luis's angry scowl deepened Michelle's feelings of rejection, but she bravely got to her feet. "It wasn't gratitude that inspired me to kiss you," she explained.

"I don't want your pity, either."

"There's no reason for anyone to pity you, Luis. I certainly don't."

Luis swallowed hard. "I've got a very good imagination, so I have a fairly accurate idea of the way I must look. Perhaps you do care enough for me to want to be with me now, but when we're rescued and you see the way others turn away from me, you'll swiftly change your mind."

"You just told me that you'd not have abandoned me today. Why do you think that I'd ever abandon you?"

Luis shook his head as though her question were absurd. "You're a beautiful woman, Michelle. It's only natural for you to want to surround yourself with attractive things, men included. I'm no longer in that category."

"You are as handsome as you ever were."

"You needn't keep up that pretense. What if I were to believe you? It would only make it that much more difficult for me later when I can look in a mirror and see the truth for myself."

"The truth," Michelle emphasized in her still-hoarse voice, "is that you are going to be shocked to discover that my description of your looks is accurate. Perhaps then you'll think of some way to apologize to me for your insufferable arrogance, but until then, I'd rather not see you at all. I said I'd be responsible for the other side of the island, and I'm going there right now!"

"Michelle, be reasonable. It's dark and you've nowhere to go for shelter."

Emboldened with anger, Michelle walked right up to him. "My goodness, are you actually pretending some concern for my welfare? You've just made it plain that you're the only one who matters here. You don't want my affection because you fear it's tainted with gratitude or pity, but it didn't even cross your mind that I might want yours."

Michelle turned her back on him and disappeared into the trees before the shock of her insult had time to register in Luis's mind. Thinking he might come after her out of spite, she did not head for the eastern bluff, but instead turned south. She would have no fire for warmth, no orderly camp to tend, not even a bucket to draw water, but those problems were insignificant when the husband she had come to adore was too lost in himself to love her.

Twenty-three

Luis stared after Michelle, but despite her dramatic accusation and abrupt departure, he could not believe she had been sincere. To appear admirably loyal one minute and then angrily strike out on her own in the next made as little sense to him as her transparent compliments. He raised his hand and gingerly traced the contours of the right side of his face. He could feel the tenderness of the still-healing skin if not the scarring, but he knew it had to be there.

If only Michelle appreciated how badly he wanted to believe in her reassuring words, then perhaps she would understand how cruel they would ultimately prove to be. To have false hopes, to grasp for even the slim possibility that his appearance would be normal, only to discover that it wasn't . . . the pain of that moment would be much worse than any the fiery sail had caused him. Flattering lies were just that—lies, and he didn't want to hear another.

That did not mean he did not want to see Michelle, however. He wondered what the chances were for her to return to camp on her own, and swiftly decided they were slim. He didn't want her wandering around the island at night. A daylight patrol was one thing, spending the night huddled all alone beneath a tree like a waif with no home was quite another.

For the second time that day, he grabbed up a

piece of dry wood, lit the end to create a torch, and started for the eastern bluff. He called Michelle's name frequently, without result. When he had crossed the island, he walked along the bluff and called down to the beach, but she was not there, either.

She had to be hiding from him, which again reminded him of a spoiled child's pranks rather than the thoughtful behavior he expected from his wife, but what if he was mistaken? What if in the dark, she had walked into a low-hanging limb and reopened the gash in her head? Could she be lying somewhere nearby, not answering him because she couldn't?

He searched for another dried branch to light and then continued looking for his missing bride. They had seen more of the southern end of the island than the north, and he turned that way. He held the torch out in front of him and hoping for a glimpse of Michelle's white shirt, peered through the darkness. When he found her, she was seated so near the edge of the cliff he feared she might have been considering leaping off. Not wanting to startle her, he called her name very softly as he approached.

Michelle hurriedly wiped away the tears she seemed to shed all too often and got to her feet. "What do you want?" she challenged.

Luis had known while he had been searching for her, but now that he had found her, his reason eluded him. "I don't want you out here all alone," he answered gruffly. "It isn't safe."

"When has anything we've ever done been safe?"

"As you pointed out earlier, no one intentionally plans accidents. We've just had some bad luck."

"When did it begin?" Michelle coached.

"What do you expect me to say, when I met you?"

"If that's the truth."

"I'm glad you mentioned the truth. That's all I want from you."

Michelle shoved her hands into her pockets. "For some reason, a mention of the truth reminds me of your Gypsy friends who could bend it so skillfully." She gleaned a certain satisfaction in seeing him flinch at that insult. "If you replace the *California*, why not name the ship something like *Gypsy Dancer*, or *Gypsy Spell*, or—"

"Stop it!"

"Stop what?"

"I've already promised you that I'll have nothing more to do with Gypsies. Now let's go back to camp."

Michelle gestured expansively. "This is my camp right here. The view is splendid and the ground is every bit as soft as it is in your camp."

"Must I carry you?"

"Do you really feel up to it after the trying day we've had?"

"No, I don't, but I won't leave you out here all alone. There are too many things you need. A fire for one."

"I've already gathered some wood. You could light it for me."

In a defiant response to her request, Luis walked to the edge of the bluff and hurled his torch as far as he could throw it. It spun end over end, creating a fiery pinwheel until it landed in the surf and was extinguished. The night was clear, the stars bright, and his scowl was easy to discern even without the torch.

"You'll not need a fire because you aren't staying here," Luis boasted. "We're all alone on this island. We ought to stay together."

"There's an enormous difference between staying together and *being* together."

"I fail to see any distinction."

"No, of course not. You see only your own situation and never mine."

Luis was rapidly losing his patience. "When we are the only two people here, how can my 'situation,' as you put it, be any different from yours?"

"You're thinking only of the day we'll be rescued. What happens before then matters very little to you. I don't think we're going to be rescued, ever. That casts an entirely different light on everything we do."

"But we are going to be rescued! Why can't you believe that?"

"As you said, we're having some very bad luck."

Luis glared down at her and attempted to make some sense of her words. "Is that why you've told me I'm still handsome? Is it because you doubt we'll ever leave here and you think I'll never discover the truth?" When Michelle failed to respond, Luis softened his tone. "It's really very kind of you to want to protect me from having to accept what's happened, but your basic premise is wrong.

"The Balearic Islands aren't isolated, and even if they were, ships would come here searching for us. My family wouldn't allow us to disappear without a trace, Michelle. They'd search for years. They'd not stop until they found out where the *California* sank, and why. They would also believe that we're alive until they had tangible proof otherwise. I'm sorry if I didn't impress that upon you."

All that he had succeeded in impressing on her was the sorry fact that he didn't trust her to speak the truth. It was too bitter an insult to forgive. "Well, when the rescuers arrive," she informed him proudly, "you'll know where to find me."

Luis nodded, as though agreeing to allow her to remain there, but before she realized what was happening, he had gathered her up into his arms and turned away from the cliff. "Next time you run away from me," he teased, "try and make it in the daytime."

Infuriated, Michelle clenched her hands into fists, but there wasn't anywhere she could strike him without fearing that she might tear open one of his burns. She then chose to fight him with words and, after calling him several extremely uncomplimentary names, she insisted that he put her down.

"Just as soon as we get home, *querida*."

Michelle fell silent, and, horribly discouraged, again had to fight away tears. Luis had come to get her not because she had appealed for his affection in a humiliatingly blatant fashion, but simply because he had decided that it wasn't safe for her to be on her own. He never spoke of love, or of caring for her. The most he did was boast arrogantly that he would not abandon her. The problem was, she already felt abandoned. When they arrived at his camp and he set her down on her feet, she turned right around and walked out on him again.

Luis had been expecting as much and caught up with her before she had left the circle of light thrown by the fire. "Must you be so damn stubborn? We've already settled this question. You're going to stay with me." He led her back to the fronds where they had spent the previous night, but this time moved her leaves right next to his. Still holding her hand, he gestured for her to lie down, then took his place beside her and drew her into his arms.

He had thought holding her close until she fell asleep would be the easiest solution to keeping track of her, but instantly regretted his foolhardy mistake. The last night they had lain cuddled together he had not felt well enough to do more than sleep. Now, as he hugged her tight, the subtle contours of her lithe form slid against the planes of his muscular body with a tormenting sweetness. She was not rubbing against him in a seductively teasing fashion. To the contrary, she was squirming in an attempt to put as much distance between them as possible, but he wanted none.

When they had last made love, they had barely escaped burning to death. How long ago had that been? The days at sea were a blur, those on the island too similar to separate. He knew he ought to keep track of the passage of time and vowed to begin doing so the very next day, but now, all he wanted was Michelle.

"Did you really mean what you said about wanting me?" he asked in a hesitant whisper.

His question both thrilled and appalled Michelle and she ceased struggling to rest quietly in his arms. "Can't a woman admit to desiring her husband?"

"Give me an answer please, not another question."

"What do my answers matter when you continually malign my motives?"

Luis did not know whether to be annoyed or amused. Perhaps he was a little of both. Then it dawned on him that whatever her motives for wanting him, he wanted her too badly to care. He raised up slightly, combed her long curls away from her face, and kissed her without making any effort to disguise his need. Her lips were soft, her taste delicious, and he didn't feel even a hint of revulsion in her response. Instead, she slipped her arms around his waist to hold him near and her unspoken vow of love allayed all his doubts most eloquently.

Kissing her was such a joy that he savored only that tender expression of devotion until their mutual need for more grew too demanding to deny. He unbuttoned her worn shirt carefully, then leaned down to nuzzle the soft mounds of her breasts. He licked the pale crests and nipped at them playfully, teasing the sensitive flesh into firm buds he rolled between his finger and thumb as he lost himself in another of her marvelous kisses.

"It was the way you kiss that kept luring me back to you," he now confessed willingly. "I have never known a woman who can convey so much of herself with a mere kiss. It was enchanting."

He paused, expecting a response and Michelle did not disappoint him. "Your kisses did far more than merely enchant me," she whispered. "They brought my most cherished dreams to life."

Luis had never had the romantic illusions to which Michelle was referring, but he could not imagine any woman exciting him more than she did. "I'm going to have to do a much better job of taking care of you," he vowed. He spread a flurry of adoring kisses over her bare breasts before easing her pants down over her hips.

Her skin was soft, and, like his, slightly sandy. He deliberately tickled her tummy with his beard and laughed along with her throaty giggles. He removed her pants with one last tug and lay them aside. The amber glow of the fire gave her fair skin the sheen of pearls and he drew his fingertips up her inner thigh in a gentle caress that made her shiver with anticipation.

"I'm going to buy the most beautiful pearls I can find for you. Whenever you wear them, remember this island as being more than a mere refuge from the sea and think of the love we shared here."

Huge tears welled up in Michelle's eyes. "Please, you sound as though I'll have only the pearls and not you."

Luis kissed away her tears. "I didn't mean to frighten you. Nothing is going to happen to me." He laughed again. "Perhaps I should promise that nothing *more* is going to happen to me, or to you."

He drew her into his arms, but she was trembling still and he wondered if she was thinking of how tragically she had lost her first love, rather than how they might one day be parted. He hoped not, for he wanted her thoughts focused solely on him as he began to explore her body with an increasingly bold caress. Gentle, intimate, provocative, his fingertips traced a filigree of exquisite sensation. He waited patiently until the tremors that shook her were unmistakably those of rapture rather than remorse before he cast aside his only garment and brought his teasing torment to an end with a shattering ecstasy.

The intensity of that pleasure convinced him they were as perfectly matched a pair as heaven ever created. He wished her sweet dreams with flavorful kisses and, their passions sated, they fell asleep in a relaxed tangle of arms and legs. The balmy night covered them with unusual warmth but they awoke to gray, overcast skies.

A skilled captain, Luis could forecast the weather with a single glance at the darkening clouds. He had wanted to spend the day with Michelle, and while that would still be possible, he had not expected to pass the time working to keep dry. He studied the angle of the lower branches in the trees surrounding their camp. Two had sturdy limbs at shoulder height that he was sure would support a crosspiece.

"If we place the longest piece of dry wood we can find between these two trees, we can form a tent by leaning whatever branches we can break off against the central beam. If we top it with palm fronds, we'll be able to keep out most of the tain."

Michelle's throat was still sore, and while she had loved spending the night in Luis's arms, she did not feel at all rested. She covered a wide yawn rather than remind him that she had proposed they build a shelter when they had first arrived. That it had taken the threat of rain to convince him of the wisdom of her plan was not something for which she would fault him aloud, though.

"When I first began to gather firewood, I came across several limbs that were too large to use for that purpose. They would be perfect. I think I can remember where they are."

She had pulled on her clothes, flipped her curls out of her eyes, and looked ready to take on any challenge, but Luis was still worried about her. "Do you have a headache?" he asked considerately.

Michelle did not want to worry him by mentioning her sore throat and so kept still about it. While she could feel the gash she had received in the cave, it wasn't terribly painful, but the reminder brought a sudden inspiration. "No, not really. But rather than build a tent, couldn't we move into the smugglers' cave?"

Luis shook his head. "You've given it the accurate name. It *is* the smugglers' cave, and if they return, I'd rather not have them find us living there. The fact we lost their lantern is bad enough. They're sure to notice it's gone, but I hope they won't be curious enough to go looking for it."

"You left the wood you'd brought for torches there."

"I know. I'll go and get it later. Right now, tell me where you saw the fallen limbs that would make good crosspieces and I'll go and fetch them. I want you to catch our breakfast while I'm working on the tent. That will make the best use of our time before the rain comes."

Michelle was pleased he had given her something to do and readily agreed rather than admit she did not really feel up to the task. "They were close to the bluff, just north of here." She picked up the spear and the bucket. "I'll get the water, too. It will take a long time for it to fill with rain."

"Fine." Luis walked her to where the path began to the beach and gave her an enthusiastic hug. "Be careful. Don't slip on the rocks and—"

Michelle reached up to silence his list of precautions with a kiss. "You just be careful yourself," she told him and, anxious to complete her work, she hurried on down to the beach. She wasn't quite sure how things had gone so quickly from strained to heavenly, but she knew better than to question her good fortune. Perhaps Luis had not said that he loved her in those precise words, but he *had* mentioned love and that was definitely an auspicious start.

Luis watched Michelle until she disappeared to fill the bucket. If it rained for most of the day, he would have ample opportunity to work on carving another and, he hoped, a better one. When they left the island, he was going to take the first one along, though. It would be something to show their grandchildren while he told them how he and their grandmother had been marooned.

That was the first time he had ever even considered the possible existence of grandchildren and, amused, he went to find the limbs Michelle had described. They were right where she had said they would be and he dragged two back to camp thinking that he might later be able to connect a second beam to a third tree to give their tent two rooms. He soon discovered that his basic structure, while a good one, required more fresh branches to cover than he could gather before the first sprinkles of rain began to fall.

Michelle had already speared three fish when the raindrops falling into the sea obscured her vision and she had to return to camp. She took the bucket of water and the wood Luis had left in the cave with her. "I was already close to the cave, so I went to save you a trip," she explained.

Luis opened his mouth to scold her, and then thought better of it. "I don't want you to go there ever again," he stated in the most reasonable tone he could manage. "It's too dangerous and the risk isn't worth it."

"But you'd left the wood just inside the first chamber and —" Michelle judged the change in Luis's expression accurately and stopped protesting. "Fine. I won't go there again," she promised. "Now, hadn't we better cook the fish before the rain puts out the fire?"

Luis had been so preoccupied building a shelter he had neglected to look after the fire. "I'm going to build another one near the entrance of our tent," he explained. "There isn't room to light one inside, but as long as it's close it should keep us warm. I'll just have to shield it from the rain."

Michelle stepped back to give him room to construct the necessary V-shaped enclosure with dry limbs he topped with green branches. In just a few minutes he had a second blaze going in the small, protected structure. "That's very clever," she complimented him sincerely, pleased that he found it so much easier to build with wood than to carve it.

"Thank you. You roast the fish and try and stay dry while I see what I can do to keep the rain on the outside of the tent."

Michelle ventured inside his newly built shelter, and while the sides were too steep to permit her to stand up straight, there was plenty of room to sit, or lie down comfortably. Considering how it was constructed, she did not think it would leak too badly, either. Impressed, she sat at the entrance to wrap the fish in palm fronds and then placed them on the coals.

She took a drink of water to soothe her throat, and wished that she had some way to brew hot tea. Luis made several trips down to the beach to cut palm fronds, and when he had layered those over the spine of the tent, the rain rolled harmlessly off to the sides rather than continue to seep through the roof. By the time the fish were ready to eat, he was able to join Michelle.

"Thank you for not berating me for not building you a shelter before now," he said between bites of breakfast.

"We haven't been here all that long," Michelle reminded him.

"Perhaps not, but I should have taken your suggestion to heart and done a better job of providing for us."

Michelle was delighted that, while definitely tardy, her ideas had made an impression on him. She reached out to pat his arm. "It isn't raining hard. The pine trees have a wonderful fragrance, and this quaint little house will be all we'll need. We ought not to argue about what happened before today. Let's just do our best to get along now."

That was such a plaintive plea that Luis quickly agreed and then he made another observation. "You look tired. Why don't you take a nap when we finish eating?"

"You wouldn't mind?"

"No, of course not." Luis winked to assure her that he would look forward to more of her company later. As she slept, the rain fell steadily, if not hard, enabling him to leave the tent frequently. He covered the dry limbs stacked in their woodpile and signal beacon with fresh branches, looked out to the sea for the ship he was so positive was coming, and attempted to catch more fish. The wood got damp despite his best efforts to keep it dry, the visibility was too poor to permit the sighting of any vessel sailing past the breakers, and the fish had all fled to the depths leaving him with nothing to show for his time when Michelle awakened. When she began to cough, he was alarmed.

By the time Michelle had stilled her cough with several sips of water, her throat hurt so badly, she was frightened. She swallowed hard, winced at the pain, and then apologized to Luis. "I'm sorry. My throat started to hurt yesterday and I'd hoped it would go away, but I'm afraid it's only gotten worse."

"Why didn't you tell me you were sick?"

Luis looked more hurt than angry, but Michelle wasn't in the least bit sorry she hadn't confided in him earlier. He had been busy, and she had not wanted to be a burden. "I'll just rest a while longer. I'm sure I'll feel better later."

"Are you warm enough?"

Michelle was lying as close to the fire as she could get, and they had no blankets, so there was no point in admitting she was cold. "Yes. I guess yesterday was more tiring than I'd realized."

Luis glanced out at the sky. The clouds were as dense as they had been at dawn. "I'll try and spear more fish later."

Michelle stretched out and rested her cheek on her arm. "I'm not hungry. You needn't catch any for me."

Luis was worried, though, and very badly. He leaned over to caress Michelle's cheek and drew his hand back quickly when he felt how warm she was. "You've got a fever. Better drink more water before you fall asleep." When she sat up he held the bucket for her, but she didn't drink nearly as much as he encouraged her to.

406

"Just let me sleep," she begged as she pushed the bucket away.

Luis knew sleep would help her, but that he could not was difficult to accept. The day was growing colder every hour, and while he kept adding wood to their fire, much of its warmth was dissipated by the rain that fell between the flames and the opening of their shelter. Finally Luis got up and, by carefully positioning additional branches, extended one side of their tent to enclose the fire but still left them space to come and go on the opposite side.

When the temperature inside their makeshift dwelling instantly began to rise, Luis was angry that he had not built the structure to accommodate the fire in the first place. He was uncertain whether that had been a mere oversight on his part or a lingering fear of fire as a result of his burns. Neither excuse was acceptable, and he again stroked Michelle's cheek and prayed that the rainstorm would be a brief one and that they would have fair weather to help him nurse her back to health.

Boris Ryde returned to Valencia full of bright hopes and ambitious plans. He immediately set about making the long needed repairs to the *Salamander*. He kept his crew busy from morning to night sanding and caulking the ship prior to repainting. He visited ships' chandleries for items he had long coveted but previously could ill afford and paid for them in gold coins.

He ordered new uniforms from the city's finest tailor and bought the most expensive pair of boots he had ever owned. He had a barber trim his hair and beard in a style that flattered his rugged features. He increased the amount of provisions for his crew, if not the quality of the fare, but he splurged on every meal he bought for himself.

He savored fine wine, drank expensive whiskey, and sought out several of the city's most talented prostitutes whom he tipped generously for treating him as though he actually were the English gentleman he pretended to be. He then returned to the docks and visited the taverns where ships and sailing were the only topics of conversation. He did not ask for news of Augustín Aragon's *California,* but he listened and waited most impatiently for word the ship was overdue.

While anxious to return home, Antoine Lareau soon discovered that extended travel was much too arduous for him. He could spend only a few hours in his coach each day before the jarring motion of the vehicle made his shoulder ache so badly he would order his driver to stop at the next inn. He was grateful for the generous hospitality of the Spanish people, and took every advantage of the courtesy they showed him. The bribe to Boris Ryde had seriously depleted his funds, but his appetite was still a poor one and he required very little in the way of food and drink to be fully satisfied.

All he truly required was a comfortable bed each night. He would have actually enjoyed the leisurely journey had the pain in his shoulder not been such a nuisance. Each morning he would start out hoping to do better and, in an optimistic frame of mind, he would entertain himself by imagining what his life would be like without Michelle. After his first few days of travel, he decided he would be wise to warn her family that she would not be returning with him.

That night he composed the first of what was to become a witty series of letters describing his adventures in Spain. He began not by sounding bitter or angry about Michelle's betrayal, but admitting only to losing her to a dashing Spaniard of immense wealth. He made it plain that he assumed Michelle had already written to them. He rather hoped that she had, but he doubted that she would be any more likely to reveal the truth than he.

He sent a letter ahead to his mother, too. Francisco had already written to apologize for the delay in his return, but this was Antoine's first effort at corresponding with her and it was not nearly so amusing as composing letters for Michelle's mother and sisters. He had always been fond of the whole family. At fourteen, Nicole displayed a wisdom far beyond her years, while at seventeen, Denise was a delightfully spontaneous creature who had always greeted him with a sweet kiss, and a compliment as well.

Antoine paused for a moment to savor his memories of Denise. She was nearly as pretty as Michelle, and far more demonstrative. He liked her more than he had ever dared admit. He knew that she already had several attentive male callers, but none had fascinated her to such an extent that she had ever neglected to flirt with him when he came to visit Michelle.

Were he to marry Denise, he would be congratulated by all his friends rather than pitied and ridiculed as Michelle's jilted suitor. The longer he considered that prospect, the more attractive it became. There was always the possibility that, despite his reputation for violence, Captain Ryde would keep his money and never make any effort to harm Augustín Aragon and the French slut he had wed.

In that case, Michelle would undoubtedly bring her Spaniard home one day and Antoine would have the exquisite pleasure of greeting her as a brother-in-law. He considered that a delicious possibility and he acted out several dialogues that amused him immensely. It was unfortunate that Ramón Guerrero had seen him before he left Madrid, for surely if Augustín and Michelle escaped harm at Captain Ryde's hands, they would learn that he had survived their duel.

Greatly intrigued, Antoine included a special note to Denise to assure her he had not forgotten her while he had been away. It was a wonderfully ambiguous paragraph, one that would seem merely a gesture of friendship to her mother, but one that he was positive would thrill Denise with the hint of affection he had barely veiled.

The next day he was so lost in ambitious plans that his shoulder did not even begin to bother him until well past noon. That he had devised a way to return home in triumph rather than the most humiliating embarrassment cheered him the whole day. That night he wrote another letter with an amusing postscript for Denise guaranteed to make her await his arrival with a breathless excitement he could not wait to observe.

The storm that swept the small island kept up a steady downpour all day. Luis did not try to fish in the foul weather, but having no other source of food added hunger to his mounting problems. He kept a close watch on Michelle and, despite his best efforts to keep her warm and dry, by late afternoon she began to shiver uncontrollably. He added wood to the fire and lay close beside her to share whatever warmth his body contained, but he was frantic with worry.

He could do so little for her now, and if she developed pneumonia, he would have no chance at all to save her life. He remembered how she had coughed when he had pulled her to the surface of the water-filled cave. What if she had come closer to drowning yesterday than he had realized? What if, despite her coughs, she had still had some water in her lungs? Why hadn't he even considered that possibility? He had been so worried about the gash in her head that he had had her lie on her back when what he really should have been doing was attempt to force out any water that remained in her lungs?

He didn't know what to do now, except pray. He held Michelle tight, thanked God for his generosity in the past, and begged Him not to desert them now.

Twenty-four

Throughout the day, the gentle rain dripped from the pine trees and trickled across the sandy soil in meandering rivulets. Those tiny streams crisscrossed the forest, then slid down the channels worn into the limestone cliffs and flowed into the sea. Off shore, the storm heightened the waves and the surf slammed against the rocky coves, jealously seeking to reclaim the island as part of the sea.

It wasn't until nightfall that the heavy clouds began to lift, but when Luis saw the stars, he felt no sense of relief. Michelle was sleeping fretfully, but she was awakened often by the cough that kept Luis too worried to sleep. He had tried to rest, but found it impossible when he kept anxiously anticipating Michelle's next breath.

Each time she awoke, she offered a wan smile and he tried not to alarm her with his concern, but it was difficult to keep his spirits up when the potential danger was so acute. He had been scorched by the flames of Michelle's temper often enough to think of her as a strong woman, but it had not been long since her grief for Antoine had shown him that she also possessed a far more vulnerable side. Sleeping in his arms, she appeared as delicate as a child, evoking a conscious desire within him to protect her from all harm.

She would not have been marooned with him had it not been for Boris Ryde, and Luis's thoughts kept returning to the English captain. He had terminated Boris's employment with the Aragon Line for just cause, and, in his view, he had shown considerable restraint in allowing the man to live. Now he regretted his compassion, for Boris Ryde obviously had been incapable of appreciating it. Instead of accepting his dismissal as justified and mending his ways, he had become even more darkly twisted and evil.

Luis would not repeat his mistake. At his first opportunity, he was going to confront the man, and this time he would show absolutely no mercy. By dawn, he was determined to see that Michelle enjoyed the long and happy life she deserved and equally committed to arranging for Boris Ryde's prompt demise. He would not need the power of the Aragon Line. No, this time he was going to handle things with a far more personal touch.

Warmed by the sun, Michelle awoke to a bright day filled with promise. She lay cradled in Luis's arms and watched him with an affectionate gaze until he glanced down and discovered she was awake. "Good morning," she greeted him, but her voice was no more than a raspy whisper.

"How is your throat?"

Michelle tried swallowing to judge. "Better, I think, even though I sound worse."

"You shouldn't talk then," Luis cautioned. "Today you can sleep in the sunshine and perhaps by tomorrow or the next day you'll be well again." He leaned down to kiss her lips lightly. "I can't wait for you to be well."

Michelle's first thought was that Luis was flirting with her, which pleased her very much, but then she saw something far more serious than a teasing sparkle in his dark eyes. He looked desperately worried and, certain that was unnecessary, she squeezed his arm and snuggled against him. "I just got too tired," she apologized. "I'm not really sick."

Luis rather liked the husky tones of her cough-ravaged voice, but he placed his fingertip against her lips to remind her to be quiet. "You needn't speak until you're well. We have so few provisions here that it will be no trick at all for me to anticipate your every need. Right now you're probably not nearly as hungry as I am, but I'm going to insist that you eat. Will you be all right on your own while I spear us some fish?"

Michelle nodded sleepily and covered a yawn. She could remember being cold, but now that the sunshine had returned, she felt warm clear through, and when Luis left her to fish, she fell asleep and didn't stir until noon. Thinking she had dozed off for only a few minutes, she thought they were eating breakfast until Luis referred to the meal as lunch. She shaded her eyes with her hand and was astonished to see the sun was high overhead.

"I'm sorry . . ." she began.

"Hush," Luis scolded. "You mustn't talk." He was amused when Michelle pantomimed sleeping and then folded her hands in prayer. "You needn't apologize for sleeping. I have plenty to do. See, I've been working on a new bucket. You were gracious enough not to criticize the first one, but I wasn't at all pleased with it."

"It holds water," Michelle mouthed clearly.

"Yes, it does, but not very much and it's way too heavy. This one will be a vast improvement."

Michelle smiled her encouragement. She had eaten only a few bites of fish and already she was full. Sitting up made her dizzy and she stretched out and closed her eyes. She had not meant to fall asleep again, but soon did. Her dreams were no more than graceful images that refused to come clear. Each time she began to cough, she changed positions and attempted to stifle the annoying impulse, but it refused to be silenced for long.

Frustrated by his inability to help her, Luis took out his anger on the new bucket and hacked at the wood with a vengeance. He kept telling himself that Michelle's cough was brought on by the hardships they had endured. He refused to consider that she might be suffering from consumption. She still had a fever, though, and he could not shake the horrible suspicion that her health was now too fragile for her to survive the rigors of their bleak island existence much longer.

She needed fresh fruit and vegetables in addition to fish, and they had no way to obtain them. He watched her sleep and wondered what if she didn't ever feel any better. What if everyday she grew progressively weaker until her extended naps became a coma? he asked himself.

Desperate to dislodge such disheartening thoughts, Luis went down to the beach and swam until he had sapped most of the nervous energy that had kept his thoughts in constant turmoil. He then speared more fish for their supper, and when he carried them back to their camp Michelle was awake again and greeted him with a smile he imagined was a bit more enthusiastic than the one he had seen at noon.

That night he had no trouble sleeping, but when Michelle was no better the next day, for the first time he began to question his stubborn insistence that they would soon be rescued. What if Encario and the rest of his crew were sitting on an equally barren island waiting for him to rescue them? When the *California* failed to return to Valencia, he was positive a thorough search would be begun. Perhaps it already had. He cursed his own stupidity in not marking the days in some fashion.

While he was still confident they would be rescued eventually, his present worry was that it would not happen in time to save Michelle. There was another alternative, however, and a plan began to take form in his mind. Deliberating on it at length, he didn't realize he was being very poor company for Michelle until she motioned for him to talk with her.

"I was just thinking that we can't be far from Mallorca. We could sail the lifeboat there, using a pine bough for a mast and can secure it with ropes woven from palm fronds. If we just had something we could use for a sail."

It took Michelle a moment to grasp the significance of his words, and then she wished that she hadn't. "You want to leave here in the lifeboat?" she asked in a barely audible whisper.

Luis knew that was an outrageous plan, but he admitted to it. "Yes. I'm getting impatient waiting to be rescued, aren't you?"

Michelle hadn't felt well enough to be bored, but she could readily understand how he could feel that way since it could hardly be amusing to watch her sleep most of the day. She quickly covered her next cough and tried to give him a reason other than cowardice for abandoning his plan. "Aren't we better off here than being adrift at sea?"

"For the time being, yes," Luis agreed, "but perhaps not in the long run. That's what concerns me."

Michelle probed for the real reason. "Are you worried about me?"

"Of course. You're not used to sleeping on the ground, Michelle. It's no wonder that you're sick."

Michelle wanted to argue with him, but she was too tired, completely drained, and all she wanted to do was close her eyes and take another nap. She reached out to caress Luis's cheek and he caught her hand and drew it to his lips. "I'm not going to leave you," she vowed softly.

Luis pulled her across his lap and enveloped her in a fierce hug. He knew that she wouldn't leave him

416

intentionally, but as she began to cough, he feared she would not be given a choice. When she fell asleep, he went down to the beach and strolled along the shore. The island had a tranquil atmosphere, but he now saw it for the deadly trap it was. He wanted to leave desperately, but even if they split the seams of their clothes, they would not provide enough fabric for a sail. He chuckled to himself as he imagined how Michelle would react to the suggestion they travel devoid of any garments.

Depressed, he kept on walking until he reached the northern tip of the island. He scaled the bluff and sat down. The Mediterranean Sea was so calm that day it reminded him of the Pacific coast where he had grown up. He wondered what his father would do in his situation, or his brother, Marc, who had been so quick to volunteer to fight for the United States. Memories of his family brought a smile to his lips. He had been away from home too long and if he didn't think of a way to leave the island soon, he feared eternity would pass before he saw any of his loved ones again.

Determined to be the conscientious husband Michelle deserved, he rose and continued on his way around the island. He had been too concerned about her to conduct the patrol he had meant to establish, but now he concentrated on scanning the horizon, searching for a ship, but none sailed into view. He returned to camp in the vilest of moods, but one glance at Michelle's welcoming smile was enough to banish his darkest thoughts.

"I'm going to light the signal fire," he announced suddenly. "Or rather, a small part of it. I can't keep a close enough watch for ships, but if we have a fire burning all the time, any ship passing by will see it. While I'm going to try and keep a closer watch tomorrow, lighting a fire will improve our chances of a prompt rescue."

417

"That's a good idea," Michelle agreed, determined to continue to praise him lavishly as long as his suggestions did not include returning to sea in the lifeboat.

Late the next afternoon, the Venetian schooner *Mattino Bello* sailed near the island. One of the crew saw the plume of smoke drifting skyward from the signal fire and called it to his captain's attention. Captain Valentino Cesari was a fair-haired young man with piercing blue eyes and an impatient nature. He had traversed the same uneventful route so often, he was eager for an excuse to investigate the source of the smoke. He ordered a change in course, brought the *Mattino Bello* in as close as he dared, dropped anchor, and sent a boat ashore.

When Luis first sighted the ship he feared it was a hallucination. He stood watching silently on the bluff while the shore party towed their boat through the surf. It wasn't until he actually saw their footprints in the sand that he was convinced the men were real.

"Someone's finally here," he called to Michelle.

Not really strong enough to do more than daydream, Michelle had been sitting by the fire. She still possessed her customary grace, though, and rose with a languid ease. She walked very slowly to where Luis was watching the shore party mill about on the beach. Five of the men were talking together while one had noticed Luis's tracks and was following them toward the bluff.

"What should we do?" Michelle asked anxiously. "Do you know any of the men? Are they likely to be friendly, or should we hide?"

"They're flying a Venetian flag. As far as I know, I haven't a single enemy in Venice." Luis knew he ought to be elated that their exile was over, but he wasn't eager to have a look at himself and thereby know, not merely fear, the worst. There was also Michelle's welfare to consider, and concern for her prompted him to end his selfish thoughts of himself. He called out to the men and waved to attract their attention. After putting out their fires and picking up their souvenir bucket, the tired and hungry couple was ready to depart.

Captain Cesari and his crew were shocked to find a woman had been stranded on the small island. They showed Michelle the most solicitous concern while she kept insisting it was Luis who deserved their attention. That she was speaking in French, while the captain spoke Italian, served to increase their level of misunderstanding. Able to comprehend the gist of the captain's conversation, Luis offered his own opinions in Spanish, prompting one of Cesari's crew to come forward to translate both his and Michelle's comments into Italian.

Captain Cesari had recognized the name Aragon when Luis had first introduced himself, but it was not until Luis's remarks had been translated for him that he grasped just how important a man Luis really was. He then listened attentively as Luis described how he and his bride had come to be shipwrecked. Valentino had never heard such a diabolical tale, and he offered whatever sympathy and promises of help he could.

Luis had promised to take Michelle to Mallorca, but he swiftly decided she would be able to recuperate far more comfortably in Valencia. He could better direct the rescue efforts for his crew from there, but his main purpose for choosing that city to allow him to deal with Boris Ryde's treachery without delay. "Take us to Valencia," he requested in the same tone he used for a direct order, "and I'll provide a substantial reward for you and your crew."

"We'll be there by tomorrow afternoon," Valentino

assured him. "Until then, I insist that you and your wife use my cabin. I'm afraid I have no feminine apparel, but I can at least provide clean garments for you both."

As Luis thanked Cesari, he had to admire the younger man's composure, for he had given no indication in either word or action that he was offended by the sight of his burns. Luis doubted that he could expect the same courtesy from others he met. The seamen in the shore party had been so taken with Michelle that they had scarcely noticed him, but Luis could not take her everywhere he went to provide such a lovely distraction his scars would go unnoticed.

"Your kindness is most appreciated," Luis enthused. "We've had nothing to eat but fish." He paused to calculate the days but became confused. "We left Valencia on October twenty-second. What is today's date?"

"The fourth of November."

Grateful their suffering had not been any longer, Luis pulled Michelle close and asked to be shown to Valentino's cabin. "If we could have some warm water to bathe and something to eat, we will both probably sleep until we reach Valencia."

"You are my guests and it will be my pleasure to provide whatever you wish. Please let me know should you require anything else." Valentino led the way to his cabin and then excused himself after promising to attend to their requests immediately.

Michelle sat down on the captain's bunk, closed her eyes, and gave a delighted squeal. "I never thought a narrow bunk would feel so good to me."

Luis replied with a distracted nod. He wandered about the cabin, wondering where Cesari kept his shaving mirror but not eager to find it. He wanted to shave off his beard, but knew if it hid some of his scars, he would be forced to keep it. After being outdoors so many days, the close confines of the cabin felt oppressive and he didn't know what to do with himself until Cesari returned.

While Michelle felt wonderfully safe and secure, she could easily see that Luis did not. "Is something wrong?" she asked. Her throat was no longer sore, but she had continued to speak in hushed tones so as not to strain it and bring on the coughing spells that still plagued her. "Don't you trust Captain Cesari?"

Luis sat down at the captain's table and folded his hands in front of him. "He appears to be an honest man. We'll just have to hope that he truly is."

Luis raised his hand to shield the right side of his face as he spoke. To a stranger it would appear that he was merely combing his hair off his forehead, but it had become a nervous habit he had not displayed before the fire. Michelle did not have to guess at what he was thinking. "When Cesari comes back, I'm going to ask him for a mirror. Then I hope you'll offer the apology I deserve for doubting my word."

Luis had set the bucket on the table and he turned it in his hands as he waited. "I think your feelings for me have blinded you."

Michelle had yet to put those feelings into words, but she would not deny that she had them. "You're right," she agreed. "You've been a wonderfully considerate husband under the worst of circumstances and I'm sure that does affect the way I see you."

That comment confirmed Luis's fears, but he did not attempt to force Michelle into speaking the truth when he would soon see it for himself. He simply sat and waited for Cesari's return and prayed he would be man enough not to weep in front of his wife when he finally saw his reflection. He got up to answer a knock at the door, and found the captain carrying a small copper tub and leading the man who had translated for them toting two buckets of hot water.

"We use this for laundry," Valentino explained as he set the tub down. "It is the best I have to offer for bathing."

"Thank you so much," Michelle replied. "Do you have a mirror and razor my husband might use? I fear he's forgotten what a handsome man he is even if I haven't."

Amused by her praise for her husband, Valentino provided all that Luis required for grooming, plus additional soap and towels for Michelle. He then searched through his wardrobe for clean garments for them both. His clothes would be a trifle small on Luis and much too large for Michelle, but they were clean and not unattractive.

"Your meal will be ready whenever you are," he assured them. "I hope you'll forgive me for not joining you for supper, but I must attend to my other duties."

Pleased he understood their need for privacy rather than amusing company, Luis thanked him again. When the cabin door closed behind the captain, he steeled himself for the grave shock he would surely have and, after a quick glance toward Michelle, he picked up the mirror Valentino had set on the table. The first thing he saw was his beard. It grew low on his cheeks, enhancing rather than obscuring his features, but he still thought it lent too forbidding an air.

Knowing that he would be sickened by the sight, he turned his head slowly to view the right side of his face. Then, thinking the mirror must be too dirty to provide a clear image, he picked up a towel and wiped it off. A second glance showed him no more than the first, however.

"It isn't the mirror," Michelle assured him. "Your

422

burns weren't severe there and the aloe helped to heal them. I'm sorry it wasn't as effective on your shoulders."

Unable to accept the proof his own eyes provided, Luis continued to stare into the mirror. While it was true the skin on the right side of his face was now a paler shade than the left, it was smooth and unscarred. To believe he was hideously scarred and find that his tan was merely uneven was almost more than Luis could sanely accept.

"I really thought—" he mumbled.

"Yes, I know what you thought and no amount of reassurance from me meant a thing to you. Do you recall the conversation we had on the way to Valencia? I said an agreeable companion would be one who would not dismiss my comments merely because I'm a woman and he's a man. To not be believed is just as humiliating as being ignored. You owe me an apology."

She had stated her case so eloquently that Luis did not even know where to begin. He set the mirror aside and went over to the bunk. After a brief hesitation, he knelt in front of her. "I am sorry. Truly I am. I shouldn't have doubted you, but I still think you'd lie to spare me if the truth would cause me pain."

Michelle thought that a pitiful apology, but apparently all that Luis's pride would permit him to offer. She knew better than to ask for more and leaned forward to kiss him. "Would sparing your feelings be wrong?"

"I don't know. A lie told for a loving reason would still be a lie."

"But if the truth were cruel, wouldn't a lie be infinitely better?"

Luis rested his cheek against her knee. "I don't want to argue any issue now. Let's just take advantage of the hot water before it cools, eat whatever

423

they have for us and sleep until we dock in Valencia."

Michelle stroked his hair. It had grown too long, but she liked the wildness of it and hoped that he would be in no hurry to have it trimmed. "I have a better idea," she offered in a sultry whisper. "Let's bathe, eat, and then make love all the way to Valencia."

Luis looked up at her. Her fair skin glowed with a newly acquired tan, but she still looked frail to him. "I didn't think you felt well enough."

Michelle responded with a slow, secret smile. She could not have walked around the deck had he asked her to, but the weakness in her limbs had nothing to do with the desire that filled her heart. Rather than describe the way she felt in reassuring terms that would surely be lies, she answered with a kiss filled with the truth of her love.

Fooled by her affection, Luis helped her out of her clothes. He poured most of the hot water into the laundry tub and then took her hand to be certain she did not slip as she stepped in and sat down. Though she had to bend her knees, it was not an uncomfortable fit. Luis picked up the soap, but rather than hand it to her, he knelt on one knee by her side and worked up a lather.

While her arms and face were now an attractive golden brown her shoulders were still the shade of rich cream and he started scrubbing her there. She had gone from slender to thin, and that pained him badly. "I should have taken much better care of you," he murmured regretfully.

Michelle covered his hand with hers. "Please don't think that," she begged. "You did your best. No man can do more."

"Things will be different now," Luis promised. "I'll not let anyone hurt you ever again."

Laughing, Michelle flicked water in his face. "Let's

424

celebrate our rescue, not dwell on the dangers of the past."

That she would brush aside his heartfelt vow insulted Luis, but only for an instant. Then her teasing tone inspired him to be playful. He chose another method, however, and slid his soapy hands over her breasts. Her nipples hardened instantly and he toyed with them between slippery fingers. Even if too slender, she still had the luscious body of a goddess. He longed to give free rein to his desires but first he paid attention to his task and shampooed the sand from her long curls.

The water lapped at her navel and Luis scooped up a handful to rinse her breasts. Then he followed the water's trickling path down between her legs. His touch was gently adoring, but taunting as well, deliberately creating a need within Michelle that matched his own. He wanted more of her than he had ever taken, and he wanted it now.

Michelle closed her eyes and savored the mounting ecstasy that Luis skillfully coaxed to the edge of the ultimate plateau. Nearing that raptuous peak, he stopped suddenly, rose, and pulled her from the tub. She was too startled to complain, but the hunger in her glance spoke for her. Luis wrapped her in a towel to blot the moisture from her skin, then carried her the few steps to the captain's bunk. Placing her there, he cast the towel aside and leaned down to kiss the taut buds crowning her breasts. He drew them into his mouth, teasing them with his tongue and teeth until Michelle arched her back to offer still more of her flavorful flesh.

Luis slipped off his pants and joined her in the bunk, but rather than lie down beside her, he moved over her, slowly blazing a trail with kisses that began at her lips and then tarried at her navel drawing forth the expected giggles. Still craving more, he moved off the end of the bunk and, taking a firm hold on her waist, he pulled her toward him. He rubbed his cheek against her thigh, parted her legs, and then nuzzled the golden triangle of curls nestled between them.

He heard her gasp, but he was past caring whether or not he had shocked her. All that mattered was that what he was doing would bring pleasure to them both and he slid his tongue along the cleft that hid the last of her secrets. He teased apart the delicate folds of her most feminine flesh, savoring her sweet, salty taste as he invaded the core of her being. Next he found the tender bud that shared his sole purpose of giving joy. Caressing it with the tip of his tongue, he felt Michelle writhe as the bliss he had hoped to create shuddered through her in convulsive waves. Still, he did not release her until he had also had his fill of this new and exotic thrill.

Completely relaxed by Luis's lavish attentions, Michelle lay unashamedly naked across the bunk. Her eyes were half closed as she watched him shave with the hot water he had set aside and then step into the tub. He was much too tall to sit comfortably as she had, but he did manage to cover himself with lather and rinse off without splashing too much water about.

It was not his neatness that fascinated her, though, it was the remarkable handsomeness of his muscular body. Even now, as he stood in a relaxed pose, his appeal was enhanced by his deeply bronzed skin. She slid off the bunk and, went to him. Taking the towel, she patted the droplets of water from his back and then placed a kiss on his shoulder blade.

"I liked your beard, but I do believe you're slightly better looking without it."

"Only slightly?"

While she remained behind him, Michelle trailed her fingertips across the flat planes of his stomach. "What about all the women you used to tell me

426

about? Did any of them prefer you with a beard?"

"What women?" Luis asked with an amused chuckle.

"The women who were going to be driven wild with jealousy when they saw the mark of my kiss on your throat."

"I've forgotten them all," Luis assured her. He closed his eyes as her hands strayed lower, but he could take only a little of her teasing before he clamped his hand around her wrist. He drew her over to the bunk and after stretching out, pulled her down beside him.

Michelle returned his eager hugs, but soon escaped his embrace. She traced a loving trail of kisses across the smooth flatness of his belly and wondered aloud if her intimate kisses would bring him as much pleasure as his had her.

"Even more," Luis assured her. He held his breath, not really expecting her to be that bold, but her next kiss was a deeply devouring one that ended all speculation on that point. His bride was not merely bold, but gifted in the art of bestowing pleasure. She had a touch that was both confident and tantalizing, while the magic she worked with her lips and tongue brought a rush toward ecstasy he had to fight to control. Unwilling to be hurled over that delicious brink alone, he pulled her back into his arms and buried himself deep within her to share the euphoria that filled his heart.

Michelle again welcomed his affection with a throaty giggle that proved her delight was as great as his. Their need for each other far from sated, they moved toward a climax that bordered on violence in its splendor. If for only a few brief seconds they were truly one, it was enough to make an indelible impression on their hearts.

* * *

Luis did not know how long they had slept, but it was dark before they awakened and recalled they were hungry for something other than the taste of each other. He donned the clean clothes Valentino had loaned him, but Michelle chose to wear just a shirt. Luis was gone only a few minutes to fetch their supper, but it had been enough time for Michelle to grow worried.

"I heard you mention Boris Ryde to Captain Cesari. I know you believe he's responsible for the sinking of the *California,* but will the Spanish authorities arrest him without substantial proof he was behind it?"

"I'm not going to trust the matter to the authorities, Michelle. I'm going to deal with the bastard myself."

Luis had spoken calmly, as though he were contemplating a business matter rather than what she feared was something as drastic as murder. He again had the haunted look she had seen in his eyes on the island and now she understood what he had been plotting then. "You can't kill the man without proof that he's guilty," she insisted.

While Luis had taken care not to mention killing Boris Ryde, he wasn't surprised by his bride's perceptive conclusion. He lay his knife and fork across his plate. "Despite evidence to the contrary, I'm not an impulsive man. If I were, Boris Ryde wouldn't be alive today and we wouldn't have lost the *California.* When we reach Valencia, my first responsibility will be to send search parties out for any of my crew who are still missing. Once that's done, I'll speak to some of Ryde's crew. He's too brutal to inspire loyalty, so I'm sure they'll tell me if he had anything to do with setting the fire on the *California.* If I can find the two men who actually lit the blaze, so much the better, but even if I do, I'm not stopping until I get Ryde himself. I know what I'm suggesting is

428

dangerous, but don't ask me not to take this into my own hands, Michelle, because our lives are too important to trust to well-meaning authorities who might investigate my accusation for months and take even longer to arrest Ryde and bring him to trial."

Luis was about to remind her that all the men on watch had been murdered by Ryde's assassins, but thought better of mentioning that gruesome fact. "I realize our marriage has gotten off to a very poor start, but once Ryde is taken care of, I want to take you on a honeymoon trip. Please trust me to take care of Ryde without landing us in more trouble. Can you do that?"

Michelle knew Luis was serious, but she was, too. "Don't go after Ryde alone," she begged. "Some of your crew may have already found their way back to Valencia. If not, hire other men you can trust to be loyal, but don't go after Boris Ryde all alone."

That was precisely what Luis intended to do, but because he would be certain to involve a few others in some facet of his plan he nodded his consent. "I plan to live a long and happy life, *querida,* and I intend to do it with you."

Michelle saw more in her husband's sly smile than he had meant to reveal. He might have promised not to go after Boris Ryde alone, but she thought he still meant to kill the swine with his bare hands. Luis was a proud man, but, as Antoine had learned, a dangerous one as well. She knew he was sincere in wanting to make her happy, but she wondered if they would ever escape the violence that plagued them long enough to make their dreams come true.

Twenty-five

Luis pointed out the office of the Aragon Line to Michelle as the *Mattino Bello* sailed into the harbor at Valencia. That his family's distinctive red flag was flying at half-staff startled him. "I hope no other ship has been lost," he worried aloud, "or God forbid, one of my family."

"There's been time for the sinking of the *California* to have been reported," Michelle reminded him. "I certainly hope we haven't been given up for dead, though. That would be very bad luck, don't you think?"

"The absolute worst," Luis agreed. "I'll take you to the hotel where we left our things and then I'll visit the office."

Michelle wanted to go along, but before she could ask to accompany him she began to cough and knew he would never agree. He hugged her tightly, and when the ship had docked, swung her up into his arms. The clothes they had worn on the island were worn out, so all they had to take with them were the borrowed garments they were wearing and Luis's first attempt at a bucket.

Captain Cesari again called upon the talents of the seaman who translated for them, and gestured graciously. "Allow me to hire a carriage for you. You cannot carry your bride barefoot to your hotel."

Luis realized the Venetian had an excellent point and replaced Michelle on her equally bare feet. "You needn't do that. Mine must still be here somewhere. Please send someone to our office and let them know that I'm here. They'll send my carriage for me."

Cesari immediately dispatched a man with Luis's message. In a matter of minutes, a commotion rippled along the docks as a frantic group of men came running toward the *Mattino Bello* shouting and waving their hats. When they drew close enough, Luis recognized Encario Vega and half a dozen other members of his crew. While he was delighted to see them, he could not help but wonder what they were doing in Valencia when they should have been out searching for him and Michelle. As a result, his greeting was somewhat cool.

It took Encario a moment to catch his breath. "I know," he pleaded. "I am as embarrassed as you must be to see you were rescued by a Venetian rather than one of the Aragon ships searching for you."

"*Embarrassed* is a poor choice of word," Luis replied.

"Forgive me," Encario begged. "Most of us were adrift for two days before we were picked up by a French vessel and taken to Mallorca. The others washed up on an island and were rescued later that same week. Every man with a boat on Mallorca is out searching for you. We all arrived here yesterday and hoped that you would have already found your way here. When you hadn't, well, we all feared the worst."

"Everyone is here?" Luis asked. "None of the men who survived the night of the fire was later lost at sea?"

"Not a one, Captain," Encario informed him

431

proudly. He then leaned close to confide more. "Captain Ryde's ship is in port. He's been spending money freely to refurbish her, and making everyone curious about where he got it."

Luis glanced down at Michelle, who was straining to follow their conversation. He suddenly wondered if she didn't understand more Spanish than he had realized. That he had never asked her such a question now struck him as a foolish oversight. He quickly translated Encario's remarks into French for her benefit.

"Does the fact Ryde has come into money so soon after the *California* was lost seem like an unusual coincidence to you?" he asked.

Michelle licked her lips nervously. "That would mean someone else was involved, wouldn't it?" She did not even want to think about her husband having so many enemies.

Luis nodded. "I hadn't considered a conspiracy, but if one existed, I'm certain Captain Ryde can be persuaded to identify his partners."

Michelle understood that what Luis really meant by that confident boast was that he would beat the information out of Boris Ryde before he sent the English devil's soul to hell. Their carriage arrived then, and Julio and Tomás ran up the gangplank to greet them.

"You'll have to act quickly," she warned Luis before his servants interrupted them, "before Boris learns that we've survived the sinking of the *California.*"

Luis had already thought of that and he nodded to signify he was in agreement with her. After responding to Julio and Tomás's excited welcome, he turned to Captain Cesari. "Thank you again. You'll have your reward before the day is out."

While the Venetian was pleased by that prospect,

432

he did not want to be excluded from the conclusion of what he saw as a great adventure. "If I can be of any further assistance, do not hesitate to call on me. My crew and I are strangers here, and our actions will not draw the same attention as yours. We have the very same commitment to justice, however."

Luis readily understood Valentino's diplomatically worded offer and he assured him that he would call on him should the need arise. Encario and the other Aragon men followed Michelle and him to the carriage. Luis helped his bride inside and then turned to his first mate.

"I'll come down to the office in a hour or so. Find out where Ryde is and have him watched. I'd like to speak with one of his crew and you can make it plain I'll pay for information. Have you seen anything of the two men you hired?"

Encario shook his head. "No, and I asked around in the taverns for them, too. Several barkeeps recognized their names, but none had seen them in the last couple of weeks. They must have known some of us must surely have survived the fire and would be suspicious of their part in it. They could be hiding anywhere."

"While you're waiting for me, check with the harbormaster. Find out when Ryde's ship was last out of port and how long she was away. I can scarcely accuse the man of trying to kill me if he was here in Valencia the night of the fire and can prove it."

Encario broke into a wide grin. "I've already done that, Captain. The *Salamander* left port supposedly bound for Ibiza on October twenty-second, apparently within minutes of our departure. She returned October twenty-fifth."

It took every bit of Luis's self-control not to move against Boris Ryde at that very minute. With Encario and six crewmen, he knew he could stop whatever opposition the Englishman might make, since the crew of the *Salamander* would undoubtedly desert rather than defend their captain. He needed to be better prepared, however. At the very least, he needed a pair of boots, and that realization helped him find the will to be patient a few more hours.

He clapped Encario on the back. "Good work. There'll be a bonus in this for you, too. I'll come to the office as quickly as I can." He joined Michelle in the carriage, and dropped his arm around her shoulders in a fond hug. "I should have asked you this long before now, but how much Spanish can you understand?"

"What are you really asking, whether or not it is safe for you and Encario to plot in front of me?"

"No, of course not. I trust you not to betray us to Ryde. I'm just curious. I assumed that you spoke no Spanish at all, but I can't help but feel that I was wrong."

Saddened by her memories, Michelle glanced out the window as she replied. "I have studied the language and Antoine and I practiced speaking it on the journey to Madrid. He was far more fluent than I and served as my tutor." She then turned back to Luis. "I can understand you if you speak slowly, but by the time I formulate the correct reply in my mind, you would be several sentences ahead of me and I would have undoubtedly missed them all. I will try to improve my Spanish, though. I don't expect you to translate for me for the rest of my life."

She seemed so terribly earnest that Luis could not help but smile. "It would be my pleasure, *querida*, but life would be far easier for you here if you mastered our language."

"*Our* language?" Michelle inquired. "You have French blood as well as Spanish."

"Yes, but no one ever mistakes me for a French-

434

man. Someday I'll take you to California and we can practice speaking English all the way there."

"Please, allow me to become fluent in Spanish first."

Luis thought that such a reasonable request that he immediately agreed. They had reached their hotel and he hoped that he would be able to continue to distract Michelle with inconsequential conversation until he left to confront Boris Ryde. He again picked her up and carried her into the hotel. The clerk at the desk appeared to be astonished to see them, but Luis greeted him warmly.

"We were away slightly longer than we expected," he announced. "I hope that you haven't sold our belongings and rented our suite to someone else."

While taken aback by their casual garb, the clerk recovered quickly. "Captain Aragon, we would not even consider taking any such action without specific directions from you." While he thought Michelle's boyish apparel and bare feet odd, he was shocked when he looked down over the counter and found Luis was lacking shoes, too. "Have you any luggage, sir?" he asked.

Michelle was holding their bucket, but she did not feel that it qualified as luggage and laughed along with Luis. "We shouldn't laugh," she scolded her husband. "That we should arrive in such a pathetic state isn't at all funny."

"I don't know," Luis argued. "I can see the humor in the way we look even if you can't. May we have a key to our suite, please? I seem to have mislaid mine."

The clerk immediately summoned a porter, handed the boy a key, and told him to accompany Captain Aragon and his wife to their rooms. The lad's eyes widened as he glanced at the fancifully dressed pair, but knowing Captain Aragon was a

435

valued guest, he bowed as though nothing about him was out of the ordinary. That sent both Luis and Michelle into peals of laughter they made no effort to control until they reached their suite. The rooms had been cleaned regularly, and the fresh flowers filling the vases provided a fragrant welcome.

Luis set Michelle down, and then dismissed the young porter with a promise that he would receive a tip as soon as Luis had some money in his possession. "I think it is good that we can still laugh after what we've been through," he confided as he shut the door after the boy. "I'm so grateful to arrive in Valencia, even wearing borrowed clothes and without a single coin in my pockets, that I'm too happy to care about how funny we must look to others."

Michelle strolled from the sitting room into the bedroom where they had first made love. The suite was handsomely furnished, but it now looked like a palace to her after living in a makeshift hut. She opened the wardrobe and was overjoyed by the sight of all her pretty clothes. She withdrew the gorgeous green-and-wine gown she had worn to the Castillos' party, held it to her waist, and twirled around.

"I can't wait to put on a dress," she called to him.

Luis followed her into her bedroom. He was glad that she was so thrilled to see her things again, but he was still worried about her health. "I think I should send for a doctor," he said in a newly sober mood.

"Yes, do. I'd like him to look at your shoulders. Your cuts and burns all appear to be healing nicely, but perhaps he can prescribe a salve that's more effective than aloe."

"It was you I wanted him to see."

"Me, but why?"

Michelle looked sincerely surprised by his concern for her, but he was certain it was well placed. "I'm

436

worried about your cough. I want you to climb into bed and rest. I'm going to change my clothes and then send for a physician. If he says you're all right, I won't mention your health again, but if he doesn't, I don't want any arguments from you. You'll follow his orders to the letter. Is that understood?"

"No! It most certainly is not." Michelle immediately regretted having raised her voice, for it brought on another coughing spasm.

Luis wasted no time in picking her up and depositing her on the bed. He then replaced the expensive gown in the wardrobe. "You've just settled that question," he scolded. "Now stay put."

A little cough did not mean she was in poor health, but Michelle fumed silently rather than waste her breath when Luis was in such a determined mood. She knew he wanted her confined to her bed to keep her out of his way while he dealt with Boris Ryde. Not that she would ever dream of interfering! she grumbled to herself. She did not want anything to do with the loathsome man who had tried to kill them. Just the thought of him made her feel sick to her stomach.

Luis had left an extra pair of boots at the hotel, and after he had traded Valentino's clothes for his own, he entered Michelle's room. "It shouldn't take me long to locate a physician. I hope you won't be terribly bored without me for a few minutes."

Michelle glared at him. "And what if I am?"

"Where is that book I got for you on Spanish history? Read that." After offering that teasing suggestion, he gave her a jaunty salute and left. He knew she was probably thinking that he was ignoring her wishes again, but he was certain when it came to matters of her health, he was right to do so.

When he took an instant dislike to the first physician recommended by the hotel, he went looking for another. The second fellow, Dr. Martín Saenz, had a far more helpful attitude and Luis told him of their island ordeal while he escorted him back to the hotel. Taking care not to be seen, he chose a narrow side street rather than the main boulevard.

Michelle had actually tried to become interested in the history book, but had soon dozed off. When Luis returned with the doctor, their steps awakened her and she quickly sat up and attempted to look as though she was intensely interested in Spanish history. Then she realized that she should have at least donned a nightgown and robe rather than remaining in Valentino's clothes.

"Good afternoon," she greeted the two men nervously. Luis's companion was no more than thirty. While his features did not resemble Antoine's, he possessed her late fiancé's fair coloring and slender build and immediately called him to mind. She had not wished to see a physician in the first place, and that Luis had found one of Antoine's size and coloring unnerved her completely.

Luis already knew Michelle wasn't pleased with him, so he saw nothing unusual in the reserve she displayed as he introduced Dr. Saenz. "I neglected to ask, do you speak French?"

"Alas, I do not," Martín apologized.

"Fortunately I do and I'll be happy to translate any questions you wish to ask so that you and my wife will understand each other."

Martín perched himself on the edge of the bed, and smiled warmly. Because Michelle's hair was thick and glossy and her complexion a lovely golden shade, she did not appear to be seriously ill to him, but she did look tired and much too thin. Taking advantage of Luis's helpfulness, he inquired as to her previous illnesses and was pleased to learn she had always enjoyed excellent health until this episode.

438

She did have one brief coughing spell while they spoke, but it did not alarm him.

"Is your wife expecting a child?" Martín turned to ask Luis.

Luis still remembered the reaction he had received when he had asked Michelle that same question as he translated it for her.

Embarrassed, Michelle rushed to deny the possibility. "Tell him we've only been married . . ." She paused when she realized she could not supply the exact amount of time. "How long *has* it been?"

"A little more than three weeks," Luis answered with the same awe which then lit her eyes. He turned to explain to Martín that they had yet to celebrate their first month's wedding anniversary.

"You had the most eventful honeymoon that I have ever heard of," the physician replied.

Luis laughed and shook his head. "No, you don't understand. We haven't been on our honeymoon yet." When the doctor cocked a brow, Luis realized he had confused the man completely. "We have been enjoying all the benefits of marriage," he explained. "We just haven't taken a trip for that purpose."

Michelle was positive Luis was saying more than he should have, and blushed deeply. "Is there anything else the physician needs to know?"

Luis relayed that query and Martín stated that he did not. "All you need is rest and plenty of nourishing food," he informed her.

"Thank you. You see, Luis, I'm not suffering from any dreadful malady. Now I absolutely insist that you ask Dr. Saenz to examine you as well."

Thinking that he owed her that much, Luis removed his coat and shirt. "My arm got the worst of it, and it's healing on its own."

Dr. Saenz was amused by the attractive couple, each of whom was convinced the other was in need

439

of his services. That Luis had suffered cuts as well as burns saddened him, but as the captain had reported, his injuries were healing well on their own. Martín noticed the loose fit of the waistband of Luis's pants and offered him the same advice he had given Michelle.

"Rest and good food will help you as well," he assured him. He opened his medical bag and removed a small jar of salve. "This is made from the juice of the aloe and far more convenient to use than the fresh plant. I'm sure your bride will not mind applying it for you before you go to bed each night."

Luis assured the friendly doctor that Michelle had always taken excellent care of him. He thanked him for visiting her, showed him to the door, and promised to send his payment to him later that very afternoon.

"You will have beautiful children," Martín assured him, and confident his bill would be paid promptly, he went on his way.

Somewhat surprised by the doctor's last remark, Luis nevertheless believed his prediction would come true. He walked back into Michelle's room and quickly put on his shirt and coat. "I'm going down to the Aragon office now, but I won't stay long. I'll be back in time to have supper with you. We'll eat it here in our room. Why don't you take a nap while I'm gone?"

Michelle was tempted to insist that she could plan her own day, but she knew he had not meant to insult her with his suggestion and thought better of it. "Just promise me that you'll be careful."

Luis bent down to kiss her goodbye. "I'm always careful, *querida*."

"Not always," Michelle reminded him.

"Well, perhaps not with you, but that's different." He was still chuckling as he left the hotel, but he again chose side streets and entered the office of the Aragon Line from the rear. The clerks greeted him with near-hysterical fervor, but he calmed them as quickly as he could, and finding Encario waiting, took him into a private office.

"We should have been the ones to locate you," Encario again began.

"That's no longer a concern," Luis assured him. "Boris Ryde is. Have you been able to speak with any of his crew?"

Pleased that Luis was not blaming him for his long stay on the desolate island, Encario stopped apologizing and leaned forward in his chair. "Ryde's crew is fond of a tavern called the Loaves and Fishes. Do you know it?"

"I've heard the name."

"On any night of the year, it can easily boast Spain's largest gathering of criminals ranging from the most villainous cutthroats down to petty thieves. Apparently the authorities are grateful to have such despicable scum congregated in one place where the frequent brawls result in deaths they greet with enthusiasm rather than arrests leading to trials. I wouldn't go in there on a dare, but that's where Ryde's crew can be found when they're not on the *Salamander.*"

"Then what are we doing here?" Luis asked.

"What do you mean?"

Luis turned toward the door. "We're stalking vermin. We'll have to walk through the garbage."

Revolted, Encario had to push himself out of his chair. "You want to visit the Loaves and Fishes?"

Luis was already out the door. He stopped at the office safe to remove the reward he had promised Captain Cesari and the payment for Dr. Saenz. He sent both off with messengers, and then counted out what he would need for the night. When Encario caught up with him, he asked for the names of the men who had been slain while they stood watch the night of the fire.

"Did they have any families?" he asked.

"No, Captain. One was a childless widower, the others had never married. The men all know the Aragon Line looks after their widows and orphans, but there are none this time."

Luis was grateful for that, as writing letters to inform loved ones of the death of a seaman had always been difficult for him. "We're not going to lose another man to Ryde," he promised as he turned away. "Now where is the Loaves and Fishes? We haven't much time and I don't want to waste it."

"Shouldn't we take your carriage?"

Luis shot Encario a darkly menacing glance. "I doubt it's the sort of place gentlemen arrive at in their carriages."

"Well, no, it isn't, but—"

Luis halted abruptly. "I plan to go in the back way, get the answers I want without arousing anyone's notice, and leave. If that's too frightening for you, then you can wait outside, but I don't want to have to listen to you complain the whole way there."

Encario did not recall Luis ever being so short-tempered, but he hastened to improve his mood. "I'll be proud to follow you anywhere. You know that, Captain." He gestured toward the corner, and without another attempt to dissuade Luis from what he considered a suicidal course, he led the way along the docks and through back alleys that stank of rotting fish and other scents too vile to identify. When they finally reached the Loaves and Fishes, Encario followed Luis's example and swaggered bravely as they strode through the back door.

The light was so dim, the two men nearly tripped over a man who had passed out on his way to the alley. They stepped over him and sat down at the first unoccupied table they came to. Luis waited until his eyes had grown accustomed to the smoky haze, and seeing no sign of a barmaid, he tousled his hair, put up his collar, rose, and went to the bar. Satisfied he would not be recognized by anyone standing nearby, he ordered an ale for himself and his friend.

When the barkeep slid two pewter mugs across the badly scarred bar, Luis handed him the coins to cover the cost plus a tip. "I have a friend on the *Salamander*," he said in a deliberately hoarse croak. "He was supposed to meet me here last week, but I missed him. Are any of Ryde's crew here?"

Usually paid for silence rather than information, the one-eyed barkeep squinted to get a better look at Luis. What he saw was a tall man who appeared to have seen better days and he weighed the coins in his hand. "There might be ten or twelve of them sitting up front. Can't remember which table, though."

Luis rolled another coin across the bar.

"Bald man wearing the red shirt," the barkeep whispered before answering a call at the opposite end of the bar.

Luis took the two mugs of ale back to the table where Encario sat fidgeting in his chair. "What were the names of the men you hired?"

"Pablo Herrera and Norberto Macias, but as I said, no one has seen them."

"Don't get too comfortable. We might have to leave in a hurry." Then, carrying his mug, Luis approached the table where a bald man wearing a red shirt sat. Certain he would recognize Pablo and Norberto, he surveyed the others at the table, but they were all strangers. Using the same hushed voice, he spoke to the bald man. "I'm looking for Norberto," he announced. "Where can I find him?"

443

Alarmed, the red-shirted man turned to his mates, who all looked equally ill at ease. None said a word, but the anxious glances passing between them revealed more to Luis than they realized. Then, almost to a man, they took a gulp of ale and continued their conversations as though he hadn't spoken.

Luis slammed his mug into the side of the bald man's head spraying him with ale and knocking him to the floor, where he exhaled in a low moan before passing out. Encario reached the table then, but Luis waved him off. He grabbed the closest of Ryde's men by the scruff of the neck and yanked him to his feet. "Where is Norberto?" he repeated.

As the captive seaman struggled to break free of Luis's grasp, his companions all leapt from their chairs, but rather than come to his rescue, they abandoned him and hurriedly filed out the front door. The other patrons of the noisy tavern paid absolutely no attention to what Luis was doing as he dragged his protesting prisoner through the maze of crowded tables toward the back door. Encario followed, frowning menacingly to discourage the opposition no one raised, but he was greatly relieved that they did not have to fight their way to the alley.

On their way out they again had to step over the sleeping drunk, but as soon as they were clear of the doorway, Luis shoved the hapless seaman against the rear wall of the tavern. "As you can see, I'm a man of little patience. Now where is Norberto?"

The seaman looked up and down the alley with a terrified stare. Finding no one about who might report what he said, he began to babble incoherently about sinking ships, fires, and murder. Luis slapped him across the face, but rather than startling him out of his hysteria, the seaman began to weep pathetically. Luis released him and he slid down the wall and landed in a dejected heap.

"Is he just drunk, or is he crazy?" Encario asked.

"Probably a little of both." Disgusted, Luis hauled the seaman to his feet, and with his first mate's help, carried him back to the office of the Aragon Line. They entered through the rear door and hustled him into the private office they had used earlier. Luis dropped his captive into a chair, and then leaned close.

"Do you know who I am?" he asked in his normal voice.

The panicked seaman wiped away his tears on his sleeve, and seeing he was in the back office of some respectable business, took courage that he was not about to be murdered. "No," he admitted shakily.

Luis adjusted his coat collar, and smoothed down his hair before introducing Encario and himself, but rather than calming the poor seaman, the man paled and looked faint. Luis hastened to reassure him. "It's Pablo Herrera and Norberto Macias we're after, not you. If you can tell us where to find them, I'll reward you well. Because Captain Ryde won't be sailing much longer, I'll guarantee you a job on one of my ships. Now do you understand? You've nothing to fear. What's your name?"

Overwhelmed, the poor seaman held up his hands to beg for a moment to collect himself. He was in his early twenties, but the fears of a lifetime shone in his dark eyes. "Jorge Morales," he murmured nervously.

"Tell us where we can find Pablo and Norberto, Jorge," Luis urged.

Jorge had no reason to be loyal to Boris Ryde and, gathering his courage, swiftly betrayed him. "I only signed on with Ryde a month ago," he claimed. "Had I known what kind of a man he was, I would never have sailed with him."

445

"Of course not," Luis sympathized.

"On our last voyage he said we were bound for Ibiza, but we had no cargo to deliver and we did not go there to pick up any. Instead, we followed another ship, then remained out of sight until we saw the red glow of a fire in the sky. Ryde was anxious to investigate the flames, but did not approach the burning ship. Pablo and Norberto reached us in a lifeboat, but Ryde refused to make any effort to rescue any others.

"The last time any of us saw Pablo and Norberto, they were on deck talking with Captain Ryde. The next morning, Ryde said that they had chosen not to stay with us, but where could they have gone? Everyone believes they're dead, but no man has dared question Ryde about them for fear he will be killed, too."

Luis glanced toward Encario, who was equally stunned by Jorge's account. "Michelle and I found the lifeboat they had set adrift. It appears they are dead."

Encario felt sick to his stomach and turned away. "What are you going to do?" he asked.

Luis handed the frightened seaman more money than the lad had expected to earn in six months sailing with Boris Ryde. "Don't go back to the *Salamander*," he warned. "Spend the night in an inn, and come back here in the morning. I'll see that there's work for you." When he opened the office door, Jorge mumbled his thanks and promptly bolted through it.

Encario waited until Luis had closed the door. "Do you really believe him?"

Luis shrugged. "I know Boris Ryde for the murdering coward he is, so the story is plausible. He's precisely the type of man who would send killers after me and then murder them. He has neither morals nor ethics."

"What are we going to do?"

"I'm going to talk with the captain who rescued us. Then I'm going to have dinner with Michelle. I want you to get the crew together and meet me here at nine."

"We're going after Ryde tonight?" Encario asked with more than a hint of the trepidation he had shown when Luis announced they would visit the Loaves and Fishes.

"You and the men are going to pick up his crew. You saw how eager they were to flee rather than fight this afternoon and they won't have grown any braver by tonight. If you can do that for me, I'll handle Ryde on my own."

"Consider it done," Encario swore convincingly.

Luis clapped him on the back. "I know you won't fail me."

Encario was embarrassed by that praise. "Not intentionally, but we should have found you. You know that."

"Must I listen to you apologize for the rest of my life?" Luis shook his head as though that were the last thing he wanted and left by the back door while Encario went out the front to begin assembling their crew for the long night ahead.

Twenty-six

When Luis returned to their suite, he found Michelle dressed in an exquisitely feminine rose satin gown that flattered her lissome figure to perfection. She had styled her hair in a cascade of curls, and when she came forward to meet him, she was so incredibly lovely that he was unable to provide a compliment worthy of her. As he drew her into his arms, the seductive scent of her perfume stole the last of his reason and he kissed her with a passion that stunned them both.

"What are you trying to do to me?" he asked when he finally had to draw away to take a breath. "Didn't I tell you to take a nap?"

Michelle laughed as though he was teasing her, even though she suspected that he was not. "Yes, and I did, but you were gone a few hours and that gave me plenty of time to not only rest but bathe and dress. Are you disappointed not to find me still wearing Valentino's clothes?"

"No, not at all, but I don't want you to become overtired again."

"Dressing for dinner isn't in the least bit tiring, Luis." She raised her hem slightly to show off her rose satin slippers. "I can't tell you how nice it is to wear stockings and shoes at long last. I feel like a lady again."

"You were always a lady, Michelle. Even when you were spearing fish out on the rocks, you were still a lady to me."

"Thank you, but I certainly didn't feel like one. I don't know for what time you ordered our dinner. Do you want to change clothes first?"

Luis was afraid that his coat reeked of the ale he had splashed on Boris Ryde's red-shirted seaman, but he didn't have time to dress in the elegant evening clothes she was used to seeing him wear when they dined. Embarrassed, he backed away from her.

"I'm sorry, but I have to go out again as soon as we're finished and there isn't time for me to change my clothes twice."

Michelle did not have to be told where he intended to go and what he would do there. "Do you have enough men to help you?"

That she would not weep and plead with him not to go after Boris Ryde was the greatest compliment she could ever pay him and he relaxed and replied with an easy grin. "Yes, I do." Before he could say more, a porter arrived with their food and they waited until he had left to continue their discussion.

Luis helped Michelle to her chair and served up generous portions of the paella they had enjoyed so much when they had first eaten it in Valencia. He poured the wine and finally found the words to toast her beauty. "Each time I see you, I don't think it's possible for you to be any more beautiful, but the next time, you always are."

"Thank you, but my parents encouraged all of us to devote as much time to our minds as our appearance. You needn't constantly flatter me or talk of inconsequential matters when tonight is so important to us both. I'd rather you described what it is you intend to do."

Luis set down his wine goblet with deliberate

care. "I'd rather wait until I know how my plans work out before I share them with you. That way, if anything goes wrong, no one will be able to accuse you of aiding me. It would be bad enough if *I* were punished, I certainly won't allow such a catastrophe to befall you."

Hungry, Michelle took several bites of the seafood-laden rice dish before replying. "Being marooned on a chunk of limestone too small to serve as a public park was a catastrophe, Luis. Nothing that can happen to us now can compare to that. Besides, if the authorities want to insist that I knew your plans, how would I be able to prove that I didn't?"

"Believe me, if everything goes as I hope, no one will be asking either of us any questions."

Michelle watched her husband eat for several minutes as she recalled how confident he had been the night before the duel. "I'm sure you know what I'm thinking."

Luis glanced up. "No. What?"

"That our lives appear to have the unfortunate habit of not going the way we've planned. I hope that you have several alternatives prepared for this evening, not simply one path which you'd blindly follow no matter how poorly it goes."

"I do indeed have several options," Luis assured her, "but I won't pretend that I make a practice of mounting attacks on my enemies. Boris Ryde is the exception, not the rule."

"Thank God."

Luis nodded and kept on eating. He had such high expectations for the evening that his appetite had been unaffected by the inherent danger. He was determined to make short work of Boris Ryde and quickly return to his bride. He looked up at her and smiled. "I'm sorry. I'm not being very good company, am I?"

Michelle was having such difficulty adjusting to

the fact they were again in comfortable surroundings, while at the same time calmly discussing putting an end to Boris Ryde, that she was not about to criticize him for being inattentive. "The paella is delicious," she said instead.

"And so are you," Luis assured her. When her cheeks filled with an attractive blush, the very last thing he wanted to do was leave her. Believing any further delay would make parting all the more difficult, he promptly excused himself. "Please don't wait up for me. I promise to wake you when I come back."

Michelle left her chair to walk him to the door, but there was only one way Luis wished to tell her goodbye. He embraced her tightly, gave her a long, slow kiss, and then renewed the mark he had once taken such a mischievous pride in leaving on her pale skin. Even with her new tan, the evidence of his passion was clearly visible. She leaned against him now, readily accepting his devotion rather than pulling away in disgust, but that didn't diminish his pleasure a bit. He winked at her, then slipped out the door without giving her a chance to whisper more than his name.

Michelle leaned back against the door for a long moment. She was proud of herself for putting on such a brave front, but now that Luis was gone, she knew she would never be able to wait for him in their suite. Positive Captain Cesari would know her husband's plans, she hurried into her room and removed her gown. The clothes Valentino had loaned her would be a far better choice for the night than her own and she donned them quickly, added her own boots, and left the hotel no more than fifteen minutes after Luis. He might not think that he needed her help, but she wanted to be certain that she was nearby to offer it should his optimistic predictions again prove wrong.

* * *

When he reached his office, Luis greeted the members of his crew he hadn't seen that afternoon and then provided all his men with the opportunity to leave rather than join him in avenging the wrong Boris Ryde had done them. To a man, they all chose to remain. Grateful, he praised them for their loyalty, outlined his plan, and asked if anyone cared to offer a suggestion.

"I don't think you should give a serpent like Ryde a chance to defend himself," one man said. "Just shoot him dead."

While that proposal met with hearty approval from his crew, Luis couldn't agree. "That's too easy a death for Boris Ryde. No, I intend to talk with him first. He'll know what's coming then, and that will make his final agony all the more painful."

"Let's keelhaul him!" another man shouted.

While that brutal suggestion had a definite appeal, Luis shook his head. He wanted to punish Ryde in a far more personal fashion. After he had assured the men Boris would not escape retribution, Encario led the way to the *Salamander*.

There was only one man standing watch and he immediately saw the value in surrendering rather than foolishly attempting to defend the ship himself. He was taken off and marched to a nearby Aragon warehouse to await the dawn under guard. Luis then stationed his crew where they would could wait unseen for Ryde's men to return after another night of revelry. They knew what to do as soon as Boris Ryde arrived, and Luis went to the captain's cabin to await him there.

A captain with any pride kept his cabin neat, but Boris's quarters were littered with cast-off clothing, wrinkled papers, and dirty plates he had not bothered to return to the galley. Luis was not surprised to find the cabin in such filthy disarray, but it made the wait for its owner all the more disagreeable. He prowled around a bit in a search for weapons, found only one pistol, and hid that where Boris would never think to look. He then turned the lamp down low, sat down at the table, and waited for his prey.

Michelle had had time that afternoon while she waited in their carriage for Luis to finish talking with Encario to note at which pier the *Mattino Bello* was moored. She made her way there, and asked the seaman who greeted her to take her to Captain Cesari. Certain the captain would be pleased to see the pretty young woman again, he smiled widely and showed her to his cabin.

When Valentino answered the knock at his door and found Michelle, he looked past her expecting to see Luis as well. Discovering she was alone, he sent her escort for the man who was adept at translation. While they awaited him, Valentino attempted to be hospitable, but Michelle declined his offer of refreshments. Once the translator arrived, the Venetian felt far more comfortable.

"It is a pleasure to see you again, Señora Aragon."

While his manners were perfect, Michelle had come for a specific purpose rather than to conduct a flowery exchange, and after thanking him for seeing her, she immediately got to the reason for her visit. "I know my husband intends to confront Boris Ryde tonight. While I don't wish to be directly involved, I do want to know that Luis is safe. If you have a part in his plans, and I feel certain that you must, will you take me along with you?"

Dumbfounded by her request, Valentino clasped his hands behind his back and frowned. "I do not think that would please your husband, señora."

"Perhaps not, but it would please *me,* and I believe

my feelings ought to be given the same weight as my husband's."

Valentino found the French belle such a charming creature that while he knew he should refuse her request, he could not bear to do so. "We'll be sailing shortly, but we aren't going far and we'll be back in port before dawn. You may come with us if you must, but I need your promise that you'll not get in anyone's way."

The mention of a voyage, even a brief one, perplexed Michelle. She had wanted to hear the plan, perhaps observe from a safe distance, but she had not expected to have to go to sea in the process. What if Luis returned to the hotel before she did? she worried. How could she possibly explain where she had been? It seemed she had a choice: to return to their suite and pretend to be the docile bride she knew she would never succeed in actually being or to remain with Valentino and risk having Luis discover that she had taken a far keener interest in his plot than he had wanted her to have.

She made her choice in an instant. "I'll stay, and you have my word that I'll not be in anyone's way."

Valentino responded with a mock bow while he silently hoped that he had not just made a dangerous error.

Boris Ryde had been celebrating almost continually since rumors had begun circulating along the docks confirming his hopes that Augustín Aragon and his bride had been lost at sea. While he had heard some of the crew of the *California* had returned to Valencia the previous day, he felt certain his mission had been accomplished and hoped that Antoine would soon send the rest of his money. The repairs to the *Salamander* were proving to be more costly than he had anticipated, and he needed the bonus he had been promised to complete them.

After spending an entertaining hour with the woman who was becoming his favorite whore because her tastes were as bawdy as his, he made his way back to his ship, but when the man on watch failed to answer his call, his ebullient mood rapidly deteriorated to the foul one for which he was well known. He stomped off to his cabin to check his roster so he would know whom to punish for deserting his post, but when he came through his door and found Luis sitting at his table with the relaxed posture of an invited guest, he came to an abrupt halt.

"Good evening," Luis greeted him in English. "It's been a long while since we've spoken. How have you been?"

Despite that friendly greeting, Boris knew exactly why Luis was there. A jolting tremor of fear ricocheted down his spine and so violently jarred his knees that his trembling legs would no longer support him. He grabbed for the back of the chair opposite Luis's and held on tightly to hide any such show of cowardice but that Luis was alive rather than at the bottom of the Mediterranean had unnerved him completely.

He attempted to save himself with false bravado. "I've been doing fine, no thanks to you," he shot back at Luis. His pistol was just out of reach, but he inched toward his desk, intent upon getting it.

"You can't imagine how pleased I am to learn you're doing well. I understand you've come into some money recently. Why don't you tell me about it?"

"An aged aunt died and left it to me," Boris lied smoothly. "God rest her soul."

"Amen," Luis murmured. "There have been a great many unfortunate deaths recently, haven't there?"

"Whom do you mean?"

"We've both lost members of our crews. That's very bad for morale."

"What are you talking about?" Boris snapped.

Luis watched him attempt to reach his desk, where his pistol was no longer hidden, without drawing notice. Luis wasn't alarmed, merely amused. He rose, and answered Ryde. "I hear you lost two of your best men—Pablo Herrera and Norberto Macias—on your last voyage. Not that such a brief trip can truly be called a voyage. Were you afraid they'd betray you? Is that why you killed them?"

Luis obviously knew too much and, terrified, Boris dove for the desk drawer. He yanked it open and, to his horror, found nothing but faded correspondence. He slammed the drawer shut, and feeling trapped, ran for the door only to find that it was blocked from the other side. Still gripping the handle, he turned back toward Luis and, knowing his life was in grave jeopardy, hastily began to bargain.

"You never had any respect for me, and I can't expect you to show any now, but you were always fair. I wasn't the one who sent Pablo and Norberto after you. It was Antoine."

For a savage instant, Luis felt as though he had been kicked, then he caught his breath and continued toying with Boris. "There are a great many men named Antoine. What is his family name?"

"That I don't know. He signed only *Antoine*."

"You have a letter from him? I'd like to read it, please."

Boris realized his error, and while his eyes darted toward his hiding place for the box of gold coins, he shook his head. "I threw it away," he lied. "When I would not work for him, Antoine must have hired Pablo and Norberto."

"To do what?"

"To cause you trouble, what else?"

456

"You call slaughtering innocent men, setting fire to a fine ship, and endangering not only the lives of my wife and me but my crew as well merely 'causing trouble'?"

"I don't know anything about that. I swear I don't."

Perspiration was pouring off Ryde's forehead, trickling down his face, and dampening his collar, giving visible evidence of his guilt despite his sniveling protestations of innocence. Luis drew his knife and took a step toward Ryde. "I don't believe you. There was no one named Antoine. You sent Pablo and Norberto after me, and now I've come for you."

"No!" Boris shrieked. "Antoine is to blame! I've done nothing!"

Luis appeared to hesitate. "If only you had some proof, but since you no longer have his letter, I've no reason to believe you."

Boris pointed with a hasty wave. "I do have the letter. I really do. I'll get it for you."

Suspecting this was another of Boris's endless lies, Luis remained alert and gestured with his knife. "Then get it."

Boris lurched past him, bent down, and after brushing the accumulated trash out of his way, reached into a dark nook for the box he had been sent. There were only a few coins left in it now, but he wasn't concerned about keeping them. From what he recalled, Antoine's letter had been vague, conveying its meaning with cunning innuendo rather than blunt demands, and he was determined to keep denying he had followed through on the treachery it suggested.

"Here," he said as he offered Luis the single sheet of stationery. "Read it for yourself."

As Luis reached for the letter, the whole ship shuddered and seemed to groan with the bellow of a wounded dragon. Boris grew even more alarmed, but Luis smiled knowing his crew had unfurled the *Salamander*'s sails. The ship was leaving the dock on her way to rendezvous with the *Mattino Bello*. Seeing Boris's resulting fright, Luis did nothing to reassure him. "I didn't want us to be disturbed tonight and I knew you'd not mind sailing with me. Now, sit down while I read this."

Boris took the chair Luis had indicated, then drummed his fingers on the tabletop in a staccato rhythm that echoed his racing pulse. He watched Luis, hoping for an instant of inattention in which to disarm him, but with the table between them, the wily Spaniard was out of reach. He gulped in air, and tried to convince himself all wasn't lost even though he feared that it most assuredly was.

Luis had never seen Antoine's handwriting, but a quick glance at the letter that bore the Frenchman's name shocked him deeply. Though it might seem to contain no more than veiled threats toward a mutual enemy, the paragraph referring to the accident that might befall Michelle was appalling. Money was offered, but again, there was only a hint at how it was to be earned. Luis eyed Boris with a disgusted glance, but he saw in him only the reflection of the hatred he now knew Antoine must bear him and Michelle.

He marveled how Antoine could possibly be alive. There was no date on the letter, but Michelle was referred to as his wife so it had to have been written after the duel. That Antoine had survived what he had assumed had been a fatal wound changed so many things that Luis had a difficult time fighting off the distraction to again focus his attention on Boris Ryde. He refolded the letter and shoved it into his coat pocket.

"There appears to be no action so low that you won't sink to it," he taunted. "The letter proves nothing, and I still intend to deal with you."

458

Like most seafaring men, Boris also carried a knife, but Luis was taller and possessed a longer reach, making it impossible for him to get close enough to cut him without the risk of having his own throat slashed. Desperate as he was, he did not want to be that foolhardy. "What do you intend to do?" he forced himself to ask.

Luis eyed him coldly. "I'm going to kill you and set the *Salamander* on fire. After what you did to me, that will be a fitting end to you both, don't you agree?"

"No!" Boris argued. "I'll help you find Antoine. He's the one who caused all the trouble. Not me."

"You can stop repeating that boring lie. I know exactly who's to blame here and it was you."

"But Antoine—"

"Don't worry about Antoine. I know where to find him and I'll give him your regards."

Hearing that jest, Boris lost what little hold he had had on his composure and again fled to the cabin door. He pounded and kicked on it, but it refused to come open. He then began to beg and plead with whomever stood on the opposite side, but there was no sympathetic reply. Luis waited until the Englishman had worn himself out and turned back to face him before he approached the door.

"If you want to go up on deck, why didn't you just say so?" he asked. He then rapped lightly on the door and instantly the obstruction was released, permitting him to swing it open. He gestured for Boris to precede him.

Fearing a trick of some kind, Boris peered out first, but when he saw no armed men waiting to attack him in the companionway, he hurried to reach the deck well ahead of Luis. Because Luis had such a long stride, Boris failed to outdistance him. He looked back toward the rapidly receding lights of Valencia and for an instant grasped the slender hope he might be able to leap over the side and swim to safety.

Reading his captive's mind, Luis gave Boris a quick prod to move him toward the bow. "I'll give you an opportunity to swim if you like," Luis promised. "But later, when the land is no longer in sight. I want you to know what it's like to fight to stay afloat when you're so tired you can no longer feel your arms and legs."

Boris stumbled, caught himself, and then continued staggering toward the bow. He saw several seamen, but they were Luis's men rather than his. "What have you done with my crew?" he called over his shoulder.

"My God, do you actually expect me to believe you care what's happened to them?"

Boris turned back to look at Luis. "I do care," he insisted. "I'll admit to being strict, but every crew needs firm discipline."

"I doubt Pablo and Norberto would agree."

They had reached the bow, and when Boris attempted to shrink away from Luis, he slammed into the rail. Cornered like a trapped rat, he was buffeted by the stinging night wind and shivering with fear. "You accused me of being cruel, but I never tortured a man like this."

"Torture?" Luis mocked. "This is scarcely torture. One of my crew thought you should be keelhauled. Now, *that* would have been torture. Fortunately, I'm far more humane. I'm going to give you a chance to defend yourself."

"How? With what?" Boris cried out, grasping for the faint hope of salvation Luis had offered.

Luis replaced his knife in its sheath. "With your fists. You talk like a strong man. Let's see if you really are."

That Luis wanted to fight him hand-to-hand astonished Boris, but even if it had been a while since he had had to defend himself in that fashion, he had grown up backing up his boasts with his fists and he was confident he could still do it with his former pride. Luis might have a longer reach, but Boris was muscular and tough and believed he possessed the more powerful punch. "Tell your men I'm to go free if I win!" he shouted.

"Did everyone hear him?" Luis asked, and a chorus of deep voices assured him Boris's demand had been understood. Boris appeared to be satisfied, although Luis had asked only if his plea had been heard, without making the promise that it would be honored. He had intended to put a decisive end to the horror Boris Ryde had caused him that very night, but now that he had Antoine's letter in his pocket, he knew this was only the beginning.

It wasn't Boris's smug expression that inspired him to throw the first punch but the thought Antoine could have offered money to have Michelle slain. He had never liked the effete Frenchman she admired so highly, and now he had an excellent reason to despise him. He slammed his fist into Boris's nose, but barely staggered the obnoxious man.

Unaware that he was about to take a beating meant for Antoine, Boris countered Luis's move with a series of short jabs to the Spaniard's midsection that proved totally ineffective. He had not believed any man possessed the strength to deflect his blows, but the taut muscles of Luis's flat stomach protected him well. Then, bent on destroying Luis's aristocratic good looks, Boris aimed for his face, but Luis blocked his punches with an ease that left him frustrated again. Losing his concentration, he began to swing wildly raining blows on Luis's shoulders and chest that the Spaniard countered with forceful punches to the chin.

Dazed, Boris reeled away. Spying a grappling hook stored in the bow, he pretended to slip, and in an apparent attempt to catch himself, lurched against the rail. He grabbed up the grappling hook and, turning, swung the wickedly barbed iron at Luis's head. With the element of surprise on his side, he succeeded in striking Luis a glancing blow that drew blood at his temple, but that small triumph filled him with hope and renewed determination to win their bout. He lashed out at Luis again with the barbed hook, and swore when the agile Spaniard dodged out of harm's way. Luis represented the wealth and privilege Boris had been raised to both jealously crave and heartily despise, and he came at him again, swinging his deadly weapon with the force of his lifelong demons.

In response to that furious attack, Luis drew his knife, and while ducking to avoid the grappling hook, he thrust upward, sending his blade into the underside of Boris's right arm. The Englishman bellowed in pain, but kept on fighting. The two men circled each other, stepping from the shadows into the pale moonlight, shifting their balance constantly to compensate for the rocking motion of the ship. Out of the corner of his eye, Luis saw the *Mattino Bello* approaching and broke into a wide grin.

Believing Luis was laughing at him, and unable to tolerate such a humiliating insult, an infuriated Boris came at him again, but his high, arching blows fanned only the air. He cursed the man on whom he blamed all his woes, and with a desperate lunge, tried to cleave him in two with a mighty downward stroke of the iron hook. When Luis leaped backward and escaped his blow, he followed, and swung at him again.

With his arms raised, Boris provided an excellent target, and taking full advantage of it, Luis stepped to the side with the grace of a matador, and raked his blade across the Englishman's belly. Boris froze, looked down at the bright-red bloodstain spreading across the slashed front of his shirt, and this time swung at Luis from the side. It was a ferocious blow that would have disemboweled Luis had he been struck, but again Luis's reactions were far more swift than Boris's and he escaped harm.

The island ordeal was beginning to take its toll on his stamina, however, and Luis knew he would not be able to continue their game successfully much longer. It was Boris who had broken the rules by using a weapon, and Luis slid his knife back into its sheath. When the English captain let out a hoarse shriek and again raised the hook, this time Luis sprang in close rather than dart away and caught the smooth grip of the iron. Before Boris could recover from that astonishing move, Luis had wrenched the evil weapon from his hands.

Luis saw Boris's eyes widen in terror, but he did not check his swing, and with one clean stroke of the grappling hook, he ripped a gash two inches wide in the side of the Englishman's throat. Blood gushed from the dying man's severed jugular vein, but before it could sully the deck, Luis caught hold of Boris's coat collar and heaved him over the side.

Finding precious little satisfaction in what he had done, as the body of his old foe was sucked under the *Salamander* and spun down into the depths, Luis flung the bloody grappling hook far out into the sea. He then leaned back against the rail and breathed deeply. This was to have been the end of it, he thought sadly, but although he had no taste for killing, he would not stop until Antoine was no longer a threat to Michelle.

When Encario reached him, Luis forced himself to concentrate on the task at hand and began the series of orders that would end in the fiery destruction of the old schooner. His crew was quickly transferred to the *Mattino Bello* in the first of the lifeboats, and he and Encario followed as soon as they had lit the

463

fires. They stood at the rail of the Venetian ship until the *Salamander*, like his beautiful *California*, sank in a glowing spray of flames.

Luis closed his eyes for a moment, but nothing would shut out the pain that filled his heart. He knew he owed Michelle the truth, but how was he going to tell her the man she loved was not only alive, but intent upon killing her? He doubted that he could find the words in any of the languages he spoke to reveal such a vile secret.

Antoine is alive and wants you dead. How could he ever tell her something that cruel when it would undoubtedly break her heart all over again? She had wept so many tears for Antoine, and this was how the foppish French dandy repaid her, Luis agonized. He had encountered several truly difficult dilemmas in his life but nothing to compare with this. Lost in thought, he remained at the rail as the *Mattino Bello* swung back toward Valencia. The wind whipped his hair and stung the cut in his temple, but he didn't care. Nothing mattered to him but finding a way to protect Michelle from a truth he could not bear to tell her.

In the final moments of the fight, Captain Cesari had brought the *Mattino Bello* in so close to the *Salamander* that Michelle had seen more than Luis would ever have wanted her to see. She had been able to distinguish her husband from Boris Ryde by his impressive height, but when she realized Boris was armed with a grappling hook, she was consumed with dread and could not bear to look, nor could she glance away. Too frightened to breathe, she had nearly suffocated by the time Luis put an end to the despicable rogue who had attempted to kill them.

The end had come quickly, but she was sickened rather than elated to have the brutal contest over. She moved into the shadows as Luis came on board and remained there watching him rather than taking in the fiery death throes of the *Salamander.* His crew were all in high spirits, laughing and recounting the fight with the enthusiasm of men who would have wagered on its outcome had they been able to find anyone willing to take Boris Ryde's side.

She wished she had had sense enough to remain at their hotel, but when Luis turned into the moonlight and she caught a glimpse of his agonized expression, she knew she was exactly where she belonged.

Twenty-seven

Michelle stepped out of the shadows and into Luis's arms with the confidence of a woman who loves her man dearly. In response, he pressed her so close she feared he might crush her ribs, but rather than raise an objection to his forceful embrace, she hugged him just as tightly. Gradually they both relaxed, but he continued to rest his cheek against her curls for a long while before drawing away.

"I know you didn't want me to be here," Michelle argued before Luis could object to her presence, "but I was too worried about you to wait at the hotel. If you're angry with me, I'm sorry, but please try and understand how it felt to be left out after the calamities we've faced together."

"I just killed a man," Luis replied. "That you disobeyed me is a matter of complete insignificance when compared to that crime."

Michelle had had the opportunity to observe Luis in a wide variety of moods ranging from seductive playfulness to a heroic determination to survive against impossible odds, but she had never seen him so depressed. He looked as though his best friend had just died, rather than his worst enemy. She reached up to comb his hair away from his face and felt the warm stickiness of blood.

"You've been hurt!" she cried.

Luis could see the dark stain on her fingers, but it was without meaning to him. If he was hurt, it was a minor wound and not one which either pained or alarmed him. "It's nothing," he assured her calmly.

Michelle was equally convinced her morose husband needed care. She wiped her hand on her borrowed pants, and then taking charge of the situation, guided him to Valentino's cabin. She found some water in a container, and she quickly wet the end of a towel. Luis had already dropped into a chair at the table and she held the dampened cloth to his temple.

"You're right. It doesn't look like a bad cut and your hair will cover the scar. I should make you lie down the way you make me, though," she said.

Luis had met more than one woman who had insisted upon fussing over him, but he had not enjoyed being the focus of attention until now. Michelle's touch was very light and loving but it brought him a deeper pain than the scalp wound. She was caring for him as any considerate wife looks after her husband, but if she knew the truth, would she believe he had a right to that honor?

Confident to the point of cockiness, Luis was a stranger to the doubts plaguing many men, but he wondered if Michelle would continue to show him such solicitous concern if he informed her Antoine was alive. She would undoubtedly be as shocked as he was by that news, but once she had accepted it, how would she react? Which would be the stronger emotion, her joy for Antoine, or her anger with him?

Would she blame him for spiriting her away from the scene of the duel before her fiancé's true condition had been ascertained? Would she accuse him of taking advantage of her grief to rush her into a marriage to which he knew she had been violently opposed? Would she charge him with the crime of stealing her innocence the night she had turned to him for comfort after realizing Antoine was shot because of her panicked cry?

Deeply troubled, Luis did not respond to Michelle's comments. He tried to see their elopement from Antoine's point of view but found the questions just as difficult to answer. Could the Frenchman have possibly assumed that Michelle had deliberately distracted him to influence the outcome of the duel? Could he actually believe Michelle had abandoned him on the field of honor after he had risked his life to defend her reputation? Could he have accepted their elopement as proof of Michelle's betrayal?

When seen in such a devious light, Luis had to admit Michelle's conduct was suspect, but Antoine's incriminating assumptions were frightfully wrong. Even if she were guilty of taking a lover and then fleeing the scene of the duel with him, was that just cause to hire a reprobate like Boris Ryde to execute them both? Antoine was obviously a proud man, but was the embarrassment of losing Michelle to a Spaniard cause for murder? Thoroughly sickened, Luis failed to suppress a shudder of revulsion.

"Have you caught a chill?" Michelle leaned close to ask.

Luis turned to look at her, but he was only vaguely aware of what she had asked. "No, I was just mulling over some most unpleasant thoughts."

Having stemmed the flow of blood from the cut grazing his temple, Michelle took the seat beside him. "Would it be unforgivably inconsiderate of me to ask what Captain Ryde had to say for himself?"

Luis caught her hand, brought it to his lips, and then laced his fingers in hers. "No, you have every

468

right to be curious. The bastard blamed everything on the two men who set fire to the *California*. They have disappeared, but one of Ryde's crew told us he killed them, and I believe it. Because Ryde would have responded with more lies, I didn't even bother to ask him why he hadn't come to our rescue the night of the fire if he had had nothing to do with it. That he sailed away leaving us all in grave danger of drowning proved his guilt."

When Luis fell silent, Michelle prompted him to continue. "Did he implicate anyone else, or explain the source of his newfound wealth?"

Luis took a deep breath, and by the time he had let it out slowly, he had an answer for her. "He claimed he had inherited the money from an aunt, which was clearly another flagrant lie. As for any other co-conspirators, he named one, but I want to investigate his accusation fully before I tell you more."

Michelle was grateful Luis was talking to her, but his expression had remained the same downcast one she had first seen up on deck. "That's what's bothering you, isn't it?" she probed gently. "Is the man Boris Ryde named someone you trust?"

"No," Luis admitted freely, "but as I said, I want to know the truth before I discuss it with you."

"You told me you had enemies, business rivals, you said. Was it one of them?"

"Don't press me to explain more, Michelle. I can't do it yet."

Michelle sat back. Had it not been for Luis's thoroughly miserable expression, she would have argued that he need have no fear of confiding in her, but when he was so morose, she did not want to add to his troubles. "Will you at least warn me if we're going to be around the man so that I may be doubly cautious?" she asked.

Michelle's gaze was so warm and trusting that Luis had a difficult time denying her request. "Please, let's just let the matter drop for the time being."

Michelle leaned forward and kissed him lightly. "As you wish, but if we're still in danger, I think you should teach me how to shoot."

That ridiculous request brought the first trace of a smile to Luis's lips. "It won't come to that, *querida*. Besides, I feel certain the danger is past. Now let's go back up on deck. We should reach Valencia soon, and we need to get back to the hotel and pack."

"Pack? Where are we going?"

"Home to Barcelona," Luis responded.

"Will we be safe there?"

"I'll make certain that we are," Luis promised, and he sealed that vow with a kiss he didn't end until Valentino interrupted them to say they were nearing the port.

As she returned her garments to her trunks, Michelle could not help but recall how upset she had been when she had hurriedly gathered up her belongings the night before the duel. Her memories of her departure from her aunt's home were anything but pleasant, and when she came across the handkerchief containing the Gypsy love charm she recoiled in dread.

She would have thrown it away, but the beribboned handkerchief held keepsakes she didn't want to lose and she sat down on the bed to untie the knot in the blue ribbon. When Luis came to her door, she made no effort to hide what she was doing. "Aurora told me how to make a love charm," she confessed. "That's what I was hiding the morning you gave away my blue suit and tossed my lingerie all over the hotel room."

Intrigued, Luis came forward. "Is that what you have there?"

"Yes, but I'm taking it apart. I had very little faith in Aurora's magic to begin with, and once Antoine was dead, I shouldn't have kept this."

Luis wasn't ready to reveal that Antoine was apparently very much alive, but he sat down beside her and took the lace-trimmed handkerchief from her hands. He found an exquisite pair of pearl earrings, two locks of fair hair, one hers and another he felt certain was Antoine's, a small gold heart, and a dried rosebud wrapped inside it. "Charming collection," he murmured, "but I don't understand what sort of magic it was supposed to work."

Michelle sighed softly before confiding in him. "I know that Antoine loved me, but he hadn't mentioned marriage and I was hoping to inspire him to propose. It all seems very silly now." She picked up the rosebud and turned it slowly in her hand. "The red rose was for passion, but this is the one you gave me, not one I'd gotten from Antoine."

Luis laughed in spite of the blackness of his mood. "You mean that's one of the roses you dropped on me?" When Michelle nodded, he continued. "You looked as though you were going to slap me with it when I handed it back to you."

"I was sorely tempted to do just that," Michelle described truthfully, but when she looked into her husband's eyes and saw an understanding rather than taunting light, she was ashamed of the way she had behaved. "I'm very sorry for what happened that night. That you wanted to sing for me was very flattering, but I mistakenly believed you were someone

471

I ought not to know. I had no idea who you really were, or that your interest in me was sincere."

Michelle's touching apology stung Luis badly because on the night in question his intentions had been anything but sincere. He had been inspired to serenade her not out of a genuine desire to impress her, but simply to tease her because of the haughty way she had rebuffed his attempts to talk with her that afternoon. He had been brazenly obnoxious, and yet none of his motives had remained clear once he had kissed her.

He plucked the tiny gold heart from the handkerchief. "Did Aurora give you this?" he asked.

"Yes, but I doubt that it contains any magic."

Luis disagreed. "You wanted a proposal, and you got one. To my amazement, Antoine referred to you as his fiancée, and you would have wed him had he won the duel."

Had Antoine won, then it would be Luis who was dead, and unable to bear such a heartbreaking thought, Michelle's eyes filled with tears. "Oh, please," she begged, "let's not mention the duel ever again."

Believing her tears were for Antoine, Luis had a difficult time not blurting out what a despicable coward the Frenchman truly was. He handed her back the handkerchief filled with treasures, but kept the gold charm. "Hurry and finish your packing. It's late and we have to get up early."

Luis returned to his room leaving Michelle with the uncomfortable sensation that she had said something wrong. Believing that he had been offended by talk of the duel on a night marred by another death, she was sorry the topic had ever entered their conversation until she remembered that Luis was the one who had first mentioned it, not her. That death

472

could be preying on his mind seemed such a natural conclusion, she looked no further for reasons for the curtness of his tone. Instead, she hastened to complete her packing.

Thinking he would prefer to be alone, when she was ready for bed, she stayed in her room rather than enter his. After such an eventful night, she doubted that she would be able to fall asleep and she remained seated in the middle of her bed brushing out her hair rather than getting under the covers. She was looking forward to reaching Luis's home in Barcelona, where she hoped they would enjoy an extended stay before they traveled again.

Impatient for his wife's company, Luis peered into her room. "How much longer are you going to brush your hair?" he asked.

"I didn't mean to keep you waiting," Michelle apologized. "I thought that, well, after tonight—"

Insulted, Luis walked into her room. "You'd rather not sleep with a murderer, is that what you're saying?"

"I saw the fight," Michelle reminded him. "You killed Boris Ryde in self-defense. No one can rightly accuse you of being a murderer. What an awful thing to say." Putting her brush aside, she slid off the bed, went to him, and again slipped her arms around his waist.

"Please don't talk that way. Don't even think it. After what that man did to us, I'd have been happy to kill him myself if I'd had the chance, and so would any of your crew. He got exactly what he deserved and I hope you'll never apologize for it."

Now understanding she had remained in her room out of consideration for his feelings rather than revulsion, Luis gave her a fond squeeze. "The *Salamander* and Captain Ryde sailed out of Valencia tonight and will never be heard from again. Ships are frequently lost at sea, and in time it will be assumed that's what happened to the *Salamander*. The crew are being confined in one of our warehouses tonight, but in the morning they'll be released and offered work for the Aragon Line.

"I doubt anyone will ever miss Boris Ryde, *querida*. On the remote chance they do, I'll never admit that I was one of the last to see him alive and I absolutely forbid you to ever tell anyone how Ryde died."

Michelle regarded him with a wide-eyed, innocent gaze. "Why, I never even met the man. How could I possibly know anything about him?" she asked with exaggerated innocence.

"Perfect," Luis whispered before leaning down to kiss her. He dimly recalled insisting that she spend all her nights in his bed, but hers was far more convenient and he wanted her so badly that he didn't waste the time to carry her into his room. He scooped her up into his arms, threw back the covers, and placed her on the bed. She laughed but pulled him down with her rather than make any attempt to escape him and he smothered her giggles with kisses.

After that teasing beginning, his mood swiftly changed, for what he wanted from her that night was the sweet oblivion of forgetfulness, not playful loving. He enveloped her in the heat of his passion, stripping her with the same urgency with which he discarded his own clothing. After dispensing with the silken barrier of her nightgown, he was free to touch and taste every inch of her luscious body, but it wasn't enough to silence the fear of losing her that cried within him.

Driven by that terror, he moved to possess her with a fervor that burned too hot to tame. He plunged to her depths, losing himself in the warmth of her acceptance until his heart beat with a joy that sang in his soul. He held back nothing as he raced his own desires to the limits of earthly bliss, and having won, he abandoned himself to that radiant splendor. He fell asleep with Michelle still clasped tightly in his arms and his deeply felt promises of love still a secret.

Stunned by the fury of Luis's passion, the peace he had sought and found in her arms eluded Michelle. She lay relaxed in his embrace, wondering what it was they had just shared. She had been raised to believe in the gentle sweetness of an idyllic love, but Luis had always had a wildness about him that frightened as well as attracted her. That he was such a passionate man thrilled her, but at the same time, she sensed he had not been making love to her so much as subduing demons she could neither understand nor name.

She supposed that she had been used by her husband, a complaint she had heard whispered more than once by her mother's friends. It had not diminished her pleasure in being with him, though. If anything, she had wanted to match his ardor rather than escape it. She ran her fingertips up his arm, taking the same delight in the vibrant warmth of his skin that she felt at his kiss. It was still too soon, but she knew she loved him and when she finally drifted off to sleep, thoughts of him filled her dreams as well as her heart.

Toward dawn, those handsome images faded to be replaced by vivid scenes of the fight she had witnessed from the deck of the *Mattino Bello*. Far more gory than the actual event, her mind played vicious tricks, and when Luis swung the grappling hook in her dream, he severed Boris Ryde's head from his neck and sent it spiraling off into the waves. The evil captain's body then tottered around the deck of the *Salamander,* his outstretched arms groping for his killer's throat until, with a mighty kick, Luis sent the beheaded corpse over the rail. Luis turned toward her then, his face twisted in a triumphant grin that was every bit as horrifying as what he had done to Ryde.

Michelle awoke with a strangled cry that instantly tore Luis from his tranquil slumber. She sat up and tried to force the hideous dream from her mind, but she was too frightened to gain control of her thoughts and continued to tremble in fear. She knew what she had really seen and what had taken place in her nightmare were two entirely different things, but that did not help to calm her, either.

Luis put his arm around her shoulders in a comforting hug. "What's wrong? Are you ill?" he inquired.

Michelle shook her head until she could find her voice. "It was just a nightmare, but it seemed so real. I'm sorry I woke you."

Luis did not have to guess what had given her the terrifying dream; he knew. "Come," he coaxed. "Let's try and go back to sleep."

When he eased her down onto the soft mattress, Michelle cuddled against him. She wanted desperately for things to go well for them in Barcelona, but she had not forgotten that Captain Ryde was not the only man with a grudge against her husband. "I'm worried about the other man," she confessed anxiously. "I know you don't want to tell me his name, but I can't help but worry that he's going to do you harm."

Luis shifted his position to look down at her. He ached to tell her the truth about Antoine, and at the same time, he was too uncertain of her reaction to

476

risk doing so. "The man's a coward" was all he would confide. "Now that his partner has, well, been lost at sea, he won't have the courage to move against me on his own. Now if you're too wide awake to get back to sleep, let's find another way to spend the remainder of the night."

Still trembling, Michelle's lips felt numb at his first kiss, but then she found herself clinging to him with the same eagerness for lovemaking that he had shown earlier. She could not bear to think of them being separated for any reason, much less parted forever by death, and it was her passion that inflamed his this time. The joy they created convinced her neither could ever be accused of using the other when the mutual desire that drew them together was a source of such endless beauty.

After breakfast the next morning, Luis made certain Boris Ryde's crew had been released with a promise of berths on ships of the Aragon Line before he and Michelle boarded the *Monterey*, a sister ship of the *California*, bound for Barcelona. When they passed the pier where the *Mattino Bello* had been moored, she expressed surprise at finding the Venetian ship gone.

"I thought we'd be able to tell Valentino goodbye," she explained regretfully. "We should have returned his clothes, too. I didn't realize he would be leaving Valencia before we did."

Luis smoothed a stray curl away from her cheek. "I paid him for the clothes, and as for his schedule, he had not intended to visit Valencia in the first place, so it's no wonder that he's already gone."

Michelle leaned back against her husband's broad chest and covered his hands with hers. "I can't wait to see your home," she enthused.

"It's in the city, *querida*. It's not an estate like the one on which you were raised."

"Still, I'll wager it's very beautiful."

"It will be even more impressive once you're there."

Michelle thought they sounded like a newly married couple who were very much in love. It was a pleasant thought, but a shadow crossed her eyes as she considered how unusual their marriage truly was. "I would just like to live a normal, happy life," she murmured softly. "It would be such an agreeable change."

Luis concurred, but Antoine's vindictiveness stood as the chief impediment to realizing that dream. He continued holding his bride as they watched the coast of Valencia again disappear beyond the horizon. The voyage to Barcelona was less than two hundred miles and could be made in half a day. They had brought their carriage and horses with them so that they could depart for the Aragon home as soon as the vehicle and team had been unloaded.

Cradled between two hills, Tibidado and Montjuich, Barcelona, boasts of a fine natural harbor. As Julio and Tomás coaxed their team ashore, Michelle stood on the dock and marveled at the activity going on all round them. The excitement that was so much a part of the appeal of a life at sea permeated the breeze as distinctly as the water's salty scent, but she kept telling herself that they were home, which was exactly where she wished to be.

Once they were ready to go, Luis helped Michelle into their carriage. "Would you mind if we stopped to pick up the mail at my office? I don't want to stay long now, and I'll bring you back in a day or two to meet everyone. I should at least announce that I've returned from Madrid at long last, though."

"Of course I don't mind," Michelle assured him, and she settled herself comfortably to await his return when they stopped at a building whose austere Gothic style was softened by planters filled with both green and flowering shrubs.

As promised, Luis entered his office, greeted his clerks, picked up several bundles of mail, and in less than five minutes, returned to his carriage. As they started up the narrow street, he quickly sifted through the letters looking for personal mail. When he came across a letter from Ramón, he drew his knife and slit open the envelope. Then he realized what the missive might contain, and regretted being so impetuous.

"I'm sorry, I didn't mean to be rude," he apologized. "I'll wait and read my mail later."

Michelle was enjoying the sights on the route to his home and wasn't at all offended. "I have no more interest in your mail than I'm sure you will have in mine. Go right ahead and read whatever you want. I'm far too interested in seeing something of Barcelona to complain I'm being neglected."

Luis leaned over to kiss her cheek, but he saved Ramón's letter to read later, in private. So as not to arouse her curiosity, he opened another envelope which he was confident would contain a letter concerned with a shipping contract and hurriedly read it. "Nothing's changed in my absence," he remarked. "Our customers are still determined to have lower costs and higher profits."

"Isn't that the concern of merchants everywhere?"

"Yes, indeed it is." Luis slipped Ramón's letter into his coat pocket and set the rest of his mail aside to peruse later. He pointed out sights of special interest, but he was grateful when they reached the corner where his home stood. Surrounded by a high wall, little but the tile roof on the second floor was visible from the street, but he had always thought it a charming residence and was eager to share it with his wife.

"My grandfather built this house for his bride. There's a portrait of her in the parlor. She's been described to me as not only a blond beauty, but a very bright woman as well. They had a wonderfully happy marriage but tragically she did not survive my father's birth."

"That must have broken your grandfather's heart."

"Yes, I'm sure it did. More than twenty years passed before he married the French widow who was his son's mother-in-law. I told you about that. It must have been very complicated at the time, but I know my mother and father have a good marriage, and from what they told us of the letters they received from their parents, they did, too."

Luis would have been willing to recount every story he had ever heard about his Spanish or French relatives rather than tell Michelle about Antoine, but he feared he was merely fooling himself instead of facing the truth as he knew a gentleman should. When Julio drove their carriage through the gate, the household staff hurried outside to greet them, but as Luis introduced his servants to his adorable French bride, he could not help but worry about how long he would be able to keep her.

When the cook realized Michelle was French and would not understand him, he raised his hands in dismay and began to complain that he feared the recipes it had taken him a lifetime to collect would not please her. He reminded Luis of several of his

480

most superb dishes and implored him to convince
his bride not to change the menus, which had always pleased him and delighted his guests. He
pointed out that a young woman with Michelle's
slender figure probably did not eat much anyway
and it would be a shame to upset everyone in the
kitchen on her account.

Keeping one secret was already too many, and
Luis promptly translated the cook's lament into
French for Michelle's benefit. Michelle listened attentively, and then replied sweetly. "Please inform
him that this is neither the time nor place to discuss
menus. It will take me a while to become accustomed to the household routine, but when I do, he
will either prepare what I request or he will be free
to seek employment elsewhere."

Luis first complimented her on her tact, and then
relayed her message to the temperamental cook who
paled visibly before nodding and hastening to assure
Luis that he had no wish to work for anyone but the
Aragons. The matter settled in a manner that had
made Michelle's determination to become mistress of
the household plain, Luis asked if anyone else cared
to raise a question. When none wisely did, he escorted Michelle into his home.

"I'll give you the complete tour of the house later,"
he promised, "but I know you'll want to unpack
first. As for a maid, I'll be happy to bring Yvette
here. Do you suppose she's gone back to your
mother's house?"

They were on the stairs, but Michelle paused as
she replied. "I need to write to both my mother and
my aunt. I can ask each of them if Yvette is there
and inquire if she'd like to join us. I've no objection
to hiring a Spanish maid, though. In fact, it might
be preferable if I did because I would be forced to

481

practice my Spanish with her. What do you think would be best?"

Luis took her hand and led her toward the landing. He had not realized making even the smallest plans required the assumption that she would be spending the rest of her life with him. It was a sobering thought that made him feel all the more guilty for not confiding in her.

"The language of Barcelona is Catalán rather than Spanish, but you'll want to know that, too. You can practice your Spanish with me anytime you wish. If you'd like to have Yvette with you, however, then we'll convince her to come here."

Michelle made her decision quickly. "Yes, I really would prefer to have her since she already understands how I like to have things done. She also knows everyone at home and would appreciate the news from Lyon."

Luis responded with a distracted smile before showing her into the bedroom adjoining his. It was an attractive room, brightly lit by the afternoon sun, and he prayed it would please her. "I realize the furnishings in my home must seem very plain when compared to French tastes, but you may do whatever you like to make yourself comfortable here. Replace the furniture, paint or paper the walls, buy whatever fabrics you require. I want you to be happy."

That was so painfully obvious in the nervousness Michelle had never before seen Luis display that she hastened to reassure him. "I think this room is lovely exactly as it is. It's decorated in the same spare fashion as the rest of the house and that's as it should be. If I were to fill my room with French antiques, rugs, and draperies it would look as though I were very homesick, and I'm not. I'll be perfectly content here. Believe me I will."

Michelle looked so delightfully sincere, Luis's burden of guilt weighed on him even more heavily. He waited with her until her trunks had been brought up to her room and a chambermaid summoned to assist her with unpacking, and then quickly excused himself. He went downstairs to his den, poured himself a stiff drink, sat down at his desk, and opened Ramón's letter.

As he had anticipated, his friend had written to disclose his astonishment at sighting Antoine Lareau. He described the elegant Frenchman as having lost a great deal of weight and looking pale, but stated Antoine was clearly recovering from the wound that had nearly killed him. Ramón confided that Antoine had not been in the least bit cordial, which could be expected, but that he had mentioned plans to return to France the next day.

Luis confirmed the date on the letter and assumed Antoine would already be home. Because Michelle had had no opportunity to write to her family, they would have heard the news of her elopement from an undoubtedly bitter Antoine. Luis winced just imagining what the Frenchman must have said about him, but it had to have been mild when compared to how Luis could now describe him.

He poured himself another drink, and attempted in a calm, reasonable fashion to come to terms with the two-edged, painful dilemma that plagued him: that Antoine had survived the duel and that he had hired Boris Ryde to carry out his revenge. As Luis acted out possible scenarios in his mind, he swiftly came to the conclusion that if he told Michelle that Antoine was alive and she no longer cared, he need never divulge how close the effeminate Frenchman had come to having them killed.

On the other hand, if she did profess her love for her former fiancé and ask for a divorce to marry him, he could show her the letter Antoine had written Boris Ryde. After she had read the murderous intentions Antoine had conveyed, Michelle could not possibly wish to marry him. But would she still ask for a divorce rather than remain with a husband she had not freely chosen?

That question ate at Luis's soul because he did not know what her answer would be. He could wait until a letter arrived from Michelle's family, for surely it would contain some mention of Antoine, but that was such a cowardly option he was disgusted by it. No, he was going to have to tell Michelle the truth, or at least the first part of it, and Ramón's letter provided the perfect means to begin such a momentous conversation.

Gathering his courage for what he feared might be the darkest hour of his life, Luis picked up Ramón's letter and went to find Michelle.

Twenty-eight

Luis waited at Michelle's door until she noticed him. She and the chambermaid were sorting her clothes with such animated gestures and frequent laughter that it was difficult to remember they were unable to communicate with words. When Michelle glanced his way, she welcomed him with an enchanting smile.

"I know you're busy," he apologized, "but I need to speak with you for a moment. Would you like to see the garden?"

The seriousness of Luis's expression alarmed Michelle, and she did not even think of denying his request. "I would love to see whatever you'd care to show me," she replied. Leaving the maid to complete the unpacking, she hurried to him and took his hand.

Luis led her downstairs, through the dining room, and out onto a charming patio that contained a table and chairs and was decorated with potted plants in brightly colored ceramic containers. "I eat breakfast here in the spring and summer and the sparrows grow so tame they'll eat crumbs right out of my hand."

"We used to do that, too!" Michelle exclaimed. "Mother always scolded us for encouraging them and

485

threatened to bake the little birds in a pie."

"Did she ever actually do it?"

"No, but she didn't think we should make pets of wild creatures. We didn't spoil the sparrows so terribly that they forgot how to forage for themselves, but she was firmly convinced that it was eventually going to happen."

The gate at the back of the patio opened into the well-kept garden and Luis selected a bench where they could talk for as long as they wished without any fear of being observed by the household staff. He was not worried about their words being translated since none of his servants was fluent in French, but he did not want the curious group observing their reactions, either. He waited until Michelle had made herself comfortable and then sat down beside her. He pulled Ramón's letter from his pocket.

"I really don't how to tell you this," he began truthfully, "but perhaps the best way is simply to get it over with quickly. I hope that you understand that I honestly believed I'd killed Antoine, but apparently his wound wasn't as severe as it first appeared. He's alive, *querida*. My friend Ramón spoke with him recently in Madrid."

For a long moment, Michelle stared at her husband in stunned silence, then she reached for Ramón's letter with trembling fingers and attempted to read it for herself. Too upset to summon the skill to translate it accurately, she handed it back to him. "Would you read it to me in French, please?"

As Luis granted her request, she listened closely, but inside, in the warm hollow where her emotions dwelled, the extraordinary news failed to bring forth any feeling other than a numbing sense of shock. She looked away toward the stark rows of rosebushes that had been pruned back for the winter. It was easy to imagine them covered with brilliant blooms come spring but she doubted she would be there to appreciate them.

When she glanced toward Luis, her eyes sparkled with the bright sheen of tears. Because Antoine had been shot while he had escaped injury, she supposed that technically Luis was still the winner of the duel, but he did not appear to be happy with the prize. "What do you want to do?" she asked shyly.

Fearing that what he wanted and what she wanted were two entirely different things, Luis turned the question back to her. "I'll do whatever you think is best," he responded.

Now overwhelmed with tears, Michelle reached into her pocket for her handkerchief. "After all we've suffered, I had such high hopes that we'd be happy here. I should have known such a romantic dream would never come true."

Puzzled by her words, Luis nevertheless pulled the distraught beauty into his arms. He longed to be able to keep her without having to reveal Antoine's treachery to influence her decision, but she had confused him completely. "Do you want to stay with me, *querida*, or go home to Antoine?" he forced himself to inquire.

That was the most difficult question Michelle had ever been asked. She knew Luis to be a gentleman, but she did not want him to remain with her out of pity, or a tiresome sense of duty. If only he loved her, she cried silently, but he had never expressed any such devotion. What if he regarded their marriage as a regrettable mistake and was eager to seize this unexpected opportunity to end it? If he would be more content alone, shouldn't she sacrifice her own chance for happiness and offer him his freedom?

Michelle appeared to be as hopelessly perplexed by this completely unforeseen turn of events as he, but Luis could no longer stand the suspense. "Why is it taking you so long to voice what's in your heart? This ought to be an easy choice. Either you want to spend the rest of your life with me, or with Antoine. Which of us is it to be?"

When pressed for an answer, Michelle offered another option. "You should have a say in this, too. After all, it takes two people to make a marriage the sacred union it ought to be."

"Yes, it most assuredly does," Luis agreed, but he was fast loosing all patience with her. "Please don't make this any more difficult for me than it already is. As a gentleman, I believe the choice should be yours. If you can't make up your mind, perhaps we should flip a coin, but the sooner the decision is made the easier it will be for the both of us."

Michelle swallowed hard, for her problem was not in making her choice, but in wanting it to be the same as Luis's. While Luis did not prompt her again, she could feel him growing increasingly restless and she did not want him to be angry with her. She had humiliated herself once before by begging him to make love to her, and that evening had ended so magnificently, the memory gave her courage to risk sharing her deepest feelings again.

"I would never leave you willingly," she blurted out in a choked sob, "but if you want to send me away, I'll go."

Luis let out a joyous whoop that startled Michelle badly until he began to laugh. "I'll never send you away," he promised. "I told you I took our wedding vows seriously. I meant for them to last forever when I spoke them and I still do."

When he hugged her this time, Michelle rested her cheek against his shoulder. That he regarded his wedding vows as a sacred promise was admirable, but she hated to think he might feel trapped. She wanted him to remain with her out of love, not because he refused to break a solemn promise, but was that merely another of her romantic dreams?

She shut her eyes tightly to force away all hint of tears and attempted to project the same joy as Luis. If it was too soon for him to speak of love, she would not beg to hear the words he was reluctant to say. Whatever his excuse for continuing their marriage, she was grateful for it.

That Ramón's letter had not prompted a difficult scene filled Luis with hope. "This is good news," he sat back to tell Michelle. "Now the hideous outcome of that ridiculous duel won't always be in the back of our minds lending dark shadows to every happy moment."

Enormously relieved by that thought, he grew bold and began to plan for a shared future. "The *California* was insured against loss, and while I won't be able to go into much detail about the mysterious fire that sank her, the Aragon Line enjoys such a fine reputation that the insurance company won't mount a lengthy investigation. I do need to submit a written claim so it can be processed, however, and then I'd like to take you home. I want to meet your family, and now that Antoine has recovered his health, there's absolutely no reason for us to stay away."

Michelle tried not to let this second shock affect her as deeply as the news of Antoine's survival. She attempted to consider her husband's suggestion dispassionately, but he appeared to be so excited that she wanted to be enthusiastic about the trip, too. It was not going to be easy to return home with a man she had married in such shocking haste, but she was positive anyone who met Luis would be charmed by him.

"I'll be proud to introduce you to my family and

friends," she assured him. "As for Antoine, I think he'll have the good sense to stay out of your way."

Luis kissed her rather than confess that while he sincerely did wish to meet her family, he was far more eager to confront Antoine.

The autumn weather remained warm, and within a few days Michelle had had sufficient rest and nutritious meals to fully recover her health. She then had to pack her trunks again, but this time she took only a few things to allow her plenty of room to transport the remainder of her wardrobe home from Lyon. She had swiftly overcome her mixed feelings about the trip and had sent a letter ahead to announce their imminent arrival. When they left Barcelona after a week-long stay, she was eagerly looking forward to seeing her mother and sisters and had only mild trepidations when she considered she might also have to speak with Antoine.

Rather than the magnificent China clipper, *Monterey*, Luis arranged to use one of the Aragon Line's smaller ships, the single-masted sloop, *Isabela*, for the voyage. While he trusted the *Isabela*'s usual crew, he added Encario Vega and several other strong young men he knew would prove useful. All fine sailors, they completed the two-hundred-mile trip to the mouth of the Rhône, which lay west of Marseille, the first day, and then made their way up the river to Lyon the second.

Located on the narrow peninsula between the Saône and Rhône rivers, which run parallel for nearly two miles before joining in a rush to the sea, Lyon was the second most populous city in France. With Fourvière hill on the west and Croix-Rousse hill on the east, Lyon, like Barcelona, enjoyed a superb natural setting. Michelle had always admired the rugged beauty of the steeply terraced hills and was pleased when Luis echoed her views.

Her family's stately home was located below the town on the east bank of the Rhône. The stone house, like many of the most impressive residences in Lyon, had been built two centuries earlier by a wealthy silk merchant and possessed the elegance common to French dwellings. Bright ribbons tied to the dock lent a festive air, and although Michelle had never felt homesick while she had been away, she was now swept with a poignant wave of longing. Embarrassed, she brushed away her tears.

"I'm sorry to be so silly. I'm really happy to be here."

"It always feels good to be home," Luis remarked with a captain's insight.

"Oh, yes, it certainly does. I hadn't realized how much I've missed everyone until this very instant. Is that heartless of me?"

Amused, Luis leaned down to whisper a teasing reminder of how exciting her life had been since meeting him. When she responded with a charming blush, he gave her a quick kiss. "I promise not to embarrass you with inappropriate displays of affection in front of your family, but I'm assuming they'll already know how fond we are of each other."

Michelle was far more than merely fond of him, but she again chose not to reveal it. "My parents were an affectionate couple, so I'm positive a discreet kiss or two won't upset anyone."

Making no promises to be discreet, Luis left his arm wrapped around her waist as the crew secured the *Isabela*'s mooring lines to the dock. Michelle had failed to notice the ship was not flying the bright-red Aragon flag that day, but its absence was intentional. Luis was uncertain how far he might have to go to repay Antoine for hiring Boris Ryde to kill them, but he did not want the proud Aragon name sullied in the process. Appearing relaxed, he scanned the gentle slope leading up to Michelle's home and was the first to spot a young woman running their way.

"Is that one of your sisters?" he asked.

Michelle waved excitedly before she replied. "Yes, it's Nicole." With an assisting hand from her husband, Michelle stepped out on the dock. When Nicole reached her, her curly blond hair went flying as she engulfed her eldest sister in an affectionate hug.

"Thank God you're here," she began, but sighting Luis stepping up to Michelle's side, she fell into an awestruck silence.

Amused, Michelle quickly introduced her husband and sister. As Luis bent to kiss her hand, Nicole whispered an aside to Michelle. *"Mon Dieu,* he is handsome!"

"Yes, he most certainly is," Michelle agreed, "and he speaks fluent French, so you must remember not to praise him too highly or he will become insufferably conceited."

Aghast to learn Luis had undoubtedly understood what she had meant as a private remark, Nicole blushed deeply, prompting him to give her a brotherly hug. Although not as tall, she resembled Michelle closely, and at fourteen would soon become as stunning a beauty as her two older sisters. Generally far more reserved and shy than either Michelle or Denise, she had had a good reason to run out to meet them and she revealed it now.

"It's a blessing that you've arrived today," she explained in a flustered rush. "Denise has eloped with Antoine, and Mother is so upset over it, she has taken to her bed and hasn't left it since noon yesterday."

"Antoine Lareau?" Luis gasped, even more surprised than Nicole had been when she had first seen him.

Nicole exchanged a worried glance with Michelle, and when she received an encouraging nod, she responded. "Yes. He told us that you and he were acquainted, if that is the proper term to describe adversaries in a duel. He explained everything in letters he mailed on his journey home. He also included sweet messages for Denise and they have been inseparable since he returned. Yesterday they eloped."

"Antoine has married Denise," Michelle repeated with a befuddled frown. It had taken every bit of her patience to wait for a proposal from her childhood sweetheart and that he had married Denise after such a brief courtship left her feeling both astonished and insulted. Denise was an inveterate flirt and had always shamelessly encouraged Antoine, but he had never responded with more than an amused smile in Michelle's presence. Had he always preferred Denise to her, but been afraid to admit it? she agonized. That possibility was truly appalling, but it was a plausible explanation for why he had been so reluctant to declare his intentions.

The dismal nature of Michelle's thoughts was so easy to discern that Luis hastened to distract her. Leaving their trunks to be transported later, he took Michelle's arm and gestured toward her house. "Your mother needs you, *querida*. Let's not keep her waiting. Tell me, Nicole, was Antoine aware that I was bringing Michelle home for a visit before he and Denise eloped?"

"Yes. We were all so excited when we got Michelle's letter that we've been talking of little else. Aunt Magdalena had written to tell us about your elopement. The poor dear was terrified that we would blame her for not being a better chaperone,

493

Michelle, but Mother wrote to assure her that wasn't the case and that she had every confidence in your judgment. When we didn't hear from you, however, Mother wasn't at all pleased. Then Antoine's first letter contained news of the duel and, well—" Nicole shrugged, as though their mother's reaction had been too frightful to describe.

"Then it's no wonder that your poor mother has had to take to her bed," Luis responded. "To have two daughters wed under less than ideal circumstances would upset anyone. Let's do our very best to be pleasant company for her and let's also invite her to come for a visit in the spring. You'll be included in our invitation, Nicole, if you haven't also eloped by then."

Completely enchanted by Luis's dashing good looks and sharp wit, Nicole again blushed at his teasing. "I've never been to Spain, and I promise to postpone whatever marriage plans I might have next spring to see it."

Michelle tried to smile, but although she knew it was ridiculous, the news of Antoine and Denise's elopement could not have left her feeling more painfully empty had she been jilted. When she looked up at Luis, she knew Antoine did not compare to him in any respect. Luis possessed not only keener intelligence, but a marvelous depth that Antoine, with his shallow preoccupations, could not even begin to approach. Still, she was doubly hurt that Antoine could have recovered from losing her so quickly and that her darling sister had been the one to heal what had obviously been only a slight disappointment, if that, rather than a broken heart.

Yvette met them at the door, and they were quickly surrounded by curious servants whose expressions reminded Luis of the gaping mouths his staff had displayed when he had first brought Michelle home. Unlike Michelle, however, he had no difficulty understanding the servants' whispered comments about him. He was grateful they were all complimentary, and hoped his bride's mother would be as easy to impress. He followed the two sisters up to their mother's room.

"Would you prefer to have me wait here in the hall while you speak with her?" he asked. "After all, if she's as distraught as Nicole claims, she might not want to meet me today."

Michelle would not even consider entering her mother's room alone. "No, I want you to come with me. Once Mother has seen you, everything will be so much easier to explain."

Flattered, Luis took Michelle's hand as they followed Nicole into their mother's bedroom. Furnished in shades of powder blue and gold with the light yet ornate touch preferred by the French, it was a charming room that on more normal days reflected the personality of its owner. It was not the lovely setting that impressed Luis most, however, it was the fact Michelle's mother was still a young woman with a slender figure that rivaled her daughter's in its classic lines. Her blond hair was without a trace of gray, and if her fair skin had even a tiny wrinkle, he did not see it.

"Why, Michelle," he chided gently, "you've never told me how closely you resemble your mother. I would mistake her for a sister if I didn't know the truth."

Despite being horribly depressed, Margrethe was greatly intrigued. Although she had heard that same compliment from others, she leaned forward to get a better look at Luis. Pleased with what she saw, she apologized for her current distress and offered a cordial welcome to her home. "I understand that you are half French," she then added.

Her accent differed from any Luis had ever heard, but he had no difficulty understanding her. "My mother is a Bourbon and raised all of her children to be proud of their French heritage."

"My children are also half French. Their father was in the textile business. We met when he came to Copenhagen."

Luis had once asked Michelle if she possessed Viking ancestors, but she had been too distracted by Antoine's presumed death to respond and he had not imagined her ties to the Scandinavian countries were actually this close. "I've sailed to Copenhagen on several occasions and found Denmark to be a beautiful land filled with intelligent and attractive people."

Nicole gave Michelle a slight nudge in the ribs with her elbow to indicate her approval of her Spanish brother-in-law. After a few minutes of conversation with their mother, Luis had improved her spirits to the point she felt well enough to leave her bed and join them for supper. Luis returned to the *Isabel* then, but Michelle remained with her mother.

"What do you think your father's opinion would be of your husband?" Margrethe then asked pointedly.

"Luis has a fine character as well as a handsome appearance. Father would have liked him very much. I imagine Antoine's remarks weren't complimentary, but all we need do is consider the source."

Margrethe frowned slightly. "Antoine did not belittle your husband in any way, *chérie*. While he complains frequently of soreness in his shoulder, he freely admits to initiating the duel and he does not blame Luis for responding to his challenge."

Because she had never known Antoine to have such a forgiving nature, Michelle found her mother's opinion difficult to accept. "Was the timing of the elopement a mere coincidence then, rather than an excuse to be away while we're here?"

Margrethe was now seated at her dressing table, and turned to face her eldest daughter. "It's true that he knew you and Luis were about to arrive, but I really can't say whether or not that influenced his decision. Frankly, I'm still astonished that a man who prides himself on his extensive social circle would elope rather than insist upon an elaborate wedding. The move was completely unlike him, which is why it was such a dreadful shock. I'm sure Denise was partly to blame, but you know she has never been as serious a person as you and Nicole."

"I had no idea that she was in love with Antoine," Michelle mused softly.

"I hope you'll not criticize your sister," Margrethe then advised. "After all, you left here hoping to marry Antoine and returned married to Luis. You can scarcely accuse her of being fickle."

Stung by that rebuke, Michelle promptly excused herself and went to her bedroom. Decorated in mauve tones, it was a feminine room filled with happy memories, but the majority of them included Antoine. She sat down on the window seat to admire the view of the river as she had done nearly every day of her life. By the time Luis arrived with their luggage, the familiar nature of her surroundings had helped her reach an important decision.

"It was so thoughtful of you to invite my mother and Nicole to come visit us," she said. "Because we'll have such a pleasant time together in Barcelona, we needn't stay here more than a few days. I'd like to get home and start planning for the holidays. It will be our first Christmas together and I want it to be perfect."

"It's more than a month until Christmas," Luis reminded her. "There's no need for us to shorten this trip. I'd like to stay a week at the very least, perhaps two. I want to meet all your friends and see something of Lyon. I'm sure the city must offer many entertainments."

"Well, yes, of course it does, but—"

Luis could not bear to watch Michelle wring her hands, and after joining her on the window seat, he grasped her trembling fingers in a fond clasp. "If what you're really attempting to tell me is that you don't want to see Antoine, it's simply too bad because I'm not leaving Lyon without speaking with him. I'm just as unhappy to find he's now a part of your family as you are, but we can't avoid him forever. We'll have to face him eventually and postponing that day won't make it any less awkward."

That Luis was taking such an adamant stance frightened Michelle. "What if Antoine eloped to avoid seeing us?"

A shrewd judge of character, Luis believed Antoine's elopement to be a far more desperate act than merely an excuse to leave town. Antoine had most probably taken a bride from the Minoux family in a bid for immunity from whatever retaliation Luis might mount had he discovered Antoine's association with Boris Ryde. Luis had no intention of revealing that he was aware of their plot, however—at least not initially.

"He could have just gone away alone had that been his only motivation. He must have wanted to marry your sister, but I doubt that he'll take her on an extended honeymoon. Whenever they return, we'll be here to greet them."

Michelle recognized a dangerous gleam in his determined gaze. "Didn't the duel settle things between you?"

"I thought so," Luis replied.

"But something changed your mind?"

"The less you know, the better, *querida*. Now let me

ask you a question. Are you still in love with Antoine? Is that why you don't want to risk seeing him with Denise?"

While Michelle knew she no longer loved her former sweetheart, it was difficult to explain the sick feeling that filled her heart. "No," she assured him bravely. "It's just that, well, I guess I'm disappointed in him, and in Denise as well."

"That arrogant lizard doesn't have a heart, so you shouldn't have expected him to pine for you. I'll bet the fact he married your sister is no mere coincidence, though," Luis speculated, but he revealed only his most obvious reason. "He must fear that he lost considerable prestige in his friends' eyes when you married me. I think he wed Denise in a blatant attempt to show them that he can win the affections of a similarly beautiful young woman. You told me Denise enjoyed flirting, but perhaps her feelings for Antoine were sincere and when Antoine showed an interest in her, she made the most of it."

"They're both opportunists then," Michelle wisely concluded.

"Perhaps. Now we need to change our clothes for dinner. I like your mother and Nicole. Let's do our best to share an enjoyable evening with them."

That suggestion made Michelle feel very selfish for having become so depressed over Antoine's elopement. She leaned forward to kiss her husband, and thought, as she always did, that she was very fortunate to be his wife.

Michelle could not help but dread seeing Antoine again, but she made no attempt to change her husband's mind about remaining home until he and Denise returned. As Luis had suggested, she made the most of every minute. They went riding each morning and took Nicole with them since she no longer had Denise for a companion. At Luis's insistence, they rode over to Antoine's estate where he admired the vineyards that were their owner's pride and joy.

"I'm certain Antoine loves his vines far more than he'll ever love Denise," Nicole confided for Luis's benefit. "Oh, but I'd forgotten that you met him in Madrid. You must have noticed that he preens constantly just like a peacock."

Michelle turned away to hide her smile, but Luis was open in his amusement. "Don't forget that he intended to marry Michelle, and he has wed Denise. So if Denise grows bored with him, he just might come courting you, Nicole. Would you hold the same sorry opinion of him then?"

Nicole made a face that perfectly conveyed her contempt for her most recently acquired brother-in-law. "I'd enter a convent before I'd accept the attentions of such an arrogant man. With all the love he lavishes on himself, I doubt he has any left for Denise."

"I had no idea that you didn't like Antoine," Michelle said. "Why didn't you say something to me?"

Michelle's question had been asked in a serious tone, and Denise responded accordingly. "I knew that you loved him so much that you overlooked his faults. It would have only been cruel of me to point them out when they didn't matter to you."

"Thank you," Michelle replied, "but I'm not certain you did me a favor."

"I am," Luis exclaimed. "If you notice my faults, I hope you'll keep them a secret, too."

"You don't have any faults, Luis," Michelle was quick to assert.

Luis glanced toward the heavens as though her compliment was totally undeserved. "Thank you, *querida,* but I know myself far better than you do. Now, let's go on home. Your mother will be waiting for us to join her for lunch."

Luis continued to encourage the banter of his two lovely companions, but he had made a point of noting the precise location of Antoine's estate and later that day conveyed the directions to Encario. He also asked him to go into Lyon and buy silk scarves, colorful vests, and anything else he might find with which to create Gypsy costumes. He would have preferred to give Antoine as fierce a beating as Boris had suffered, but he doubted the Frenchman could take more than one punch before collapsing, and that would only frustrate rather than satisfy Luis. Because the vineyards were Antoine's most prized possession, Luis had decided justice could be better served by destroying them.

At supper that evening, Luis casually suggested that when Antoine and Denise returned, they hold the wedding reception the couple had missed. "I've yet to meet all your friends, and I'd be more than happy to assume the cost of entertaining them as well as your daughter and her new husband. It would also allow me the opportunity to meet with Antoine in a formal setting to assure him that I hope the duel can be forgotten. You have such charming daughters, madame, it would be a tragedy if their husbands could not get along."

"I think a reception is a superb idea," Margrethe agreed, "but you and Michelle should be guests of honor as well and I won't consider allowing you to pay for such a party."

"At least allow me to provide the champagne then," Luis offered, and he was delighted when Margrethe agreed. "Why don't we send the invitations tomorrow, and state the party will be a surprise celebration given on the day of Antoine and Denise's return? After all, their elopement amazed everyone, so I think it's fitting that we prepare a surprise for them."

Margrethe looked first to her daughters and when they had no objections, she began to smile. She had grown fond of Luis in the brief time they had shared, and his soothing presence had calmed her outrage over Denise's elopement to mere dismay. "Yes, it would be fun to surprise them. Let's do it."

Luis sat back and nodded approvingly as his companions began to discuss the details of the party. When Antoine and Denise returned four days later, the preparations had all been made. The couple went first to Antoine's home, but sent word that they would visit Margrethe that evening. They had anticipated tears and recriminations from her over their impromptu nuptials, but when they were greeted by the laughter and good wishes of their family and friends, they were relieved and delighted rather than disappointed.

Luis and Michelle stood aside as her sister and Antoine were embraced by their guests, for each wished to speak with them later, and without an audience intent upon catching their every word. Luis successfully masked his utter contempt and loathing for Antoine, and Michelle also observed the pair with a detachment that surprised her. She gave her husband's arm a loving squeeze, grateful that he had insisted they face her former sweetheart and sister now.

"They look very happy together, don't they?" she observed.

"Yes, they certainly do, but she's not nearly as pretty as you are."

Luis was content to bide his time, but in a surprising show of courage, Antoine and Denise swiftly sought them out. "I hope that this is merely the first of many fine celebrations we'll share over the years," the Frenchman offered with a disarming smile. "We both hope that you'll visit Lyon often."

"We intend to," Luis assured him. *He doesn't know about Boris Ryde,* Luis quickly surmised, for Antoine's manner was far too confident. At that moment, the musicians began to play a popular dance tune and the guests insisted Antoine and Denise begin the dancing again, leaving Luis and his bride alone to observe the others.

"Would you care to dance?" Luis invited.

"In a minute," Michelle replied, and as soon as several other couples had joined Antoine and Denise, she and Luis moved out among them. Luis was as marvelous a dance partner as she had always assumed he would be.

"Will you teach me to dance like the Gypsies do?" she asked.

"I'm sorry, but I gave you my promise I'd have nothing more to do with Gypsies, so I can't possibly do their dances."

"I thought they were Spanish dances, though. From Andalusia, I was told."

"Yes, that's true. Does that make my teaching them to you permissible?"

"Yes, I believe it does."

Luis was delighted his bride was so relaxed and happy. She was wearing the lovely wine, ecru, and green gown she had worn the night he had danced for her, but this evening there was a serenity to her mood she had lacked that night. "I do love you, *querida,*" he bent down to whisper in her ear.

Astonished, Michelle would have tripped over her own feet had Luis not caught her. "Oh, Luis, I love you, too!" she responded with a joyful cry, and the next hour passed in a blur of happy conversations with her friends, music, and dancing. When the party was interrupted by a fierce pounding at the front door, she was as alarmed as the other guests. Luis, however, had a difficult time hiding his smile.

Twenty-nine

Anxious to see who had announced their arrival in such frantic style, the revelers spilled into the foyer only to find a soot-covered workman from the Lareau estate excitedly babbling about a fire. When Antoine reached him, he repeated his tale in hoarse sobs.

"The fire's still raging, monsieur. We tried our best to stop it, but failed. There will be nothing left of the vineyard. The vines will all be destroyed."

The magnitude of such a tragedy beyond his comprehension, Antoine grabbed the front of the man's blackened jacket and shook him. "How could there be a fire?" he asked accusingly. "There's been no rain tonight, no lightning. How did it start?"

Weary and heartsick, the workman mumbled all he knew. "Pierre saw some Gypsies near the vineyard tonight, monsieur. It must have been their carelessness, a cooking fire, perhaps."

At the mention of Gypsies, Antoine released the workman with an angry shove that sent the poor soul careening into the door. Making no apology for mistreating the man, he turned, and his face filled with rage as he searched the crowd for Luis. The Spaniard's height made him easy to locate and Antoine started for him, cursing with such vile expletives that the badly embarrassed guests immediately parted to let him through. With Denise running to keep up with him, he hurriedly reached Luis and, unmindful of how his accusation would sound to the others present, he began to berate him.

"This is your doing, isn't it?" he shouted. "Your heathen Gypsies set fire to my vineyard! While you fooled everyone here with your charming lies, your thieving Gypsy friends were out to ruin me!"

Aghast at her husband's temperamental outburst, Denise grabbed his arm and attempted to pull him away, but he shook her off as though she were a troublesome hound and again screamed at Luis. "I know you're responsible for the fire. Don't even try to deny it. No one else would stoop to such an execrable trick."

Luis regarded Antoine with a sly smile. Momentarily tempted to demand an apology and force the livid Frenchman into another duel, he swiftly discounted the idea as unwise and replied so softly that those people crowded around them had to strain to hear. "Why would I wish to ruin you, Antoine? What harm have you ever done Michelle and me? If you mounted a plot against us, it must have failed, because we're completely unaware of it."

The Spaniard's voice was low, but his taunting words pierced Antoine's heart with the chill of a frozen dagger. When he had heard Luis and Michelle were coming to Lyon, he had regretfully assumed Boris Ryde was a worse scoundrel than he and Francisco had supposed and had merely kept his money and made no attempt on their lives. Now it was obvious that Luis had somehow discovered his bargain with the English captain and thwarted its completion.

Not daring to continue his insults when Luis could rightfully accuse him of attempted murder, Antoine was forced into a near-strangulating silence. He had given Michelle no more than a polite smile earlier in the evening, but when he glanced toward her now, his venomous gaze revealed his true feelings. Despite the fact he had just rudely shoved Denise aside, he reached out to grab her hand. Without bothering to thank anyone for their company or bid them a good night, he turned and started for the front door, where his bedraggled workman awaited him.

Denise looked back to cast a frantic glance toward Michelle, and her tearful gaze revealed her dazed confusion. Michelle doubted that Denise had ever seen Antoine angry before that night, so it was no wonder she had been badly frightened to discover he was capable of a murderous rage. While she had never been envious of Denise, now Michelle felt truly sorry for her sister.

Once Antoine had slammed the door shut, the guests' attention swung back to Luis. None was certain just what they had seen and heard and that confusion would fuel their gossip for weeks. Seeing he was the subject of curiosity, Luis gestured toward the musicians to encourage them to play another tune.

"It's a shame Denise and Antoine were called away, but that's no reason for us to end the party. Let's enjoy ourselves." With Michelle in his arms, he started the next round of dancing, and from the admiring glances they received, he was convinced Antoine had embarrassed only himself that night. Confident as always, he did his best to continue to charm Margrethe's guests, and he prided himself on doing it without telling any lies.

Michelle also noted the admiring glances and while she was pleased her husband was becoming popular with her friends, her earlier joy at having won his love was clouded by the questions his brief conversation with Antoine had prompted. "I want to talk with you," she whispered anxiously.

They were dancing to what Luis considered a particularly pretty waltz, and he shook his head. "Later," he promised. "After your guests have gone."

Michelle grew more insistent. "Now," she stated firmly, "or I'll create an even worse scene than Antoine, and you know I'm fully capable of doing it."

507

While Luis doubted she would go to such theatrical lengths, he knew he owed her an explanation. He took the precaution of escorting her to her bedroom to ensure he would have the necessary privacy to provide it. Michelle sat down on the side of her bed, folded her hands primly in her lap, and nodded to encourage him to begin. Grateful for an opportunity to sit, Luis joined her on the bed, stretched out beside her, and propped himself on his elbows.

"I thought I handled Antoine rather well. I think everyone will assume his petulant display of ill humor was prompted by the fire rather than having anything to do with me."

"Regardless of what the guests believe, I want you to tell me the truth. Did you have anything to do with the fire at Antoine's?"

"Wasn't there a mention of Gypsies being careless with their cooking fires?"

"I want the truth, Luis, not teasing evasions."

Luis wasn't ashamed of what he had done, but it was still difficult to admit when the truth would only inspire more questions. "All right. On my orders, Encario and the rest of my men dressed as Gypsies and torched the vines."

Michelle opened her mouth to ask why he had done such a thing, but the defiant sparkle in his dark eyes proved he had just cause. What could it be? she wondered. Then, with sickening insight, she knew. "Was Antoine Boris Ryde's partner?" she asked.

Because he had not had to use that information to keep her with him, Luis was willing to reveal a part of it now. "Yes. He apparently discovered Boris also had a grudge against me, and offered him money to make my death appear accidental." He recounted Boris's pathetic attempt to blame everything on Antoine, but did not mention her life had been threatened as well.

No longer in a festive mood, Michelle kicked off her satin slippers and lay down beside him. "That's so awful, I don't want to believe it. Did you see the way Antoine looked at me before he left? I think he hates me even more than he does you."

"No, *querida,* he couldn't."

His mood becoming increasingly lazy, Luis began to pull the combs from her hair, spilling her bright curls over her shoulders. They could still hear the music, and he hummed along with it for a while. "You needn't worry about Antoine. He'll undoubtedly find replanting his vineyards so absorbing he won't have time to make any more dangerous alliances or get himself into further trouble."

"Let's hope not, but burning his vines was fiendish."

"Killing the men on watch and setting fire to the *California* was far worse. Antoine got only a small part of what he really deserved." Drawn to the warm, soft sweetness of her skin, he began to nuzzle her neck.

Michelle snuggled against him, encouraging him to renew the mark that had become their own secret sign of love. "Now I can't go back to the party," she scolded in a throaty giggle.

"Did you really want to?"

Michelle combed her fingers through his hair. "No. It was a wonderful party, but I'd rather stay here with you."

"Good." Luis withdrew a long string of beautifully matched pearls from his coat pocket and slipped them over her head. "Let me help you out of your gown, and for the rest of the evening, these are all you'll need to wear."

Michelle hadn't forgotten his promise of pearls, although she had thought *he* had. She was deeply touched. "Oh, Luis, these are so beautiful. Thank you."

"I didn't mean to make you cry."

Michelle hurriedly brushed away her tears. "This has been the most amazing night. I've learned that you love me and that Antoine was Ryde's partner. I don't know which was the greater surprise."

"It can't have been much of a surprise to learn that I

509

love you. I've never made any attempt to hide it."

"Perhaps not, but tonight was the first time you've spoken the words."

"You had never said that you loved me, either."

"Well, no, but a woman just naturally waits for the man to declare himself first."

"Really? I thought it was the magic in the gold heart Aurora gave you that inspired you to finally admit the truth."

Michelle laughed. "Is that why you kept the charm?"

"Yes. I would have relied on any magic to win your love."

"I can't recall when I didn't love you, and if only you had said that you loved me, I would have told you so."

"Do the words mean so much to you, *querida?* Can't I just show you how I feel?"

Michelle made the mistake of pausing to give him a proper answer, and his next kiss was so long and delicious that, completely distracted, she forgot the question. All she knew was that if there were any magic involved in their love, it was a spell of Luis's own creation. A long while later she arrived at the dreamy conclusion that he was right about feelings being so much easier to convey in the language of love, for it was the one spoken by every heart.

Note to Readers

Michelle Minoux and Augustín Luis Aragon were born of my imagination, but the royal wedding that drew them both to Madrid in October 1846 was an actual historical event. The marriage of a Spanish princess and French prince was cause for enthusiastic celebration and provided the perfect background for a fictional romance.

I had long wanted to include Spanish Gypsies in a story. My research revealed them to be a closed society which forbid intermarriage with outsiders and I remained true to their customs. The *Hokkano Baro,* or great trick, described in this book was one of the Gypsies' favorite ploys. In what would now be called a con game, an enterprising Gypsy would convince some unsuspecting person, usually a wealthy widow whose fortune she had told, to bury her valuables in a spot where the Gypsy swore they would magically double in volume. The Gypsy, who quickly stole the buried treasure, was the only person to profit from the magic, however. Amazingly, some trusting souls actually believed their belongings had disappeared because they had failed to follow the Gypsy's directions closely, and fell for this same trick twice!

I love to hear from readers and invite your comments. Please write to me in care of Zebra Books, 475 Park Avenue South, New York, NY 10016. Include a legal-size SASE for an autographed bookmark.

FEEL THE FIRE IN CAROL FINCH'S ROMANCES!

BELOVED BETRAYAL   (2346, $3.95)

Sabrina Spencer donned a gray wig and veiled hat before blackmailing rugged Ridge Tanner into guiding her to Fort Canby. But the costume soon became her prison—the beauty had fallen head over heels in love!

LOVE'S HIDDEN TREASURE   (2980, $4.50)

Shandra d'Evereux felt her heart throb beneath the stolen map she'd hidden in her bodice when Nolan Elliot swept her out onto the veranda. It was hard to concentrate on her mission with that wily rogue around!

MONTANA MOONFIRE   (3263, $4.95)

Just as debutante Victoria Flemming-Cassidy was about to marry an oh-so-suitable mate, the towering preacher, Dru Sullivan flung her over his shoulder and headed West! Suddenly, Tori realized she had been given the best present for a bride: a night of passion with a real man!

THUNDER'S TENDER TOUCH   (2809, $4.50)

Refined Piper Malone needed bounty-hunter, Vince Logan to recover her swindled inheritance. She thought she could coolly dismiss him after he did the job, but she never counted on the hot flood of desire she felt whenever he was near!